Brothers

The translation of this work has been supported
by a grant from the Goethe-Institut.

GOETHE
INSTITUT

This book has been selected to receive financial assistance from English PEN's PEN Translates programme, supported by Arts Council England. English PEN exists to promote literature and our understanding of it, to uphold writers' freedoms around the world, to campaign against the persecution and imprisonment of writers for stating their views, and to promote the friendly co-operation of writers and the free exchange of ideas.
www.englishpen.org

ENGLISH
PEN

Supported using public funding by
ARTS COUNCIL
ENGLAND

Brothers

JACKIE THOMAE

Translated from the German by
Ruth Ahmedzai Kemp

DAS EDITIONS

A publishing imprint of Afropolitan Digital Limited

Praise for *Brothers*

'With utter nonchalance, the book tackles topics such as skin colour, success, love, the question of living right and, above all, the meaning of fate, origins and influence. *Brothers* is an incredibly gripping read, but Jackie Thomae also manages to weave existential questions and themes into it with great ease, almost in passing.'

2019 Jury of the German Book Prize

'*Brothers* spans a wide arc and follows both life stories, which are also tales about love, family and cities, to the present day, fanning out debates, fashions and the depths of the decades featured. Thomae describes all this with a mixture of seriousness and relaxed storytelling that poses major questions without big words.'

Sabine Rohlf, *Berliner Zeitung*

'*Brothers* is a major social novel where Thomae deals with the heaviest themes with astonishing lightness.'

Kölner Stadt-Anzeiger

'Jackie Thomae's characters Mick and Gabriel claim for themselves what is natural for white males in European society. They do not want to be defined by their skin colour, and yet it continues to determine their lives.'

Mechthild Lanfermann, *Deutschlandfunk Kultur*

'This highly observant social novel shows that skin colour and racism are more complicated than the social justice warriors think.'

Ijoma Mangold, *Die Zeit*

'A cross between *Trainspotting* and *White Teeth*.'

Silke Lührmann – Literary translator

'Jackie Thomae's novel is as funny as it is tragic, touching on topics like racism, family and love. It is about a bygone era – from the mid-1980s to 2017 – and is surprisingly topical. A very readable book with a variety of dimensions in which the reader can become immersed.'

Karolin Kolbe und Lena Stönberg, *Litaffin* Blog

For all you black sheep

CONTENTS

PART I

THE PASSENGER

Yes, one year flowed into the next. But not without beauty. A fleeting beauty you can't hold on to.

1985-1994

Why, Mick asked himself many years later, why had the nineties blurred into a nebulous haze in his memory, even though it was his first decade as an adult? When he zoomed into this fog, a disco fog, even though no one said disco anymore, he saw that actually a lot had happened that was worth remembering. I was there, he thought, as he crouched down in front of the evidence: the boxes full of photos, vinyl records, magazines, CDs, and VHS tapes. Along with his piano, these were the only possessions that had travelled with him throughout his adult life. The only official proof of his participation in the nineties was his pension statement, which clearly confirmed that he hadn't paid any social security contributions on his earnings at the time. He flew under the radar back then, with no verifiable qualifications or certificates, but also no debts, bankruptcies, criminal records, or divorces. He had emerged unscathed. With no visible wounds or scars, not even a single tattoo. Fortunately, along with every other failure, he also failed to settle on any half-baked idea long enough for it to be etched into his skin.

The photos from that time were much like his memories. Blurred and hazy, at night with the flash on, red eyes, closed eyes, concentrating eyes waiting for the self-timer, bad colours and contrast, no ambience at all, just a jumble of people looking lost in dingy rooms, although the parties they were at were legendary. No, these photos wouldn't inspire nostalgia in anyone. And as documentary evidence of the zeitgeist, the only people they might evoke something in were those who had actually been there. Desperadoes of the club scene like

Mick. But there was also photographic evidence of his daytime existence. Mick with the people who were close to him, Mick with animals and children, sporty Mick, holiday Mick. Photos of a boy who thought of himself as buff and tough, but who later seemed as harmless and chubby as a porcelain Hummel figurine.

In 1990, he was twenty. The years that followed were cushioned by a sense of maturity and perspective which, by his early thirties, turned out to be entirely baseless. He could forgive himself for his age-appropriate megalomania, but not the careless way he had frittered away his life – a negligence that, although also linked to age, had emerged from the childish illusion of his own immortality. In essence: a beautiful feeling, a gift called youth. Which he had squandered. Like he had squandered everything that had been offered to him back then. Even friendships, even love. After a certain point there was nothing left.

Prior to all that, he was just a little boy who learned to speak late, and then, when he did, the proverbial dam broke and he chattered away like the proverbial waterfall, prompting the kindergarten teacher to stick a plaster over his mouth – she'd be reported for that today, but not back then, in the seventies. He was the one who was the first to learn to ride a bike, who stayed in the water until his lips were blue, who was a pro with anything to be thrown or caught. He broke a lot of things, but he didn't torture animals. He was the one who didn't have a father. The longing for a dad had an equal ranking alongside many other things in the universe of things he wished he had, making it something distant and abstract, something that orbited around him and only made an occasional close-up appearance. He was the one whose face came up a different colour in the class photographs. A shade darker, light grey, because the photos were black and white. He stood out, and because of that, people noticed if he messed about. Who did this? people would ask. It was a couple of kids messing about; the little Black lad was one of them. Ah, yes, that little Michi Engelmann's always one of them, isn't he, and enjoying the attention by the looks of it. Engelmann, angel man, but not exactly true to his name. *Nomen non semper est omen*. Sometimes it was his idea, sometimes he followed someone else's lead – the instigator, as they always put it. 'No entry' signs always had that magical lure.

And yet, he was the dearest child imaginable. Well, that was what Martha said, his mother's favourite aunt, who had taken on the role of grandmother in his life. Martha's view wasn't shared by many. He was sixteen when she said it; his vandalism days were behind him, giving way to a development phase that might have made anyone worrying about him wonder: was this still puberty, or already depression? Not that anyone actually asked him, and neither did he ask himself. Martha, who he rarely saw after they moved to West Berlin, didn't use the word 'depression', but she could see he wasn't having an easy time of it.

Minors who left East Germany, the German Democratic Republic, were allowed to return to the country, unlike adults. After visiting Martha, he went back to the western part of the city via the Friedrichstrasse border crossing and spent the entire S-Bahn journey fighting back what would have been a flood of tears if he'd let it. Martha's joy at the flowers he bought her at Bahnhof Zoo was so unexpectedly great that he had to step out of her hospital room for a moment, at which point he was hit by the realisation that she wouldn't leave that bed again and that, most likely, this was the last time he would see her. He went to the bathroom and leaned over the sink, unsure what to do. Cry? Throw up?

Hyacinths, Martha had exclaimed. Oh, how I miss my garden! She was pale and small as she watched him place the flowers in water, and he wondered if she had been trying to protect him from the truth – he wouldn't put it past her – or maybe people always assumed they would live on forever, maybe that's why we're programmed to never give up. And because he was only sixteen, with all his love for Martha, it was hell to have to even contemplate such thoughts. He punched the wall a few times. And then, when he emerged from the phonebooth-sized bathroom and went back to her bedside, she told him what a good boy he had always been and told him a few little stories to prove it, as if she had to remind him of his lovable nature deep down, currently swamped under a mass of chubby teenage insecurity. Not yet any good at dealing with compliments, in this case compliments directed at a person he no longer was, and possibly had never been, he smiled bashfully, looked at Martha's straight, bright white teeth, and wondered for the first time if they were real. Stay as you are, Martha said, never mind what anyone else says. There's no point worrying about what other people think, she said, repeating herself several times because she was a talkative old lady, and in reply all Mick could say was okay, because he was a taciturn young man. She asked him to pass her the wallet from the bedside table and pulled out fifty GDR marks. The dark pink banknotes with the bushy-bearded Friedrich Engels, eternally condemned to second place behind the even more bushy-bearded Karl Marx on the blue hundred.

Here you go, dear, for the compulsory exchange at the border.

No, no need.

Take it. What am I supposed to do with it?

But the compulsory exchange goes in the other direction. When I come over here, I have to exchange West German marks for East German ones.

Oh, then these are of no use to you.

Yeah.

I always forget that our money is worth nothing. That's sad.

Yeah. It's dumb.

Money that nobody wants. Who came up with that, then?

And then she laughed. Probably because it was the best thing you could do when you'd seen so many things come and go. She winked at him, then asked for a glass of water.

Is anyone ever more than a reflection of what others see in them?

Martha died two weeks later. He came over again for the funeral, this time carrying a wreath bearing his name and that of his mother, who wasn't allowed back into East Berlin for the occasion. But this time, when crying was officially sanctioned, he no longer felt anything, just the unease that funerals bring and the urgent need to make a quick getaway from the subject of death.

The centre of Berlin is surrounded by a circular railway that politicians called the *Hundekopf* because it's shaped like a dog's head. When Mick's mother said, Wolfgang and I, we're getting married, it meant moving from Treptower Park, at the base of the dog's head, to Halensee at the tip of the snout. It would take twenty-five minutes by S-Bahn if you could go straight along the lower jaw, but the train no longer went all the way around because the city was divided. It took a year and a half between applying to leave and leaving. Mick's mother had lost her job at an academic publishing house and was now working at an Evangelical church preschool. An act of mercy for which Monika was grateful, although she could hardly have felt more out of place if she'd joined the circus. Meanwhile, Mick was living his teenage life, which outwardly, at least, looked mostly the same as always. But while he still went to rowing practice or hung out with his gang in the woods at Plänterwald, he was already inwardly saying goodbye to his turf and his mates. His consolation lay in the endless material possibilities that awaited him on the other side of the wall, and in reassuring himself that there would be people there, too.

By the time they moved, or crossed over, as they said in the East, he had just about put the pain of leaving behind him. The feeling of being dragged away was masked by excitement. He was only moving a few kilometres away; it was still the same city. One way or another, he assured himself, he had absolute control over the situation.

Which turned out to be wrong. Mick spent his first three years in the West facing his first serious addiction. An addiction he had never heard of. Not once did it come up when the myriad evils of capitalism were enumerated by the East's propaganda, so it took him a while to understand what was happening to him and what had triggered it.

To everyone else it was obvious: in the East there were fewer cars, less advertising, and less stuff to buy, no bums, no junkies, and a cityscape entirely free of any hint at sex. In the East, there was no immigrant community to speak of that had settled down and opened shops and restaurants, there were only foreign contract workers and students who came for a while, then disappeared again, like Mick's father. In the West, they didn't have trams but double-decker buses, and there was an entire underground network instead of just two puny lines. It didn't need to be a glittering metropolis to shine in comparison with East Berlin. It just needed a little more of everything, and that's precisely what West Berlin had to offer. Mick had anticipated all of this. But he wasn't ready for the addictive power of a certain substance. He was fifteen, the time of the great growth-induced hunger, and because he hadn't yet grasped the connection between consumption and combustion, he cultivated the eating habits of the athlete he'd been as a child, although he now spent his afternoons slouched in front of the television. He needed to taste everything, the intense flavours – nothing was too artificial. Chimeras of barbecues, fresh pastries, and fruit that nature could never produce. Fantasies conjured up by fat, sugar, and a chemistry lab. He guzzled his way through the city. At every U-Bahn station he was drawn to the kiosk, and at Bahnhof Zoo station, he was tempted not by the infamous back entrance but by the forecourt, where the golden M gleamed so seductively. In the East, everything had so much less taste, there was none of the addictive alchemy that turned food into designer drugs. Sophistication was an ingredient in short supply back in the East, making culinary habits way ahead of their time: everything tasted like it was 1946 or like it came from a health food store. Whether it was better, or worse, or healthier didn't much interest Mick. What he cared about was how he looked all of a sudden. Would he get picked for the team? Would they let him into *Dschungel*? What would the bouncers say at the sight of his underage chubby face? How would they know that this was where he belonged? Because the real Mick definitely belonged in the nightclubs – and in the beds – of the cool people. But for the time being, unfortunately, you couldn't tell that from looking at him.

Interestingly, he didn't get the idea from anyone else. His mother did let slip the occasional comment about his weight; he'd been such a beautiful little boy, after all, and of course – a crucial point in this context – her son. His classmates, on the other hand, were hardly in a position to be cruel. Cursed with their acne, braces, and sebaceous and sweat glands, they were stuck in the same proverbial glass house. The GDR was never actually as grey as it looked in the films they made there, and definitely not as bad as the Cold War secret agent movies made it look, but neither was West Berlin actually the epitome of cool, at least not at Mick's high school.

Before they left, his school in the East was swept by a goth wave of black that spread through all the upper grades and even gripped the nerds. The adults were unprepared for this epidemic, though they were less alarmed by the Depeche Mode fans than by the Cure devotees with their white-powdered faces. What did it all mean? The younger teachers probably appreciated the provocation, the sequel to their earlier long-haired rebellion. The hardliners certainly didn't think black lipstick suited the face of socialism, yet at a certain point even they got used to the New Wave festival in the corridors. Because as far as ideology was concerned, it was business as usual, with events for the good of the collective, like parades, ceremonies, and sports contests, being held with the same regularity as Mass in a Jesuit boarding school, and what motivated these pubescents was beyond anyone's control anyway, as every good teacher knew. And so they wore their Free German Youth T-shirts with Robert Smith hairstyles, except for Mick – the eternal exception when it came to hair – who had a frohawk, an Afro version of the mohawk, all the time envying the straight-haired ones, while they envied him, because his hair stood up by itself. Everyone else was surrounded by a highly flammable cloud of hairspray, until at some point someone found the ultimate setting agent in their parents' medicine cabinet: plaster spray. Hurray – finally, hair like concrete.

Mick had assumed that style-wise, things would be much wilder over in the West, what with clothes and things being easier to come by, and because *over there* it wasn't some stuffy little West German town, but West Berlin, the home of the hip. But no. This was no Kottbusser Tor; he had ended up in leafy Wilmersdorf, where you came to class in your quality knitwear and natural hair colour, and where the girls found everything *totally hilarious*, with their nasal voices and lack of ironic subtext. The fact that he had come from East Germany wasn't an issue; it was no big deal that he didn't look how they imagined someone from the East would look. They assumed he was the son of an American soldier. A G.I. kid? No, he wasn't. Really? Oh, whatever. At least it spared him the irritating questions about *over there*. Irritating because he'd already had to answer enough stupid questions in his early life, surely enough for several lifetimes. The where-are-you-really-from? question and the you're-from-the-other-side-of-the-Berlin-Wall?! question at the same time? No, thanks.

Instead, Mick recovered from the shock of his total life change cushioned amidst an innocuous bunch of squares. They snoozed and mumbled their way through class, shuffling along the corridors, hoping to one day stumble upon a personality. This apathetic crowd included a few other immigrants besides Mick. Some you could spot straight off, some's names gave it away, and with others you only knew when you asked them a question or two. But happily enough, there weren't too many questions. Someone might mention in passing that they didn't eat pork, that they celebrated Christmas in January, or not at all, that they went to their parents' home country for the summer. They didn't form a minority gang exactly; some of them liked each other, others didn't, and Mick quite soon felt like he had felt before, like he'd been washed up from somewhere else. And yet he was quick to adapt. Within a couple of days, he'd figured out the dress code and passed it on to his mother, who bought him the requisite brands as if they were a school uniform: Diesel? Stüssy? Chevignon? Uh-huh. Fine. All right. Monika could quite well have refused, especially at those prices. A Chevignon leather bomber jacket scuffed up to look old? Perhaps she really ought to have said no – after all, how would he learn? In the West, the school grades went not only from one to five, but down to six, which opened up new depths for Mick, an opportunity he was quick to seize. But luckily for Mick, Monika didn't conflate these topics. For her, as a fashion-conscious East-German woman, getting the clothes she wanted had always involved sacrifice, especially when it wasn't her money she was spending but Wolfgang's, her new husband, a bon vivant of the seventies, with a blonde centre parting, a serious moustache, and gold-rimmed, tinted glasses.

What else did you need for a passable social life? Gift of the gab, good taste in music, a bit of dough for the movies, and somewhere to hang out undisturbed. Not so different from his old gang. The pressure to quickly shed his fast-food chub grew within him, within his boxer shorts to be exact, because how was it going to work with the girls if he looked like this? The future he had envisioned for himself was not one of someone dependent on the mercy of semi-attractive women. He had been picturing more of a selection to make your head spin. And first things first, the major breakthrough, because what he had cleverly disguised through knowing grins and vague hints was the fact that he was still a virgin, even if this wasn't how he had planned it. His target, a girl who looked like Billy Idol, had finally agreed to go camping with him just as their application to leave the country was – also finally – granted, which meant that Mick and his mother not only *could* leave the German Democratic Republic within a week, but also *had* to leave. Damn it, thought Mick, as he left the girl his brand new 501s and the five mixtapes he'd recorded for their sexy time in the tent. But his romantic feelings for Billy Idol from Baumschulen Lane weren't quite strong enough to leave behind his leather jacket. Neither were they strong enough for a long-distance over-the-wall romance, because there was a clear and, he assumed, mutual understanding that it was about bodily contact, not about a border-crossing meeting of souls. When he wrote her a postcard, completely black with the caption *Berlin by night* – totally hilarious – and had trouble filling the blank space with anything halfway meaningful that avoided either boasting or raising her hopes, her face had already evaporated from his memory. All he could picture was her stiff, silver-blonde hair. *Hair without a face.* And her flexible gymnast's body, which he'd had to leave behind practically untouched, an omission that didn't make him sentimental, but tense and – no other word for it – horny. Then there was the move, the settling in, the overeating, all of which left Mick stuck in his virginity for the time being.

It was he and he alone – one sunny June day when he normally would have gone to the open-air swimming pool, but which he was avoiding for reasons already outlined – who decided it was time to go cold turkey. He opted for hunger.

And he went through with it, too, even though he was still growing. The idea of losing weight slowly seemed like a torture to be avoided at all costs. He decided to steer clear of his so-called study group: his classmates he was supposed to spend the afternoons with, catching up on the schoolwork they had slept through, but who had instead discovered how intense their favourite albums were when you smoked Black Afghan. Only once a week, and only as much as you could get away with nicking from your older brother without him noticing, but enough to experience delayed time perception, paranoia, unrestrained fits of laughter, and a craving for Nutella that dwarfed his previous binges. Mick realised that these afternoons were having a negative impact on his weight and decided to cut them out.

And he identified that his number one enemy was sugar. It took Mick, bottom of the class in chemistry, a mere afternoon to grasp the essential features of sucrose and saccharin, proving yet again that it wasn't the subject matter he had a problem with, just the way it was taught, which was no more engaging in the West than over there in the East. Once he had unmasked sugar in its many guises, he avoided not only sweets, but all carbohydrates. What was harder was reactivating his dormant urge to exercise.

Team sports? No thank you, he was no longer in a fit state for group exercise. Join a club? No way. A gym? Not in this condition. So he kept to himself and started running. Amazing how much woodland there was in a walled city. After school, or during, he would ride into the woods on his road bike, an ultra-thin contraption, hoping he didn't look like Baloo the Bear, or at least not for much longer. And to round things off: pull-ups.

What do you want for Christmas, big guy?

A horizontal bar.

A what?

A bar across the door frame. Or rings in the hall.

Crossbar, okay. Can you talk about it with Wolfgang?

Sure.

Will you do that, honey? Do you promise? That's sweet of you.

That was typical of his mother, making his request sound demanding. Monika was training to be an alternative practitioner; she was good at delegating. So was Wolfgang, an estate agent who managed several apartment buildings. He sent a handyman to accommodate his stepson's request for a home gym in the box room, because Mick had added to his request wall bars, a rowing bench, a punch bag, and a collection of dumbbells and expanders. He stuck a Rumble in the Jungle poster up on the wall for motivation. As he worked his punch bag, gazing at Muhammad Ali and George Foreman's defined muscles, he finally understood the lyrics of the song 'In Zaire'.

Everyone kept out of each other's way. Which is to say, Mick avoided Monika, and Wolfgang avoided Mick. Wolfgang didn't do much to hide his indifference towards children, especially male, pubescent ones, and Mick preferred that to feigned interest. The fact that Wolfgang had space and money made everything easier. They lived in a six-room apartment in Halensee, where Mick had his own entrance to what would once have been the servants' wing, with his own bathroom, and two of the smaller rooms where he spent his peaceful afternoons with MTV and masturbation. He was supposed to be 'in the front' during the day, by which Monika meant the sunnier, smarter part of the apartment. But he loved his add-on, the quiet, and the view of the courtyard, where it never really got properly light, but which had something Mediterranean about it with the creeping vine. Every now and then the peace was interrupted, either by the neighbours' music, Bon Jovi or Angelo Branduardi, evoking a deep aversion to both, or by the screech of cats fighting, their savagery reminding Mick of the meaning of life. At night he slept either in his bed or on the mezzanine, a sort of loft bed, a hangover from the servant days, and he would lie awake imagining the girls who had slept there in the past. Servile, rosy-cheeked, and so clueless that they had to be taught everything, oh yes, everything. Some innocent, light relief from his daytime fantasies. At some point, though, he had the disturbing thought that those servant girls must be at least ninety by now, or dead, so he swapped them for more contemporary visitors: female cat burglars in black leather, for example, caught red-handed, or tradeswomen who had come to repair something in the apartment.

Twice a year they flew to Spain, where Wolfgang and Monika either drove around with estate agents, or just sat there ordering wine, while Mick, deprived of his diet of porn and MTV, picked up his training regime again. And at a certain point, he was rewarded for his efforts. Psyched up from his permanent fasting and his regular runner's high, Mick received a juicy bonus from Mother Nature: he was still growing and was already over six feet. The mirror became his friend again. His once chubby form became angular; he could see tendons and muscles, and finally a man's face, finally proper stubble. He'd ended up good looking. Operation Man was a success, at least visually. A reason to celebrate. For several years, as it would turn out.

His final departure from school was, in contrast, just something that happened in the background. He paid about as much notice to the start of his carpentry apprenticeship as to a casual acquaintance at a nightclub. A proud vocation, said Monika; her dad had also been a carpenter. Try it for a bit, then see, said Wolfgang. Why not, as an interim solution, thought Mick, thinking of it as something to do with design, and picturing that natty black corduroy outfit they wore in the Guild of Carpenters. He could rock the Zorro get-up with the floppy hat, he told himself. Euphoric from his first major triumph in life, a triumph over himself, Mick galloped through his new existence as a good-looking young man. Life was one dopamine rush after another. Then the Wall fell, the nineties began, and the city became a playground that developed more and more to his liking.

The sun had come out.

Time for ladies. Time for parties. Time for new friends.

What happens when two highly virile males of the same species are trapped together in a small cage? Do they become aggressive or fraternal? The cage was an Audi Quattro, the males were Mick and Desmond, crammed into a car buzzing with revved-up revellers on their way to Unity, an unmissable Sunday club night whether you were gay or not, or undecided. Sandwiched between them was another male and a female, also dolled up to the nines, also high as a kite. Because even straight women knew that queer parties were the best parties, plus they were the perfect place to meet non-gay men. Some women found it *totally chilled* to be surrounded by so many attractive men and not get hit on. Bad flirting, ladies, Mick thought. If you don't want to get hit on, why not put a bag over your head or stay home?

Mick and Desmond clocked each other in the back seat over the other two now unimportant heads. They rose from the whooping crowd and flew into their own formation, a courting dance, you might say. But that wasn't it, because one was into men and the other women. Friends, then. Or brothers. In any case, from that evening on, they were inseparable.

Mick had found someone in whom he could see a reflection of himself. Desmond offered him a glimpse of the future if things went well. A little darker than him, a little shorter, nine years older, American, and therefore endowed with a natural advantage when it came to being cool. A brother, yes. As Mick saw it from the rose-tinted perspective of the only child, a brother formed an inextricable unity with another, a covenant against the rest of the world – a world that also reflected them as brothers, constantly commenting on how alike they were.

Mick and Desmond shrugged it off, even though they knew they looked about as alike as two random blondes in Beijing or Nairobi. Mick and Desmond looked alike in Berlin. Also because they liked it that way. Also because Mick took on Desmond's dress code as his own; he was one of the most stylish guys he had ever met, which was no great feat in badly dressed Berlin. When he thought about Desmond later, he would picture him in the back of a cab, or ordering drinks at the bar, leaning in close to the bartender, or in bed, a remote control in his hand, an ice pack on his forehead. He, Mick, the friend at his side.

Mick, who shortly after moving out of Monika and Wolfgang's place had also abandoned his apprenticeship, was now free of any supervision, so free that it bordered on bewilderment. And here was Desmond showing him how a life could look with as few responsibilities as possible, to as high a standard as possible.

Times were good for talented photographers. Desmond took great photos but hated being a service provider, and was, to put it politely, somewhat awkward to deal with, which is why people tended to book him less frequently than others and often only once. The mad thing was that he had somehow made a name for himself as a fashion photographer in spite of it, and that got in the way of being recognised as an artist. So Desmond claimed. His speciality was provocative fashion shoots or fashion-inspired art shoots exploring themes like heroin, hedonism, HIV, homosexuality, homelessness, holy saints, horror clowns, haute couture, hermaphrodites, and the house & techno scene of Berlin, Chicago and Detroit. The apparent fixation on the letter 'H' was a coincidence.

Mick was more interested in Desmond's current status than his future vision of himself as an icon of photography.

His tastes were extravagant, as was his unabashed manner of dividing the world into things he either desired or despised. Mick would see Desmond go out on a bender for days at a time, come back, yank the phone out of the socket, and emerge after two days in bed to find a fax offering him a five-figure sum. Whereupon Desmond would whine and curse, and Mick would tell himself, that it surely couldn't be that hard to snap a few shots of a couple of good-looking people in front of an expensive backdrop. Desmond accepted some jobs, turned down others. So he must be able to afford it, Mick concluded, hoping to pick up some crumbs from this generous pie. What if Desmond made him his assistant?

No, was his reply.

Desmond was standing in front of the mirror, Mick sitting behind him.

Why not?

Desmond pulled a scrap of tissue from a razor cut and took a step back.

Because I need an assistant I can yell at.

Their eyes met in the mirror. Mick laughed.

I mean it.

Desmond moved a little closer, poked his cheek out with his tongue and stroked his bulging skin. A spot?

You can yell at me.

Desmond dabbed some concealer on his cheek.

I know. But I don't want to.

Desmond nodded to himself, ready to go.

I think being yelled at is preferable to having no money.

Desmond laughed and called a cab.

Mick kept on asking. He was touched that Desmond wanted to protect him from himself as his boss, but the money question was getting more urgent. And beneath his acute need for money lurked the question, more pressing with each year that passed, of what he actually wanted to do, who he wanted to be. He envisaged some kind of late-starter career, the only thing missing was the field of expertise. And Desmond's field was creative, with room for a little mayhem, otherwise it wouldn't be Desmond's field. Whereas Mick felt miscast in his current array of part-time jobs: at an arthouse video rental shop, at a record store, and as a sporadic assistant to a stage manager. He wasn't in a position to call himself overqualified, certainly not out loud, but he didn't see himself as a shop boy or someone's dogsbody. He just needed a suitable opportunity to come his way. But Desmond stuck to his no. A few times they flew away together, to parties and friends in Paris, Bologna, and Barcelona, where Mick did everything he could to prove to Desmond how indispensable he was to have around. How good he was at driving, at organising, at persuading random people to give them something cheaper, bigger, faster.

And then all of a sudden Mick's drifting, carefree days were over.

Monika and Wolfgang split up. For Mick, that meant having to pay his own way on what he pieced together from his odd jobs. He could just about manage it, but it wasn't fun. It was precarious.

He had lived through his mother's break-ups before and had always accepted the change, just as children do accept the world their parents present them with. Now, a few years late, he was gripped by an infantile rage at his mother. What brought her to this preposterous, financially disastrous decision? Who did she think she was? His own pain was unexpected. For a short time he even asked himself that naive question, what could he have done to prevent it? He was almost twenty-three and wasn't exactly in close contact with his mother or her husband, now ex-husband. Monika grasped his arm, a little too tightly, as she answered him.

Wolf and I, we had our differences. He's a good guy, but very conservative in his attitudes, you know? Almost reactionary at times. Do you understand?

No, Mick didn't understand. The restaurant where they were sitting was run by a Turk passing himself off as an Italian, which wouldn't be a problem in itself if he could cook like an Italian, or even like a Turk. The place and its cuisine both seemed to point towards a bleak future.

I'm doing my own thing now, and do you know what? I'm excited about it.

Can't things just be *normal* for once?

I beg your pardon? Monika kept on pretending to enjoy her iceberg salad. What kind of dressing was that – kebab sauce?

You know exactly what I mean. I can't keep constantly readjusting. Every few years you have to change your life or change your husband, and I'm supposed to be super happy about it.

I'm not forcing you to be super happy about it. I just think it would be nice if my son understood me, said Monika. And you don't have to *constantly* readjust. You're an adult, at least on paper. You could have a career by now. How are things looking on that front anyway?

Not a topic Mick was keen to go into. A sore point. He had spent two nights in a row at a club called The Planet. After a shower, he'd felt surprisingly sprightly as he headed to meet his mother. He had even coped pretty well with the abrupt change of scene between the fire and brimstone of techno fluorescence and this restaurant, with its grotto walls painted with cypresses, donkeys, gondoliers, and a stone oven. He was wearing sunglasses with yellow lenses. I've been at a party – his standard summary for the weekend, always followed by the come-down of having to step back into the world like you were descending from an overcrowded UFO.

Have you been out clubbing? Monika asked, and they exchanged a smile, each picturing their own idea of a good Saturday night. The first beer had grounded him while also picking up his mood, but beer number two and his mother's bad news sent Mick into a tailspin.

I want a Coke. He sounded like it was 1976.

Order one, then.

For once in my life, I felt like I had a home.

Is that right? If I remember correctly, it was a home you couldn't move out of fast enough.

Yes, but I had somewhere I could come back to.

Oh honey, said Monika, you can come to mine anytime.

Mick wasn't about to confess that he was about as happy with Monika's poky new apartment in Moabit as he was with the abrupt end to Wolfgang's monthly allowance for his 'apprenticeship expenses'. That would have made it a bit too obvious that Mick was less interested in a home in an idealistic sense than in the high standard of home he was used to with Wolfgang.

Nobody's stopping you from staying in contact with Wolfgang. To be honest, I wasn't aware you were so attached to him.

Mick nodded sadly to himself.

Don't you like the pizza?

The ham is from Penny and the mushrooms are from a can.

Oh please, you don't have a penny to your name and you want *La Paloma*?

You asked.

Yeah, but do you know what? If you think you belong in a fancier Italian restaurant, then get a job where you can afford a fancier Italian restaurant.

It'd be fine if it was actually Italian.

Mick half-listened to Monika putting a positive spin on her downward trajectory and blamed himself for never having nurtured his relationship with Wolfgang. He could have asked him for an apartment in one of his houses, for example. He could have been a permanent tenant with protected rights. Maybe not in his ideal district, but still. And a generous guy like Wolfgang wouldn't have kicked him out even after separating from his mother. No, never. Why hadn't he thought of this before? Suddenly he missed Wolfgang. Too late, and with unexpected intensity.

How is Wolfgang, anyway? he asked, the first time it had ever occurred to him to wonder how Wolfgang was.

Oh, you know him. Busy with everything he's got going on. He's cutting back on work a bit and he's bought himself a boat. That wouldn't have been me, anyway; I'd be seasick all the time, remember? Yeah, well . . . Anyway, we parted on good terms, you know? No claims or demands, that's not my style at all.

I see. What is your style?

What's with that tone? My style is that I don't just *say* I'm emancipated, I live it. And if I've got one thing from this shitty country, it's the attitude that a relationship between two people doesn't mean that one of them has to compensate the other for his absence in the form of alimony.

I'm sure Wolfgang thought that was great. Think of all the money he'll save because you insist on being emancipated. You could have got away with it, too. No one would have noticed. It's not like Wolfgang publishes his bank statements.

Oh, honey. Monika waved the waiter over. The point is I can look at myself in the mirror and see an independent woman. Something a lot of Eastern bloc women could benefit from. What are you grinning about?

Have you ever seen what the Russian women get up to on the Ku'damm?

No, what?

Buying designer clothes like potatoes.

So what?

So much for Eastern bloc women.

Firstly, I get it. If women want to dress well, good for them. And any other way of catching up on what they've missed out on. And secondly, maybe it is their own money they're spending, we don't know.

For sure. Saved up from their wages as crane operators in the Soviet Union.

Monika laughed and tried again to wave the waiter over. Mick's friends had always liked his mother. They thought she was cool, modern, and attractive, precisely how Monika thought of herself, in fact. She placed a hand on his arm. Mick noticed she was still wearing her wedding ring, a decent-sized rock.

You, with your comedy rhetoric, how you wander off topic but always hit the nail right on the head. There's talent in that. You should use it somehow. Professionally, I mean.

Mick nodded. You had to hand it to her: she saw him as a glass half full.

That's been your strength since you were a kid. I think it's great.

Monika was still laughing, Mick smiled. She looked good, his mother, except for her habit of wearing Birkenstocks with an otherwise elegant outfit, something she must have picked up from the alternative medicine scene.

Signora? the waiter asked.

Un otro Pinot Grigio y una Coca Cola, por favor, said Monika.

A German speaking Spanish with a Turk who doesn't even seem to notice that it's not Italian, what a shitshow, thought Mick. Diet, he added as the waiter walked away.

I think he thinks you're my lover, Monika said, pleased. What were you up to on the Ku'damm, anyway?

I was out with Desmond.

Desmond. How is he?

Great.

Tell me, what's with the leather trousers you've got on? Are they new?

What he had on was a pair of leather trousers that were exorbitant when new. They were too long and too tight for Desmond, who had nevertheless worn them for a while and stretched them, which didn't add to their appeal and meant they would only fetch a laughable amount in a second-hand shop. So instead, Mick was wearing them, somewhat reluctantly.

Yeah. Why?

No reason. You know, I've wanted to talk to you about this for ages, only the thing with Wolfgang got in the way, and the move and so on. Ah! My wine! Anyway, it's absolutely fine with me, I'm really pleased for you, the important thing is that you feel comfortable . . .

Mick didn't feel comfortable and focused instead on the hoo-ha with the wine tasting. A level of ceremony that didn't quite match the establishment or the wine. Monika took a sip and nodded approvingly.

Muchas gracias.

Prego.

Anyway, I always thought, though maybe I'm wrong, but I always imagined I'm the kind of mum you could come out to straight, I mean without beating about the bush, that you could tell me that you're with a man. Wolfgang's another matter. But he's gone now.

I'm not *with* Desmond.

No? But you do everything together. Desmond's a great guy. Good looking, too.

Look, if I was with a man, I'd tell you, okay?

I'm not so sure, but I just want to stress that I'm a hundred per cent *d'accord* with it.

Monika had this way of not believing him that he was powerless against. She was right to be sceptical: the lifelong evidence of lies was irrefutable. The lies had indeed existed; it was true. And they gave her the right to decide, depending on the situation and her mood, whether or not she believed Mick. The Coke did the trick. He slurped noisily around the ice cubes. Reverting to prepubescent mode, nice. His problem wasn't being in love with a man. His problem was the abrupt end to his extended childhood, which, as he was discovering only now, in this crap restaurant, was dependent on the good will of a man whose presence in his life was in turn dependent on his mother's whims. His pain may have lacked justification, but it didn't change the fact that he still felt it. It was an old pain, new format. Whenever they had these conversations where Monika insisted they were having a fresh start, presenting the two of them as a team, and revealing to him that Arndt, Friedhelm, or whoever it was, was no longer on the scene, a desire arose within Mick for nothing to change; he wanted to cling in panic to the status quo that he had previously perceived without any strong feelings. And when he looked for the origins of this catastrophe, which wasn't actually a catastrophe but his mother's love life, it seemed like everything needed to have been very different from the very start, although he had no real idea quite how. And inevitably he couldn't help but think about the man he usually only thought about when other people asked about him. Where's your father? Where was he from? Have you ever been to Africa? Do you miss him? Questions to which Mick had no real answer. He longed for a state of being more than for a person he didn't know. And now here he was, an adult man, hearing about his mother's divorce with Eros Ramazotti crooning in the background, the echo of the bass that weekend still reverberating through his body. When Monika started harping on again about her progressive stance on homosexuality, he had to interrupt her.

But soon I'm going to be working with Desmond.

Ah! That sounds good. As what?

Photographer's assistant.

Well, that's great news. I always thought you should find an artistic line of work. Let's drink to our new start, then, she said, raising her empty glass towards the waiter. *Por favor*?

In the Wolfgang era, his mother, who couldn't drive, would have called a cab. Instead he walked with her to the bus. It ran so infrequently that they had a fifteen-minute wait in the unbearable, biting wind. Monika turned her coat collar up and kept chatting away, freezing but resigned to her fate. When she got on the bus and went up to the top deck, it occurred to him that a taxi wasn't just more comfortable, it also spared you this kind of awkward farewell. Monika waved down at him, made her *Venceremos!* fist and laughed. She wrinkled her nose and scrunched her eyes up into smiley crescents. People said he had her laugh. And when he finally pulled his hand out of his jacket pocket, unsure whether to wave or do the Che Guevara gesture back at her, she was already off, heading into her new life, which he didn't like but which she had chosen for herself. Who was he to say how she ought to perceive happiness? When he finally burst into tears it was hard to say why. Biochemistry or sadness? Not that it made any difference.

From now on, anything you do can be used against you. That's what people should tell a woman who decides to have a baby, Monika thought as she waved down to her son, his face deep in his hood like the Grim Reaper. No, she thought, it's not just that it can be used against you, it *will* be used against you. You breastfed? You didn't breastfeed? You let him cry it out, you made a tyrant of him with your fussing. Too much attention, too little attention. You were overprotective, you weren't there for him when he needed you. You were too young, too old, too preoccupied with yourself, too focused on him, too anxious, too careless, too strict, too lax, you had no clear limits. Whether you did things the same as your parents, because that's what you knew, or took a different approach, whatever you did, the response was how could you? Too little time, too little structure, too little love. Or too much. You're not even safe when it comes to love. Sooner or later it's thrown back at you, like everything else.

Monika didn't see herself as a bad mother. Things were the way they were, she thought, I did my best. The fact that later on she was called courageous and contemporary turned out to suit her well. It felt like belated recognition for something that had in fact just happened to her, but looked, in retrospect, like she'd been actively making a point, a liberated young woman, rebelling against the stale establishment by raising her child alone. It might have been the case, but it wasn't deliberate. She got pregnant, that's all there was to it. She didn't have to decide whether to go it alone; it was always clear that Idris wasn't going to start a family with her. He had never promised her anything, which wasn't to say that he didn't break her heart, but that was no one's business but her own. And then it was up to her to put the right spin on things. Something Monika was good at. Was she a helpless young woman who some guy had got pregnant and then abandoned? Or was she a woman who wanted a child and could manage perfectly well without the father? Of course, the latter. No one saw her after she found out she was pregnant, feeling like she'd been given a fatal diagnosis. Hardly the herald of a new life. No one ever asked her how she spent the weeks that followed. She lay in her apartment on Veterans Street and read. Lowbrow paperbacks from the West, thrillers and tearjerkers that were passed around surreptitiously like something from a conspiracy, when in fact they were simply well-plotted potboilers that exerted a calculated tug on Monika and offered the perfect counterweight to her compulsory university reading list of Engels, whom she preferred to Marx and Lenin but who was far from being a page-turner. For two weeks she subsisted on macaroni and tomato sauce, and potatoes with quark, ignoring the doorbell when it occasionally rang. She would stand in the hallway of her apartment, hot tea in her hand, or she would freeze in the shower, shivering and covered in soap, until she felt safe to turn the water back on again, or she would step back from the window and stand there motionless holding the nail scissors she had been using to cut the chives for her quark – until her meddlesome visitor had finally stopped pressing their ear to the door and walked away. Then she would creep into the stairwell and check the little notepad on her door to see who had come by.

That was our answering machine back then, Monika thought, looking out at dark Berlin.

Moni, I was just passing by, Ulla. Wanted to bring your boots back, will try again next week, Annegret. Dearest Harmonika, I came by with wine, but you weren't in, too bad, see you soon, Werner.

Moni was popular. And now she was pregnant. She sped through the books like they were movies, and every time she reached the showdown, she knew she only had a few pages to go before she was alone again with her truth. I'm having a baby. What?

Later, when it all looked like it had been Moni's life plan from the start, those weeks were reduced to a vague memory that seemed to her like a particularly bad cold, which was how she explained her disappearance at the time.

It was ages since she had thought about that time. The bus driver shouted up at a couple of kids who were messing around at the front on the top deck; he could see them in his mirror. That's enough up there, gentlemen, he said. Monika grinned to herself in the window.

No, it hadn't been about being seen as a strong woman. What was that even supposed to mean: a strong woman? She was well-versed in worn-out clichés, dead phrases. It was years before words like *peace*, *friendship*, or *solidarity* had any meaning again, they'd been robbed of their soul in the East. The word anti-fascism was so overused that for some people any sense of the real horror of the Nazis was lost. In the collective, they let these meaningless phrases rain down on them without any thought. Appropriately enough, critical thought wasn't welcome anyway. Their propaganda, which was no good at manipulating people, only sedating them, was so counterproductive that Monika, the daughter of a Communist who had been persecuted by the Nazis, decided even before graduating from high school that she wasn't going to stay in a country that treated its people like idiots.

When she arrived in the West, the key facts of her motherhood took on another meaning. Especially the fact that she had never received any child support from the father. *Wow* or *oh no*, depending on who you were talking to. The question had only come up for such a brief time that Monika could hardly remember the details. Was it Idris who had raised it? Had she asked? Not that it made much difference. She didn't get a penny from him. When fathers from non-socialist countries sent money for their children, the hard currency was retained by the state and passed on to the mother in GDR marks. That could have worked well, Moni thought, ah sod it. And anyway, alimony wasn't really an issue in the East; it wasn't a question of the father as the main earner. If there was a suitable father, great, that helped regardless of the system, but the idea of a sole breadwinner was largely passé. Instead, mothers worked full time and did the housework, too. Equality, yes, but hardly cause for celebration. You had children early. Another reason Monika's path seemed less exotic at the time than it did in hindsight. Her child looked exotic, sure. And not every absent father vanished with such finality as Idris. Not every father left a permanent question mark behind in his child's looks. What an adorable little boy, where was the father from? What a cutie, did you adopt him? Still, it would only have been a drama if she had seen a drama in it. But as it was, there she was, the tall blonde with the Black baby, the nuclear family that was just a bit different. And anyone who had a problem with it could either talk to Moni or keep their mouth shut.

Her boy seemed to understand what it was all about right from the start. As if he had picked up the signal while he was still floating around in the amniotic fluid: listen, it's not going to be easy, but if you and I stick together, we'll figure it out, okay? Maybe she really had talked to him while he was in the womb, she didn't remember, but it was quite possible, given how isolated she was during her pregnancy. And then there he was. She named him after the brother she would have had if he hadn't died of meningitis. Michael. Michi. An uncomplicated baby. He hadn't turned her life upside down; he had just joined her. An undemanding little guy who didn't seem to need much, so quiet and easy to love that it was hard to believe. Sure, she was grateful that he slept through the night and hardly cried, until her mother started taking him to the specialists. Could he hear okay? Could he see? Was everything all right with him? Monika, if you had harmed him by smoking or drinking, you would never forgive yourself. But no, he was healthy. He was perfect.

She played with her ring. An amethyst. She never took it off, the only precious thing she had from her mother. She died before she'd had the chance to settle into being a grandma. Michael was only three.

I always did have strange timing, she thought. I didn't feel alone when I ought to have done. And when no one cared any more, when my child was almost grown up, that was when I longed to get married, when I wanted someone to look after me, in the most conservative sense. But when I was still a student, it was all about railing against the East. I didn't want Idris to marry me; I just wanted to get away. To be alone. I was several times on the verge of being kicked out of the university. I took all their lies and threw them back in their faces. I harangued my professors, wrote letters to the editor of *Neues Deutschland*, and complained to my member of parliament, because after all, we were supposed to be living in a democratic republic. Either get on with being democratic or get a new name – as simple as that, comrades. But nothing was simple, really. Even though I enjoyed being an active citizen and getting on their nerves. Until two comrades came to my door and asked me if I wasn't ashamed to be putting my father through this when he was seriously ill. Those perfidious bastards knew my only weak spot. I shut up. And then, when I was allowed to leave the country, I suddenly didn't care anymore. All that mattered was my marriage and my peace. I no longer had a political opinion, I started reading *Vogue* instead of *Spiegel*. I didn't vote, not even when it finally made sense to. It was as if it had taken me all those years to recover from the rampage I'd been on. And now, when I should be worrying about ending up a lonely old woman, here I am living alone again in student digs. Maybe that's what Mick is so upset about? Children have bourgeois sentiments. Even when they're grown up and live under dubious circumstances themselves, they expect their parents to offer stability.

Raindrops trembled along the bus window as if following predetermined paths. Monika looked at the rows of houses, the large bay windows, the warmly lit living rooms, middle-class cosiness – at least that's how it looked as she passed by.

Why don't we have a real dad, only Arndt? he had asked her again and again. And she had always answered, with a laugh, because Arndt was a great guy, and she was a mama who always had an answer.

Why are you going to parents' evening in your cowboy boots?

What have you got against my cowboy boots? Don't you think they're cool?

Yes, but not for parents' evening. You're supposed to wear normal shoes like the other mums.

I don't like the other mums' shoes. Do you? See.

And later, when Monika had already risen to the status of cool single mum in other people's eyes, and she saw her younger colleagues scrabbling around for babysitters with hardly any money to pay them, she thought, hmm, I've been leaving mine alone since he was five. I'm not going to tell you that, and I'm certainly not going to encourage you to. It'd be a case for the youth social services, if not a criminal offence. Antisocial behaviour at the very least. I didn't tell anyone at the time, but often I couldn't help it.

Monika asked herself if her situation had made her as sad then as it did now that it was only a memory. No. Back then, she couldn't afford the luxury of sadness. Which, in hindsight, was even worse.

Once Mick had tried to bake her a cake. He had thrown together everything he could find in the cupboards and mixed it up with some eggs. She came home moments before he might have blown the house up. He was already on a stool in front of the stove, reaching for the gas tap at the back. Mama, it was supposed to be a surprise, he shouted, as she pulled him down from the stool, trembling. After this incident, she briefly put her faith in that idiotic saying that children and drunks must have a guardian angel, but all the same she took him to stay with her aunt in Grünau when she needed to go out.

Mama? Why do I have to stay sleep at Aunt Martha's again?

Because I don't want a burglar to get you.

A stupid reason, which she immediately regretted when he stared at her with his wide eyes. Great, Moni, you idiot, she thought, just one sentence and you've destroyed his secure home. The burglar she had just blurted out became a permanent fixture. A state that lasted until after her father's death, when they moved into his larger, brighter apartment in Treptow.

Actually, we were a good team, me and my little buddy, she thought in her upbeat Moni way, and it felt like she was addressing someone who was nodding along kindly while not believing a single word she said.

But that's really how it was, she thought. He only became aloof and difficult later, when I was married, as if he had been waiting until I was settled. And then? Well, then he had withdrawn from her life, a gradual process she barely noticed, it was so unexpectedly painless. She was barely forty and had an adult son. Finally, a payback for becoming a mother so young. And now that he was older than she was when she had him, she once again felt like she couldn't leave him on his own.

Even before the cigarette smoke had reached her in the back row of seats, the bus stopped abruptly, and the driver appeared on the upper deck. He didn't hang about. That's it, guys, end of the line. The teenagers giggled, but did what he said, without a fuss. Such a tender age, thought Moni, in a group they're a nuisance, but on their own they're more vulnerable than younger children. They huddled in the bus shelter and lit new cigarettes. Monika looked down at them, children in adult bodies who'd been given a dose of authority.

It's a bit late now, in retrospect, to wonder whether he missed his father. She stood up, wobbled down the aisle, sat in the front row, and looked down at the river of red taillights. Seriously? she thought; I was always there, and now I'm wondering if I was there enough?

It had been a nice evening, really. Mick had seemed a little out of sorts, and she assumed he'd had a lot to drink that weekend and not much sleep. She assumed that he took drugs from time to time, something she'd stayed out of. He was an athlete; he could keep a lid on it. And she would always accept his relationships, too, which he knew, even if he had acted silly when she said that. All the same, something troubled her about the evening. Something shook her so deeply that she had to rifle through her bag for a tissue. She who could hardly remember the last time she had cried. It wasn't his snooty grumbling about the nice restaurant. Or his edgy eyes behind those ridiculous sunglasses. He had looked pale, almost wan, which only she would notice because to everyone else he was just brown, but it wasn't even that that had worried her. It was more how insecure he had seemed. When he was the same age as those kids on the bus, she'd had the feeling he seemed mature for his age. Good manners, nice friends, confident and friendly around adults. She had been spared the boorish teenager, she was glad to say. It seemed like his social nature would open doors for him, including those he studiously ignored. His charm would see him through. But today he seemed like he was in free fall, as if he had forgotten what he had known since he was a toddler: who he was.

Help Desmond? She had no problem with him being an assistant. She had no problem with any job. On the contrary. She'd had more of a problem with seeing herself as academic. Not every path to a college degree was illuminated by intellectual brilliance, not in the East or in the West, either. All the same, Mick would have had it easier if he'd earned some official certification of his intelligence, that much was clear. He hadn't wanted to, and that might have had something to do with the way she raised him. But what she had always taught him was that he was something special. You're smart, you're good, be brave. And if you don't feel brave, ask me and we'll find a way.

But maybe there was another way of seeing self-confidence, Monika thought, looking at herself in the window and wiping traces of mascara from her face. Maybe he was so self-confident that he didn't feel he had anything to prove to anyone.

You're smart, son. I know, I've heard it a thousand times. He seemed to be good enough for himself. And despite being the one who had done everything she could to let him feel that way, she was now worried that he might not be good enough after all. But for whom? For her? For the cold world out there?

Next stop Kirchstrasse/Alt-Moabit.

I don't live in Halensee anymore. I live near the Moabit correctional facility. *Where?* Opposite the prison, she'd explained. Mick wasn't thrilled. She shook her head and pressed the stop button. We always accuse each other of making things harder than they need to be. Why? Because we're afraid of falling. Because we've always known we're on damn thin ice. Because we love each other.

Mick had added to his list of lies. This one was a fib, a white lie, because Monika had clearly been thrilled about his creative job with Desmond. Failing to mention something didn't fall under lying. Withholding information was simply withholding information. Otherwise, anyone who asked a stupid question would have the right to know the truth. Are you an alcoholic, do you think I'm beautiful, do you like it? Of course, it didn't work that way.

Anyway, the thing about him not being with a man was true. Okay. There had been that one inevitable incident. Desmond and Mick realised at the same time that there was nothing else left to do besides sex. Mick was on the bed and Desmond was on the floor. Everyone else had left, the bottles were empty, all the drugs had been taken, everything had been said. There was only Desmond, who had successfully scared off his last boyfriend, and Mick, who at this point was successfully avoiding several women and unsuccessfully chasing another. The Cocteau Twins were playing. *But is it Heaven or Las Vegas?* An elfin voice over a synthesiser dreamscape. Yes, what was it that they had going on here? The sun slanted in through the corner window overlooking the courtyard in Desmond's spacious 'Berlin room' that was as large as Mick's entire apartment at the time. Then the elf fell silent; the record had finished. What now? asked Mick, and Desmond laughed. From that moment Mick's memory blurred with other memories of sex from those days. That Desmond wasn't a woman hardly mattered – only in that it was the moment that Mick knew for sure that he wasn't gay. And neither was he a homophobe. Well, he was already confident about that, but this was bulletproof.

Being neither gay nor homophobic wasn't exactly a big deal in the company he kept, but all the same, he was glad of the confirmation. It was an important life experience that made his life richer, making him more grown-up, and cooler. But he still wasn't planning to talk about it with anyone.

Mick's long hoped-for opportunity followed shortly thereafter. Desmond had worn out several personal assistants. Ghastly stories, ghastly people. All ties cut; the proverbial tablecloth ripped in two. The last assistant he did get on with was now a fully fledged photographer in her own right with her own assistant. Desmond rejected the people the agency suggested on principle. So, it fell to Mick after all. Andalusia. Bullfighting and Semana Santa. Models against a backdrop of bulls and matadors, and the Easter processions. Mick didn't mind, he couldn't care less. But passing on his details to a secretary, he was filled with a wonderful new businessy kind of feeling. When his airline ticket arrived, it felt like a covenant that could open up his future. As it turned out, the trip was a disaster.

Everything about putting on a photoshoot in Málaga's bullring wound Desmond up. He didn't articulate the cause of his wrath, though he made a point of making everyone in the team suffer. It wasn't very pleasant, but it was at least democratic. Mick, ever loyal to Desmond, kept out of the mudslinging. He tried on his own to work out why Desmond was going around with his sour-lemon look, finding everything unbearable. The models, the stylists, the smell of the arena, the hotel bed, the catering, the client, and especially the producer – a sly bitch, as Desmond had discovered. Mick, on the other hand, thought it was great. He liked this job and was getting better day by day at handling Desmond's grumpy work persona. His serf status as assistant was bearable because everyone on the set was frantically running around in a sweat – a group experience that Mick had never been part of before. A missing hat had to be brought in by next-day delivery from Milan, and one day they just sat around speculating where the bull trainer was and if he was coming; the next day, a new model had to be flown in because the original one had been stung by a bee right between the eyes and her face had swollen up like the Elephant Man, which gave everyone a bit of entertainment and helped with the team spirit. There seemed to be an inexhaustible budget for unforeseen deviations from the plan. The dinners were fun and stretched into the night. It was just before Easter, and Andalusia was already hot and dazzlingly sunny. The cherry on top was a little flirting with the styling assistant and the hotel's rooftop pool; it all left Mick firmly convinced of his future in Desmond's working world.

I'm sick to death of these dead-end jobs, Desmond grumbled, undoubtedly in the midst of an existential crisis; from everyone else's point of view he was the despot, not the dogsbody. In the evening at the bar he told Mick about the bounty they'd earned as a reward for this hellish trip: Desmond was to shoot his own photo series. They'd tag it on at the end, an idea he'd been toying with for a while, the time had come. Finally. The hooded cowls of the penitents, with the hints to BDSM, Catholicism, and the Ku Klux Klan (who all had a similar dress sense incidentally): a conglomeration of provocative elements that was crying out to be translated into Desmond's visual language. Semana Santa was the perfect backdrop. The surprise for Mick was that *he* was going to be the naked Black man in religious-sexual ecstasy at the feet of the hooded men.

Have you asked them yet if they'll take part? asked Mick, who had never envisaged that a job offer as a model could make him feel so uncomfortable.

My friend Xavier will ask. By the way, we're staying at his mum's place, she lives in an old palacio. It's going to be amazing.

Mick also wasn't exactly enamoured by the idea of staying in some old ruin with the mother of someone he didn't know. In some respects, he kept noticing, he was probably too young for Desmond's tastes. Perhaps bonding with another guy's mother was also a gay thing. The simplest explanation for the plan, however, was a lack of money.

I haven't got through to Xavier yet, but it's fine. We'll go anyway and ask them there and then.

How? During the procession?

Yes, the best thing is to talk to the abbot or whoever is in charge of the choreography.

Desmond's long fingers signalled 'two' to the bartender. They didn't bother with a jigger here in Spain, they just poured it by eye. After two *vodka limón*, Mick felt like he did after six in Berlin.

Yeah, but Desmond, they're not dressing up as Catholics, they are Catholics, celebrating Easter.

Exactly. Let me do it. Relax. You're just the model. You'll see, it'll be great.

And then it was as if God had heard Mick's prayer, or as if He had simply had enough of all this blasphemous fucking about with his symbolism, because on the last night of the fashion shoot, they went to a particularly nice restaurant and were struck down by a seafood platter. Out of the entire team, only two people, a vegan and a woman who only had dessert, managed to catch their return flight. Desmond and Mick had to keep postponing their onward journey to Seville as they lay whimpering in their hotel rooms, which were getting pricier by the day, because in Málaga, too, Holy Week was one of the tourist highlights of the year. The onslaught on their digestive organs was over by Good Friday, but they were too weak to watch the procession, at least out on the street, and stayed sprawled out in front of the TV, feeling fluent in Spanish by now.

Next year, then, said Desmond. Mick had never heard him speak so softly, and he seemed diminished in other respects as well. Mick did his best not to let too much relief show through in his words of consolation. Look at it this way, Desmond: the whole thing seemed doomed from the start, there were lots of downsides, a, b, and c weren't quite clarified, firstly, secondly, thirdly, plus getting sick, plus money worries, and no sign of Xavier, but sure, you could think about re-enacting this Easter procession, and of course, Seville made more sense than Berlin, but wouldn't another setting be even more provocative? And as he was saying all of this to Desmond, who was nibbling plain sliced bread and watching the Spanish version of *Blade Runner* – the entire film seemed to be dubbed by just one voice actor – it occurred to him again just how much he cared about Desmond, his adopted brother.

His first meeting with Delia was much less magical. She was the roommate of a woman Mick bought an amplifier from. He got it cheap because the woman was keen to draw a line under a difficult relationship which the amp had been a part of. At least, that was how it had sounded on the phone. He arranged to pick it up that Wednesday morning, near Savignyplatz. It all happened very quickly. Mick rang the doorbell and a woman opened the door in a robe, turquoise seahorses on midnight blue silk, very beautiful, before immediately disappearing again into the depths of the labyrinthine apartment. Another woman appeared. She was wearing a light pink negligée with paratrooper boots and looked as if she had recently been crying. Over the previous owner of the amp, Mick presumed, a thought swiftly followed by: not my problem. The woman greeted him, sounding annoyed as if it had been his idea to come over in the morning. Then she bent over the stereo and tore at the cables, stressed and cursing. Her leaning forward in her negligée had the effect that, within a split second, the answer to the question of whether she was wearing panties underneath fluctuated from a yes, to a no, to a oh yes, maybe. Mick looked around the room: dark green velvet curtains, two red chaises longues, a folding screen, a disco ball on the ceiling, deer antlers on the walls, a butterfly collection behind glass, art by David LaChapelle, and Pierre & Gilles: Boy George as Krishna with a flute and the Archangel Michael with his sword. Should he start calling himself Michael again?

Did he want the equaliser too? No. Or the record player? The speakers maybe? Seriously, that's enough now, he thought.

No, thanks, said Mick, the amp's great. Could you just grab that end? Oh, yeah, sure.

Would he like a coffee? The first woman was back again. Now with wet hair, wearing jeans and a fluffy, mailbox-yellow sweater. Why not, I'd love one. Big Bird disappeared again, leaving behind a haze of shampoo and body lotion. Mick loved the aromas women filled their apartments with in the morning. That was true for woman one, anyway, while woman two smelled like an old down duvet, plus she had a cigarette dangling from the corner of her mouth. So, she said, tapping ash into a huge flowerpot containing a Ficus benjamina, what did we agree?

Two hundred marks?

Oh, do you know what? Just give me fifty, she said, waving it off sulkily.

Her roommate came in with the coffee and spoiled Mick's bargain with a startled: why are you saying that now?

And there stood Mick in this kitsch cabinet of curiosities between the perky fluffy jumper woman and the dozy negligée woman, sipping his espresso with the irritating feeling that this ridiculous cup of coffee was costing him a hundred and fifty marks. All the same, the fluffy jumper woman offered to give him a lift; she had to go to Dahlem, to the university, what about him? He didn't, but great if she could drop him off on the way. He walked behind her down the stairs, a splendid Charlottenburg staircase, all red and gold stucco bling and polished mirrors: how did he look? Not bad. Careful on the marble steps.

She held the front door open for him, tottered along quickly beside him, needing three steps for every one of his, while he lugged the amp in silence, until she rudely left him standing like a porter in front of Butter Lindner while she popped in to buy cinnamon pastries, providing him for the second time that day with something he didn't need. Sitting next to her in her Golf GTI, he saw her in profile for the first time. A sculptured profile that from the front was pretty but nothing like as spectacular as this side view. She chatted away, looking alternately at the street and at him, really embedding this thought: perfect, okay, awesome, well, guess so, sensational, quite nice, actually.

She didn't drop him off on the way; she drove him to his front door. Thank you. You're welcome. Later, he couldn't remember what she had told him, if he had even replied, and it then wasn't long before he forgot all about her too. Mick had a very fixed idea of what it would be like when he fell in love. He didn't picture a woman in this visualisation, it was more a vision of himself seeing a woman who would trigger in him a kind of explosion on all levels, an explosive awareness that this was the real deal. Yes! his body and soul would scream in unison. It was a scenario he'd experienced several times and it usually turned out to be an ecstasy-fuelled delusion, yet still he clung to the notion that this was the supernova that love began with. Whereas with this woman – who had ruined his bargain with her stupid question, but who was otherwise nice enough and also pretty in her own way – there was no big bang moment. In that phase of Mick's life, everything of importance and worth took place at night, meaning he moved through the daylight hours with his antennae withdrawn. He ate, got some exercise, and, out of necessity, did the chores that were associated with business opening hours, but he didn't have the energy for anything bigger, certainly not for something like an unforgettable encounter. Besides, he was already seeing an overly sensitive photographer with a permanent cold and a highly competent booker at a modelling agency through whom he hoped to make a few contacts, which she clearly suspected was the case and was blocking. Plus he was playing a bit of cat and mouse with a DJane who made out she had a boyfriend, an obstacle Mick preferred to see as friendly competition. Outdoing supposedly steady boyfriends was one of his favourite sporting disciplines. At night, of course, when else?

A week later, Delia showed up at his door with a pair of sunglasses which he hadn't left in her car. A shame, actually, because they would have suited him. There was never a clear answer to whether Delia had really assumed they were his.

Rather than the sunglasses, it was her name he had forgotten. For him, she was a brief episode the previous week. He didn't under any circumstances want to invite her in, so he thought up an excuse, an appointment: he had to go, right now, sorry, had to dash. Where to? Swimming, at the Olympic Stadium. Really? Great. He grabbed a sports bag with dirty laundry for the laundromat and pulled the door shut behind him. Again he followed her down the stairs. Again he looked at her shoulder-length, light brown hair, which this time he filed under 'pretty'. Again she gave him a lift. Again he toyed with her profile. Again she had the competitive disadvantage that he had no desire to be interested in women during the day. Although he did notice that her uni outfit seemed shorter, tighter, lower cut that day. She drove him across the city to the Olympic pool. He went in and did actually swim a few lengths in his underpants. As penance for his lie? Or because she had been so enthusiastic about his alleged swimming routine that he couldn't bring himself to head straight back on the U-Bahn? Hard to say. He lapsed into a front crawl meditation on the DJane and her latest idiotic and at the same time cryptic message on his answering machine. *Hi Mick. So I thought if I catch you now that would mean something. But the fact that I can't reach you now, that means something too, right? Seems that way, anyway. It's a sign, right? All that remains is how to interpret it. Okay, speak soon, that's enough from me!* Yep, that's enough from you, Mick thought.

The third time they met was at Delia's apartment, where she was hosting a farewell dinner for her roommate. She had invited him on their second encounter, with friends if he wanted. Mick wasn't sure why he would want to go to a leaving party for the amp woman, but on the other hand, his approach at the time was to say yes to every invitation and give it more thought later. Afterwards he was glad he hadn't brought a date, because now, in the evening, he finally saw Delia, the student with the Golf, with his night vision. Mick and Desmond, the double act that always made Mick feel so comfortably complete: two emissaries from the realm of night. And Delia: the dazzling host. She consumed vast quantities of roast beef and tiramisu, drank even vaster quantities of wine and then onto spirits. Mick, conditioned to calorie counting, was astonished. Was she trying to counteract her girlish looks with this Viking appetite? A tactic, perhaps, like the forgotten sunglasses? On the other hand, why shouldn't women have their own tricks? Besides, she was an eloquent and witty conversationalist, and that couldn't all be an act. She was bright, that much he could see even in this substance- and hormone-fogged phase of his life. And in her iridescent way, she was beautiful, too. Mick sat next to her and looked: at her sweet, childlike forehead, her nose, a slender sail catching the breeze, and her chin that hovered with a proud Nefertiti line above her long neck, making him wonder why there were so many songs about eyes and lips, and none about this fascinating part of the face. Anyway he couldn't think of one. A jaw-dropping jawline, he thought, and watched on as she rose from the mass of nice girls to the smaller circle of radiant ones, and it also helped that she made Desmond laugh. When people started to get up from the table, she stayed right at Mick's side, a clear signal, and all the same he hadn't expected how electrifying her hand on his thigh would be. Later, when Desmond had organised the assembled guests – by now all completely off their heads – into four cabs to Schöneberg's *Ninety Degrees*, he stayed behind with Delia. They'd clear up, maybe join the others later. Desmond gave him a knowing nod. How good that their hunting grounds didn't overlap. Desmond had found himself a new following. And Mick now had another woman in his life.

He hadn't chased her; she had just happened. Mick and Delia accumulated the various factors that defined being a couple. She was enterprising, she had a different style to Desmond, but definitely a style, and she had an irresistible talent for beautifying his life. He hadn't realised until then how susceptible he was to comfort. He had freedom in Kreuzberg but hadn't realised just how much he missed the immense comfort of Halensee, with the nice cleaning lady, the fragrant laundry and fridge full of nice things. Delia restored these conditions, in a deluxe version: with him as the centre of attention, with sex. He maintained an irrepressible desire for freedom, he squirmed away from commitment, vanished to Desmond's, vanished back to his austere one-room apartment, didn't answer the phone, but Delia was a siren and he was easily seduced: stay a bit longer, I've got this for you, come to mine, I'll make that, you'll love it. And he did love it. He soon stopped wondering whether he loved her too.

Desmond was taking a break from the unbearable Berlin autumn and was visiting friends in California and his mother in New Jersey on the way back. After three months he returned like a resplendent saviour, at least that's how it seemed to Mick. No one had offered him the prospect of a job or money, but all the same he was convinced Desmond's return meant both would be forthcoming. He had already said as much to the various people he had borrowed money from.

The next job they did together was small and took place in Hamburg; the next one would be bigger, but it wasn't official yet, still in the pipeline. So, vague prospects, but still, enough to melt away Mick's existential fears like a medicine you could rely on. It was all just a question of time. Desmond was keeping a low profile; he seemed busy. Christmas was approaching and time seemed to be running away, as it always did in December, the time of year when, if someone asked his age, Mick started rounding up. He would be twenty-four in January. Also, everything seemed to be getting pricier, another December effect, and when Desmond finally told him he was planning his next trip, Mick said yes before he had even heard a single detail. He nodded enthusiastically over his *duck à l'orange* (Desmond was an excellent cook) while Desmond outlined a plan that only slowly percolated through Mick's mind. He ate and nodded and ate.

You know, this is just a suggestion, and you can always say no, Desmond said in conclusion, with a wink as he tossed him a bag of coke next to his plate. In a minute, Mick said, gnawing on the duck carcass. Cocaine, he had discovered, was the new espresso. The perfect after-dinner chaser.

Desmond wasn't suggesting a little sniff after dinner, but rather procuring a large quantity of little sniffs directly from the producer. And the plan seemed so simple and well planned that Mick wondered why he hadn't been part of something like this before.

Step 1: They would take a charter flight to a Caribbean island that was part of Colombia, as tourists on a package holiday. There they would do whatever tourists did.

Step 2: On the last evening, a helicopter would take them to the mainland. There they would meet the pros and do whatever they were told. The helicopter would take them back to their resort, then they would board their charter flight the same night along with all the ruddy, drunken tourists and fly back to Germany.

Step 3: After landing, they would deliver the cargo at a price that had already been negotiated. If Mick wanted to earn more on the side, he could sell his share himself, i.e. become a small-time dealer in Berlin. Though Desmond advised against it.

Mick said yes.

He now realised how it was that Desmond had better cash flow than anyone he knew, even though he didn't work more than anyone else. The phone rang. Desmond's mother. Here was another version of Desmond, a tender, gentle version that only emerged in the context of his mother. He had a completely different tone of voice when he spoke to her. This son version of himself was now murmuring cheerfully into the receiver, leaving Mick facing the duck bones, deep in thought.

You could (and indeed many did) look at the matter this way: people who make their bodies available for the transportation of illegal substances are at the very bottom of the food chain. They're the ones bearing the risk, the ones who have no choice of how to make a living other than to make available the only thing they possess, their body, to help everyone else above them on this miserable ladder to make more profit. Not only do they put their lives on the line, but they also earn the least from it. These people are such poor bastards that even the officials who nab them see them as victims, only to condemn them as perpetrators all the same.

You could also see it this way (and this was how Mick saw it): when your life is a financial disaster that you can't escape by legal means, despite years of trying, then you turn to illegal means. And when you've been on the illegal route long enough, even if only as a consumer, it doesn't seem quite so illegal anymore. Illegal could be taken as a synonym for courageous, determined, resourceful. And this method had one advantage: speed. It was as quick as a flight to another continent. And if it went well, and it would go well, of course, it would also make a really good story with him, Mick, as the hero.

It was only when Desmond came back into the room and began to clear away the dishes that it occurred to Mick that he could have done that. He was so bad at these things. Again, he told Desmond he was up for it.

Now all we need is a woman to join us, Desmond said quietly, carefully scraping the leftover food onto one plate. Mick looked at him.

They don't check those all-inclusive charter flights so closely, sure. But we look like a couple of dodgy Black fags.

One attribute too many.

Indeed.

I'm straight.

Congratulations, darling. Get it stamped in your passport.

And checking us because of our skin colour would be racist.

Oh? Is that right?

Desmond laughed his laugh that could be a blessing or an annihilation.

We'll go as two couples. I'll fly with Sascha, you find Little Miss X, and we're off.

Mick now had two people cooking for him on a regular basis. Delia lifted the pan lid, stirred, tasted, and nodded approvingly.

I'm in, she said.

Delia took drugs in Mick's company but she wasn't massively into them. Her maxim was that she could do whatever she wanted. Take it or leave it. Delia had no financial worries and no energy for criminality – she was studying law – but she didn't even take a minute to think it over before she said yes. He should have known. The Girl with the Pearl Earrings was nurturing her dark side.

One plus, she said, I want to go away with you.

Another plus, she said, I speak Spanish.

Winter was cold, she needed a break, everyone needs money, Colombia is supposed to be beautiful, plus, plus, plus. Mick went to the bathroom and came back. When he sat down, she picked up her fork and ate as if he had fired a starting gun.

He looked at her. She was essentially exactly what Desmond was after: good cover. On the other hand, provided they kept their mouths shut, he and Desmond could pass as locals you'd better not mess with, while Snow White here looked like ransom.

And my addictive disorder would be an advantage for once, Delia said as she piled on more spaghetti. Mick looked at her and had the sense that she had thought about this revelation for some time, probably even rehearsed it. He wasn't sure he should talk about addictions with a woman who thought she was a hoarder because of two piles of clothes in her bedroom and that a couple of drinks made her an alcoholic. But anyway, he did her the courtesy of asking.

Your what disorder?

Delia inhaled sharply through her nose.

So: I have bulimia. Or had. It's in the past. All the same, I can swallow, gag, keep it in, whatever you need. Might be convenient in this scenario.

Shit, Mick thought, and said nothing.

So. That's the way it is.

She laced her fingers together, rested her chin on them, and looked at him expectantly. Wow. Talk about inner demons. He still didn't know what to say, so he stood up and stuck his head into her large refrigerator, staring at her neatly arranged groceries, wondering if it was genuinely all in the past like she said. Then he sat back down in front of his plate, added some salt, joylessly twirled the spaghetti onto his fork and forced it down his constricted throat. Delia crossed her arms and looked at him encouragingly. He had the feeling that the innocent, carefree times were coming to an end. Desmond was a criminal; Delia was dysfunctional. And he wasn't interested in playing Bonnie and Clyde; he was just broke.

Don't you have any qualms at all? I mean, like, none at all?

Sure, but they would be counterproductive. If we started going down that route, we could forget it right away.

You're studying law, he said.

Right. But since we're assuming that it'll go well and that, if in doubt, we can still get out, it's not a problem.

Mick felt a surge of panic. Sometimes she radiated this we're-in-it-together determination that had him cornered. Strangled. She cleared the dishes away.

Look at it this way: we fly to the Caribbean with Desmond, and then we'll see.

Caribbean, flying, Desmond – the surge subsided a little. Delia had a way with bullet points. Mick didn't like to admit it, but sometimes he was a bit of a pushover. He nodded. She beamed, pleased with her powers of persuasion.

We're the ones who don't *need* to do anything. I definitely want to go away with you.

He carried on nodding. Delia turned up her hip-hop and nodded to herself, too. Not chin up and down, but back and forth, yo. And why shouldn't she be allowed to nod like a scowling Black dude? The world was diverse and tolerant. The world was upside down. He'd intended to ask her if she might possibly want to join him in this Desmond madness, and now she was the one trying to convince him. He had two little devils sitting on his shoulders, both shouting: Jump!

When she came back from the bathroom and offered to pay up front for the trip and the product, and to his great relief she still smelled good and tasted good, his anxiety dissolved. Time to take a leap.

I like Delia, she fits, was Desmond's terse response over the phone. They talked through the rest of the details the week before the trip.

And if something happens, which I don't think it will, but if one of us, for whatever reason, gets held up, what do the others do?

Carry on, said Delia, the swot.

Exactly, said Desmond, nodding to Mick.

No looking back, no discussion. From that point on the others don't know them. Right?

Delia had her wine glow again, and the candles were reflected in Desmond's eyes. They expected a nod from Mick and instead got a shrug. That seemed to be enough. They clinked glasses. When Delia disappeared into the bathroom Desmond got up and poured Mick more wine. He then took Mick's head and pressed it gently against him, and stroked it. It's going to be alright, okay?

Mick nodded at Desmond's belt buckle and inhaled the smell of his fabric softener. What was this? It wasn't erotic, but it wasn't just a hug between friends, either. Was it paternal? When Delia returned, Desmond sat back down and raised his glass. Here's to our trip!

There would be three of them flying. Sascha, Desmond's companion, had pulled out, which Desmond accepted with uncharacteristic forbearance. If you're not sure, you shouldn't do it, was all he said. Delia nodded. Mick gulped.

Their flight from Berlin was on a lousy February morning. The island, which looked like it had been dreamed up by a travel agent, was a popular getaway for mainland Colombians, who came here to stock up on duty-free alcohol and cigarettes, as well as for package holidays like them. He had never had a holiday like this before. His travels usually took him wherever he would meet like-minded people: ravers and festival nomads. Now here he was at a beach resort. First, relax and have fun, then work. But Mick didn't manage so well at the having fun part. The first few days he struggled with jet lag, his suffering compounded by the sight of Desmond and Delia, who were going to irritatingly extreme lengths with their seasoned tourist camouflage. Beach volleyball, renting a jeep, virtual deep-sea fishing, diving – great. Plus: jumping into the pool, hand in hand and screaming, dividing the day up into aperitifs and meals. And finishing off with a spot of salsa. Where had they learned to dance like that? Desmond simply expanded his usual house stomp with a few courtship elements. Four-four time. What was there to think about? All you needed was to throw off your inhibitions for a moment. Delia came up trumps by not only having the perfect choreography, but even going so far as to make it look effortless. All this one-upmanship – so out of place on a straw-hut dancefloor – left Mick powerless, and wound-up. Desmond walked around in a bandana, looking like a genie let out of his bottle, while Delia showed up for every entertainment slot on the itinerary in a new outfit with a matching hat or hairband. The other holidaymakers loved them. Which meant they stood out. Which meant that they would be missed when they set off for their little jaunt to the mainland.

Desmond, the attractive solo traveller, toned down the flamboyance compared to how he was in Berlin, allowing him to become – in the eyes of the other Germans – a recent divorcee holidaying with his brother and his brother's girlfriend. The fact that he spoke German with an accent, but his brother Mick didn't, didn't occur to anyone until a few days in.

Because they're idiots, said Desmond.

Because they're racist, said Mick. Of course we're brothers. All Black people are brothers. They all look the same.

Desmond waved it off and ordered another frozen margarita. What would happen, Mick thought, if I flew home just like that? Desmond would be pissed off, but what could he do? Sure, I'd have more to pay him back, but I could work that out with Delia.

The reason for their trip hung over them like a stench that only Mick seemed to notice. He, usually the constant chatterbox, became the silent one. He, who usually repressed everything, became the worrier. Whatever he tried as a distraction, to take his mind off it, it never worked for longer than an hour. Then Mick saw his distorted egghead in Desmond's mirrored shades and heard him say, they don't check US citizens. They all bow down to our embassies. Desmond said, I know South America, of course. It's my side of the world. His side of the world? According to this longitudinal logic, a Norwegian ought to automatically know Nigeria like the back of his hand. It occurred to Mick that Desmond had never told him why he had moved to Berlin from New York. But for all his hot air, Desmond really did give off an aura that made people sense it might be best not to mess with him. The best table in the restaurant, getting in without paying, without an invitation, getting credit without even having a good credit rating – these were Desmond's birthrights. And presumably it was also his birthright to glide through security, because who would stop a man like Desmond?

Oye cómo va? Frankly, a bit shit, thought Mick. The trouble had spread from his head to his skin. He'd been attacked by sand flies and had bites all over his legs. He took an antihistamine to soothe the itching, which made him sluggish and drowsy, a brief respite from the anxiety.

Whatever you took, that's enough. We need to be sober and clear-headed, Desmond said, a daiquiri in his hand.

Then you guys go without me.

Desmond crunched an ice cube and said nothing. I might actually get out now, Mick thought, as good a time as ever, I'm sick, *basta*.

Man, I can't do it, I got fleas – is that it? Desmond teased, shaking his head.

Mick laughed wearily. Desmond placed his ice-cold cocktail glass on Mick's stomach and ran into the water. That didn't help.

So, do you guys actually tan, I mean, get even browner? a fellow holidaymaker asked him. It was the woman he had danced with two nights ago, a mistake, because since then she had followed him around like a shadow. You guys, she had asked, although he was lying there on his own, and now it was up to him to answer. On behalf of his people. The question wasn't meant to be malicious, but it was naive and tedious, and he had answered it a thousand times.

No, you silly cow, we don't get tanned, and we don't get wet and our fingernails don't grow either, thought Mick with a yawn.

Sure, I get a tan, don't you? he said, showing her his winter colour under the waistband of his trunks, which she immediately reached out to touch, like it was a miracle. The woman would surely be amazed if he told her he could even burn. It amazed Mick too, as he had always thought himself invulnerable in this respect. Desmond was using sunscreen, which in the early nineties was only used by redheads and children. He doesn't want to get any darker, Mick realised, rubbing himself with oil for a deeper tan, as he found that a shade darker gave more contour to his muscles. It wasn't only in the southern hemisphere that people talked about the aggressiveness of the sun. It wasn't the seventies anymore, when Mick's great-aunt's neighbours used to barbecue themselves using an aluminium sheet to direct the blazing sun into their faces, always with a cigarette dangling from the corner of their mouths.

Now, twenty years later, he got sunburnt for the first time. Four days of lying around sulking had been enough to turn his upper torso into a painful map of pink continents amidst a bronze-coloured ocean. Languid and pumped at the same time, he lay in the shade in Desmond's long-sleeved shirt from India and a straw hat Delia had bought, and for the first time, he understood the meaning of the word *sombrero*.

Three was not a good number. He might have been mothered by Delia if it hadn't been for Desmond. And Desmond might have cheered him up if it weren't for Delia. He should have known that they would get on so well; Desmond couldn't resist a champion and Delia couldn't resist competing, and winning, in every discipline. The others would carry on, Desmond had said, no looking back. By that point it was crystal clear that when Desmond said 'the others', he meant himself.

Seeing the Colombian mainland appear down below, for a moment Mick felt free. The helicopter flight, up front beside the unnamed pilot, briefly had the air of a casual daytrip with the jet set. How had he never heard before about how stunning Colombia was? Someone had mentioned it – was it Desmond or Delia? Unfortunately their itinerary didn't include stopping to enjoy the scenery, and his spirits sank.

The man who picked them up from the helicopter called himself Juan. He looked like a family man. There were thousands of possible ways you could provide for your family. The car that he drove them in to their destination had mirrored windows all round. Better than a bag over your head, Mick thought, his day trip feeling gone for good. The trip was now an operation; even Desmond was keeping his mouth shut. Underground parking, elevator, *hasta luego*, Juan. They were met by a woman named Pilar. She was around forty, in jeans that looked tailor-made, a pistol on her belt. She knew Desmond but was equally monosyllabic with them all. She led them into a room that looked like a doctor's surgery and introduced them to *el médico*, a soft-faced, very young man who might have studied medicine, or he might have been self-taught and *el médico* was a nickname. He was going to give them some capsules and injections that would help with swallowing and immobilise their digestive systems. Mick was a fin-de-siècle junkie who regularly indulged in excess, followed by indulgence in nursing himself back to health. He would take everything for the sake of a party but feared legitimate medicines like other people feared illicit drugs. When his soul craved destruction, his athlete's instinct told him when the fun was over. What was happening here had never been advertised as fun.

While the young guy injected him, muttering reassuringly to himself, Mick stared at Pilar, a woman who had nothing inviting about her, but besides Delia, who he didn't want to look at, she was the only woman in the room, and staring at women was the best distraction technique he knew. As if obeying a silent instruction, Pilar turned first her profile to him, then her rear view. From behind, her figure was even more guitar-shaped; she had the largest waist-to-hip ratio Mick had ever seen. A comic-strip heroine, he thought, distracting himself from wondering what he had just let happen to him. As a final touch, *el médico* gently stroked the inside of his forearm, his hands soft and warm, and when Mick raised his head, he looked him straight in the eye. The young guy nodded to him. He feels sorry for me, Mick thought, why? Because I'm a miserable bastard. A mule, a poor beast of burden. And on top of that I'm a mulatto, the term for people like him, derived from 'mule'. Was the world nothing but a dark, nasty shithole? At that precise moment, yes.

You okay? asked Desmond, and Mick looked at Delia. The slightest sign of misgivings on her part and he'd be out of there. He could be the Prince Charming who rescues Thumbelina from her predicament. He would even take it upon himself to reimburse Desmond for all expenses. Why did they call them expenses when they were actually costs?

But no, Delia didn't seem put off, and she was the first to swallow the little white balls that looked like tampons, as she noted with a giggle. Her gag reflex was no longer a reflex, she claimed, but a bodily function that she could control, whereas for Mick even the phrase 'gag reflex' triggered the gag reflex.

Brava, said Desmond, and Pilar watched her, stony-faced.

Delia's professionalism again came across as pushiness. He had had an idea, she had gone along with it, and it turned out she was better at it than him. He didn't even want to think about her previously concealed eating disorder, which she whipped out here as her secret weapon. He would never mention it again in Berlin. If he ever got back to Berlin.

During the flight back to the island, Mick, who was again sitting next to the pilot, reassured himself that he was not about to die. Why not? Because then surely he would feel something: rapture, melancholy, ecstasy, some kind of sign. Numb, he stared down at the dots of light below and at the helicopter cockpit. It didn't look so complicated; he could probably take over in case of emergency.

They must have spent the next few hours packing; their flight left at four in the morning. Desmond and Delia remained firmly in tourist parody mode. Farewells with the hotel staff, handing out tips, exchanging addresses and phone numbers with other holidaymakers. See you in Kiel. Definitely. I have a cousin in Berlin. Be sure to stop by when you're there.

Couples from near Bonn would soon be showing up, ringing Desmond's doorbell, worlds would collide.

The travel agency Desmond booked everything through was called Titanic Travel. A joke for fatalists. They had the nice professionals there to thank for their seats with lots of legroom and the perfect timings. No other flight left them with as short a gap between loading their cargo in Central America and unloading in Europe, Desmond said. They even had a time buffer, not that they would need it. The plane wasn't fully booked. Delia and Mick sat just the two of them in a row of four, Desmond was on his own in a row of two by the window. Before take-off he had put on a sleep mask, making it clear he wasn't to be spoken to. Delia put on her headphones and lay her book on Mick's lap.

As they departed from Colombia, Mick read Gabriel García Márquez, the Colombian. He turned to the table of contents and read: *Nabo: The Negro who Made the Angels Wait.* Very apt. He read the story, which was awful and disturbing and ended with the aforementioned Black man, a former saxophone player, spending fifteen years of his life languishing forgotten by the world in a horse stable, where he is vertiert, as the German translation put it, although they were waiting for him in the choir, the choir of angels, as it turned out. Mick read the word *vertiert* about ten times before he realised it referred to a man becoming an animal. Negro, music, animal. Great, thank you, Mr Nobel Prize winner.

I hadn't realised García Márquez was so dark, he said to Delia, though she had fallen asleep and was leaning on him with her mouth open. Poor little thing. Seeing them both asleep helped him make his peace with them. They weren't his enemies; they were his friends. When he heard the tinkle of the serving trolleys, he realised that even in their sleep, his friends were pros, always one step ahead: they had avoided the food question, which he had to answer with no, thank you. The stewardess responded with an incredulous smile. What could he safely ingest? He asked for crackers and black tea, which tasted as if it had never been in contact with any tea leaves, but which nevertheless kept him awake. He leaned against Delia, breathed in the scent of her hair, and began his negotiations with a higher power. If She or He let him get through all this without any complications, what would he sacrifice? A body part, which one? A relationship, with whom? Years of his life, how old would he become? Exhausted by these thoughts of self-blackmail, he finally fell asleep.

He was woken by the end of an announcement. He woke with a start, and when he saw that the plane was stationary, he was startled again. Had they arrived? No one stirred; everyone was asleep. Desmond was slouched in his seat like a Z. His window blind wasn't pulled down. Outside, Mick saw a night somewhere wintry. Snowflakes swirled in a cone of yellow lamplight. The announcement was finished before he'd had the chance to understand it. He thought of the man in García Márquez's story who thought only a moment had passed since he was kicked in the head by a horse's hoof, though it had been years. He had no idea how long he had slept; he wasn't wearing a watch. He took Delia's arm. She twitched in her sleep and then, with a sigh, changed her position. It was too early; they weren't at their destination. They were somewhere else.

Fear spread through his body, freezing his hands and feet; it crept up his spine and wrapped around his head, making his throat throb and pressing behind the eyes, making his hair stand on end. Then he felt where it had centred itself, a seething, bubbling pool where everything coalesced. His body commanded him to stretch and take a deep breath, to loosen his belt and stand up, quickly. Delia woke up, looked at him, startled, and then out of the window at the snowy ghost airport. I'm going to go to the bathroom, he said, a sentence that in an enclosed space like an aeroplane cabin was even more superfluous than usual. Delia was startled, and asked, for a pee? Also superfluous information that a woman like Delia would never request, but which jolted Mick from his sleep like a siren and raised his fear to a conscious level. He stared at Delia, who also realised at that moment that the thing he desperately needed to do was what he was not allowed to do under any circumstances. Across the aisle, Desmond sighed in his sleep.

Desmond woke up in the middle of nowhere, somewhere over the Atlantic, and asked for a black tea. He checked his watch, which he hadn't changed yet, and figured out the time. They should have had the technical stopover at the provincial airport on the US East Coast by now. It wasn't mentioned on the ticket because they wouldn't actually get off the plane, they'd just stay put while they stopped for refuelling or for the next pilot to start his shift, fresh as a daisy.

He stretched and yawned, and as he did, he caught a whiff of shit. He shut his mouth, irritated. The downside of sitting at the very front, right by the toilets. For fuck's sake, Desmond thought, sipping his exceptionally bad tea. Mick and Delia were asleep. Their heads were resting against each other, her right arm linked with his left. He had spared them both a few unnecessary details. They should have flown straight to Berlin from the Caribbean, but their scheduled flight was overbooked. This flight went via London, which meant their cover as package tourists wasn't quite as watertight as planned. London's better than Madrid, he'd reassured them. They could have asked, in what way? But even Delia just nodded.

Another waft of shit blew in his direction. A blonde with a deep tan walked by and looked him straight in the eye. Yes, Desmond wasn't bad to look at, even after over ten hours crumpled into an economy seat. But who starts flirting in the presence of the unmistakable stench of their own shit? He gave the blonde a withering glare and looked out the window, yawning.

Asleep, Mick looked even younger than when he was awake. He looked like the little boy he must have been not so long ago, vulnerable and sweet and alone. Delia, on the other hand, unable to control her appearance in her sleep, unmasked the person Desmond had seen her to be over the last ten days: a sly old hag. A furrowed forehead, nasolabial folds as deep as canyons, and shit, she wasn't even thirty yet, thought Desmond, who had nearly a kilo of cocaine in his stomach. These mundane passenger thoughts helped him exude the vibes of an ordinary passenger irritated by the exertions of a long-haul flight.

His nerves had mellowed – normal when you pull something off several times in a row without incident. If he hadn't already decided this was his last job, he might almost think of it as routine, but he wasn't about to push his luck by cutting corners, because one thing he definitely wasn't, and that was a fool. If you go through with a plan, you have to expect an element of uncertainty and be ready to improvise. Last time, one of the guys had dropped out and flown back empty-handed. He had given the impression in Berlin that he never missed a chance to break the law, like he couldn't even buy a pack of aspirin without threatening the guy at the drugstore. But he lost his nerve. Maybe it was because of Pilar. By now, Desmond was used to her intimidating air, like a frosty barmaid. Or more likely – and Desmond's misjudgment was to blame here – the problem lay in the nature of the criminal act, which required not reckless bravado, but self-control. Looking back, he had no idea how he'd persuaded himself to expect this mental capacity of a short-tempered fighting dog.

Mick was different. An erratic desperado with – seemingly – nothing to lose, but who also loved life to the max. An unusual combination, it seemed to Desmond, appealing and useful. But to what end? Desmond glanced again at Mick's sleeping face. When Mick thought something was funny, he'd throw himself back and shake with his own laughter. And no doubt he was an animal in bed. Desmond had had a glimpse of that in their little, um, interlude, that finally drew a clear boundary in their friendship. Yes, Mick was straight, period. Desmond could have anyone, so he didn't usually bother seducing anyone who was still on the fence about their sexuality. Guys who were probably thinking about women the whole time. Sure, there were queers who got a kick from converting straight guys; Desmond wasn't one of them.

Mick was a good companion. Not reliable in the usual sense; he could barely rely on himself. You could take it for granted that he would turn up late. He got there when he got there. He drifted along with the flow. Sundance Kid. With the soul of a Samaritan. Desmond had seen him drive no matter what state he was in, and he was with Mick the time he hauled a homeless man who'd fallen asleep in the snow all the way to the emergency room, getting an earful from the guy the whole way. Outrageous. For Mick, on the other hand, it wasn't exactly helpful, but in view of the bum's overall situation, it was understandable. Sorry, dude, but we have to get to the hospital now, okay. He laughed so charitably, like it was a freshly bathed little boy hanging off his back, not some degenerate old man. Mick, who was always broke, was a big tipper. At night, he was always there for anyone who was out of it or dehydrated or in a bad way, and in the daytime, he would stop to help anyone old or slow or disabled: basically, anyone who, for whatever reason, couldn't keep pace with the survival of the fittest and who had generally resigned themselves to the fact that no one gave a shit. No one did, except Mick. Give me that, I'll carry it, sit down, it's fine, sure I'll buy a rose from you, here, Desmond, for you. If it was helper syndrome, he'd be hooked on gratitude. But that wasn't it. He came, he saw, he helped.

Then he moved on, once again engrossed in his own little world. He was a sunny boy in a man's body. Desmond had no problem with men's bodies. But boys, hmm, no thanks. He used to hate the way his younger brother looked up to him; it was even more irritating since Desmond was forced into the role of not just big brother, but also the bad one.

Again, he looked over at Mick and Delia, who seemed to form an inseparable unit when asleep, nothing like when they were awake. If this wasn't his last trip, he would have to change how he did it next time, because even this group had turned out to be problematic. Sascha's backing out at the last minute had turned a sturdy quadrilateral into a wobbly triangle, with him the boss at the top. Or the kindergarten teacher. Desmond had overestimated how callous he could be. It didn't work with Mick. On the island, he was conscious that he felt responsible for him, an unfamiliar, disturbing feeling that he couldn't easily switch off. Desmond could look out for himself just fine. He'd always needed to. As one of two sons of an overworked single mother, it had become a way of life that others just had to accept. If you're going to have anything to do with Desmond, you need to look out for yourself. If you can't, don't burden Desmond with it. At best, you're someone who can bring beauty to Desmond's life. Once you've grasped that, assuming you're also independent, rich, influential, sexually attractive, highly entertaining, or all of the above, you and Desmond will get along just fine.

And what did Mick have to offer him? He wasn't part of Desmond's VIP circle, characters from the world of art and fashion, whose lifestyle Desmond always aspired to until he saw there was no legal way he could afford it. Nor was Mick part of the crowd who were less affluent, more creative and cosmopolitan. But he was so thoroughly loveable and entertaining in his coltish way that, against his principles, Desmond spent a lot of time with someone who was actually no use to him. Mick reminded Desmond of himself, not that that made him more generous or indulgent. He abhorred naiveté. It was a luxury only women could afford. Some. Very few. Mick's proving himself as naive and whiny as he had been on this trip – making Desmond feel he needed to protect him – was worse than the damage done by that small-time crook he had inadvertently brought with him last time. And it left him no choice but to cut Mick off and turn instead to Delia, who wasn't close to him and whose fearlessness had been a pleasant surprise. She seemed to be under permanent pressure to prove herself, but never mind. Sure, let her strut her stuff, and try to drink him under the table. Very amusing, all that swagger.

The anonymous wholesaler wasn't going to get his supply. Desmond would take over the distribution himself, to boost profits. It would still be far from the kind of money he had in mind, but it could finally cover a deposit on a house in East Berlin. He was amazed people weren't scrambling to get their hands on those crumbling nineteenth-century *Gründerzeit* tenements. Their value was sure to skyrocket. The Germans seemed to have lost their nerve when it came to taking risks, an instinct driven out of them by dictatorship in the East, and in the West by a narcotic mix of bourgeois prosperity and longing for security. Before they stirred from this twilight state, Desmond would have invested in a Berlin rental property that would give him ongoing financial stability. Buying real estate in a prime location wasn't even a risk. Unlike this operation here.

Yes, it was hideous, but the end justified the means, because for Desmond poverty was even more hideous. The feeling of being unjustly condemned to poverty had been with him for as long as he could remember. He found it depressing to see people set their sights too low. Modest goals weren't a sign of good character, just lack of imagination and self-respect. People who valued themselves didn't settle for mediocrity, did they? Desmond had always wanted the best for himself. Because he saw it and identified it. And then he always had to accept that the best wasn't meant for him. First, it was toys and clothes; later, art, furniture, houses, and places that belonged to a parallel world that everyone around him seemed uninterested in. His mother was astonished by his refined tastes. Whenever she was getting dressed up, she'd ask his advice, laughing. His innate desire for quality seemed like a funny quirk to her. Desmond wants to get back to his real parents on the Upper East Side, she'd tease, whenever he wanted something beyond their reach. Desmond's dream career was to be a millionaire: that was the running gag among the adults. No one wondered whether or not there was a route to achieving this goal. As if it was more far-fetched to become an investment banker than an astronaut.

He eventually went to art college, while Dashiell, his nerdy rock-collecting brother, stayed true to himself and studied geology. When Dashiell received his doctorate, their mother, a nurse, beamed as though she had achieved her life's goal. No one asked about Desmond's childhood dream anymore. Why not? Because you weren't supposed to long for wealth as blatantly as Desmond had as a child. Because it wasn't the done thing for poor people to cite wealth as their goal, while for rich people it was to be expected. Wealth was for keeping, multiplying, and donating ostentatiously. While many people climbed *one* rung of the social ladder within a generation, very few succeeded in climbing several. So, if he busted a gut like his mother, his children might manage one more rung. The thought depressed him, even though children didn't feature in his plans. His current venture, after several wearisome years as a photographer when he had at least surrounded himself with people who met his aesthetic standards, was so far below the threshold that it was, Desmond reasoned, actually unclassifiable. He was just sidestepping the rules by which he was supposed to humbly work his way up. An illicit but necessary step.

His long-standing taste for wealth had brought with it a nice standard of living, but also a mountain of debt. He could hardly lower his standard of living any further; after all, anyone who seemed hard-up was shunned, and that would negatively impact his commissions and his reputation as an artist. Besides, there was the fact that his mother needed him, even if she strenuously denied it, and strangely enough, this responsibility didn't annoy him but drove him on. In fact, he wasn't even annoyed by his dozy brother Dashiell at the moment; he could mess around at his institute if he wanted to, at least he lived near Mom. Meanwhile, Desmond, the distant son, with no doctorate and no wife, would single-handedly pay off his mother's mortgage.

Desmond put aside his book, *American Psycho*, a bloodbath of a thriller that was hailed as satire because the guy behind the bloodbath wasn't some antisocial weirdo but a bored Wall Street yuppie type. A reminder of the career in finance Desmond hadn't had. He stood up and stretched, smoothed his trousers at the knee, put on his suit jacket over his Armor Lux shirt – Gaultier and Picasso might not have worn a suit jacket with this kind of shirt, but Desmond thought the look worked. Not playfully serious, not deliberately casual, not too easy to pigeonhole – perfect for this trip. Just as he reached for his toothbrush, the seat belt signs came on. Thank God, he was spared having to brush his teeth in that stench.

The captain began with his multilingual announcement. And Desmond sincerely hoped that he had misheard the time.

Delia let the cabin sounds drift into her semi-consciousness for as long as she could before giving up on sleep and opening her eyes to find Desmond staring right at her. Looking back, past Mick's chest and the crook of his arm, she caught Desmond's uneasy gaze and wondered how long he had been looking at her like that. She smiled at him, his grin impossible to interpret, but it certainly wasn't reassuring. It couldn't be that she was the only one here who felt in control. And it was almost uncanny how normal she felt physically. She looked at her watch, fumbled around for her ticket, looked at it. The times didn't make sense. Never mind what time it was in the air where they were, the question was what time it was in London. If she'd worked it out right, they ought to have been checking in for their Berlin flight right now. Desmond was sitting with his head cocked. He seemed to be thinking.

Desmond?

Reluctantly, he looked at her.

Are we going to make the connection?

He shrugged, as if he couldn't care less.

If we don't make that one, we'll get the next one. No problem.

It is a problem, Delia thought, feeling her normal physical state tip towards maximum nausea. She pictured herself walking through Heathrow, sitting around for hours on end on an airport bench. She saw herself collapsing and dying in agony. Shit shit shit, she thought, rummaging in her handbag for a Valium. She didn't find any, which was a relief, because who knows what that would lead to. Instead, she tucked her deodorant stick under her blouse, and the familiar smell calmed her down slightly. If they left the airport in London, they would have to cross another border, and with contraband luggage instead of body cargo. Then they might as well have travelled the whole way with a suitcase of coke. Fuck it, Delia thought, and fuck what Desmond thought, she needed to get out the second they landed. But then what? There was only the ferry. She didn't need to justify not showing up for her flight. She would simply walk out of the airport and find a good hotel to do what she needed to do. There are only two choices, she thought, and immediately she felt better: either we make the scheduled flight, or I'm out. Either way is fine.

She leaned forward and glanced again at Desmond. He was looking out the window with the same fascination as a little boy. Fortunately, for the flight, he had swapped his common-as-muck holiday disguise for a pale linen suit that suited him perfectly. But please, Desmond, don't wear a hat with it, keep it subtle. Mick sat next to her in jeans and a polo shirt, fine. He could pass for a nice young man, a professional athlete, a dancer maybe, at best a trainee teacher on a semester break. She herself heeded her father's advice more often than she let on. She didn't like to mention him, since realising that a father who was present, a role model even, who supported her morally and financially was such a rare thing in her new circle of friends that she almost needed to justify it. Desmond's father was said to have been a suave bigamist, which you could believe when you saw Desmond, though he hadn't seen his father since he was four years old. Mick's father had disappeared before he had any memory of him and was replaced by his mother with a string of successors. Mick spoke neither disparagingly nor particularly warmly about them; they were just part of his childhood, not something he had strong feelings about. It was what it was. He didn't seem to see any deficit in his lack of a father; perhaps that was why she saw it all the more clearly. Poor Mick. Other friends of hers also struggled with father issues, which in essence boiled down to: under no circumstances do I want to end up like mine.

Delia, on the other hand, loved Bernhard, her father, unconditionally. Bernhard was an active part of his daughter's life, also offering a safety net in the form of a credit card for emergencies, although she could define for herself what counted as an 'emergency'. Bernhard had taught her how to keep a cool head, because hysterics never helped, on the contrary. Bernhard had taught her how to control her emotions by taking a deep breath and looking at things from another perspective. Bernhard took her with him to his office, where she saw how you could exude authority *and* be nice. When you find yourself in a new group, Bernhard had taught her, immediately identify the best person there, and become better than him. Bernhard had taken her hunting, and by the time her mother objected, she could already use a shotgun, and had downed a wild goose from the sky. Among Bernhard's less belligerent life lessons was the advice that one should always dress well. You could make people reconsider their first impressions later on, but better to steer their first impression in your favour. Delia was wearing a lightweight, powder-blue Armani suit, with a white blouse that she'd put on in the toilet cubicle of horror.

She now heard, in three languages, that they had made up only forty-five minutes of their three-hour delay, which meant they wouldn't make their connecting flight to Berlin.

End of the line, she thought, as the cabin crew finally prepared for landing. At her side, Mick was grinding his teeth. She leaned over him and whispered to Desmond, let's get out in London, I'll pay for a hotel, we can relax. He eyed her silently, apparently not interested in hearing anyone else's suggestions. There's a flight from London to Berlin almost every hour, he said, eventually.

As if you could get on any flight just like that. Should she try and reason with him? No, Delia decided. Desmond leaned back in his seat again. He had not come through this flight unscathed; he looked pale, as far as that was possible with him, oh yes, it was definitely possible. Mick seemed to be having another bad dream; he clung to her forearm, breathing heavily. When the plane touched down and applause broke out at the back of the cabin, he opened his eyes.

Waiting for the plane to reach its final stop, waiting for the seatbelt signs to go off, waiting to be hooked up to a boarding bridge or until some steps were dragged over, waiting for the disabled passengers and those in business class to disembark first. They also had a disability, a hidden one that was nobody's business. They should have flown business. But Desmond had been categorically against it. We need to be your average package holiday tourists, he had said in his Yankee drawl, which Delia had loved so much that it cheered her up when she imitated him. Oh my gawd, that feels gooood when you oil my back, Delia! She slowly stood up. She had shown ample mental and physical strength; she couldn't take any more. The hunter had sewn the boulders into the wolf's belly in place of the little goat kids which, strangely enough, he had swallowed whole. Along with Little Red Riding Hood and her grandmother. Delia, the animal lover, had always felt sorry for the wolf, which she had assumed was the same one in both fairy tales, not *a* wolf, but *the* wolf. And now she was the wolf with the indigestible, lethal cargo in her belly. Not in her grandmother's nightgown and bonnet, but in an Armani suit, with Grandma's pearls around her neck, which had a similar effect to Dad's Amex: very comforting.

They exchanged very few words. We've missed our connection, Delia said. Mick nodded. We'll get the next one, Desmond said. Or we'll get out, we'll see, Delia said, and again, Mick only nodded feebly. For days, she hadn't been able to read him emotionally. Delia tried to catch his eye, but he put on his rucksack and stood in the aisle, where he stared down at the floor.

When it was their turn to disembark, Desmond went first, followed by Mick, and Delia let a few other passengers come between her and them. On the steps, the English winter blew in her face. She boarded the bus and looked over several weary heads up at Desmond's fingers full of silver rings gripping the ceiling strap. What was her body saying? She'd lost contact. She rummaged in her handbag for a cough sweet and chewed on it, just in case she had bad breath. One less thing to worry about, albeit a comparatively small one. The bus driver seemed to spice up his monotonous job by waltzing around in great loops, and a few tighter ones, perhaps he was a former champion in the giant slalom. There was no end to the twists and turns. Heathrow was gigantic; it felt like they'd been round the whole of Corsica on a serpentine road. Delia wanted to scream. To just open her mouth and scream. Her sense of time was out of kilter; her tenacity was depleted. She stared at the stationary planes, at the trailers full of luggage, tankers, men in neon hi-vis vests. Were they content with their jobs, looking after the jet fuel and suitcases? She slowed her breathing, breathed more deeply; it helped. Mr Slalom's final flourish knocked the passengers off their feet, minutes after they'd had to learn to stand again after sitting for fourteen hours, then the bus swung to a stop in front of the glass door to the terminal.

She got off and followed the herd, keeping the back of Desmond's head in view. He had a fast stride anyway, a natural frontrunner, and the question now was: which was the best strategy? Being part of a group, part of a couple, or alone? At the moment, Desmond was still in a pair with Mick, which could have been two friends or brothers. Desmond stopped abruptly in front of the display board. She stopped, too, though she had already decided. With throbbing temples, Delia read her way through the cities of the world until she found Berlin. Just under three hours. Mick stared paralysed at the board; Desmond gave her the slightest nod, turned and walked towards the exit. Mick caught up with him; Delia regretted wearing her pumps rather than keeping her Chucks on – they only had a medium heel, but still. Click clack, click clack. At passport control, she breathed deeply again and visualised her face, the face that the man up ahead was about to see through the glass window. Miss Hoyer, Cordelia Bernadette, born on the twentieth of March 1966 in Hanover, resident of Berlin, one metre sixty, eyes: grey-green. Had she known that her description would be printed in every single passport thereafter, she would have said green. Green like hope, like jade, like the silent ocean. Her eyes were grey.

She walked up to the border guard and smiled at him. A quick glance. A dour-looking South Asian with an Elvis haircut. He read her passport closely and asked for her ticket. Why aren't you flying on to Berlin, Miss, um, Hoyer? Because I want to take the chance to visit my cousin. Quick glance. She's studying at Oxford. Quick glance. History. A nod, passport with the ticket inside. No more glances. It was no crime to skip your flight, but it didn't hurt to have a plausible explanation. Two counters along, it was Mick's turn, hopefully he would get through easily enough. She wasn't sure if he was even really awake yet. There was no need to worry about Desmond being able to explain himself, just as there was no need to worry about Desmond in general. He was through. They had made it. Mick caught up with her, put his arm around her shoulder and said, let's talk at the hotel. She nodded. Talk about what?

The other passengers walked toward the baggage carousels, then on towards the exit. What else was still to come? Anything to declare? Ha ha. Good joke. Desmond, who was in the lead again, had a small Rimowa aluminium cabin bag, Mick had a backpack, Delia had her handbag and her vanity case, a popular item of hand luggage for women at that time, full of bottles, tubes, and jars. They didn't look like they had anything to declare. The older passengers they had just overtaken did, on the other hand: the woman with waist-length, white hair, in sandals and a baffling mess of layers of fabric, and the man, in a large-checked wool suit, bright yellow sweater, and a ridiculous little trilby. Their luggage looked more like immigration than a holiday; she had more on her trolley than him, though to make up for it he had more teeth than her. A younger man seemed to belong with them, with plaited hair and a goatee, taller than the two oldies, with a rakish, bare chest covered in necklaces, under a velvet jacket. Delia pulled past him, sensing a smug whistle and his gaze on the back of her neck.

Then came the moment Delia would later remember only in slow motion. Uniformed men. Airport police officers with padded vests and short machine guns. And other officers in regular police uniforms. Two women among them. Two were talking to each other. One was speaking into a radio. They were standing there because they had to stand there, nothing to be alarmed by, just doing things by the book, right? If you need to justify your presence, check the Gipsy Kings – they've brought their entire village with them in four suitcases. Delia saw an official step into the corridor; Desmond was walking towards him with long strides. He said something to the officer standing next to him, who looked like a fourteen-year-old with a machine gun. Desmond raised his hand like a businessman on his way to work waving off a beggar, sorry, no time to stop. The policeman kept his friendly expression and pointed to Desmond's aluminium case. Behind Desmond, Mick slowed his pace though he was supposed to keep going, that was the arrangement. Did they look like people who knew each other, or was Desmond far enough ahead of Mick? Then a policewoman with a bright red ponytail under her police hat shouted something. Mick stopped. A tall, broad woman, Delia later recalled, who had been talking to a colleague on the other side of the corridor. Excuse me, Sir? she called out, beckoning Mick over, with what seemed to Delia in this dream sequence an endlessly slow wave and an official smile.

Delia's get-out-of-there instinct was so strong that she could already picture herself running back. Back to where? Through the roar of her own blood, as loud as a waterfall, she heard the polite voice of a British official, presumably addressed – as it occurred to her later when she reconstructed the scene – to the white mane woman and not her. Please go on, ma'am! And Delia was off.

Her heels clicked as she paced to the exit, where she could already see the people waiting. In her peripheral vision she saw Desmond, flanked by uniforms, and heard him say, I'm an American citizen. His mantra, with which he granted himself worldwide immunity. She had already lost sight of Mick behind the redhead and a young Black man. The waiting hordes in front of her were peering into the arrivals area, hoping to see their loved ones. Delia walked faster; they were waiting for her. She raised her arm and waved to the throng of strangers: Yoo-hoo! Here I am! She caught the gaze of a young, uniformed officer, who eyed her for a split second. Did he find her edgy, did he find her suspicious? She continued to beam at the crowd out there, just four or five more large Desmond strides. One, inhale and wave again. Two, inhale and bat your eyelashes. Three, exhale, run your hands through your hair. Four. If the policeman was still watching her, who was she waving to? Probably not the family with the small children, who were waving paper flags of a Caribbean nation Delia couldn't place right now, and not the chubby couple in the matching anoraks, nor the group of nuns holding up a sign that didn't say anything monastical like *Father John* or *Monsignor Domenico*, but simply *Barry*.

She plunged herself into the crowd as if stepping into dough, hoping to sink into it. They could still pull her back out, this woman who had been destined for Berlin-Tegel and was instead pacing towards the Piccadilly Line. Delia couldn't help thinking of the 'wanted' posters of childhood, the creepy black and white mug shots of the Baader-Meinhof Group, a violent guerrilla gang with an unusually high proportion of women. She felt like she had a flashing neon arrow floating above her. She forced herself not to look around, forced herself to drop her shoulders, forced herself to breathe. Then something occurred to her, and she turned back and went against the stream to a bureau de change, where she exchanged a hundred deutschmarks for a paltry thirty pounds, which would vanish into thin air in no time at all because this was London. She exchanged another hundred and fifty deutschmarks then dashed back towards the Tube. She would get off at Piccadilly Circus or at Leicester Square, head to one of the hotels there, and finish this operation alone, which was perhaps better than with the others. Buy a ticket, get on a train, sit down, one passenger among hundreds, a face easily confused with someone else. She woke up at Russell Square. There must be hotels there, too. But she switched platforms and headed back to Piccadilly Circus, anyway. She had her Discman on and was listening to Massive Attack, and years later she would have the feeling that Massive Attack was her soundtrack to the whole of the nineties.

The hotel was called Every Hotel, which suited her, and no one seemed particularly interested in her, which suited her even better. For the time being, a double room for three days. Just you? Yes please. Do you have any luggage? Not yet. The airline will send it on to me, I hope. Oh? Yes. Good luck and have a pleasant stay.

She went up to her room, finally took the laxative that Desmond had got for them in advance in Berlin, lay down naked on the bed and waited.

After he had been examined and X-rayed in a make-shift medical centre, he was left for what seemed like hours, sitting alone at a table in a white room with a grey carpet. He sat there with his eyes closed, because there was nothing to look at anyway, presumably part of the policy of attrition, composing stories testifying his innocence, each one more incoherent than the last.

I didn't know what I was swallowing, it was a dare, I lost a bet, we were drunk. The amount would determine the sentence, and there couldn't have been much left in him. Involuntarily, he thought of the toilet on the plane where he had experienced one of the various worst-case scenarios. A nightmare, hideous yet human, while Delia's reaction had been superhuman. She had washed off the shit and swallowed it all down again, while Mick, the originator of the shit, had squatted, wretched and shivering, on the quarter of a square metre at her feet. He wondered if he would have done the same for her, or if Desmond would do it for him, or he for Desmond, and the answer was always no. Delia, in heroine mode, had even spoken to the stewardess through the closed door in a perfectly normal passenger voice, at which point the stewardess had disappeared to go and fetch anything that might help. And then, still frozen and incapacitated, he had forced himself to look at Delia with the thought that he would never be able to kiss this woman again.

The stewardess had offered them a selection of harmless emergency remedies for the gastrointestinal tract, as well as bananas and oral hygiene kits, which Delia grabbed before disappearing again, while Mick was relieved to find, beneath the surface of the horror, that his cramps were subsiding. He closed his eyes to avoid having to respond to any concerned questions from the stewardess, and when Delia got back to her seat, he had already passed out, exhausted. When he came round again, they were just landing. He didn't know what the other two might have discussed. Desmond might already know, if Delia had filled him in. Had she?

It was quite possible that his response when they pulled him out at customs was the instinctive *Me? Why me?* of his childhood. The associated reflex was to shout something that had, fortunately, stuck in his throat: Delia! She had tottered past him with the slick panache of a frequent flyer. She hadn't hesitated for a second but had saved herself for the other side: wealthy, carefree, legal. Bravo. He didn't know if he could have mustered that professional level of callous detachedness. But he knew that she was out.

He stretched his legs out, jiggled his thighs, inspected his fingernails. Didn't you get assigned a lawyer right away? They must have had good reason to be suspicious; they didn't X-ray any old passenger as part of routine checks. Mick began to picture life in prison. Clearly influenced by Hollywood, he saw himself in the slammer, sitting behind a window in an orange jumpsuit, his mother facing the window with a telephone receiver in her hand. What have you been up to, then? she would ask, as she always did whenever he was in trouble. Most of the time he even told her the truth, because Monika's punishment was the questioning itself. She wouldn't stop until she knew everything, then she would leave him alone. He had been up to a lot. He'd been in trouble a lot.

After being given a paper cup with lukewarm water and then a plate of dry cookies, which he didn't touch, he was left alone for another indeterminate amount of time; he couldn't tell how long. He suspected that he was being observed, although there wasn't a window or a camera in the room, assuming the thing on the ceiling was a smoke detector. An official came, stuck his head through the door, excused himself in a cheerful, officey tone of voice, and left. A woman came, told him someone would be along soon, and left. He heard voices in the corridor. The woman popped her head in at the door again and asked him if he spoke English. He wondered if he should ask for an interpreter, to have someone on his side. But why would an interpreter be on his side? The woman asked again and he said, yes, I do speak English. Why would that have been his one strong subject at school if not as preparation for an interrogation by Scotland Yard? Was it Scotland Yard? Whatever. He felt too young for this. He had fallen in with the wrong crowd, a bad influence. Where was his bad influence now, and what was he saying?

When the woman came a third time, this time accompanied by a man with a shrewd piggish face, Mick had forgotten all his excuses. They asked him if he knew Desmond, and how, and he stuck relatively close to the truth, because he couldn't tell what they knew about them and what they didn't. What files were shared between the IT systems of the travel agencies, airlines, banks, and immigration offices? Was it a spot check or had they already had their sights on Desmond? In any case, better to admit that he knew him. How well did he know him? Not very well. Through work, he had been his assistant. Who had had the idea of flying to this island? Desmond. Why hadn't they taken their connecting flight? Because they wanted to spend a few days in London.

The man looked like he didn't believe a word he was saying. He nodded and looked at a stack of papers in front of him. Mick resisted the urge to rock back on the chair, an urge triggered by the government-owned furniture with its tubular steel legs. Mick as delinquent, nothing new. Wouldn't an innocent person ask what all this was about? But the English section of his brain's language centre seemed to have been deleted with the exception of the words *yes*, *no,* and *what*.

The man cleared his throat. The woman sat beside him smiling like a social worker and interrupted the silence by asking Mick if he was okay physically. He said yes and looked directly at the woman, who fortunately exuded neither authority nor sexual attractiveness. The man clasped his hands together and looked him straight in the eye as if he were following the choreography of an interrogation; Mick presumed such a thing existed.

Did he know, ahem, that Desmond was a drug mule?

No.

A simple no. A shocked no wouldn't help, either. In his daze, he registered a sense of incredulous relief. They thought he was Desmond's accomplice. But apparently, they couldn't prove anything. Because nothing had been found. They had X-rayed him and seen nothing except, it seemed, a completely empty intestinal tract.

He expected a question about Delia. How was he to explain that one half of a harmless couple vacationing together had simply disappeared when her partner had been picked up? An innocent woman would have stood outside, distraught, waiting for her mistakenly arrested boyfriend to be released. Or called the German embassy. Or found a lawyer. In any case, she would still be there. We had an argument, he would have said. But they didn't ask him about her.

The pig-faced man looked at his colleague and snapped the folder shut. His colleague pushed her chair back and asked Mick to wait again. Mick nodded. And waited.

After another eternity, an older officer came in, handed him back his passport and backpack, and asked him to follow him. They walked along a neon-lit corridor he hadn't noticed earlier, up a flight of stairs, along another corridor, and finally stopped at a door. The officer unlocked it and, with a friendly nod somehow unsuited to the situation, let him out. He was free to go.

And Mick sidled away. He staggered off, feeling like he had been hurled out of a moving car, onto the street. As if they could change their minds and come back for him at any time. Outside, he lit a Lucky that was supposed to calm him down, though it completely failed; it felt like the first cigarette he ever smoked. He stamped it out and just stood there for a while. An approaching police car made him turn and head back into the arrivals hall, which he wandered through on shaky legs. Artificial lighting and a milky light from outside, gongs and announcements, people moving in all directions, all decisive and purposeful, except for him. This could be what it's like to have died, arriving disoriented in a new place. This place, Heathrow, would be a relatively comfortable hell, or a completely underwhelming heaven. You couldn't tell anything about the weather outside from what people were wearing, something he had noticed before in London. Sandals, woolly hats, Hawaiian shirts, duffle coats, and shorts all existed in parallel. Which would also be the case in the afterlife, assuming you arrived in hell or heaven dressed the same as when you died.

He was drawn back out into the drizzling rain. The idea of taking a bus into the city seemed less claustrophobic than an endless ride on the Underground. Then he went back inside, where he exchanged the last of his cash, Colombian pesos and German marks, for seventy pounds. He remembered that he could ask about the next flight to Berlin, but he was still reeling from the shock of the arrest. Would they know in Berlin and would they question him again? His digestive tract was apparently so offended by the ordeal that it was on strike;

it refused to give him the slightest hint of thirst or hunger. He bought a bottle of airport water at an eye-watering airport price and drank it just in case. He followed the signs to the Tube and got off at Covent Garden. There he wandered around a few stores that would have appealed to Desmond in his tireless search for beautiful things. Delia had said something about a hotel – had she mentioned the name? He found a phone, called his Berlin landline, entered the code for the answering machine and listened to twelve unimportant messages. He would keep trying until he heard from Delia, because it had to occur to her that this was the only way to reach him. He wandered through Hyde Park, then went onto Regent's Park, where he would have liked to visit the zoo, though he didn't, for financial reasons. Where was he going to sleep? Where was Delia? What would happen to Desmond? His fears lined up one after another, switching places, becoming quieter then louder again, before starting their little dance all over again. If he had a device to measure his fear, it was his fear for himself that would be sounding the loudest alarm. Hardly very heroic, but what could he do? Every man for himself. That's what they'd both said, and now it had come to pass. And, viewed objectively, wasn't it fairer that Desmond, as mastermind of this operation, should bear the consequences, rather than them, his tag-alongs?

A new, disturbing thought burst in on these deliberations: how would Desmond react when he heard Mick had been released? It could well feel like a conspiracy, being stuck inside while his accomplice was freed. Assuming that Desmond hadn't known that he, Mick, had unwittingly become innocent. He imagined Desmond, distraught, desperate, and alone.

It was getting dark, he was freezing. All he had on was a hoodie, only intended to get him from Berlin-Tegel arrivals to Berlin-Tegel taxi rank, and instead he'd been wandering around London in it for four hours on a damp day in February. That his fear of sleeping on a park bench was greater than his relief at being released was perhaps not a typical reaction, but it was true all the same. He'd have to find a bar to sit at or a club and drink away his last fifty or so pounds with strangers. Here's to freedom, cheers mates. But that wasn't what a survivor would do. Unless, like Mick, they walked past a pub at the right moment that looked so inviting and unpretentious that there was nothing he could do but go in.

The landlord's watery blue eyes, with white lashes and heavy tear sacs, looked like there was nothing they hadn't seen before. He didn't look benevolent exactly, more like he rose above things, and what several hours of walking hadn't achieved was now brought about at the sight of this contemplative, boxy guy in a check shirt: Mick felt calmer. He would sit at the bar until last orders opposite this Zen master behind his row of taps. An ale, please. A nod and an ale, which Mick eked out for an hour, while the place gradually filled up with people who looked like they'd come from their cushily paid jobs, and other people who looked like sitting around in the pub was their job, and young people whom Mick would later ask about a club. Because the miserable idea of the park bench had been replaced by a much more appropriate solution, a sign that he was slowly recovering from his shock: he would head to a club and while the hours away on the dance floor. At some point he would hear from Delia, and until then, why suffer?

Beside him were two men in overcoats who had placed their mobile phones on the bar in front of them. Mick envied their prosperous lives, so secure that they could leave a small thousand-pound device lying around while they got drunk. The definition of manly success. It was time for a serious way to make money, Mick thought, savouring his pint slowly with small sips, while Mr Nokia and Mr Motorola each downed three gin & tonics in twenty minutes. But how? These guys were about Desmond's age. Desmond. He was almost ten years older than Mick and still hadn't found the answer to this conundrum. Desmond. At the other end of the bar, an old man called out a toast to Tottenham Hotspur, apparently an inside joke here in this pub. Mick laughed along, trembling, telling himself he'd check in with Desmond as soon as he could. Two women joined the men with cheerful hellos, Mr Nokia ordered a round, and Mick wished he were an acquaintance of these carefree strangers. He would come here from his good job, buy rounds, glance at his Patek Philippe, and head on to dinner, pleasantly tipsy.

He left three pound coins beside his empty glass and went out. Across the street was a phone booth. A horn jerked him back to his earlier state of high alert. Fucking tourists, the driver must have thought, because he refused to stop honking. Fucking left-hand driving, Mick thought. The iconographic status of the red telephone booth didn't change the fact that the mouthpiece stank. How could bad breath have such a high molecular density that it ate into plastic? Still no word from Delia. Breathing shallowly, Mick stood in the singular haze of damp phone book and cold smoke and tried to concentrate. He went through all the people who could wire him money from Berlin, but it would take days and would require explanations. He pounded the receiver against the phone a few times, then hung up. This couldn't be happening.

He met her in a club that he had no chance of ever finding again, and where he immediately felt at home. The smell of the fog machine and the red lighting had the same impact on him as the sound of the sea or a glimpse of a mountain range might have on someone pining for their homeland. No wasting money at the bar, straight to the dance floor, right in the crowd, drum'n'bass, the heart's rhythm disrupted. It felt good. He let himself be swept along. Everyone around him seemed to be moving to a different level of the multilayered composition. Layer by layer, every element its own rhythm, every clubber their own raison d'être: those who moved gracefully to any music were surrounded by those who writhed like they were in pain, the marchers stomped alongside the hip-swingers and the standers and those who seemed to be dancing to a much slower tempo, while others were raving to an even faster beat, which was hardly possible. What was also a relief was that people danced in the evening in London, not waiting 'til the early hours, like in Berlin. Mick joined the jumpers. Drum'n'bass had an incredible athleticism to it if you played it right. A jump or kick for every note, and after a while, the effect set in for which this kind of dancing was created: a state of absolute completeness. The body felt at peace, the soul let go, the spirit gave its blessing to the personality: you're okay! Years later, Mick would insist that at no time had there ever been such egalitarianism on the dancefloor as in the nineties and that this egalitarian spirit had a liberating effect on society as a whole. Within one track, Mick's isolation dissolved, and he bounced his way to being an equal member of this peaceful tribe.

The bedroom where he woke up the next morning looked like it belonged to a woman forty years older than Lynn, the woman lying next to him. Hopefully she rents fully furnished, Mick thought. Or it's her grandmother's place. He lay beneath a poppy-patterned quilt; next to him was a bedside lamp shaped like lily of the valley. A fat Maine Coon cat was sitting on his chest, staring at him. Hello, said Mick.

Lynn was cute, blonde, and easy-going. That wouldn't be a compliment she'd love to hear, Mick knew that much about women, but it was the truth. He'd scored some weed from her, and she'd been generous with the vodka shots. Nothing about her was intimidating. Everything about her was sweet and cuddly. Her blue eyes, her bare shoulders, her denim bum, her fingers drawing spacey shapes in the air as she jumped up and down to the bass. Everything about this woman was welcoming. Unlike her friend. Jeez, thought Mick, who perceived himself as tall and Black, but seeing this woman he realised that everything was relative. As if hewn from stone and polished, she leaned against the bar, talking to the two guys next to her – one built like a suitcase, the other like a jumping jack – peering down at them and laughing majestically. Her name was Nona. And even though Nona proved a few hours later that she too was a mere mortal by throwing up in Lynn's car, Mick still couldn't have slept with her. Somehow, it just wouldn't have been right, he thought, stroking the Maine Coon. Mick was well versed in lazy comparisons, but he wouldn't let himself think of Grace Jones, a reference Nona had surely heard plenty of times; maybe she even liked the comparison – what did he know? But all the same, that way spelled danger – no thanks. Best stick with lovely Lynn. (Was there even a choice? Mick liked to think so.) Also out of respect for Delia. Because this, he thought looking at Lynn's soft, white, girlish back, wasn't cheating. The cat looked him in the eye and had a big yawn. A feline predator. No, it was sleeping over at a friend's house.

The thought of Delia jolted him up; the cat took a startled leap and retreated to the foot of the bed. Mick climbed into his jeans and crept downstairs. During the night, he had seen the phone on the mezzanine. It was on a table next to a stack of music magazines and a dry flower arrangement full of artificial birds and butterflies.

Delia was on his answering machine. Twice.

Hi Mick, it's Cordelia here. I hope you got our invitation to the wedding. We've reserved some rooms for you, you'll need to confirm them. At Claridge's or the Every Hotel. I'll get back to you. Ciao ciao.

Mick stared at the music magazine at the top of the pile, which he didn't understand, just like Delia's message. The typography and graphic design were so experimental that he wasn't so much trying to read it but decipher it. The beep between messages was painful. An invitation to a party, two questions about a guest list, and a question about a DJ's phone number that probably also amounted to a guest list. Saturday night messages. Then his ancient landlady who had found out he had a piano. A piano, she said, clearly vexed at having to leave messages on his answering machine, was forbidden, not only because of the noise, but more importantly because of the structural condition of the apartment. Did that mean that a maximum of four people were allowed in his living room? He grinned for the first time in days and felt homesick for his dilapidated house, his harmless Berlin problems. Then Delia again: *Good afternoon. It's Titanic Travel. Just confirming your booking at the Every at*

Piccadilly Circus. Please contact the hotel directly with any special requirements. Thank you and have a nice day.

The daytime Lynn was just as nice as the laughing girl in the night. Under the feeble shower, he heard her clattering dishes and cursing amiably. When he came into the kitchen, she was sliding fried eggs onto a plate from a cast-iron skillet and asking him if he would rather have coffee or tea. A question that shut down Mick's flight instinct for another twenty-four hours.

To Lynn, it may have seemed like he was finding it difficult to leave her. Her warmth, her body, her sense of humour. Aside from the fact that the messier part of the truth was none of Lynn's business, there wasn't in fact one direct truth, but rather an inexplicable web. No one knew where he was. He knew where Delia was and that she was alive. He fell into his old habit and made her wait. As if he had done his job. As if he was safe. And so he crawled back into Lynn's bed again and again. Then at some point when it was already the next day, and she was telling him what she liked about Black men, he managed to get his clothes on, which felt like capitulation.

Don't get me wrong, it's not like you're *black*-Black, said Lynn, turning over onto her stomach, laughing. What's convenient about your situation as biracial people is that you can choose which stereotypes to embrace and which not to. Do you know what I mean?

Mick did, but he wasn't into stoner monologues. She licked her finger and lovingly dabbed the end of the spliff.

Want some?

No, thanks.

Basically, it's about my bum. Black men don't have a problem with big bums. You?

With a shake of his head that could mean anything, he glanced at himself in her old, polished mirror draped with a collection of necklaces, taking in his stubble, the dark bags under his eyes, and Lynn in the background, catching his gaze in the mirror and then falling back into the pillows, laughing. Lynn was okay. People talked a lot of crap when the body was busy breaking down toxins and the mind was wandering when it ought to be asleep. Yes, maybe this whole after-hours culture came about for the sole purpose of abusing people you picked up at parties as psychotherapists. You reveal yourself briefly, open up, offload, and then disappear back into your life until the next time. Lynn had stood up and wrapped herself in her towel again. He continued to stare in the mirror. He had just arrived from the Caribbean, and he looked Caribbean. Had his skin colour played a role in his arrest? Had his German passport had an influence on his release? Maybe both.

So then, Lynn said almost ceremonially, leaning her forehead against his chest, it was a pleasure, German man.

The pleasure was all mine, he said, and meant it.

The cat had a good rub against his trouser legs. Lynn put her arms around him.

Where are we here?

Golders Green. Go down the street and then turn right and you'll see the station. Do you want me to take you?

No, thanks.

Stay in touch, okay?

It was so hard not to say something like that. Even if it was a lie, even if it was so seldom true, if neither of you said it, there was just an ice-cold chasm that only the most cold-blooded could endure. He was glad she had said it.

Yeah, he said, wondering, how? Are you going to write me postcards? Will you call me in Berlin? And then what?

He took a pen from the dresser that was strewn with make-up paraphernalia and wrote his phone number on a neon-coloured flyer for a club night. He couldn't bring himself to do his trick of replacing the final one with a seven. A trick for women he needed to keep at bay, for reasons that, despite that strange last half hour, didn't apply to Lynn. He gave himself a fake surname: Michael Buttmann. The butt guy. An impeccable German surname and his little farewell joke. Lynn rummaged in a pile next to the radiator and shoved a few magazines into a plastic bag for him.

Here. That's what I do in the day. You're into music, aren't you?

She put her arms around him.

It's funny how quickly you can get used to someone, she said. When you're gone, it'll feel like you were here for years.

Mick knew that feeling. It was what made you call again the next night.

I'd better go.

He took her wrists from his neck and guided her arms gently back down. Like a python, he thought.

She walked downstairs in front of him; he stared at her bum. In proportion to her delicate torso, it was actually quite large, though he hadn't noticed until she mentioned it. Why did women do that?

Don't stare at my bum, she said, looking ahead, down the narrow staircase. He laughed. She turned to him and laughed back. Her loud and lovely laugh. Mick could hear the news coming from the ground floor.

My uncle, Lynn said.

Lynnie? The voice came from indoors. Mick had no idea how the last day and a half would have turned out if he'd known that a – judging by the voice – elderly man was prowling about downstairs. He kissed Lynn, a polite, terse kiss.

Take care, she said.

You too, said Mick, feeling pulled out of the house. He ran through the front yard. Golders Green, Lynn called after him, and he nodded without a glance back. He didn't slow down until he was out of sight.

As he travelled along the Northern Line, the rapidly fading Lynn was immediately replaced with a reappearing Delia. This meant that Mick didn't have a moment's respite, and that he wasn't so much riding the Tube as riding a wave of guilt that swelled from station to station until it finally broke and crashed into anger. Why, he asked himself, full of self-pity, as he got off at Leicester Square and headed in the wrong direction at first, why are people always harassing me? Why is someone always waiting for me to show up? When he realised that he wasn't supposed to be going in the direction of Cockfosters, funny name, he briefly felt a profound empathy with the rejects who shove their way through the crowds jabbering and cursing because they can't take the torment anymore and they've run out of self-control to hold back their despair, letting it flow unfiltered. This is what they must feel like, thought Mick, as he finally got on the right train to find himself staring at a back in a Burberry trench coat and wondering what he was going to say to Delia. If she was still there. If she had already headed back to Germany alone, which was quite possible, his problems were even worse. He would be left with barely ten pounds on an expensive island whose main airport he would never set foot in again. If she was still there, then hopefully she would put it all down as an emergency and that it wouldn't make any difference if he showed up at her hotel a day earlier or later, or where he had spent the intervening time, and with whom. It could also have been that they had held him for forty-eight hours; anything was possible. The thing with Lynn was something he would have a guilty conscience about in Berlin, but here it was different, he had done nothing wrong. And she wouldn't be able to find fault with him, either. He inhaled the thick rush-hour smog and affirmed to himself: Delia hadn't accused him of anything! She had gone through with the thing and, smart cookie that she was, she'd let him know where he could find her. Tough cookie. Not long now until he'd see her again. His petulant, defensive grudge gave way and instead he was so excited to see Delia that it gave him goosebumps. She was alive and she was waiting for him. And he, too, was alive. He tore his gaze from the Burberry coat and smiled at the train carriage full of unsuspecting strangers. When he got off the Tube at the next station, the pathetic figure muttering to himself had morphed into a slick professional. And as he strode up the steps into the city, he was, for the first time since he had left Berlin, almost free of fear. His body was giving him the all-clear, he was sober, he wasn't freezing, he was intact, and his balanced hormonal state put his mind at ease – thanks

Lynn. Mick looked at the roundabout, the neon signs against the indigo evening sky over Piccadilly Circus. Wasn't it gloriously kitsch, after this trip, to meet up here in this textbook location?

Hello, my name is Mick.

Are you a teacher?

No, I am not a teacher. I am a hero.

Delia's transformation from gangster's moll to gangster in her own right went more smoothly than any of the other metamorphoses she had undertaken thus far.

The realisation of being alone was not new to her, that helped. She knew that self-pity was counterproductive, which also helped.

Shifting her body cargo had been scary, yes, but it would have been much scarier not to shift it. Delia spent a day between the bathroom and the bed. She imagined herself as someone having to hold out in hiding under the harshest circumstances. She imagined herself as a woman having to give birth to a child alone. She imagined herself circumnavigating the globe, alone at sea with dysentery on board. I can do it, she'd told herself, in a cold sweat, who can if not me? At least I was alone, how could I have done that with anyone else around? I would have had to leave the planet in shame, she thought, when she finally lay in the bathtub, transforming herself back into a fragrant woman. Afterwards she ordered tea, toast, and all the newspapers, and lay down in front of the television. The arrest at the airport didn't seem to have been significant enough to make the news. And if the police were looking for Delia, then at least the media didn't seem to know about it. She put her freshly dry-cleaned suit back on and had her hair cut and dyed at Toni & Guy. The stylist, an enviably slim young man with a dangerous-looking piercing, a bolt through the bridge of his nose, looked at himself in the mirror constantly throughout the cut, was much less chatty than the hairdressers in Berlin, and managed, after barely glancing at her hair, to cut Delia the sharpest bob of her life. After that, she went shopping. She worked her way through the stores from top to bottom, which was a mistake, but a forgivable one. She started at Selfridges and ended up at Tesco, feeling better with each bag of purchases. A bulimic buying slop for a vomit orgy, she thought sarcastically as she piled the last load up at the checkout. Not being able to talk to anyone was the hardest bit. The construct of lies she would have to trot out for her parents was too precarious to risk. Instead, she would just say they had got the date wrong for her return flight. She wouldn't call again until she was back in Berlin.

The hotel staff were illiterate, it seemed. The *Do Not Disturb* sign did nothing to keep them at bay, someone knocked on her door at least once an hour. Poor choice of hotel, not that she could have foreseen that. Delia hid her cargo in the safe and, after almost two days of fending them off, finally let them in to clean her room. She had decided she would take the train to Dover the next day and then the ferry to Calais. No more Heathrow. And as it looked so far, no more Mick either.

She rewarded herself with a pair of black patent leather trousers and a floaty silk top with an open back, both so perfect in cut and finish that for a moment she could believe she was thin enough. Perhaps it was also due to the extreme loss of fluids. Or wait, no. It was because of the transformative power that comes with life-threatening situations. It was also the contrast the hefty platform boots made to her legs. Her hair was no longer the colour of wet sand, but of dark chocolate, and her new haircut, cut to the chin, elongated her neck; length was always good. Except with noses. No, long noses were good, too. She had had enough of constantly putting herself down. She rummaged in her bags and buttoned a black leather band around her neck. She took off the silk top and laced herself into a corset. She didn't look like a dominatrix;

she looked like a woman who liked indulging herself with BDSM-inspired designer pieces.

She spun around in front of the mirror, thinking of all the phrases she had heard and even said to herself in connection with her distorted body image. None had worked. Even now she didn't believe in ever being able to eat in the carefree way she could before puberty, but she felt she was on the threshold of something new. At least she liked herself in front of that hotel room mirror. She resolved to maintain this soothing complicity with herself, if not constantly, then at least to celebrate it on a regular basis.

She crouched down on the floor and laid out her grocery shopping in front of her. Chutneys, pickles, sauces, jams, jellies, mustards, spreads, oils, spice pastes, curry sauces, pesto, baby food, diet meals. Of Delia's furious love-hate relationship with food, only love remained. Five continents in tins and jars, kosher, halal, and indifferent, set, wobbly, and creamy, brightly coloured, vegetarian, seductive, repulsive, some natural and unprocessed, some packed full of glutamates and heavy metals: all in all, a much more diverse selection than you'd get in Germany. She would send herself a glorious hamper. She would set off after sending it, blithe and innocent, and get home before it arrived. Perhaps one day she would calmly come to terms with why her hunger for love and affirmation had been so great that she had got herself drawn into this madness. But not now.

Delia fetched the plastic bag from the safe, unscrewed a jar of pickled ginger, gave it a sniff, and was just sinking the first portion of cocaine into it when someone from room service knocked again. And then, an unforgivable habit that she abhorred in her mother, and that her mother had passed on to her sister, and that should be condemned at least as severely as slapping other people's children in the face: entering a room at the same time as knocking. It drove her crazy. And in this case, it triggered the nervous breakdown she'd been suppressing since the layover at the unnamed snowy airport somewhere in North America. Delia jumped up, kicked over several open jars, yanked the door from the person's hand and shoved him back into the hallway, screaming. She had spent four hours in the rain so they could finally clean this shitty room, she was paying a hundred and thirty pounds a night for some peace and quiet, and she had had enough of people sticking their fucking head through the door the entire time saying *excuse me*. No! Enough *excuse me*! Now get out of here!

There's a man at the front desk who wants to talk to you.

1996-2000

Mick pulled down the sun visor and deliberately missed the exit. He'd go for a bit more of a spin, in honour of the day, in honour of the music that was never better than when he was driving; there were even some tunes reserved for the autobahn. Sometimes he wondered if other people listened to music the way he did, if they experienced it in its entirety, until it became the only message that could be understood by anyone if they only listened properly. Yeah, it was just a question of time, he thought. He spent a lot of time with his music. Whenever he had to brake hard, it sounded like he was entering a city of plastic toys, his car was so full of tapes and tape boxes. He only shoved them aside when he was giving someone else a lift, which he avoided whenever possible, not because he had a problem with driving other people around, but because this was his space, and he liked to keep it for himself. He sang, he smoked, he talked on the phone. He drove barefoot, he leaned his elbow out of the window, and when he saw himself in the rearview mirror, he tended to be pleased with the look. His thoughts flashed by like the streets. Since when has that street been closed off, where's the shawarma takeaway gone, why haven't I been to the Philharmonic lately, and that Ethiopian place – must check out the menu – since when have there been hookers here, the light's green, come on slowcoach, ooh, nice legs, jeez, what a shithole, always has been round here, nice old Peugeot, get off the road, idiot cyclist, shit – it's red. At red lights he'd flirt with ladies, try to catch their eye, and almost always managed it, even women with their husbands, or with children, or women in headscarves. Or he'd use the red light to pick his nose, his ears, between his teeth, stroke his scalp, crack his neck, a few intimate moments, but visible to anyone passing. Sometimes guys would pull up next to him, eager for a race, and Mick might take them up on it if he was in the mood. He could have written a Berlin city guide, and could definitely have passed the taxi driver test, but why would he? He rarely went to a car wash, although he loved his car, which, like most things in his life, came to him without him having to do much. Adel, someone he knew from the club scene, had owed him money. Owing Mick money was nothing special; Mick was always feeling sorry for people who were in a fix. Having a few thousand deutschmarks spread out over the city seemed a better idea to Mick than keeping it in his bank account; he chucked the statements into a shoebox without bothering to open them. It'd find its way back eventually; money followed its own laws, one of which was that it had to keep moving. In Adel's life, that movement had stalled, but he liked Mick better than his other creditors, so he left him his black BMW 3 series before he skipped town. That was 1995. Looking back, that time seemed like a stream of things flowing in his direction, sometimes sticking around, sometimes drifting on. The BMW guzzled fuel, but it was a beauty. And Mick was a good driver, criss-crossing his city. At night he drove to the club – he was now one of the owners through a certain sequence of circumstances and encounters – and by day he drove around buying records, which suited him as perfectly as the club did and felt just as much like a hobby.

Complaints about the soullessness of the CD format didn't stop people from parting with their decades-old vinyl collections, which Mick bought up and sold on to southeast Europe, via Darko and Axel, though Mick didn't know precisely which countries, just as he wasn't sure what

Darko and Axel did for a living besides that. He'd met them at the gym, which was also called Axel. What did it matter? Everything about this business was gloriously casual, the stream of cash that he thought of as his pocket money, and the trips to meet clients. The sellers, mostly middle-aged men, advertised their collections in the classified ads and lived in parts of the city Mick would never otherwise have reason to visit. At first they used to stand on the clients' doorsteps, the three of them together, and only Mick seemed to wonder what kind of impression they must have made on the suburban family men. A shady one, most likely. Darko looked like he was on a trip he'd never come down from; Axel's enigmatic grin seemed to stem from the period of his life, now behind him, as a heroin user. Even with the patina of clubbing that seemed to cling to him despite his attentive personal hygiene and pricey togs, in the company of these two, Mick had the rare feeling of being the most respectable. And so they found themselves in living rooms and basement hobby rooms, among ski equipment, car parts, and tool collections, standing before built-in storage units and sofa landscapes, meeting wives and children of every age, with dogs jumping up at them and parakeets buzzing around their heads, examining their masters' records. Perhaps it was the subject matter, the music of their past, or perhaps it was coincidence, but these men were invariably very relaxed. Once, Darko walked into the living room of a complete stranger, headed straight for the windowsill, and sat there staring at the sky until it was time to go. The client's response was to say: Like in *Birdy*, remember? Peter Gabriel. Here it is. And he pulled the film's soundtrack out from his collection, neatly arranged by alphabet. Axel had, as always, retreated to the bathroom, and as they said goodbye to the Birdy man,

Mick decided he would do these visits alone in the future. He liked his partners, especially Darko with his murky name and his resolute distance from reality. Same moolah, less work, he put it when he suggested the new arrangement. Why, they asked, as expected. Better that way, Mick said, and they both accepted it with the placid indifference that ran through their entire relationship.

Going it alone – and this wasn't new for Mick – meant he could be whoever the situation demanded. He could do High German or Berlin slang, he could be loquacious or monosyllabic, offer praise when needed, ignore whatever was best ignored, and then get down to business. He didn't do anything strange, didn't show contempt or greed, no, he was someone who loved music, and who was surprised to find that he enjoyed talking to people who were bidding farewell to the treasures of their youth and, perhaps, to their former carefree selves. He didn't haggle. He approached them with the reverence of a funeral director. He chatted with the records' owners about the backstories to the albums, the fates of the band members, and the life stories of the men who had once bought these records. With their pocket money, their first wages, or their student grants, because they were in love, because they were electrified, because they were young and this LP was all that mattered. Sometimes he would also have a listen with them, and he'd find himself hanging out on a sofa, bleary-eyed, next to a man in slippers and a Dead Kennedys T-shirt, or snakeskin boots, or corduroy trousers, or tracksuit bottoms, men with gold-rimmed glasses, moustaches, and grey ponytails, and he felt as close to them as he did to the countless people with whom he had spent the early hours of the weekend nights, and who he didn't know any better than these vinyl collectors. Yes, here was a guy who had a clue about the music and a good heart; their LPs were in safe hands. For most people, Mick found, that was more important than the amount of money he eventually handed over.

And that was nice. With every visit, he honed his method of coming up with a quote. He saw the diamonds sparkle amidst the clods of earth, rarities that were sometimes worth more than all the rest put together. He would sell them on to a collector, while the rest would go to Darko's southeast European connection. But more and more often the good records stayed with Mick, who told himself that this was his financial investment, they were gems after all. His business ethics dictated that he couldn't leave anyone sitting on a heap of rejected records, so he bought almost everything, including garbage, at a price that both sides could be content with.

Nicely done, he thought, as he said goodbye to Frank. Frank – who had offered him a beer the moment he walked in and suggested using the informal *du* – was just as surprised, and delighted, by Mick's offer as Mick was by the quality of the collection. Frank was clearing out his father's apartment; he'd clearly not seen much of him in his later years. While Mick knelt in front of the record collection, the son stood in the middle of the living room, drinking his beer and shaking his head. I had no idea, he kept saying. What do you say to that, he asked Mick, pointing around the room. Mick looked up from the stack of records and shrugged. It's . . . um . . . creative? The old man collected dolls. He bought Trolls, Barbies, Kens, Big Jim, and his Black brother Big Jack, and sewed little celebrity outfits for them. He'd made his very own *Who's Who*. Mick recognised Kiss and Queen, an excellent Jimi Hendrix, or was it Lenny Kravitz, and mafia mobsters, dictators, astronauts, tennis players. He had built a ledge that ran through the entire apartment, at eye level, full of his dolls. They hung from the ceiling on mobiles, they filled every shelf, every surface: the kitchen cabinets, the windowsills, the sofa.

Did he have friends, Mick asked, or did he do it for himself?

I have no idea, said Frank, taking a sip. I didn't even know he could sew.

And suddenly Mick was giving a crying man he didn't know a comforting hug. Of course, the apartment looked like the lair of a maniac, but on the other hand, as Mick reassured Frank, it was spotless, and somehow this manic costume making also suggested he was having fun, he had a passion for his hobby, he was doing his own thing, wasn't he? Frank regained his composure and Mick gave him a bit more than he had planned, because the record collection – another indication that Frank's father might have been a bit off his rocker but not off the scale – was excellent. He had started buying in the sixties and never stopped. There are worse ways to spend your retirement than listening to good music while sewing, Mick said as he patted Frank on the shoulder and left him alone with his questions about his father in Friedenau. He turned up the volume on the mixtape he had just recorded, headed straight onto the autobahn, decided to miss his exit and extend his drive with a lap of honour.

Delia was waiting for him.

After Colombia, Mick had imagined that he and Delia would avoid each other, that it would be over. That was the logical outcome after everything that had happened. He had also counted on saving up some of the proceeds, which might not make him rich exactly, but could take the pressure off for a while. None of that came to pass. They came back to Berlin, something had happened between them that was no one else's business, they stayed together. For him, that meant he carried on sleeping with her on a regular basis. She called him, she cooked him dinner, she planned things for them to do together, and when she saw something he might like, she would buy it for him and get a buzz for a few days from seeing his reaction. But we can't just go back to business as usual after everything that's happened, he thought. This thought developed into a mantra that looped through his head whenever he saw her, and he was seeing her more often than ever. One evening, they were coming out of the cinema, he'd had this phrase going through his head non-stop throughout the entire movie, and he lit a cigarette and said it out loud. Delia acted like she was living the film through to its culmination. A coked-up romance: a couple on the run from the mafia with the case of cocaine they find, who end up playing with their son against the backdrop of a Californian sunset. *True Romance*. Exactly Delia's kind of thing. Her beautiful profile strained towards the screen, spellbound, while Mick unexpectedly found himself trapped in a headlock, unable to free himself for the full hour and a half. This oppressive feeling was worse than when people occasionally asked him about Desmond, to which his response was always a shrug. When Dennis Hopper was shot by Christopher Walken's companions, Delia stroked his cheek comfortingly, and he cursed her for the fact that nothing escaped her notice.

Excuse me?

I said, we can't just go back to business as usual after everything that happened.

What business as usual? Her question sounded surprised, without any irony. They stood facing one other in silence, cars whooshing past them down the damp Kantstrasse. She looked him in the eye. He looked her in the eye and carried on smoking. A Mexican standoff where only one of them would prevail.

And what do you think we should do? she finally asked, resolving the scene in her favour. He didn't know. If he had known, he would have already done it.

Delia had addressed the food package from London to Desmond. It had been delivered, as she had hoped, to Desmond's neighbour, a somewhat timid woman who was a physiotherapist and whom Mick had helped at some point with building her IKEA shelf. She was happy to see him, and didn't ask him for the delivery slip. Neither did she seem particularly interested in where Desmond was. Staying in the US a bit longer, Mick said as a precaution.

Delia took the package from him and placed it, unopened, in her closet. It's hers, thought Mick, who had nevertheless calculated the potential profit on direct sales. I'll deal with it, she said, muttering something about a Hanover connection. She was very prudent about it, like a secret service. Mick had his own thoughts on the matter: it wasn't Delia who had a construction company, it wasn't Delia who sat on the board of every association and committee in the state of Lower Saxony, and therefore it wasn't Delia, either, who was owed a favour by everyone in Hanover. But Delia claimed she could tell her father everything, really everything. The longer he thought about it, the more certain he was that Bernhard was in the picture. He knew her father, because Delia had taken him to Hanover so early on that it hadn't even occurred to him that she meant something by it. That is, things are getting serious, I'll introduce you to my parents. A coffee and a chat, why not. Then that evening Mick joined Delia and her sister Cosima at a party, something he was good at. Since that weekend Bernhard always invited not only his daughter but also Mick to his favourite restaurant whenever he was in Berlin on business. For Christmas, he got a cashmere sweater, which presumably wasn't chosen by Bernhard but by Ingrid, Delia's mother, but it was clear to Mick what status he now held in the eyes of her family. And he could also see which members of this family formed an inseparable team. Mick could picture the father-daughter conversation as well as if he'd been there.

You'd think I would have raised my daughters to know the difference between a little prank and serious crime, Bernhard would have bellowed. And in the event that this was an oversight on my part, then you might have learned the difference in law school, Cordelia. You were there long enough.

Delia would have dished up some nebulous version of events, some cock-and-bull story. The truth didn't matter; the important thing was the outcome, that she had ended up with the package. What was also important was who else knew about it.

And so, during this imagined Delia-Bernhard dialogue, Mick found himself wondering for the first time what Bernhard actually thought of him.

Haven't I always told you? Keep away from that Black guy! No. That didn't fit with Bernhard's cosmopolitan view of himself. He might not have dreamed of having a Black son-in-law, but he was firmly convinced that he was a friend to Black people. A conviction based on his innate love of jazz, and bearing in mind his background and his age, you could take it at face value. I might have known, he would have grunted, and Delia would have had to wait as contritely as possible until he shifted from reproach to something more solution oriented.

Yes, well, given the circumstances, I'm hardly faced with a choice. A swift resolution is what's needed here; it's no good waiting for the mouse to bite the thread. (Yes, Bernhard really said things like that.)

Afterwards he would have given some thought as to who he could rely on for one hundred per cent discretion. Facing the floor-to-ceiling windows of his executive office, standing with his hands on his hips, thumbs pointing forward, fingers on his kidneys, gazing on to the tranquil woodland outside, his square skull rattling with thoughts of Hanover's high-fliers. He'd have made a phone call, setting off a chain of calls, from snow-white to slightly off-white, to somewhat dodgy and not quite kosher to unambiguously shady, and finally to the point where all the fun ended or where it all began, depending on your perspective. Bernhard would be untraceable as the origin of the silent missive. That much was certain.

Then at some point, as if by some magical intervention, the money appeared. Delia, who never again mentioned that she had taken on the transportation alone, handed him, without comment, an envelope containing several thousand DM notes and a few hundreds. It was the thickest bundle of cash he had ever held, but even without counting it, he knew that it wasn't going to change his life. What's more, it was dirty money. Best get it shifted. He bought a sound system for the club as his official contribution to their unofficial entertainment business. He spent the rest on drinks, cab rides, records, and clothes, and no one batted an eyelid because it was no great change from how he was before, just more generous. No one questioned it, because everyone knew Mick as someone who liked to throw his money around. Leave it, I'll get it, come on, let's go straight for a bottle, let's have a *good* bottle, life's too short for bad food, why have the worst option when we could have the best? When you've racked up a hefty bill, the thousand-mark bills fit the bill – the brown ones with the Brothers Grimm – and Mick took a brotherly approach to dishing them out to his friends.

If the money had had a different origin, he would have most likely bought a gram or two of coke with it. But to spend this money on crushed painkillers, lactose, and wall plaster – no, no way. And so, despite its brief appearance in his life, the cash did at least have the long-term side effect of making him steer clear of the white stuff from then on.

Thinking about Desmond also helped. It was Delia who had contacted his mother a few weeks after they had got back. Mick didn't know exactly how the conversation had gone or what Delia had told Desmond's mother, but it yielded the information that Desmond was doing well, considering the circumstances. As well as you could be when you were doing time in a penitentiary called Wormwood Scrubs. His mother and brother would be flying to London and then on to Berlin to deal with his apartment. Desmond's mother, Mrs Mills, had seemed touched when Delia asked her for her bank details, but declined the offer of help, Delia told Mick, who was also touched by the gesture. She got hold of a phone number for Desmond's brother, Dashiell, who – in a perfectly polite way – seemed to take it absolutely for granted that he and his family should get support for Desmond's lawsuit. He read out the numbers she needed as if it was something he did several times a day. After the bank transfer, Delia dragged Mick to Abricot, one of Desmond's favourite restaurants, which felt like a memorial service for a dead man. But Delia's relief was so contagious that he, too, told himself that it was all over.

It took him just under a year to fritter away the money in bars and boutiques. When he had almost finished, Delia announced that she was buying a house. It felt like she'd been saving up the whole time; it felt like a cocktail of reproach and betrayal. But Delia didn't need a bundle of cash of ominous origin; she had her father and the German Bank for Development, eager to help people like her buy real estate in the East. An opportunity not to be missed. That was how they thought, the kind of people who invested in themselves and in their future, people like Delia and Bernhard, while people like Mick, at best, made plans for the following weekend, all the while allowing for the possibility that those plans might be scrapped at any moment.

I'm not moving to some gentrified fat cat East district, Mick said, as the house-buying process evolved from searching to finding. He had never had any desire to live in Pankow. In Mick's eyes, this city, that had once been so dramatically divided into east and west, still had an equator running through it, making him a resident of the southern hemisphere, though he would have preferred to be in the centre, in the tropics, while the north, especially the northeast, made him feel like the world was a flat disc and if you went any further you'd fall off the edge. Not exactly a valid argument against Delia's favourite of the properties she was considering. In 1996, he moved to Pankow with her.

Delia was persistent in calling the house *our house*. It was not his house and they both knew it, but he let her say it because he did also live there. The house, the former embassy of a tiny nation, was a special edition GDR prefab: a two-story concrete cuboid with panoramic windows and a garden that actually exuded a certain charm, though Mick would never admit it to Delia. He found the conquest of the East as a playground by so-called 'creatives' from the West extremely irritating. Not because the creativity in question consisted primarily of money – quite clearly there was no conquering to be done in any real estate market without cash – but because he couldn't bear the entire spiel that came with it. Ooh, we live in a prefab now, isn't that funny? No. Prefabs have never been funny. Not in the East nor in the West. You didn't need to have an opinion about living in one; it wasn't bad and neither was it avant-garde. You could just be indifferent, like the many people who just lived in them without feeling like they were making a statement. Delia found it marvellous. Not only did she have a *Plattenbau*, a prefab, but it also used to be an embassy, making it an elite GDR relic with an international history, and to top it all, it was in a leafy suburb. Such clear lines, she exclaimed in the empty house, like a professor of Bauhaus, I don't need stucco. As if he needed stucco, as if anyone *needed* stucco. As if she was even asking what he thought.

There was no mention of any alternative to moving in together, to this place precisely. This was the house Delia had fallen in love with, and no other joint living arrangements were up for discussion. Delia was still in love with Mick, so moving in together was just the next step.

And so, like their diplomatic predecessors, they became a couple living on foreign territory. Ludicrously close to his old stomping grounds, just a couple of U-Bahn stops away. He felt like an emigrant coming back to visit the old country. He had emigrated within a city, and the country he had left no longer existed. Yet it seemed so determined to live on in Pankow that he took every grumpy pensioner for a bitter GDR official, though he would object if Delia were ever to utter the same suspicion. He accused her of stumbling around in this ex-republic like a development aid worker, too pleased with herself to be able to see things for how they actually were. She diagnosed him with paranoia, even post-traumatic stress disorder, a re-traumatisation, which he denied. The East was irritating in every respect, it always had been, but it wasn't anything like as creepy or quirky as people like Delia made it out to be. No, the main problem of the GDR was always its insipid mediocrity.

Nothing's changed, he said. I'm suffocating here.

Delia was as serene as ever. She had what she wanted. Her house and him. Cheerfully squeezing her fresh orange juice every morning, she acted like it made no difference to her getting up an hour earlier to trek all the way over to Charlottenburg, where she now worked in a law firm. Her neighbours two houses down, a gay couple with top jobs, were supposed to be proof that they lived in an up-and-coming hip neighbourhood. Mick rolled his eyes. You didn't need up-and-coming hip neighbourhoods; you lived in whatever neighbourhood you lived in because it was what you could afford.

Not wanting to travel in a big city is provincial, Delia said at one point, and for once he didn't disagree with her. Provincial? Touché. No, he wasn't that. So he started getting out and about again. He drove to Mitte to his club, to Schöneberg to his gym, to Kreuzberg to see his old friends, and to the outskirts to see the old men with the record collections. He drove his car in every conceivable state, he rode his racing bike, and though he took public transport as rarely as possible, he found that getting out and about was good for him. Because Mick needed his parallel existences. He needed to be able to do things that were none of anyone else's business. He needed to cultivate relationships that belonged only to him and didn't cross over with anyone else. He started to appreciate the long distances. Once again he had ended up somewhere he hadn't chosen. Doesn't have to be forever, he thought. What's forever, anyway?

Silvio Kurz couldn't say if the past week had been a success or not, given that success wasn't exactly a category that featured prominently in his life. The one good thing was that he was signed off sick. He got the extension – so far so good. The bad thing, though, was all the bleeding stress that came with it because they wouldn't accept a doctor's note from his GP, that mangy cow who was always in such a rush to get him out the door. It wasn't enough to be signed off by that fucker from the job centre, no, now he had to go to an external assessor. It all depends on the case worker, Schmitti had told him, that big mouth who must have been screwing his own case worker, how else did he get away with never having to show up there? And he'd been getting his benefits through for years, no fuss. But it made no sense. They surely didn't seriously think they could get away with it, how they've been taking him for a ride. A job in a nursery. A job in a canteen. A job in plasterboard construction. Retraining programme here, reintegration initiative there. And never once did anyone ask him about his back or his dizzy spells. Instead, they were always asking him how much he drank. Like anyone ever counted how many beers they'd had? Like crap they do. The only ones who counted how many were the guys behind the bar serving them, the same for spirits. But there he was showing up at this dumbass appointment, at seven in the morning, because they must have been hoping he'd miss it, which'd suit them right down to the ground, and looky here, the assessor was a woman, fucking crow-faced – gah, can't say cunt, already made that mistake, cost him dear. So this whole fuck-up had cost him his driving licence and a twelve hundred DM fine for insulting a bastard official, because the stupid cow and her shit colleague had even counted how many times he shouted it, eight times they reckoned, and of course there were two of them and he was in the car on his own. So, that was it: his licence – poof! – gone. No way he'd pass the medical, the fucking 'idiot test', and the only decent job he'd had in his life, driving cars with red licence plates to Ukraine and Russia, was also gone, just like that. Not that he was a big fan of the *Russkies*, but it was a good job. Cash in hand, plus expenses. And then it turned out that no one was interested in his few scraps of Russian, because the *Russkies* preferred to speak sodding English. The same old crap: years of fucking around with supposedly essential Russian at school, yeah, thanks a sodding lot for that and a Molotov cocktail up the arses of the comrades of the GDR's People's sodding Education. Besides, he'd enjoyed chugging around the Eastern bloc. Something different for a change, seeing the world and all that. But as mentioned: gone. Sabrina, the chancer, told him that he should stop drinking at least for a while and get his licence back. Yeah, and then what? Peace, love, and harmony, and all is well again, yeah? Er, nope. Sabrina had fallen in love. Some guy from the West. Nothing for it, she had to bugger off over there to have babies. Sorry, but since when were the *Yugos* from the West? The *Yugos* are as far East as it gets, for chrissakes. If there was something he knew by heart, it was the world map. The atlas was his favourite book, way back when – that's right, his mama was a geography teacher. Whenever they had a long car journey, they'd play the capital cities game until he knew them all. Name a fly-shit tiny island state and Silvio will tell you the capital. Yeah, well. Those were the days, Mama and him driving around in her Dacia. Turned out how much he missed her was what got that mangy cow to sign him off sick in the end. It went to her heart, and it was the truth as well, but still, he wouldn't have come out with it if she hadn't been getting on his nerves like that. How come he was constantly surrounded by grisly old hags, one grottier than the next, and he didn't have a girlfriend? Oh, yeah. The *Yugo*.

So there he was at seven on the dot waiting to see this fucking crow hag with the double-barrelled name – she'd strung some foreign *kanake* name on the end, like one German surname on its own wasn't shitty enough. Like, what the fuck? There he is rocking up at this appointment practically in the middle of the night, so they have no reason to cut his sick pay, and he's shaking like mad, because he's feeling really fucking wretched, which is perhaps just as well if he's going to convince them to keep him signed off sick, and this Frau bleeding Lehmann-Mubarak leaves him there waiting for a whole half an hour. Wasting his time like it's hers! He says to her: Ready when you are. And he thinks to himself, I'm going to smash this place to pieces if they don't get a fucking move on. And she's like: If you could just wait another ten minutes? Thank you. And please close the door, I'll call you in shortly. And he's like: Right, if you say so.

And then she calls him in when he's just about to go out for a smoke because he's sick and tired of waiting by this point. She's flicking through his records, this massive Stasi folder covering his entire fucking welfare back story, and she's asking him what he would like to do for a living. Holy moly, that's a new one. Like, what is this, he's suddenly on the *Make a Wish* show. Hmm, okay, flick, flick. You've threatened violence or administered violence to every one of your supervisors so far? Administered – that's a good one, he almost had to laugh, must remember that one, fucking hilarious. Yeah, that's right. Why? Well, certainly wouldn't be because it was pure joy to get fucked around by the wankers treating him like Karl Asshole, would it? He held back from saying that, though, because this *Frau Puppendoktor*

Pille had the upper hand here, you might say. All right, let's see: Because there was nothing else he could do? Because he was overwhelmed? Overwhelmed could work. Uh-huh. She keeps on making notes and flicking through and asking questions. School, education, home. And then he said that he hardly had any contact with his father and he used to get on so well with his mother, and it wasn't even eight in the morning and he couldn't believe it when out of the blue he started bawling, not for show or anything, but because all of a sudden he really felt that all this shit might actually be to do with his mother dying. The crow-faced witch hag handed him a handkerchief and carried on scribbling away. And he carried on blubbering away. A snivelling fit of the first order, no idea when he last cried, it must have been before the Wall came down. He couldn't believe the masses of snot that were streaming out of him. She didn't seem to be the least bit surprised – dread to think what kind of disaster cases she saw on a daily basis. And then she suggested he should be sent to some kind of residential rehab – what an utter load of horseshit, but better not say that – and then start seeing a therapist, i.e. a fucking shrink, which sounded even worse, but he kept his mouth shut, firstly, because he was still blubbering away, and secondly, he had to play along, co-operate as they called it, to keep getting the bleeding money. Of course, he didn't get to see his sodding file – it was sent straight on to the next fucker he was supposed to see, as if his own life was none of his own damn business, like it didn't concern him, and now he had to wait and see what they decided, and how things would pan out for him. In any case, the witchy crow hag didn't see anything criminal in his outbursts, just saw it as a kind of illness, an incapacity to work. How good or bad that was, time would tell. It was like a flipping Anatolian wedding out there in the waiting room. Even if she signed half of them off, the rest had it made, out there driving around in their Mercedes-Benzes all day. Poor old Germany. God, he was sick to death of all this bullshit.

All that was on Friday. On Saturday he went fishing, to get away from it all and have some downtime, and on Sunday he went up to Niederschönhausen, because Schmitti was hanging out there and maybe he knew what to make of it all: the appointment with the old crow hag and the sick pay. Therapy. At least not more fucking retraining. Turned out Schmitti wasn't even there, the wanker, but Lutz, Olaf, Reimar and two other guys were, and some broad – *not* his type. So much so that he sat down next to Olaf, knocked back three Sternburgs and wondered, when did people here in Prussia start having to drink fucking Saxon beer? And for about an hour or so, they had a bit of a laugh with Norbert in the corner shop. Until suddenly this Black lad came in the door, looking all smug like he thought he was a world champion. Dressed like a whole Nike store, just creeps in, doesn't say hello or anything, just gets some blue pigswill drink from the fridge and practically jogs into Norbert's space behind the counter. People like that, what are they even thinking? Olaf shouted something and the fucker didn't react, of course. Hiding under his hood. Norbert took the money and the fucker didn't even look up at him. What about a thank you? Not a chance. Don't you know, this lot, they've left their manners back at home in Africa. I'll sock him one, Silvio thought, and then the guy turned around and Silvio saw his face for a moment before he turned to walk out the door. Silvio said to Olaf, if that's who I think it is, he ought to at least say hello, and if it's just some foreign *nigger*, I'll show him what for. He ran out after him. And immediately faced his next hurdle: Black guys might not be good for much, but when it comes to running, they are the champions.

The strongest argument against the eastern outskirts of the city was handed to Mick on a plate, when he had just started to come to terms with his new neighbourhood. It was the day he found himself pinning down Silvio Kurz with his knee on his chest. He had just been to the corner shop at the end of his run. He'd popped in for a bottle of Gatorade. The store was used as a pub by a few locals; they spent their days sitting there in their own fug. Mick ignored them, easy enough with his hood up and headphones in. He bounded over to the fridge to grab a bottle and paid the owner, a mean-tempered hulk of a man, barely making eye contact. He was the stranger in a saloon bar, met with collective animosity; he let it bounce off him because he was just passing through. A newsagent with no newspapers. None of this lot came here to read; the newspaper rack was just random junk. One of them shouted something at him, which he also ignored, because he had his music still at running volume, turned up high. Why should he react to them, those pissheads who were already drunk by midday? Maybe he should send Delia down here for a little reality check. This, baby, is your neighbourhood. Enough of a festival of aesthetics and culture for you?

Outside, he broke into a trot. Then he postponed his cool-down phase and picked up speed again. A few strides on and he was flying over the asphalt again, heading for the park. It was the second day after two nights out clubbing, and he congratulated himself on his indestructible body. If it weren't for his Discman, he would have heard the wheezing and cursing behind him, but as it was, the jolt in the back came out of nowhere. A shove that turned out to be a kick. A flying kick that could have come straight out of some Asian martial arts movie if Mick's attacker hadn't been in such poor shape. It hurt all the same, a dull ache overlaid with terror. He turned around and saw a skinny little man lying on the ground, laid out flat by his own attack. Further back, the guys from the newsagent stood in the street smoking. One of them raised his right hand. A Hitler salute? What the fuck? Mick tore the headphones from his ears and bent over the scrawny little git. *Sieg heil, nigger,* he shouted, and Mick kneeled on his chest as if in a trance, pressing his knees into his ribs. The scrawny Rumpelstiltskin held his hands defensively over his face, still croaking on. It sounded like he was laughing. Mick looked down the street at his buddies. Foreigners out, came from under him. The idiots in front of the paper shop were just standing there. Mick ripped the guy's hands off his face and thumped him, a half-hearted punch. Like it was a chore to get over with. His knuckles hurt, the other guy's nose started bleeding instantly, the whole thing was repulsive. What was he doing here?

Michi, the guy suddenly shouted, just answer me when I say hi, or do you think you're better than me, you Black bastard?

Mick got up in slow motion and pulled the guy up with him, the guy he now recognised. Silvio Kurz. Pyromaniac, class clown, had to repeat the year, big mouth, could take a beating. He could have taken a real punch. And he carried on lashing out, because that was what he was best at: not giving up, showing no fear, the titch without fear. Kurz had always been a wacko, but somehow he was kind of okay too, if he remembered correctly. That was way back then, a thousand years ago in Treptow, when they were a mob of little boys who were expected to train for a vocation, do their military service, start a family. GDR lives that weren't identical, but similar enough in their predictability. None of it turned out like that. Mick left the country, and not long after, for all the others, international politics intervened. The same international politics that Silvio Kurz wanted to blame for the fact that he spent his days hanging out in a corner shop with some crappy rhinoceros tattooed on his neck, which, on closer inspection, turned out to be a map of the Third Reich. Apart from this self-sabotage, Kurz looked almost exactly the same. Like a girl, which is why they used to call him Silvia, either that or Furz – fart – or Shorty, not particularly original, but obvious, since Kurz was short, after all. And he always laughed along, because he liked to laugh, even at himself. Mick's mother once described him as a very sweet boy, and Mick now saw that that sweetness was still there. Especially in the top half of his face, because he had big brown eyes with long curved eyelashes, while he'd tried his best to botch up the lower half with a fuzzy moustache and a serious dental problem. He pulled out a checked handkerchief, pressed it to his nose, and eyed Mick up and down. The other guys had retreated into the newsagent. What if they came back out armed?

What the fuck? asked Mick, a perplexed, rhetorical question, and he was suddenly back in the eighties, the bigger guy pushing the smaller guy around. Pushing was all right, just humiliation, no physical harm. Kurz sneered, like he used to sneer back then when he was other people's punching bag. He had been kind of funny and he'd had some crazy ideas; today he'd be thought of as a creative kid, but back then he was just considered mischievous and a fidget and a pain in the ass for the grown-ups. He was middle class in a supposedly classless country: his mum was a teacher, his dad some big shot in the army, an asshole if Mick remembered rightly. Proof of this was the fact that West German TV was banned in the Kurz home, which is why Silvio spent the afternoons at Michi's, where anything went. They'd lie around watching what the then so limited and therefore incredibly exciting medium of television had to offer them: *The Fall Guy*, *Hart to Hart* or *The A-Team*, and they'd play stuntmen, and make cap guns and pea shooters, and throw water bombs at passers-by. Kurz seemed to remember this, too, because he chuckled to himself, shaking his head, which didn't make it any easier, the fact that he'd just taken a flying leap and kicked his old buddy Michi in the back.

I asked you a question, Mick said. Are you out of your mind?

They looked into each other's eyes, both unsure how much to joke and how much to be serious. Kurz pulled a filterless cigarette from a crumpled pack, lit it, and took a deep drag.

Are *you* out of your mind, he said. You didn't even recognise me, you monkey's butt. Who do you think you are? The lot of you! I'm telling you, you come here again and try that crap like you own the place, I'll take you down.

Annoyed, he huffed the smoke out through his nostrils. Mick crossed his arms and rocked back and forth: ball of foot, heel, ball of foot. Then he laughed. Kurz laughed too.

What you doing here then, he asked Mick, in a conversational tone now.

Mick needed an answer that gave Kurz nothing. He had no intention of reviving this old connection.

Stealing your women, what do you think?

Yeah right, said Kurz, sniffing back his snot and spitting on the ground between their feet, between Mick's new Nikes and his worn-out moccasins. The fact that it had even occurred to him to sprint after him in those faux-leather things showed the fighting spirit Mick had once admired, in more harmless contexts. He decided that this was nothing but a chance meeting with a childhood acquaintance. Not a Nazi attack. And therefore something he could bring to a swift end and forget about.

Do you live here then or what? Didn't you go to the West? said Kurz, chatty now, more relaxed, almost cheerful.

The wall is gone, Kurzer, go take a look.

They both laughed again. Michi Engelmann – Mick – could have asked Silvio Kurz what in his life made him end up getting wasted in a corner shop, but he wasn't prone to nostalgia and neither did he have any ambition to be a social worker. No, he wanted to get out of there as quickly as possible.

I've got to go. Ciao, take care.

He put his headphones back in and started running, backwards. Waved at this little guy he had known as a kid. Kurz blinked into the sun, waved back, and for a moment looked so much like he did back then that Mick couldn't help but think back to their childhood afternoons, even recalling the name of his guinea pig, Mucki, but then the spell dissolved and Kurz tensed up, stretched out his arm, and yelled something that wasn't necessarily the greeting from the evil empire, it might have been the Pioneer greeting, *Immer bereit!* or a curt *Sport frei*!, some GDR way of saying goodbye that you never heard any more. Jeez, thought Mick, poor Silvia, as he turned back in the direction he was running and jogged away.

What now? Should he not feel safe in his own city anymore? Should he wonder if other school friends were now his enemies? No way. He didn't tell Delia about the incident. He wouldn't have said anything even if the police had come by and asked why he, a tall man of 'southern heritage', had been kneeling on a small man with an anti-constitutional tattoo and a bleeding nose. Victim, perpetrator, foreigner, right-wing radical, racially motivated assault – Mick wanted nothing to do with any of it. He wanted to stay in his happy little bubble, keeping the world with people like Kurz in as far away as possible, further than the moon, ideally. And he thought it was, at least until a few weeks later, when he was on the tram, unusually, going past Pankow Town Hall, where a demonstration of clearly recognisable Nazis was taking place outside.

Unconsciously, Mick slid his shades from his forehead onto his nose and glanced at the cluster of black bomber jackets and pale bald heads of every shape and size. Mick looked back down at the sports pages and had the uncomfortable feeling of being jabbed by stares, of standing out as someone who was the focus of all that, of them expecting a reaction from him. Anger, horror, or fear. Like he was supposed to decide who he wanted to be in all this: fighter or victim. The truth was he was on his way back from a party, and he still smelled like it. He'd fallen asleep there, annoyingly, and hadn't woken up until eleven o'clock in the morning, and riding this stinking tram home with windows steamed up with stale breath was already unpleasant enough. The truth was that, as far as he was concerned, this nonsense had nothing to do with him. He thought the Nazis should just fuck off, while the Nazis thought he should just fuck off. Which, in fact, he would have liked to do, to one of the many places where these people and their worldview played no role whatsoever, places that weren't perfect but were leagues ahead of here in one crucial way: urban coexistence was a matter of course, the polar opposite of this regressive backwater. Yeah, as far as he was concerned, they could absolutely keep to themselves. If they were going to show up more often, then he no longer belonged here. He was just living here for some stupid reason. The tram was held up. Mick couldn't see why, if it was the police or demonstrators on the tracks. Mick glanced at the unambiguous symbols.

Just before they moved to West Berlin, he had started hanging out with a couple of skinheads, older boys who were already doing apprenticeships and would have sent him packing if he hadn't been the perfect mascot. Firstly, he was a wickedly cool dresser, as they put it, in the full get-up with braces, work boots, button-down collar shirts or polo shirts plus a bomber jacket, some of it inherited from his grandfather, some from his mum's boyfriend in the West. Secondly, his skin colour provided a welcome air of East London in East Berlin, making it immediately and unmistakably clear who the boys wanted to be, namely traditional skinheads, the anti-racist kind. So Mick was allowed to go along to their rocksteady parties and adopted his next adolescent look, the only one his mother was genuinely concerned about.

What is this, are you crazy?

Mum, I'm a redskin, not a Nazi. That's not exactly going to work for me, is it?

Precisely, said Monika, who showed no sign that she was really listening when he told her about the proletarian Jamaican roots of the skinhead movement, though he assumed it would interest her, after all, she was the one who was always calling herself a child of the proletariat, and she'd chosen to be with a Black man, hadn't she? And now, when he had found the perfect combination that he could identify with, not only in terms of heritage but also musically, his mother just shook her head and interrupted him.

You look like you've had chemotherapy.

She looked at him with such horror, as if he were really sick, which ruined his enjoyment of his shaved head so much that he grew his hair out again, after all, originally, skinheads didn't go as smooth as a bowling ball anyway. He left a short velvet rug, which the girls liked better, too. It was a brief phase; he was a kid. How was it that even as an adult some people clung to the uniform of youth culture, of whatever persuasion? Except that wasn't youth culture out there, that was just hate and it had nothing to do with age.

When he got off the tram a few stops on, back in his tranquil neighbourhood, he walked into the local bakery that managed to make its entire range taste of nothing and bought one of each type of bread roll and pastry, a Sunday ritual that helped him and Delia indulge in the illusion that Mick hadn't been out all night but had just popped to the bakery. He was almost at the house when he saw them, the Africans who were up there at the top of Delia's Pankow highlights list: always well dressed and out and about with several children in tow. They were attached to one of the embassies that was still here; Delia hadn't worked out which country they were from, but they literally made her heart sing when she saw them. Positive racism? General human kindness? In Delia's case, it was a mixture, combined with the desire that Pankow should have the most diverse population in Berlin. Fine by me, Mick thought.

They were walking towards him on the other side of the street – did they have anything to do with him, or not? This journey home had become an obstacle course of moral quandaries. He stopped, then crossed over and caught up with them. He called out: Excuse me? and when they turned around, he stopped at a safe distance – their dapper look made him feel even grubbier. Perhaps they were on their way to church or a diplomat's children's birthday party. The woman, too young to be a diplomat or the wife of one, presumably the nanny, wore a tight dress with a loud pattern under a jacket, with high heels. The man was wearing a dark blue suit, a pale-yellow tie, and a white shirt so bright Mick would have struggled to look at him without shades. He told them in English that he didn't want to worry them, but just to let them know that there was a Nazi rally up ahead, just so they knew. The youngest of the children tried to get out of his buggy and whined a bit; the other two looked at him wide-eyed. Delia would have loved them. The adults glanced at each other and then back at him. Then the man nodded, came up to him and shook his hand as if they were concluding a successful business meeting, while the woman leaned down to wipe the toddler's face. None of this was unkind, but it seemed as if neither he nor what he had communicated to them were of any great concern to them. They floated away in their aura of diplomatic immunity.

The following week he donated two hundred and fifty marks to a charity supporting the victims of far-right violence. Then again two weeks later. And a month after that, the proceeds of an exceptionally busy weekend at the club. Good idea, Delia said, when she saw the donation receipt, and set up a standing order.

Job, house, partner. Delia had her first good job in a large law firm and was living with Mick, who had finally stopped complaining about it. Just when she had nearly got the house the way she had imagined it, her progress onwards and upwards came to an abrupt end. Out of nowhere came an attack of mysterious rashes and swollen skin, which neither genuine doctors nor charlatans could diagnose or treat. One doctor advised her to come off the pill. Your hormone levels are out of kilter, said another; I'll prescribe you a different pill to get them back on an even keel; change your diet, take this, stop eating that. A mushroom from Japan, some tree bark juice from the Amazon, Grander water, her own blood, tablets, ointments, injections. She did what everyone said, at the same time: clearly yet another mistake. Nothing helped. At which point she moved onto the hard stuff, leaving her with a puffy cortisone face. It was truly grim. Please calm down, she begged her skin every morning, what have I done wrong? It was like a hostile takeover from within. To her surprise, Mick not only suffered with her, he still found her beautiful. It'll go away he said, gently kissing her swollen eyelids, you're not ugly, that's nonsense. He meant it the way he said. Thank you, she thought, feeling ashamed all the same. There was an obvious downside of his gift of recognising beauty everywhere. There were just too many people, half of them women.

Then he said he needed to get away. That was how he put it. And actually, she always found it funny the way he expressed this urgency. He was never just going to a party, but he *had* to go to a party, he needed to hear this one song right now, he urgently needed to eat something specific and would drive across the city to get it. And now he desperately had to go to Goa. He needed some sun, he needed to help his friend Chris through a break-up, and wasn't she just about to go to the USA without him? True. He could have extended his list of his reasons endlessly, but why should he, he had already made his plans and she played no role in them. Her skin calmed down a bit, only to literally explode shortly after. It wasn't even related; at that point he'd already booked his ticket. Still, it was hard to see these events as unconnected. It was practically impossible to look in the mirror, see a monster, and convince herself that it was only winter that Mick was running away from.

Why Mick? A question her mother asked her every now and then, always in a roundabout way, and only when she caught her alone. She did it again when Delia showed up at her parents' at Christmas, scarlet-faced and alone. She regretted even mentioning Mick's trip. She regretted not heading out to the game butcher with her father.

He's really delightful, don't get me wrong. Ingrid rolled out all the clichés, and Delia shook her head in silence. No, no. Delia did understand. This wasn't about racism, this was about significant flaws in the overall construct: he wasn't a lawyer, a doctor, or any other profession that her lifelong unemployed mother could make sense of. And on top of that, he was younger than Delia. The four-year age difference, which would be considered optimal if the genders were reversed, was such a deviation from Ingrid's standards, set in concrete, that Delia was effectively Mrs Robinson.

She could set out her case to her mother, a blazing address to the court so thunderous that she would have wrecked Christmas. Instead, she swallowed it down.

I'm with the man I like, she said, period.

If that's enough for you, Ingrid said.

It is, said Delia, and disappeared behind the Sunday paper.

But she wasn't as thoroughly the opposite of her mother as she liked to make out. She needed to keep her man, at all costs. A schema she had clearly adopted from her mother, a textbook example of learning from the model. However, in her mother's case, it meant maintaining her status and standard of living, while Delia got nothing in return for putting up with Mick's chaos and messing around. No one is forcing you to be with me, Mick had told her at some point in an argument. Sorry, but it's true. And she thought, irritatingly, he is right. Irritatingly, she was alone in her faith in their relationship.

Everything hurt. We have to get to the bottom of why your skin, your external protective layer, suddenly wants to destroy itself, said one alternative practitioner, who couldn't help her either, but who finally pushed her to tears with this ghastly sentence worthy of a horror movie, tears that were months overdue, it felt. Still, the army of doctors agreed on only one thing: that she would have to adjust to a life with chronic skin disease, like millions of other fellow sufferers, incidentally. As if that was any consolation. She would have liked to go to work wrapped in a full-body bandage to cover the inflamed patches and stop herself from scratching. Instead, she wore long cotton underwear under her office clothes, covered her face with antiseptic make-up, and dreaded spring for the first time in her life. Through the receptionist at the office, she found a Chinese doctor who practised in her living room while her husband occasionally sat there chatting on the phone or watching television. She hardly spoke any German, but she took her skin problems so seriously that Delia could see a faint light at the end of the tunnel again. Who could say if it was down to Mrs Lu's pungent ointments and teas, but after over a year of Delia desperately willing it to stop, it finally did.

When Mick returned from India, her skin had almost completely healed, and she had seen in her thirty-first birthday, alone, in the bathtub with a bottle of champagne and the prospect of better times ahead. She had spent her thirtieth, which had fallen in the cortisone phase, with Mick at an art house cinema, three nouvelle vague films in a row. His idea, because she hadn't wanted to see anyone. Her illness had shown that her fear of turning thirty was the most trivial of all her worries in her younger years. Now, a year later, she looked almost the same as before, but felt better.

Why Mick? She asked herself now that she was better, after hearing the word psychosomatic more than her own name, and after deciding that she no longer wished she could change Mick. An honest desire that, in theory, sounded like the solution to her problems but proved more difficult in practice than any of her state law exams. Because I love him, was the answer to her own question. I can't change that. At least not at the moment.

We'll see, she told herself, when she went to Stanford for six months the following summer. She'd save herself the torture of winter in Berlin, at least some of it, and besides, unlike Mick in Goa, she wasn't going there for a holiday but for a fellowship. They wouldn't see each other for half a year, the longest time since they had known each other. Delia saw it as a test; Mick wasn't keen on tests. Cash flow was tight again and he had a lot going on in Berlin, which meant he wouldn't visit, which in turn made Delia's time in the States a little less burdened. Different people, different climate, different language, different Delia. Flying back to Germany felt like a journey into the unknown. If she didn't like what she found back home, she had the option of heading straight back. Even as the plane came in to land, this seemed like an utterly realistic option.

And then there he was waiting to meet her at the airport in Berlin that seemed so tiny, like a doll's house. She had told him her early morning arrival time – not really his time of day – not expecting him to come and meet her. Just as little as she had expected him to be thrilled to see her. Why not, she wondered, as he lifted her up off the ground and beamed at her. Because I can love, but I have a problem with letting myself be loved, and that's my problem, not his. Over there, she had regularly driven sixty miles to San Francisco to see her housemate's therapist, which had felt like a date every time. A date with a dishy guy twenty-five years her senior who, for a hundred and fifty dollars a pop, she could spend an hour telling who she was: a woman who insisted on an unequal relationship where her partner soaked up her love like a sponge and gave nothing back. Pretty pathetic, she thought, as she listened to herself, staring at her therapist's bare ankles, the same cognac brown as his suede loafers.

In Mick's embrace, everything she had told the handsome shrink seemed as surreal as a drunken bender where you end up passing out. Their reunion was so overwhelming that Delia had no idea what an adequate response would be. Embarrassed, she let herself be kissed. I was really scared you wouldn't come back, said Mick, throwing her heavy luggage over his shoulder like a gym bag. As she walked beside him, everything about him seemed so familiar. His stride, which she could hardly keep up with, even when he slowed down for her, his scent, which she could just make out amid the smell of damp and snow. His allure depended on being in his magnetic field; they were both fed up with talking on the phone. By the way, I brought someone else with me, he said, stopping so she could catch up with him. Okay, she thought, suddenly thrown back to Berlin, biting wind, smokers huddled under umbrellas, not a palm tree or a sunny smile in sight. She imagined one of his friends, who he'd brought with him because he thought it would be more fun than coming on his own, because it perhaps didn't occur to him that she didn't treasure Chris or Darko's company as much as he did. He unlocked the car. Do you want to say hello? He was sitting there in the passenger seat, his ears cocked and looking up at her with his beady eyes. Mick had named him George. She loved dogs, especially Airedale Terriers, and she loved George Michael, always had, although Mick wasn't a fan. So from the looks of it, Mick loved her.

A big grin on his face, he threaded his way through the traffic while she stroked and tickled the pup. He turned the radio up louder and sang along, then told her about going to the dog breeder with Chris, and they both laughed. He was laughing at his mad story, she at his laughter. He gave her a kiss at every red light. Icy freshness just masking his slight, but not repulsive, bad breath from his night out. Everything was so delightfully the same as before that it struck her how thoroughly meaningless it was to wonder what he had been up to in her absence. The continuation of that thought was, that in future, even in Berlin, she could stop wondering what he got up to when he wasn't with her.

After three days he went out without her and didn't come back for days. She found a coat she didn't recognise hanging up in the hall, for which there would surely be a reason, and then a lipstick under the sofa, hmm. The bed sheets in the laundry basket smelled so strongly of L'eau d'Issey that she felt sick. This was also Mick. She crouched down in front of the washing machine and refused to let herself cry. Her sister was away, and there was no way she could complain to a friend – Delia knew what they'd say: he's a bastard, you're a victim, a simplistic assessment she could do without. You're always welcome here, it suits you here, her new friends had said, it was six in the morning now for them. She could only stand Lufthansa's hold music for five minutes. She took the contaminated laundry out of the machine and walked with the puppy to the old clothes charity collection point.

When she woke up, he was lying next to her, looking at her. Here I am, he whispered. They lay there, face to face. She let him fondle her, tickle her, love her, amazed at how quickly she freed herself from the stranglehold of her anger. Something is different, she thought, as he fell asleep breathing into her neck. Her new feeling persisted. His joy at seeing her again, and the freshly imported California lightness that she wanted to keep hold of as long as possible, had broadened her idea of love. From now on the question wouldn't be whether Mick would change. She would change and so would their relationship. Which, as it turned out after this break and chance to take stock, was going to continue.

Love needs freedom – something she'd heard a thousand times, and a thousand times not understood. Now she did. Fidelity was a question of how you defined it. He is faithful, just not in the way it is generally understood, she told herself, as she let him out into the night like a tomcat. He always came back. She had known that for years, now she understood it too. It wasn't the Micks of this world who left you behind, said the newly detached voice in her head, giving her strength, it was the so-called faithful men. They were the ones who moved on to be faithful to the next woman.

Better to stick with Mick, then. The other women would come to realise after a few days that he wasn't going to call again, that he'd move on after the deed was done. Mr Happy-Go-Lucky was gone. Back to her, Delia.

At some point she forbade herself from thinking about the others, the unknown, faceless women, and switched to approaching their relationship as if they were both monogamous. A refreshing decision. Delia regained her dignity and Mick could stop acting like a child avoiding his prying mother.

Most likely, her handsome American therapist wouldn't have thought it possible, but Delia's paradigm shift had turned a childish wrangling into a happy relationship. Almost a family, she thought, when the three of them lay on the sofa, a contented tangle of two people and a dog.

One more year at the firm at the most, then a baby, and after that I want to become a partner or I'll go for a job somewhere else. That was Delia's medium-term plan for the future, which only her sister knew.

And Mick? Cosima asked. What does he want?

Mick would know what he wanted when the time came. I'm off the pill for good, she had told him. It wasn't a conversation; it was a remark she put out there in the bathroom, toothbrush in her mouth. Right, great, he said, glancing at himself in the mirror, an approving glance, and walked out. Was he listening? Did he think she was talking about some random pill, not *the* pill, or did he mean what he said? She didn't ask, taking it as a murmur of agreement. Right, great.

Mick's with me, Delia said.

Right, great, Cosima also said, curiously, smiling at her sister thoughtfully.

Really, it would be. It all made more sense than it looked at first glance. Mick would be the perfect dad, and not just in terms of his genes. If she married someone from her professional world, it would be clear after a few half-hearted stabs at modernity that Delia's career would be put under general anaesthetic once children came along. With Mick it would be different. It wasn't that she wanted to make him a stay-at-home dad, after all he wasn't going to be moulded into anything. He would just have to stay the way he was. When she saw how laid-back and relaxed he was with children, it turned her on more than any of the fancy hanky-panky he came up with in bed. And it was no secret why kids loved him so much: he was one of them.

When Mick opened a small club in the mid-nineties with two friends – by the end of the nineties it had already moved to its fourth location, each time providing the occasion for legendary closing and opening parties – he was confident that no industry suited his personality as well as hospitality. You come up with something, he said countless times, drunk or sober, and that same night you get real-time feedback on whether or not your concept will catch on. One on one.

What concept? said Eddie, a battered figure who had roamed the nights since the seventies. You buy beer in the day and sell it to me at night. A concept, yes. But is it yours specifically?

Eddie laughed. Mick brushed it off, affronted, but he kept at it. Nowhere did you work one on one like in hospitality. And who was Eddie, anyway? Eddie had acquired his status as an institution through squatters' rights, no more no less. As one decade and one music scene after another passed through the city, Eddie was still there propping up the bar. His was a way of life that Mick was so familiar with that he was quietly working on another plan. The intermediate steps were still missing, but the ultimate goal was clear: get out of working nights. But how?

Having fun is harder to fake than an orgasm, Delia said to him once on the way home. Outside, the traffic was approaching peak rush-hour; inside, the taxi was pungent with a particularly aromatic tree-shaped air freshener. He took her cold hand in his warm one and rested his head on her shoulder. This world had never been hers, and now she'd had enough. And why would a woman who worked in a heavyweight law firm by day, party at night as if there were no tomorrow? It would have been futile to wait until Mick had had enough, because Mick never had enough. He played the same old movie week in week out as if it were brand new. Pounding music, feet pounding the dancefloor, abundant drinks, idle chatter, unbounded emotion. Yes, one year flowed into the next. But not without beauty. A fleeting beauty you can't hold on to.

When the closing-time mood set in, and with it that inexplicable, almost palpable fear of daylight, where would he have gone if it weren't for Delia? He would have moved on with strangers until he passed out. He would have woken up next to strangers. Okay, he woke up next to strangers, anyway. But he knew where he belonged after all that. The weekend started on Thursday, the night for the connoisseurs, they left Friday and Saturday to the amateurs, and it ended on Monday at some point later rather than earlier. He devoted Tuesdays to his sideline, writing music reviews, and Wednesday was his day off. Those days were all about diligent self-care: eating well, exercise, forest, lake, dog, Delia. Then it started all over again with the parties, every one of which felt unmissable, unforgettable, but in fact they were so interchangeable that he needn't have bothered with many of them, had it occurred to him at the time.

The truth was, working at night suited him. And spending the night in places where he would hang out anyway, with the advantage of earning money at the same time, suited him well. His business, or to be more precise, his third of the business, saw a strong turnover. Which was enough for him at the time, because for a long time they weren't much interested in the difference between takings and profit. It was all: mega takings last week, big night last night, the till's looking good, cash is king. It was all: Can I pay myself more this month? I'll pay it back, no worries. It was all: I think we should spend more on some cool flyers, I don't think DJ Whatshisname is better than DJ Whatsherface, but what the hell, he brings in the punters. It was all: We should have better visuals; I know a guy who did the visuals in the early days of techno. By the end of the decade, people were already nostalgic about the early nineties, the old skool.

You look like a Benetton poster, one of the barmaids had said at some point when the three of them stood behind the bar. Fabian, the Vietnamese with German adoptive parents, in the middle Mick, and next to him Chris, the redhead with so many freckles that he was almost brown. Mick found that his background was never less of an issue than at that time. He also thought the three of them made a good team – okay, maybe not quite the dream team – and he liked them both, although with Fabian it was more a rational decision in favour of him as a rational person, while his connection with Chris had more of an intimate quality that made him wonder sometimes what he would call this feeling. It's more of a brother thing, Mick thought, when he didn't check in with Delia for days on end and he wasn't with another woman, he was with Chris. Sometimes it reminded him of the best times with Desmond, memories that were interrupted by wondering how he was doing now.

With Chris, nothing was ever pointless or dull, everything was alive: the music, the conversations, their culture and where it fit in the grand scheme of things, because Chris was a master of good taste and a philosopher. And a patron of the arts, which Mick also appreciated. As a matter of principle, he overpaid the DJs and the bar staff, which Fabian turned a blind eye to, also because both groups were often accompanied by a throng of attractive women. But Chris also overpaid the cleaners and dishwashers, who Fabian cared less about, and sometimes he even hired people for purely social reasons who didn't do anything, except enjoy an hourly rate of twenty-five marks, an untypically high wage in Berlin.

In the first few years, it was all about fees paid cash in hand, only just covering the rent, and taste as the defining factor. A time when they could act like friendly animals without any predators. At some point they were sitting opposite a caseworker at the trade supervisory board who asked them, astonished, how it was that they had been running a business for years and hadn't thought to register it. So they registered it as an art association. They did actually display artwork by their artist friends at the club, so, great idea. They continued to grow. Yes, the growth was wild. One of the mistakes they didn't foresee at the time was with the PR, managed by the agency of a friend, a woman who, looking back on the nineties, would claim to have been Mick's steady girlfriend for two years. Essentially, a club in this city didn't really need PR at that time. But articles in city and music magazines helped, as did a national reputation and the occasional mention in international magazines.

A quarter of a year before the last big party of the century, the tax office got in touch via their company address, which in the absence of anything official was Fabian's home address. As they might have realised earlier but hadn't grasped until the moment they opened the letter, the tax office couldn't care less if your business was part of a subculture unknown to the fiscal authorities. And it didn't matter if their undeclared income, on which tax was due retrospectively, had been spent entirely on their own living expenses. Their tax bill was estimated retroactively, in favour of the tax office, naturally. Which, in the case of a bar that had been open four days a week for almost five years, as was evidenced by the flyers and ads in the press, resulted in a tax arrears sum that was difficult to contest due to the non-existence of any bookkeeping.

There was a payment slip right there, with the tax bill. The amount written on it was so large that Mick had to blink and stare at it several times, and finally count the zeros with his thumbnail. There were five zeros, at first he had counted six, but all the same there was no sense of relief. The digit before the zeros was also five. Half a million. Deutschmarks. Not that he had it in pesetas, either. Or schillings or lire.

It would be crazy to wind up now, Fabian said.

It would be crazy to pay for it unasked, Chris said.

What do you mean unasked? said Mick. They're quite specifically asking right here.

It would be cool to be able to pay this before things get uncomfortable, said Fabian, who had just teamed up with some guys for a retro chart hits club night that was doing amazingly well, and even more amazingly, hadn't affected their credibility as a cool venue. Going out is getting more eclectic, the boundaries between the scenes are more porous, Fabian liked to say, a keen sociologist of clubbing tendencies. No, tubby, was Chris's response, it's because you can take any garbage that was garbage in its day and sell it as retro now, and that's because if you're not into it everyone says you don't get the irony, because every piece of shit is ironic now or, crap word alert: cult. His thesis on the topic of tax arrears was punchier: Stephanie ratted on me.

What?

At least ninety per cent of all reports to the tax office come from pissed-off girlfriends or ex-wives. Obvious.

Chris showed Mick his Nokia Communicator, where he deleted the entry STEPH from his saved numbers. Mick gave Chris the thumbs up. Although he wondered how useful it was to delete Stephanie when he had a three-year-old daughter with her. Fabian got out his flip chart, which he had recently started bringing along to meetings. Chris found it a bit over the top; Mick was ambivalent. Flip charts had that sense of hot air, but on the other hand, hot air seemed to have considerable market value at the moment.

Fabian pulled out a marker and scrawled the six digits on a sheet, circling them with a flourish. After them he added a question mark.

We have two options, said Fabian, scribbling a Roman numeral I on his flip chart. We put together a brand package and sell it to people who want it or need it to improve their image. To big brands that are afraid of missing out on our peer group, for example. Either way, we sell to people who have money to buy a club, but no street cred, no direct access to the target group, and no drive.

Chris packed as much contempt as he could into his facial expression, while Mick felt like a maiden faced with a choice of two gentlemen, stuck between Sense and Sensibility. The chaos that he had believed would be transformed, by whatever route, into a financially sound future, had grown to around 167,000 DM in debt, coupled with the question: what now?

I'm going to Thailand, Chris said.

Thailand, thought Mick, whose flight instinct had been triggered the moment Fabian opened the letter, excellent idea.

Or, said Fabian, circling II on his flip chart – he seemed psyched up by the bad news – we'll build our own brand. He wasn't in the slightest bit interested in Thailand. Or Vietnam, where he was from. Fabian is the most German of all three of us,

Mick thought, wishing he had more of Fabian's innate get-up-and-go. But what was German about it? Or Vietnamese? Was it hereditary or instilled through upbringing? The instinctive drive to succeed. Whatever it was, Fabian had it. And Mick? His tended more to the ostrich approach. Head in the sand, or run away. It made no difference where that instinct came from.

So, we could set up an internet community. And there, on the web, we have access to an infinite number of people. A virtual club on the internet in parallel with the real-life club as a home base. That way we'll finally have a source of income that can be expanded ad infinitum. Where we're not counting beer crates, but users. What do you think?

I could be a user. I could use a beer. You?

It wasn't the first time that Mick and Chris had jumped ship like this. Chris determined, Mick more hesitant. All this talk of the web, where everything was heading, it required this ability to think in the abstract, it required faith that soon there would be enough people willing to pay to be in a place that was still fictional. Mick didn't have that faith, but he envied Fabian's ability to see the current disaster as mere teething problems in the development of their business. For him, the future seemed so bright that he didn't care what his partners thought, and that in itself should have convinced Mick, who did think Fabian had a talent for detecting trends.

Think it over, said Fabian, and Mick did indeed think about it briefly, only to realise once again that his imagination was alarmingly limited when it came to the internet, if not entirely defunct. A phone call interrupted his musings about whether he could really be that much stupider than Fabian, and he jumped down from the bar, relieved. It was the contact for the best sound system you could get your hands on at the time. Finally calling back. Could they pick it up now? Totally. He and Chris ran out into the unfiltered noise of Berlin. Four o'clock in the afternoon, everyone wrapped up tight, breath visible in the cold, rush hour. They piled into Chris's Volvo estate – the interior smelled of dog and the windows were iced up, a multipack of Red Bull and a leather skirt on the passenger seat. How did she get home without her skirt? asked Mick, and Chris laughed as he let the engine rev. The burdens of the past and visions of the future were forgotten because the present was calling: hyper-sharp, ultra-precise, and mega-loud. The end of the millennium was going to sound bombastic.

Mick hustled his way through the second half of 1999 with the feeling that he had to do everything he had so far failed to do before the one became a two. The countdown to the millennium made him feel like his whole life was a countdown, a thought that, in weaker moments, gave him deathly premonitions that he battled off with extended diversionary tactics that mostly didn't work. Things can't go on like this, he thought, all the while neglecting stuff, repressing stuff, ignoring stuff, increasingly trying not to think about it when he was out having a good time. If he asked himself *what* couldn't go on, a labyrinth opened up in his mind that he preferred not to venture into.

Everyone seemed to be racing toward a furious finale and no one had any idea what it was supposed to look like. No one could credibly exclude the possibility of a Millennium Bug. If, at 00:00 on 01.01.2000, all systems calibrated to the old millennium really did collapse, this could at least have the advantage that Mick's mountain of debt might be wiped out. From that point of view, it would be crazy to pay anything before that date. Perfect if Y2K meant everyone was sent back to square one.

Would everything be turned on its head? Probably not. While it seemed plausible that millions of other people might conceivably be right, Mick didn't believe it himself.

After all, the world, as far as you could tell, seemed stable. It didn't look like a matrix. You could throw the term cyber around as much as you wanted, nothing looked like Philip K. Dick or William F. Gibson. You went on the net, and while you did, the landline was engaged. You made a note of the best web addresses from magazines and typed them into your browser. People wondered if any imbecile would be able to compose music with the help of new software, and the answer was yes. People were always going on about Prada, always saying *galore* and *-o-rama*. If you discovered a trend too late, you could claim you'd rediscovered it. With all the irony flying around, no one knew anymore what you were still supposed to take seriously. Everyone was publishing lists of the ultimate books and records of the century that was coming to an end, lists that were even more elaborate than the bookshelves and record collections of the posers who wrote them. The same with the lists of the most important personalities, movies, events, and even websites of the past century, if not the millennium. You wondered if the time had come when everything that could exist had already existed, and the answer seemed to be: probably. From now on, this was the age of the reload. Sequel, prequel, whatever else. You felt like you were on the threshold of something brand new. Like so many decades and centuries before, you had that feeling of living through a particularly significant era. You put Prince's *1999* on again. 'Millennium' by Robbie Williams on repeat. You couldn't stop listening to Buena Vista Social Club. Electronic music was subdivided into so many subgenres that you lost track. Everyone was going on about how the best rapper right now was White and the best golfer was Black: Eminem and Tiger Woods. An observation that everyone seemed to find noteworthy. Everyone expected that Concorde would be followed by something even faster crossing the Atlantic, because acceleration was the logical consequence of almost everything. Large, respected companies sponsored every kind of madness, panicking about losing touch with the future, predicting that access would be the new ownership. Everyone was raring to go, trying to work out what they were supposed to do with all the portals that were mushrooming across the internet, even though most people had no idea how other people were already becoming immensely rich. People Mick's age. It felt like everyone else had found the entrance to some vault full of treasure – open, sesame! – while he was still messing around in the antechamber, with only a glimpse inside, before the door swung shut again. The feeling of missing out on something but also, unlike in the past, the accompanying sense of it being almost within reach, triggered something in him that Delia called his 'hyperactive apathy'. It manifested itself in too little sleep, a large radius of activity, and an almost manic need to communicate, while at the same time severely impaired concentration and shoddy results. The term burnout wasn't yet in everyday parlance, but it described the state that Mick was hurtling toward the autumn before his thirtieth birthday.

He had spent a lot of time with Delia that summer, after seeing so little of her in the spring that it could be described as a long-distance relationship. It was a while before he noticed she was scheduling sex, because after all, it was never the wrong time for sex. When he did start to spot the pattern, he realised they both had a problem now. This was the first problem of his life that was more powerful than his libido. So powerful that he feared becoming impotent. Not in general, just specifically with her. It was hell to reject her. The need for a conversation hung in the house like puffs of smoke. But he wanted this conversation even less than sex by appointment. His comings and goings were no longer dictated by what he felt like at the time, but by a fixed schedule. Whenever possible, he wouldn't come home until she was asleep or at work.

We hardly see each other anymore, I miss you, she said after a few months in this rhythm, no reproach in her voice, which might have been a deliberate tactic, and even if it was, it worked. He had just walked in, as she and George were on their way out to the park. *You say goodbye, and I say hello.* Oddly enough, it was the dog who looked offended, not Delia. He saw her straw bag with a few files and magazines in it. She was going to spend this scorching Sunday alone in the park in the June sunshine, while he lay around on his own in a darkened bedroom. He was the moon; she was the sun. He saw her freckled shoulders, her little feet in flip-flops, he smelled her sunscreen and wanted to cross over to the other side. To her. There are strawberries in the fridge, she said, and he watched her as she got on her bike and rode away. It was painful to keep avoiding her; not only that, it was exhausting to make it look like he wasn't. Their reconciliation without a prior argument felt so good that he had almost told her the truth. Almost. He kept up his stellar performance the whole summer, sometimes even convincing himself that everything was just like it was before. They went to the lakes together and to Italy. It shored them up. After all, they weren't just bodies with XX and XY chromosomes; they also existed as two people who still had something to talk about. And the fact that she only seduced him when it fitted with her timing didn't mean she didn't want him in general, did it? We'll talk at some point, thought Mick, just not now.

As this Summer of Love slowly burned out, he was pulled away again. Like being called up to the front. I've got to work, baby. But not three nights in a row. I've got to go. I'll see you later. New Year's Eve was approaching and with it the pressure to throw a party befitting the date. No victory without training. When he got home in the early hours of the morning, when the rest of the world was still asleep, or already asleep, he would smoke and scribble to-do lists on Post-its, which he left scattered around the house and could hardly decipher later, when the next day rolled around. I need a rest, he thought, alternating with: I need money, *mucho* and *pronto*. Delia mirrored his problem back to him. She had drive. So did he. Only she used hers to progress whereas he was going round and round in circles. As soon as he had an idea, as soon as he devoted himself to something during the day, the next night came along and got in the way, and pulverised not only his fears for the future but also his plans for the future. Your horoscope for the coming week: Desolation. Anguish. Despair, as Delia had texted him at some point, sick of waiting for him. Unfortunately, it happened more and more often. For years he'd been reassured that it was the same for everyone. That's the price we have to pay, he thought, until he asked himself: for what? He could have been more like Fabian, who was becoming ever more professional in his approach to business: swing by, take a look, go. He could have done things like Chris: swing by, brief but big hello, go. Because Chris had acquired two large dogs and, with his little girl, Fee, he now had three creatures to look after in the day. Mick was finding it harder to ignore the party's-over-now mood that the others exuded. The thing now was to say you had plans, that you really had a lot on, not that you had anything better to do, to say you had to put your health first, that you were getting a bit old for all that now. The gigantic bill to pay felt like the final rejection, like being chucked out at the end of the night. It was only bearable because the other two were in it with him. The end of the year began to race by like every year, like Mick's heart when he thought of the two most ominous tasks on his to-do list. First, talk to the tax office. Fabian would take care of that. Second, talk to Delia. He was alone with that one. He was glad that she was so busy, and whenever he saw her he was so affectionate that she would giggle in disbelief when he hugged her and wouldn't let go. It was winter now, and he wanted to lie next to her until it all sorted itself out. Her head on his chest, she asked him from time to time if everything was okay, and he always replied: everything's great. When he drove through the city in early December to pick her up from work, and when he yet again heard the background noise of everything that hadn't sorted itself out bursting in on any halfway positive train of thought, he interrupted himself. First see this millennium out, then we'll see, he said to himself, clearly and out loud, and the gigantic timescale immediately made his worries smaller. Windscreen wipers on, turn the music up, switch lanes and mood at the same time. It'll sort itself out, Mick thought, reverting to his classic optimism. He was turning thirty in the first month of the new millennium: wasn't that the perfect time for one or two changes? It almost felt like he was chosen. Unclear by whom and for what, but he stuck with it: it was symbolic.

It wasn't just one or two changes. Everything changed. Mick spent New Year's Eve in the Charité hospital. He slept through the party, the fireworks, the historic arrival of the new millennium. When he woke up, he saw Delia sitting at his bedside, telling him who else had visited him. Chris and Fabian, Darko, Axel, and people she didn't know, she said she'd forgotten their names. The room was full of flowers as if he had died, as if he wasn't in a bed but in an open coffin. After four days, he was discharged, but with no clear diagnosis; no one could tell him if he would regain his full hearing. His sense of balance was so disturbed that he needed to hold onto a wall to walk. Delia led him into the multistorey car park, gently helped him into the car.

You're always there, he said, hearing himself like he was talking under water. Delia gave him a lacklustre smile, before glancing in the rearview mirror as she reversed out of the parking space. It was strange, but the way that she looked at him made him realise for the first time that he could lose her. Even though, for once, he hadn't done anything that she would have to forgive him for. The thought had to be part of the overwhelming fear that had terrorised him since he woke up; he'd been trying to dull it with painkillers and sleeping pills. The doctors had interpreted this fear as unbearable pain. They increased his dosage and gave him a two-week supply of pills to take home, which was fine with him.

He zoned out in the passenger seat, gazing fondly at Delia's slender hands on the wheel, for the first time noticing her confident driving style. Isn't it the unconscious gestures that you fall in love with? Isn't everything we do consciously to please someone else just a meaningless performance, but something we still have to go through because we never know what it is that the other person is actually moved by? He had never thought of it that way, at least not in Delia's presence; he'd so much taken her presence in his life for granted and now, so suddenly that he had to wind down the window in a panic, he realised he couldn't take it for granted. He slumped into the passenger seat, feeling as vulnerable and exposed as if he'd had his skin ripped off him. He was still gazing at Delia, who was now pulling up to the barrier, parking ticket between her lips, and putting the ticket in the slot, and he had never loved her so much as at that moment when the barrier opened and she accelerated. Spontaneously, he reached into her hair and tried to kiss her.

Let go of me, please, she said, and he might almost have cried, he felt so rejected. She glared at him, a probing look, then concentrated on driving again.

We're going home now, and you're going to have a lie down.

He nodded. She stroked his knee briefly, glancing in the rearview mirror, then looked at him. We'll get you fixed up, okay?

Her hair had an almost saintly glow, although it was only a dim winter light in the car, her skin shimmered, her snow-white teeth were set in dusky pink gums that looked so clean and appetising that he wanted to touch them, with any part of him, his finger, tongue, dick.

Okay? she asked again, and he nodded and looked out the window. Nothing suggested a new millennium. Everything was the same as ever: even in this historic January, Berlin was hard to beat for dreariness.

It was only four days in. The streets were still full of the debris of New Year's Eve, but he felt as if he had been away for ages. At war, in prison, in a coma.

Mick, Delia said. Can you actually hear me?

And as she handed him a handkerchief, he wondered when the last time was that he really cried his eyes out.

And then he slept. He slept through his mum's visit. He slept through the chance to have the conversations he had spent the last few months so deftly avoiding. Which meant those conversations were had without him, out of his control, and heading in directions that he couldn't influence. At least that's how it seemed later.

The Christmas tree was still there. Mick had hung CDs on it, having forgotten to buy any decorations. They had friends over for Christmas Eve, friends who were also staying home in Berlin for the holidays and had nothing else planned. Delia's duck wasn't *à point*, but their guests were so happy that it made her want to spend every Christmas like this from then on. The police showed up at around three in the morning. A resounding success.

Now, a week and a half later, everything was different. Delia was alone, waiting for Mick's mother. She had aired all the rooms out of her horror of receiving guests in a house that stank of who knows what. She had thrown open the windows, lit incense, sprayed tiny spritzes of her best perfume, and placed a bowl of tangerines on the living room coffee table. When Monika's cab pulled up, she opened the front door and stood in the doorway, shivering, until Monika had finished her conversation with the cab driver and paid. The man carried her suitcase through the front garden and up the five steps to Delia, not a matter of course for a Berlin taxi driver, but natural when you're with Monika. Monika, who then decided that her tip was too small, opened her suitcase and took out a camel-shaped leather bookmark, for his daughter perhaps, she said. Monika had moved close to Frankfurt-am-Main two years ago, and had spent New Year's Eve in Marrakech, where she had heard Delia's message and got on the next plane. The cab driver made a fuss of refusing her gift, but Monika insisted, while Delia stood on the doorstep in her silk blouse, shivering.

Monika. She had for years referred to her as her mother-in-law. A woman she had tried to get to know time and again and yet never really knew, because she wasn't someone you could decipher with any ordinary code. She had no doubt presented to the cab driver a repertoire of personalities in the twenty minutes from Tegel to Pankow. Diva, ruffian, buddy, snob, and now, for good measure, doting mum. No wonder Mick gets on so well with everyone, Delia had thought when he finally introduced her to his mother, no wonder he likes everyone, but never really gets involved with anyone. Monika had raised a social butterfly – one that was now flightless, hence why she'd come. After the cab driver had finally let her force the camel on him and had driven off, Monika gave Delia a big hug. She pressed her against her Afghan shepherd's coat, which she described as a timeless piece and which still, after over twenty years, smelled faintly of goat.

In the kitchen, she leaned against the sink and rummaged through her handbag for cigarettes. The only thing you could rely on with Mick's mother was her seventies-inspired aesthetic. She was ever loyal to her crafted, designer hippie look, copious suede, patterned fabrics, ethnic jewellery, her blonde hair always long with a girlish fringe. And she didn't waste a single thought on giving up smoking, although she had been an acupuncture specialist for several years and a large proportion of her clientele consisted of smokers who wanted to quit. Her response to Delia's question about her flight was a counterquestion, what did the doctors say, and Delia remembered: she wasn't one for small talk. She shouted over the sound of the espresso machine, he'll be able to hear again, that's the good news. One ear is fine so far. The other one – we'll see.

Smoking, Monika looked down at her stockinged feet. She had insisted on taking off her boots.

Oh, Michi, she said to herself and to Delia: Do you think I can see him?

He's asleep, but later, of course. That's why you're here. He'll be pleased to see you.

The idea that Monika – usually so confident and headstrong – had flown all the way from Morocco only *then* to ask if she could see Mick, was part of the mystery of this woman that Delia found most baffling. Why was she even asking? Was it out of respect for Delia? Was it a sign of the distance between mother and son? Or was it a rhetorical question, and Monika was just about to stub out her cigarette and rush to his bedside regardless? They sat down in the living room, where Delia opened a bottle of white wine, which in Monika's presence didn't feel like daytime boozing but *savoir vivre*, as sad as the reason for her visit was.

So, basically, Delia began, it seems like they rented some kind of special sound system, and all they'd done was add more and more watts, or decibels, or more volume, I don't really know how it works, but it sounds like Mick and Chris were in some kind of fetish community for stereo equipment. They paid crazy money for differences most people wouldn't hear.

That sounds a hundred per cent like my son, said Monika and let the smoke out through her nostrils.

Anyway, at the sound check, Mick stood right in front of the speaker, which was about three times his size, Chris connected it to the amp and apparently didn't notice that it was on full volume, and then this noise came out of the speakers, a wave so strong that Mick went flying into a pile of chairs a few metres away and didn't wake up for two days.

Monika massaged the bridge of her nose.

For years I was afraid something would happen to him on New Year's Eve. And now he's nearly thirty and he's almost deaf.

No, Monika, one ear's completely fine. He can hear, said Delia. Please don't cry, she thought.

When he was a baby, my mother thought he might be deaf because he was so quiet, Monika said thoughtfully. Again she rummaged in her bag. Speaking of babies, I brought you the photos.

She was the only one from whom Delia occasionally got snippets that might help complete the Mick puzzle; never completely, but still. Monika took a stack of photos out of an envelope that had *Michi* written on it. Mick in 1970, 1971, 1972, sweet, cute, wide-eyed, a darling, an angel in whose innocent face Delia searched for the man she lived with. Here he was as a toddler on the lap of a rotund picture book grandma who wasn't his grandmother but his great-aunt. Here he was at about five, in front of a llama enclosure, holding hands with a rather stern-looking older man. Monika lovingly stroked his face in the photo.

My dad was a carpenter, she said, I thought it was a real shame Mick didn't finish his apprenticeship, but what can you do? Whatever you say it falls on deaf ears.

They glanced at each other, Monika alarmed at what she'd said. A motherly truism, which was now the clinical truth, at least partially, and Delia, who didn't know what to do with all this new information from Mick's past that, after all these years, really shouldn't have been news to her. Should she let Monika see her surprise? Should she admit that she was having a hard time with her son?

Who was a carpenter again? she asked, because she couldn't think of anything else to say. Bob Dylan?

Bob Dylan's *name* was Zimmerman – carpenter. Harrison Ford was a carpenter. I always thought he was chic.

And Jesus, said Delia.

As I said, a great vocation, said Monika and handed her a colour photo with a green tinge.

Here he is at school. East German colour film.

Did you name him after the Nina Hagen song?

No, no, Monika laughed. She poured herself a generous refill and said no again.

Monika was undeniably a stunner in her short dress and high boots, with Mick standing next to her with his school bag and looking sceptically up at his beaming mother. And there was something else. Delia held the photo up to her face. She had never noticed how alike the two of them were. A blind spot that must have had something to do with the fact that she had taken it for granted that he looked like his father.

He looks like you, she said to Monika, who even now looked like him, or rather he like her.

Yes, of course, he's my son.

Yes, of course, Delia thought, and saw that she hadn't been colour-blind so much as colour-misguided.

To be precise, he looks like my father, that's who we have to thank for our hooters.

Monika turned to show her her profile. In her case, her nose would be described as Roman, in Mick's as Arab, although both came from the gene pool of the stern old carpenter.

Delia went upstairs to where Mick lay gnashing his teeth. When she came back into the living room with the second bottle of wine, Monika was standing at the open patio door, smoking. The photos lay spread out on the table. Including some later snaps that Mick probably wouldn't have shown to anyone. Delia recalled a recurring nightmare: she's sitting in a conference room where her mother is showing slides with naked photos of her, to an audience that changes from dream to dream.

Was it a betrayal of Mick to carry on looking through his past? Ah, it's nothing, Monika would say. Without looking at them, Delia tidied the photos into a pile like playing cards, feeling a little protective of him.

I have to take the dog out, she said.

Go carefully, Monika said, closing the window. I'd better get going and come back tomorrow. Maybe he'll be in better shape, what do you think?

Have you booked a hotel?

No, goodness, I'm staying out at Martha's.

Mick's great-aunt Martha had died in 1986 and lived on through the bungalow she had left Mick and Monika, not much more than a summerhouse or a dacha. They didn't call it that, they always said 'at Martha's'.

Out of the question. You'll freeze to death out there. And there are wild boar. No, really, you must stay here with us.

I don't have to walk, I'll get the S-Bahn the whole way. I'm perfectly at home there.

Monika's balancing act between luxury and frugality – she had flown back on the most expensive Lufthansa flight after a week in a high-end riad in Marrakech, and now she wanted to spend the night in a garden shed that smelled of an old air mattress – reminded Delia of Mick. It was this permanent clash of worlds within one person that was so jarring, and yet also kind of touching.

Moni, don't be silly, she said, hearing herself slurring a little. Stay here.

OK. I'd better have a bath, then.

Delia stood up, swaying slightly, and wondered if she should give the bathroom a clean. Then decided against it. Don't be so obsessive, she told herself, it's fine. She called to George.

Make yourself at home, she said to Monika, before heading out with him into the cold.

Sometimes George stood by his bed in the half light, looking up at him. Hey George, what's up, he must have said it out loud, because George perked his ears up into perfect triangles, waiting for more. Action, love, or at least attention, but Mick was too weak. The next time he woke up, it was pitch black and he wondered how long you could lie there without drying out, at what point you'd be eaten away by the bacteria that proliferated in the oral cavity. Little icy clouds seemed to hover above him. He was hot; his face was cold. All he could hear was the noise from the pipes; it might have been coming from his head. Still, he could tell that someone was there, someone was downstairs with Delia.

He stared at the ceiling until the black became a graphite grey mist, and through it he could see the pendulum. It was a game he'd taught himself as a child, inspired by 'The Pit and the Pendulum', the Edgar Allan Poe story. The trick was not to block out the fear but to leave the light off and wallow in the horror of your own creation until you fell asleep, a completely exhausted survivor. Poe's shackled prisoner sees the pendulum descending on him from the ceiling and realises it's a scythe, and sooner or later it's coming for him; the pendulum comes so close he can smell the metal. Mick was so enthralled as a child; he could smell the metal too. Now, it smelled of Delia, strangely, indirectly. His heart began to race. Had his sense of smell already taken over from his hearing? Or had she been in the room? She could have left some water by his bed. He reached beside him and knocked over a bottle. She had.

He drank, slept, awoke with a jolt, and sat straight up. The chorus of a song they sang in the GDR popped into his head.

Eins-zwei-drei-vier-fünf-sechs-sieben, alles dreht sich, nichts bleibt stehn, lasst uns fahren, lasst uns fliegen, Mond und Sterne zu besehn. One-two-three-four-five-six-seven, we're all spinning, up to heaven. Ride to Venus, fly to Mars, we're off to see the moon and stars. An eager choir of children's voices belted it out over and over in his head. Strangely, the rest of the song was deleted from his hard disk. This line had been too, until that moment.

He must have dreamed it. Delia's visitor was holding him captive. There was someone downstairs, and he couldn't get down there, where there was food, and light, and television, and Delia. He missed her so much since his accident; it was like she had disappeared.

You always know, Delia thought later. You always know deep down. The wine hadn't fogged her mind; it had left her in a seismographic mood that forecast to her that a storm was brewing. Rigid as if paralysed, she followed George down the street, staring at his rear end as if hypnotised by the black hole below his upright tail. George stopped, tilted his head. Are you okay? he seemed to be asking. No, nothing's okay, thought Delia, picking up a damp stick and throwing it. What do we know? The fact that the computers had kept running didn't mean that nothing would change. No, all it showed was that *that* had been a false alarm. Her hands were clammy and her guts were rioting, like before her worst exams. She stood by the flashing lights of a house whose occupants had gone full Las Vegas for the Christmas season. How can they stand it in there, she wondered. She whistled for George and walked back home with the disappointed beast, a hopeful stick clenched between his teeth. She trudged home with him, about to pick up her own disappointment, a stick she would gnaw on for years.

Directness was Monika's forte.

So, tell me, she called from the bathroom, just as Delia walked into the house and started drying George off.

Has Mick had his vasectomy reversed, then?

Delia let go of George's front paw, straightened up, and looked at herself in the mirror in the hall: straight out of one of those TV shows where they drop a surprise on you out of nowhere, her features frozen, her brain unable to process the information it had just received.

Monika appeared in the doorway in Mick's bathrobe and unravelled the towel turban to dry her hair. In slow motion, Delia pulled the hat from her head. Her hair crackled. They smiled at each other.

Well . . . Delia heard herself say.

Monika went back into the bathroom and carried on talking, brushing her hair by the sound of it.

Sorry for asking, but it's obvious the second you walk in the bathroom that you're trying for a baby. It's great. I did think it seemed a bit hasty when he told me. I asked him, how do you know you don't want kids? At your age, I mean. Is it so hard to use contraception? It's easier than having a vasectomy and then having it reversed, if you change your mind later. But if it worked out, then, great.

Monika appeared in the doorway again.

Yeah, yeah, Mick, said Delia, needing all her strength to draw her eyes away from George's back.

I'm done in the bathroom – do you need to come in? I'll go check on him now.

Oh? Yeah. Sure. Thanks.

She turned the key as quietly as possible, as if locking the door was somehow impolite towards Monika. She wiped the last of the condensation from the mirror with her coat sleeve and had one of those moments when you not only look at yourself, but you truly see yourself. I'm thirty-three, nearly thirty-four, and I'm not doing so well today, but soon I'll be fantastic, she thought, looking herself straight in the eye. She wished she could summon tears with the same ease that she used to throw up. Just like that, out with it. Command a bodily function and feel instant relief. Instead, her jaw felt like it was locked in a steel clamp, and there was nothing she could do except swallow a few times and wonder what she looked like, though that hardly mattered right now. She forced herself to look herself in the eye again. It's better I find out now than later, she told herself. I can do this. I've lost a few years, but I still have six years until I'm forty. A good six years. And they start today.

So, said Mick, after they'd taken Monika to the station, and driven home in silence, and Delia had gone straight to the living room and sat down, not once taking her eyes off him, which meant that she wasn't letting him postpone this conversation a second longer. It was happening now.

I never wanted kids, he said, hearing himself in mono like he used to after swimming, only worse because now it felt so permanent.

She was on the sofa. He was at a cautious distance in an armchair that he never normally sat in. She looked at the carpet as if she were reading it, then straight at him again.

Sorry, this is how it is, he said. Was that enough?

Clearly it wasn't enough, or she would have nodded.

Maybe it's because I was an accident myself.

Is that how you see it?

It's how it was. Monika wouldn't say so now, but a student getting pregnant at twenty-two, no partner. Doesn't sound like a master plan, does it?

Delia shrugged. She chose to have you, and as far as I can see, she never regretted it.

Her eyes bore into him, and suddenly he'd had enough of this tribunal nonsense.

Do you think she enjoyed doing everything on her own? Do you think it's not lonely when the only person you have to talk to is a three-year-old?

The idea of his mother being alone – he had never thought about it before, and he didn't even know if it had been the case for Monika – suddenly made him unbearably miserable.

Kids just want to fit in, you know. They want to be like everyone else. It's exhausting being the neighbourhood freak.

Yeah, I get it. You're the only person in the world who didn't grow up in a family like in the Rama advert. Diddums. Have a good cry about it.

He wanted to cry and he wanted to lie down in bed. With a pizza and a movie.

Would you feel differently if your father had been there?

I don't know. Maybe.

I didn't know you were so negative about your childhood. Besides, every idiot brings kids into the world. Wasters, drunks, thugs – nothing stops them having kids.

What have they got to do with it? I can't. Or I don't want to, which amounts to the same thing.

And it wasn't just that you wanted to screw around without consequences?

He crossed his arms. A shitty question. Answered with another question: What do you want a baby for, anyway?

She glared at him.

What kind of question is that?

See, you don't know.

Let's spare ourselves this part of the discussion, she said, her voice shrill. Don't start making out I'm egotistical because I want a baby while you're saving the world from overpopulation. Forget it.

Fine, he said, it's not about the world, it's about me. I'll be happy if I can get my own life halfway sorted. Isn't that enough?

Okay, she said, hoarse. When?

What?

When did you do it?

When you were in the States.

She nodded, and finally found something on the carpet. A piece of fluff she picked up angrily, then glared at him again.

You never go to the doctor, they practically have to carry you to the dentist, and then you voluntarily go and have your tubes cut?

It sounded so awful that he moved his hand to his crotch; it was so soothing he would have liked to stick his hand down his trousers. What if, he wondered, we just moved on to sex? That would be the best exit from this interrogation. Delia's face smouldering, like an infrared lamp. He heard her scream, muffled and in mono, and his horniness subsided.

And it's not just that you made yourself infertile, which by the way I cannot believe about someone who's practically a talking cock, but you just stand there for years watching me stuff myself with hormones, buying all this crap, structuring my entire life around my fucking hormonal cycle and running from doctor to doctor, because, once again, I assume it's me. I assume I've fucked up my body so badly with my eating disorder that I'm now infertile. Do you know what I have been through?

No, he didn't. Talking cock? That's how she saw him?

No, because you've never told me about it. Seriously, sweetheart, get a grip, and enough of all the martyr talk!

He had known, though he would rather not have known. But all the same, the word 'baby' had never been mentioned specifically.

If you'd told me before that you wanted a baby so badly, we could have talked about it. But this . . .

Mick's method of shifting blame was intolerable, he knew, and yet he couldn't help it. He knew she was going to hate him now.

Instead, you've been quietly trying to get pregnant and then you completely freak out when you realise that for once you don't get what you want? This isn't about feelings; it's about control.

Was he right? He was. Go on.

You're planning a family without me, Delia, and you want me to be the dad? What am I? Your stud?

You're disgusting.

Yeah, she was going to hate him, but he was on a roll.

The big Black stud, that's right. You're the brain, I'm the body, that's how it is. That's racist, Delia, that's fucking low. But maybe this talking cock isn't at your beck and call. Deal with it.

He expected a slap in the face, but she got up, trembling, and walked over to the sideboard. She was so shaky that he wanted to get up and take her in his arms.

She pulled a bottle of cognac out of the Christmas hamper from her law firm and held it out to him, asking him with her eyebrows if he was joining her, and he nodded. Please let's get drunk and calm down, he thought.

She handed him a generously poured brandy snifter.

Nice glasses. Who are they from?

Don't change the subject. She tilted her head and knocked back the cognac.

Baby or no baby – you would never have told me, would you?

I would have told you eventually, but I didn't think it was a big deal. After all, women use contraception, too, and they decide that on their own. I thought it would be one less thing for us to worry about.

One less thing to worry about, she echoed. They looked at each other. Normally, no matter what had been going on, and there had been a lot going on, when he smiled she always smiled back. Not today.

You didn't notice that I put on weight? she asked. What made her think that now? She pulled up her sweater.

Side effect of the hormones. You didn't care, did you?

He took her hand, pulled her close, and caressed her belly. Yes, it was round, and yes, he didn't care. He loved her the way she was – that would sound like a platitude if he said it now. Instead, he put his ear to her belly button, he meant it as an affectionate gesture, but it was the trigger that made her lose it. She shoved him back, knelt on him, and thrashed out, thumping him, raining blows at him just like she used to shower him with kisses. Hey, he shouted, usually if she was on top of him it meant fooling around or sex, but now it was like she had a demon inside her, lashing out at Mick with a tirade so grotesque that he heard himself laughing in disbelief.

Delia was always so genteel with her words: she didn't call other women dirty whores, and she didn't say fuck, at least not with this frequency. She didn't call herself the stupidest woman on the entire fucking planet who had been so fucking stupid that she'd sat at home alone waiting to fucking ovulate. This wasn't Delia; she would never call him a lying piece of shit who could just fuck off, right now!

He grabbed her wrists. Delia? It's me, he shouted, like an exorcist trying to reach the gentle soul inside the raging demon. She didn't look at him; she turned her red face to the side. He babbled away, quietly.

Delia, we'll work it out. I'm sorry I didn't say anything, and I'll find out what I can do. It can be undone. Okay?

I was so stupid, she said in disbelief, and slid off him like a jockey after losing a race. Her lips pursed and eyes open wide, she walked back over to the sideboard and fiddled with the Christmas presents, her hands trembling. She stifled back tears, why?

I love you, he said, to her back. The words hung in the room, among the others that shouldn't have been said. They didn't get through. They were too feeble, too new. In their purest form, these were words he had never said before.

It sounded stupid and it really was: he had finally fallen in love with her because she had had enough. It's too late, Delia kept saying, in every possible tone of voice. It could have been a lawyer trick, threatening the worst-case scenario to strengthen her negotiating position. But Delia didn't want to negotiate anymore. For years she'd believed in him. Now all she believed in were the words *too late*.

He was broke. He was sick. Nothing he was involved in at the moment gave any sign of a bright future. None of that had mattered as long as Delia loved him in her unwavering, unconditional way. Unconditional, what a word. A word fit for gods, not humans. He was incapable of procreation, and by the looks of things, that had been her only condition. Presumably he could have carried on doing what he was doing as long as he didn't betray her. But now she needed something that he didn't have to offer. For the first time in his life, the question arose as to what he did have to offer.

Could he somehow fix this mess? He didn't know. In his desperation, he did all the things she had asked him to do for months, maybe years, like repairing things around the house and a bit of decorating. He saw himself drift into DIY drudgery.

Delia worked even harder than usual and stayed out of his way. He presumably had the high standards she set for herself to thank for the fact that she didn't kick him out. Fairness and decency meant she could hardly throw her long-term companion out on the street. He feared she would suggest downgrading to just friends. Which at any other time he would gladly accept, but now it seemed like only the slightest mitigation to the maximum penalty.

The situation reminded him of his teenage years. No more fighting, he was told. One more time and you're out, they said. It can't be that hard not to attract any negative attention for a few weeks. Except it really was. Delia didn't say anything along those lines. But she still didn't give him any credit for his new loyalty and domesticity. She could hardly expect anything else from someone who was practically housebound. The unspoken agreement seemed to be that they would leave each other in peace until he was better. Not that their truce made any difference to the rest of the world.

For years, he had been so discreet. For years, Delia had looked the other way. And now, of all times, some woman showed up at his house thinking she and Mick were a couple. Delia opened the door for her, and Mick acted clueless, which neither of the women were taken in by. The stubborn fling, whose name he couldn't recall, demanded an explanation, and Delia, who might quite reasonably have demanded an explanation, too, just pushed past them and stormed out with the dog.

The woman was genuinely attractive in an ostentatious sort of way. Everything about her was large. Huge eyes and glossy lips, almost obscenely large. Glittery top under a white leather coat and fair hair in a short style that stood out around her tanned face – she looked like she'd come straight from some high-end club. She'd sprayed herself liberally with some summery perfume. A sunflower in January. Where have you been? she asked him several times in a row, with such earnest indignation that he had to sit down. Where should he have been? He had been here, where he was unmistakably living with his partner. And this woman was standing on Delia's carpet, making a scene. She kept running her fingers through her hair; for some reason she couldn't leave it lying flat against her head. He remembered this gesture. Her name remained elusive, but the weekend with her resurfaced. A beautiful weekend that had begun on a Thursday night and ended with a Sunday afternoon at the lake. The boat rental season was already over, but the boats were still there, reminding Mick of his days as a rower. The sunshine glinted in her shades. That unexpected afterglow that October still sometimes had to offer, with an awe-inspiring sun low in the sky, a gift you could hardly refuse before sinking into the darkness and cold of winter. And she'd been there, this woman, and she must have got the wrong end of the stick. It was all cheerful and psychedelic, if he remembered correctly, and fleeting, he had thought, but he was apparently wrong about that.

Before I flew to Gran Canaria, you said we'd talk on the phone after. Before and after formed units of time in Mick's mind that almost sent him back into a psychedelic state. When? He had no memory of any conversation about Gran Canaria.

And then you said you'd call me back when the stress was over. That was almost five weeks ago now.

What stress? Mick asked without meaning to.

I don't know. I told myself, I'll leave you be, we're adults, you'll get back to me.

Sorry.

This woman needed to be gone before Delia got back with George. She winked at him encouragingly, as if everything would soon fall into place, now that she had finally found him.

What, um, were we going to do?

You're not seriously asking me that now? Well, among other things, we were gonna spend New Year's Eve together.

I had an accident.

Yes, Fabian told me about that at least. That's why I wasn't angry. Are you feeling better?

Listen, he said, you've got it wrong, we're not a couple . . . or anything like that.

You could have used the phone to tell me that.

That's right, he thought, if I'd known there was a woman sitting somewhere, staring at her phone for weeks, I would have texted. Possibly.

Sorry, he said again.

Not only had he made all these promises, but he also had her charger, apparently, which he looked for in his desk to no avail, until he finally gave up and gave her his. And he owed her money, around fifty or a hundred marks, but they could just forget about it now, she said. He went into the kitchen, where the envelope lay on the worktop with his share of the takings from the bar. Andi had brought it over yesterday, Fabian's new loyal assistant. He pressed five twenties into her hand. Then he led her to the door, where she tried again to summon up the cosy atmosphere of a couple, a couple with problems, but a couple all the same.

So, you call me when you're feeling better, and then we'll see, okay?

He didn't reply, because anything he said would force him to commit to some new obligation with a waiting period and a telephone appointment.

Get well soon, won't you? What's wrong with you, anyway?

Too complicated right now.

Well, anyway, get well.

Yeah, thanks. Bye.

Not nice, but unambiguous, he hoped.

She was already outside when she reached into her coat pocket and pulled out a small package that she handed to him. Clearly a tape.

Here, we talked about it. If you remember.

I'll have a listen, he said.

The tape had LoveMixxx written on it. He threw it straight in the bin. The long-forgotten sunflower had managed to make herself unforgettable after all, with this farewell scene that was so bizarre that he felt the urge to tell someone about it, but also so pitiful that he couldn't mock her. Fuck, she'd just had really bad timing. Just like him.

When Delia came back, he would have loved to grab her by the top of her arms and shake that unbearably smug expression off her face. Yes, he was guilty and she was perfect. On the other hand – though unfortunately, this wasn't an argument he could use in the current circumstances – wasn't it a miracle that a woman had shown up at his place only once in all these years? What did that mean? That he had presented himself as unambiguously attached? He didn't think he had. That as a lover he was a flash in the pan? Harsh.

Delia demonstratively threw open the windows and shooed away the cloying, fake summer freshness. Without saying a word, he went down to the cellar and went back to staining the old bureau he was doing up as a way of saying sorry to Delia. He heard her on the phone, laughing hysterically, endlessly blithe and cheerful. She was reactivating her old circle of friends. Mick stood there brooding in the solvent haze. The fact that all those other women had left him alone after no more than a couple of unanswered text messages showed they had style. Even if they had hoped for more, they bore their defeat with dignity. Ms LoveMixxx's crass behaviour made her tactful sisters shine in a new light. Thank you, ladies.

He had ignored Fabian's calls until then. But now this ill-fated three-night stand had shown up at his place, thanks to him. Mick called him back and laid into him for his indiscretion. Yelling at him felt good.

Man, are you out of your mind? What the fuck were you playing at? Why'd you give her my address?

It sounded urgent, and you weren't answering the phone.

I cannot believe it! Did you think about Delia?

Of course I did. Did you?

Prick.

Ditto.

Dude, you can't do that, said Mick, utterly convinced he was in the right. Fabian remained unconvinced.

Someone else called. From London. Liz? Lynn?

Who? London? Fuck, that's all I need.

Fabian, if you don't stop this shit, I'm out.

Fabian laughed his scornful hissing laugh and started up again with the tedious topic of tax debts, and the advice he'd been given by his tax advisor, and the question of how best to proceed, and when Mick thought he would be well enough to come by the club again, and how he envisaged them paying their debt, and what he thought about if they first converted everything into a limited company so they could at least be making a legitimate turnover.

Mick was in no position to negotiate any of this. Not while Chris was in Thailand. Chris. The sly git. Mick really missed him.

No, Fabian, no way, he tutted, without even knowing what he was referring to. The girl? The debts? Fabian? All of it.

And later he had to admit to himself that he had once again chosen the path of least resistance, which Fabian had willingly revealed to him, because Fabian was a businessman, and businessmen are only interested in people they can do business with. When the usually so calm and collected Fabian lost it and shouted, he may as well get out, then, Mick – who was in every respect up shit creek – was more than happy to acquiesce.

Great, then I have no more debts.

If you say so.

Fabian, you can't work with business partners. You need people you can boss around. But then you have to pay them.

That's what I'm doing. And it's working out better than with my so-called partners, one of whom urgently has to bugger off snorkelling and the other one never answers the phone and then can suddenly talk just fine even though officially he can't hear.

Mick said nothing. An aggressive silence. The club was his source of income. As part of a limited company, he would be part of the official business world for the first time, but his business debts would also have been official. If it were up to him, Andi would still pop round all chipper bringing him the cash from the bar, while Fabian would take care of the old debts and all the official crap. A business model he could hardly present to Fabian because of its blatant audacity.

Mick? Are you still there?

He remained silent. He was already exactly what he wanted to be: a silent partner.

What about this: I'll run this place alone until spring. Then we'll see. Deal?

What about my share?

What share? The five hundred thousand mark debt?

It didn't make sense. It wasn't a choice between plague or cholera, it was a decision between plague *and* cholera or nothing. He went for nothing. And hung up.

For reasons of repentance, and because he was avoiding the club, he announced that he wasn't celebrating his birthday. No party. A sacrifice that Delia would have tried to talk him out of in the past, but now she just shrugged.

She baked a cake, which she left in the kitchen for him in the morning and which made him so miserable that he went out and drove around for an hour until he found a café that didn't make him even more miserable. He had breakfast alone, and flicked through some magazines, feeling like Léon: The Professional.

Delia had invited a few friends to a restaurant for the evening, an act of mercy. Like a mother buying playmates for her unpopular son, he thought. She drank a lot and spent most of the evening chatting to Fabian, which was fitting: naturally, Fabian was interested in legal issues, and naturally, Delia was interested in an entrepreneur's perspective. And thus, on his thirtieth birthday, Mick had the frustrating sense that he was liked but not taken seriously.

His other guests behaved the same as always. So he launched himself on them, pulled out his phone, and rounded up a few more. Get Thingy and What's His Name to jump in a cab and get over here. Him, and her, and that lot, where are they? On their way over? Great! Then everyone get your phones out and call your dealers, whoever's quickest gets the tender. This wasn't some lightweight night out; this was going to be the real deal – it's Mick's thirtieth, after all! What gave him the crazy idea that he didn't want to celebrate? The paralysing question of his competencies lapsed into silence. He went back to doing what he was good at, while Fabian and Delia sank deeper into their rational discussion and ordered more wine. She wasn't trying to make him jealous; she was long past that, he noted with regret. The way she was acting was just who she was. She was reorienting herself and now merely tolerated him as a hangover from a past phase. And hopefully she hadn't suddenly noticed how good-looking Fabian was. In the shadow of this dark thought cloud, taking cocaine wasn't a great idea. But the occasion, his guests, the product that had just arrived, and the relaxed hospitality of the Italian restaurant owners, who acted as if the stampede to the disabled restroom was part of a normal evening meal, all meant he could hardly say no. So, let's go – big time!

As was the way with coke, he briefly had the feeling that his load was lightened. Even his trouble balancing seemed to disappear. He climbed up on a chair and made a speech. Delia looked up at him and laughed. This was the Mick she knew, and for years this was the Mick she wanted. And now she was genuinely happy for him, she was always good at that. She was the best thing that had ever happened to him.

Then she poured herself some more wine and turned back to Fabian. So cosy and engrossed – Mick felt like he was about to explode. He was rescued by a bawled serenade, as others poured in, bringing the cold from outside and gifts of random crap from the petrol station, showering him with their affection. Eventually, the restaurant was empty except for the last two tables, his table and one filled with distant acquaintances who became firm friends in no time. In the past, it would have been one of those evenings that started in a restaurant and ended in a club, but this time the night ended for Mick where it had begun. The Italians turned up the volume, though, and opened friendly fire with grappa, their most lethal weapon. And then Fabian covered the bill. A parting gift from the club to its co-founder.

Mick was too out of it to reflect on the meaning of this gesture. And too broke to turn it down. Mick wanted to believe that things could go on as before.

Outside in the shower of sleet, amid everyone staggering off and fumbling for car keys, making a bit of a racket, and kissing goodbye, Fabian handed him a thick envelope. Mick tucked it into his jacket and gave Fabian a hug. He had never hugged him before; the moment was charged with so much meaning that it almost made him cry. Fabian's cold ear against his, he knew that this was the end of the line for the three boys from the Benetton poster.

Chin up, fatso, Fabian said, then he shoved his hands in his pockets and hurriedly walked away through the cold night without a single glance back.

What made him think it might be a wad of cash? Because he was an optimist. Written on the envelope was Michael Buttmann, the fake name he'd given her. And the address of the club, and a return address for Lynn. Lynn Bishop. London Lynn. He had never seen her or spoken to her again, but he had stayed in touch with her anyway, in his own way. Lynn, too, was one of those relationships that Mick hadn't shared with anyone else. Here, that's what I do in the day, Lynn had said, in his memory always laughing, as she handed him a stack of music magazines as a farewell gift. And he had indeed had a look at what she got up to. She wrote the best music reviews he had ever read.

Mick could tell, not just as a reader, but as a writer. His most demanding and worst-paying part-time job was precisely that: writing record reviews for music magazines. He was opinionated and eloquent, but he was slow at writing, which decimated his meagre fee, not that he cared when he was living off the cash flow from the bar. Besides, he was used to the bonus of being sent records and CDs and didn't want that to stop. So when he read Lynn's lines, he translated them and used them for other, newer records. It wasn't with malicious intent or anything, it was more on impulse. This material was too good not to be used again. From then on, he subscribed to the English magazines and modified Lynn's reviews for similar-sounding new releases; he didn't make much effort to change them. Then just the finishing touches, names, dates, references to previous records, all done, great, off it goes. The editors loved his new style. Outrageously funny titles, witty homages to the good records, even wittier scorn for the bad ones, sharp as speed crystals, just awesome. Yes, it was Lynn's record reviews that secured Mick's reputation as a music journalist.

Worrying about getting caught was something so intrinsic to Mick's life that this one more thing hardly made any difference. Music reviews were taken very seriously, but it hardly seemed likely that anyone would compare the reviews of different magazines. In any case, someone would have to read something in a German music magazine and realise they had read something very similar a few months earlier in English in a different context. Brits didn't read German magazines anyway. Germans read the British ones, sure, but they probably leafed through then left them in the bathroom as evidence of a trendsetting household. It was the internet that made him feel uneasy. At some point, everything was going to end up on a website. Besides, he had a very short attention span. Translation or not, he no longer had the time or patience for writing; it felt more and more like homework towards the end. After nearly six years of his side gig covering the stars of the underground, he brought it to a close around a year ago. Too late, it would seem.

After all, what else would Lynn want from him now? Suddenly it seemed perfectly logical to him that he had been caught. Some kind of super checker must have read everything, maybe the press person at one of the record companies noticed when they were collating reviews. The envelope was stuffed full. If Lynn was suing him for plagiarism, this was likely to be a summons plus the evidence. Intellectual property was Delia's speciality, but even Mick realised he couldn't even entertain the thought of asking her about it. That this was a legal summons from London seemed so plausible – it absolutely fitted with the big picture – that Mick placed the envelope unopened in his box marked *Pending* where it would slowly but surely grow to menacing proportions.

Grief or rage? Mick spent the last few weeks in the house alternating between these two states; no other state was possible. Grief, because he had lost something. Anger, because there was nothing he could do about it. Who would ask a man in his twenties to live like a suburban dad, and then, when he was finally cautiously starting to accept that way of life, go and throw him out on the street?

Delia had accepted a job at a law firm in Hamburg. She would be gone before the first spring of the new millennium had even sprung. She had no need of Berlin anymore, there was nothing she couldn't do just as well in Hamburg, if not better, and in her case, also better paid. She would rent the house out to some friends of friends whose second child was on the way. This was a rampant pace of life planning that Mick couldn't keep up with. He was still enquiring about the possibility of reversing his vasectomy, which would cost him several thousand marks, with uncertain prospects. It was possible, he was told. But now it was too late. Delia no longer needed proof of his love; Delia no longer needed him. And she was in a rush.

I'm sick, Delia.

I know, and I'm sorry about that, but I've still got to get on with my life.

And suppose we try again?

Try what? We've tried everything.

I'll come with you to Hamburg.

What would you do in Hamburg?

For years, everyone had turned a blind eye to this vagueness in his life. Ah, Mick's like that, he's into this and that, cool guy.

Now he was a flawed man. A man without a profession. A man with useless sperm. A man without a future. A man on the run with a bullet he has to carve out of his own flesh. With no anaesthetic to numb the pain, just alcohol, and all alone.

Avoiding Delia, Mick hacked away at himself, trying to cut her out of his system. Deep down, he was searching for that bygone state where he merely liked her, back when she was still madly in love with him. He tried to recall those times – when he just thought she was okay, and used to make her wait until he was in the mood. It didn't work; it only hurt more because it reminded him of what he had thrown away. It might have helped if she had been annoying, but for that he would have had to get close to her. From this new distance, Delia attained perfection. She lived alongside him, as luminous, cold, and out of reach as a star. Juddering like a fool in love, he breathed in her smells, her voice, every trace of her presence. He used her toothbrush, lay down in her bed during the day, read her emails. The shortcut to madness.

Delia's professional fairness became an additional torture. She still went shopping for two, occasionally holding expensive kitchen utensils under his nose asking him if he wanted them and insisting that he should stay in touch with Bernhard, Ingrid, and Cosima. They had known each other so long, and her family liked him, that wasn't going to change. They were parting on good terms. Really? Yes, of course.

Besides, everyone could see how things were developing.

How are things developing, Delia?

I don't know yet, that's why it's a development.

Hmm, great, now I know where I stand.

What do you want me to say?

Yes, what? That everything could be how it was before. The desire of a child of divorced parents, a desire he had never articulated. She was so considerate; she resisted showing any sign of looking forward to Hamburg. The dog, did he want him? No, George belonged to her.

Do you want to come and visit him?

I'm not going to be a part-time dad to a dog.

With his last ounce of strength he wrestled down his grief and gave himself over to anger. It wasn't a hurricane, more a defiant energy that finally made him pull himself together and pack his things. He would move into Chris's old place for the time being. Delia registered this decision with a friendly nod. There was nothing they were going to argue about then – that was awful too. He was about to disappear from her life without a trace. When he came across his shoeboxes full of photos, he thought of mentioning Colombia to remind her. The two of them, young and in mortal danger, her swallowing his shit, literally, in that aeroplane lavatory, that story was so hideous, so disgusting, so criminal they couldn't tell anyone, and maybe that was why it was so romantic that it literally screamed at them to stay together, right? She had swallowed his shit metaphorically, too, you had to give her that, for years – his fuck-ups, his nonsense, his womanising, everything. He flicked through the photos. He saw the beautiful couple she must have seen in them, at birthdays, on camels, on beach loungers, on ecstasy, in front of the Sagrada Familia, in front of the Louvre, in front of sunsets, in front of DJ booths. All that time ago.

His life's possessions fitted into a small van. After he had packed it all away, the house looked the same as before, fully furnished, fully equipped. If he left any void behind it was ludicrously small, like he'd just been visiting. The question of whether he left a void behind at all depressed him even more than the question of why he had filled his life with nothing but records, sneakers, and a few bits of junk fit for the bin.

Christian Cordes, thirty-five, lay on his stomach and surrendered. The man standing over him, muscular, perhaps in his mid-fifties, knew what he was doing. Ever since he'd met him, Chris didn't want anyone else. His hands understood Chris's body better than he did himself. So did his feet and elbows. It was the dance of two bodies: Chris, the passive partner, melting into the tatami mat. Male feet were a body part that back in Europe he would have said should always be covered; they were so ugly, in most cases. Yet here, he enjoyed the intense feeling of their touch, like now when they exerted a pleasant pressure on the soles of his own feet. Next, his feet would be worked on with the masseur's hands. His pain was already much less. The masseur barely spoke any English, but on the anatomical maps in his practice, Chris had seen that each internal organ corresponded to a reflex point on the foot. He assumed that it was his liver that had hurt so badly the first few days that he howled like a dog that had been kicked. Now, after more than two weeks of coconut water, the pain had subsided. In his head, too.

His email correspondence with Fabian as soon as he had arrived here had been as unpleasant as the exchange with his ex. In the past, he would have been out of reach. Out of office, see ya. Now people kept on pestering you with emails. What was next? Permanent access to everyone everywhere? According to Fabian, the World Wide Web was going to make them millionaires in some mysterious way that wasn't yet clear. Wow, great. But right now they were in the red, and Fabian was just the bearer of bad news, which in the meantime had evolved into a serious threat. The idea of being arrested at Berlin airport as a tax dodger, for the sake of a few paltry bucks, spoiled Chris's first few days, especially after a few spliffs. So he decided to put the fire out right there and then from Bangkok, by asking his parents to give him an advance on his inheritance, which went surprisingly smoothly. We'll save a lot on inheritance tax, and it'll mean I can pay my tax bill without interest. I'll give you the details later, this is a long-distance call, he shouted down the line, and his mother grasped the seriousness of the situation faster than ever before. When the money finally arrived, he transferred it almost entirely to Fabian. Having to pay a foreign transaction fee was really the last straw. Here you go, he thought, choke on it. That enormous sum, that he had had to pass on without seeing even a penny of it, begged the question of why he was scrimping to live in a backpacker hostel. He hopped on a motorbike taxi and headed to the Mandarin Oriental for his last night in Bangkok. The cool bastard of a driver weaved his way through the traffic at breakneck speed, Chris inhaled the smog like it was mountain air, and thought to himself: screw it, it's only money. The tax office let up, for the time being, and he was part of a *GmbH*, a limited company; the contract was ready to be signed, and if they were to chance upon the promised vein of gold, Fabian would share it with him. Until they reached the gold, they'd make do with the silver from the bar takings like always. By all accounts, Mick was out. Well, hey, his decision. Would have come down to his liquidity problem, most likely. Poor old Mick. He should have a good lie down in the sun and get a massage every day, Chris thought as the backs of his thighs were pummelled. The strong thumbs working their way up his energy lines were the opposite of a caress, but this man wasn't just some wellness freak, he was a medical practitioner.

Motionless, Chris drifted toward his optimum physical state. Mick will love it, he thought, filled with tenderness for his friend. No problem, I've got plenty of time, Mick had said, when Chris thanked him for helping him out with sanding the floors and plastering the walls in his old apartment. As if that devil of a job was only a question of time. As if there was a compelling reason for Mick to play handyman for Chris, and do his old apartment up for him, so that he, Chris, could sublet it in the future. First, his ex had to move out, of course, but that was another story. Chris had heard from Stephanie that Mick had shown up with an assistant, whom she described as funny if a bit nuts, from which Chris concluded it was Darko. When she said that Mick had roped up like a mountain climber to do the walls and ceiling, it took Chris a few minutes to work out what she meant. Stephanie was already on the next topic, money, when Chris realised that Mick was still having problems with his sense of balance and must have secured himself somehow to stop himself falling off the ladder. Man, Mick is a dude, Chris thought. The masseur pressed a point on his right buttock, which brought tears to his eyes every time. Ooh, yes! He would look at the chart later to see what the dots in the buttocks area meant. Why's Mick even doing it? Chris asked himself as the pain blissfully subsided. It's fine, Mick would say, no problem.

Chris didn't exactly feel guilty about his accident, even though he was the one who had turned the amp right up, but he thought about it more often than he would have liked. They had been joking around and laughing, and a few seconds later Mick was lying on the concrete floor looking like he was dead. He can't be, he thought, as Fabian felt for Mick's pulse, and he, Chris, almost shat himself. And now that Mick had been chucked out of his comfort zone with Delia, who had justified her decision with Mick's voluntary inability to procreate, he was for the first time in nearly three years forced to recall that he was the one who had encouraged Mick to get the snip. Though, strictly speaking, that's bullshit, Chris thought. With the heels of the masseur's hands on his shoulder blades, he exhaled until his lungs felt completely deflated. Ah, that was good. He, Chris, hadn't wanted children, then he had Fee, and he loved Fee, but he decided that one was enough. That was 96, 97 – a god-awful time, money was tight, everything was a mess, and to top it all he'd lost his driver's licence. Mick, Mr Happy-Go-Lucky, who drove him around, must have heard his rants as often as his favourite songs. And when the time came for the op, he came along too. Not as a friend, but as another patient. That annoyed Chris at first, but then he forgot about it. Mick didn't always know what he wanted, but he was straight up when he didn't want something. No one could have guessed that years later she would go batshit and chuck him out. Delia? Seriously? Wasn't she the one who'd been all over Mick for years, worshipping him like some crazy chick from a Polanski film or something? Hundred per cent. And then, boom, game over. Poor Mick. Even Stephanie had never pulled off anything like that, a mood swing on that scale, and that was really saying something. The masseur gripped his arms above the elbow, and Chris, a massage pro by now, knew that he was supposed to grab hold of the masseur's forearms. I have the spine of a yogi, he thought with a thrill as his upper body was pulled upward and he hovered in the air like a cobra. Should he have talked Mick out of it, he wondered as he was gently lowered back down. Chris was older, and his situation was different, yeah. Still, Mick had been old enough to think something like that through on his own.

A peaceful warmth flowed through Chris's body, accompanied by gratitude. Gratitude for this gifted professional who had concluded his divine massage by placing his hands on the crown of Chris's head. And for Mick, the best friend he could imagine.

Imagine that you have to go back to square one. Imagine that everything that your life consisted of no longer exists. Imagine becoming homeless, unemployed, and single, all at the same time. Imagine that you're only thirty and you've already lived through the best time of your life, and you've only just realised it. Imagine that no one else gives a shit. What would you do?

Mick flew out to join Chris in paradise.

On the way there, he spent two days alone in a hotel room in Bangkok, telling himself he was jetlagged, though of course it was fear. Fear seeped out of the air conditioning and licked him like a big cold tongue. Fear of being alone, fear of what was to come, fear of everything. Hunger finally drove him out into the big city that smiled kindly back at him. He followed the river, bought himself some knick-knacks and some street food, and strolled into the wind – it was as warm as body temperature and he started to feel pleasantly anonymous. Then he took his flight to Surat Thani, followed by a boat that looked like this would be its final trip, and out on the water on this scrap heap he suddenly felt so much better. Everything was so beautiful, so simple, so affordable, and so warm. He stood up on deck, looking back at the spray, and the troublesome voices became quieter, like someone angry and ranting that he'd left behind on the shore.

Chris had found the island of his dreams. He had joined a Thai reggae band where he played bass. He was the DJ at a bar that was basically a bamboo hut, he had a massage twice a day, he looked like Robinson Crusoe on a good day. It took Mick a few days to get into his friend's rhythm. He dozed off on the beach, admiring the rock formations and bikini bodies. The island provided little reason to dwell on downsides such as poverty, architectural eyesores, or prostitution – you could indulge in the hippie dream that everyone was just here to have fun. The murky shaving mirror in the darkest corner of his bungalow showed him what good shape he was in; back in Berlin it would have taken him weeks of fasting and training to look like that. Everything was so perfect that some tropical disease seemed inevitable, but it didn't materialise.

It was his ears that plagued him from time to time. You couldn't blame the people here for not noticing the noise. Or for their enjoyment of music, which they turned up as loud as it would go, going around with it in the background like it wasn't even there. Eurotrash, Scorpions, reggae, Thai pop, the main thing: full blast. Mick, who had once been so proud of his good hearing, could no longer judge how loud or quiet the sound was, or how well modulated or how badly, he perceived it just as a wave of noise. From time to time he would hear things twice, a scary phenomenon that felt like a bad trip. Imagine hearing everything with an echo, he said to Chris, who reassured him that it would pass, it was probably a symptom of stress. Chris rocked in a hammock, mixing Thai grass and tobacco in his belly button. He'd had something similar. All that trouble with Stephanie had triggered tinnitus in him.

Chris's ex had been Mick's flatmate for two months. After he had moved out of Delia's, he had gone to live with her and the little girl, which Chris arranged, as he was still the named tenant there. Stephanie didn't seem to have a problem with Mick staying. She let him have the largest room and used him as a babysitter for her daughter, Fee, who not only looked like a tiny version of Chris, but she also had a surprisingly good sense of humour for a four-year-old. Mick went along with it all; it was only temporary, after all. The apartment was filthy, things were constantly getting lost or broken, the phone line was cut off, the electricity too at one point, and although Stephanie didn't look particularly happy about it, she also acted like it was part of the script she had to teeter through in her heels, before she reached the grand showdown. It could be worse, Mick thought, it's good that I can stay for a while. When Stephanie announced she was going away with Fee for two weeks, he decided to return the favour and spruce the place up a bit, after all it was badly in need of a bit of TLC. It would be good for everyone, including him, as it would get him out of his mental loop for a bit. When Stephanie got back, it only took her a few days to suck the immaculate white flat, and also Mick, back into her vortex of chaos. He felt like a middle-class kid who had joined a gang of punks. And in this village of three and a half million people, news of his situation spread faster than expected.

Before Delia left town, they had one last go at a night out together. Mick had hoped for an ultimatum, even though the prospect was worrying, because no matter what she asked of him, he would have gone along with anything. But then this one last go fell through on the phone before they had even met up.

So, you're a dad all of a sudden? Congratulations, Mick!

What? Fee is Chris's daughter. I'm staying at Chris's, in case you'd forgotten.

Fee is the daughter of what's-her-name? Steffi?

Stephanie.

Right, Stephanie. Well, congratulations on finding a new host animal so quickly.

Delia, that's enough.

Yeah, I think so too. Bye.

Could it really be that there was nothing left? *Dust in the wind?* Like magic. A miserable kind of magic.

Delia saw him as a parasite. And Stephanie wasn't a host animal; she could have done with one herself. When Fabian talked to him about an idea that he presented as a generous offer, Mick realised that he preferred not to think about what his true intention was. He couldn't afford to. Fabian was offering him a contract where he would cede his share in the club's brand new company. Mick skimmed over the paragraphs, which he could have done with Delia's help to make sense of, trying not to think that it might even have been her who had drawn the contract up in the first place. If he signed it, he would also transfer to Fabian the rights to the name of their legendary club night *I Sing the Body Electric*. It wasn't his idea anyway; it was the title of a book by Ray Bradbury, but fine, go ahead, Fabian, take it all. He was also forbidden from using the name of the club to his advantage, in the press, for example, or in a book title, in promotional materials, or any publication of any kind. He had no intention of publishing anything. This was what was called a buyout. Mick knew that Fabian would never buy anything from him that wasn't worth something. He thought of the graphic artist who had designed the Nike logo for which she got, like, two hundred dollars or something. He thought about the money that he didn't have. This was money he would get for *not* doing anything.

Mick signed and booked a ticket to Bangkok.

So, have you signed Fabian's buyout contract, then? he asked Chris, who dropped out of the hammock, stood up and stretched.

Of course not. Did you?

Without a word, Mick stood up and made his way over a large boulder to take a piss out of sight. He concentrated on the warm rock, its hollows and protrusions. No more questions, no more thinking about Delia. She would be thirty-four in a few days. It was good to be here. He hadn't flown halfway around the world to feel the same as he did in Berlin.

After a week, when time started to slow down so pleasantly that it felt like a month, Chris went to another island for a party. The idea of a rave, the booming speakers, howling at the moon in a sea of sweaty bodies, once he would have been psyched at the prospect, but now it felt like some kind of compulsory event like a funeral that he would go to great lengths to avoid. He gave Chris a lift on the scooter to the landing stage, which was rather generously signposted as MARINA. They sat in the shade for a moment, and Mick wondered what would become of him if Chris didn't come back. When he got back on the scooter, he felt as if the next few days might change him.

He did a circuit of the island. And another, and another, because it wasn't very big. For the first few days, he was compulsively overtaking everyone, until he realised how pointless it was to be tearing along at speed. After all, where did he have to get to in a hurry? Once he had adapted to the island's driving culture, he started to see it better. Rubber tree plantations, mangroves, birds he didn't recognise, the sea to his left, the sea to his right, rocks you could see pictures and faces in, like in the clouds. Once there was a water buffalo in the middle of the road. It was so colossally beautiful that

Mick abruptly understood the human desire to paint cattle. He stopped, the engine running, not thinking whether he should turn back or keep going and go round him. The buffalo, almost completely blocking the road, turned its head and seemed to look at its own flank. Mick wondered what he would like to do with him if he had the choice. Hug him? Ride him? Slay him? Definitely not provoke him. He stayed there unsure what to do, until Mr Sunny, a Thai version of Harvey Keitel and the owner of the bungalow he was renting, came up towards him on his motorbike, waving, and rode past the buffalo as if it were a truck or a tree, or just not even there. Mick passed the buffalo too now, and as he did the buffalo turned to look at him, a majestic movement that could mean anything, including that he was about to come chasing after him huffing and puffing, and Mick felt so alive that he whooped into the airstream.

One morning, one of Chris's bandmates was standing outside his bungalow. Like Mr Sunny, this fellow had abbreviated his presumably long Thai name; his international *nom de guerre* was Tom. Mick explained his ear problem in a long-winded way, and Tom nodded as if he was agreeing with him. The band was called Catch the Snake and they were currently without a bass player. With Mick filling in for Chris, the band now consisted of four brown men of the same skin tone. You look like Bob, said the three others, laughing and pointing at Tom's T-shirt, Mr Marley, even though they were the ones with the dreadlocks and Mick had his one-millimetre fuzz. Thanks, he said politely. Looking like Bob was a nice compliment, practically a coronation, coming from a reggae band, even if it wasn't true. Once again he fitted the bill, just as he had back in the day with his ska skinheads, who had also given him the idea of learning the bass instead of the guitar. It was a while since he had played, but it came back to him. And despite his hearing problems, he could still play by ear. From time to time he wondered who in this band was supposed to be the lead, who was the crazy one, the heart throb, the sensible one. He was there as the guest, a role he felt comfortable in. Good, good, said the others when he ventured to have a go at singing. When Tom told him that they would be playing at a festival soon, perhaps even in Bangkok, he wondered if he was now slipping into his next form of existence, from the bankrupt Berlin club scene big shot to king of Thai reggae, just because he was in the right place at the right time.

Smoke? Yes, thank you. Good? Very good! Ha ha. Good for you, my friend. They used very few words, and incredibly it didn't feel like anything was missing, just that everything was reduced to the essential. Human communication in its purest form, which worked as well as it did because it was based on a foundation of goodwill and respect. Mick found himself sitting in a circle with these men he didn't know, getting goosebumps from the idea of a world where everyone interacted with each other like this. Where did people even get the idea of fighting in the first place? Well, there were certain themes: religion, money, land. But hey, why go there? Inspired by his peace-loving mood, Mick decided to write two songs. One for his new brothers, one for a world without envy, greed, or rivalry. Admittedly not the most original song lyrics, but that wasn't the point. The song for his lovable new bandmates could also work as a love song to a woman. Which woman? It had been done plenty of times, this ambiguous addressee format, but still, nice idea. Unfortunately in combination with the word *love*, everything sounded like you'd heard it all before. *One, my, your, greatest, true, the power, the look, addicted to, is the message, the drug, in the air, the answer.* Okay, he thought, something will come. All in good time. And there was plenty of time. When he heard his bass and behind it the drums it was like being under water; this was what it must sound like in the womb, Mick thought. Whether they were playing or talking, the band did his ears good. Especially now that he'd started putting the foam earplug from the plane in his healthy ear. It had felt like he was hearing too much with it, and now he could live completely cocooned in this embryonic soundscape.

Chris came back from the rave unattached, and Mick was glad. Because who was to blame for mankind's expulsion from paradise? Exactly. Not that he begrudged his friend's desire and wanting to be desired under these almost perfect conditions. But since he wasn't after any himself, he thought it was better that they were both single. They spent their evenings surrounded by sun-kissed women from all over Europe and Australia, drank Singha beer, and then went back to their cabins alone, where they fell asleep to the calls of the geckos. This is the way to live, thought Mick. Finally a break from all the drama.

There was a new luxury resort on the other side of the island, Chris said, the Sanctuary. They had a helipad, and you could get cash out on your credit card and check your emails. But surely their massages weren't better than here, or the cocktails and the food, and a beach was a beach. Why would you spend several hundred marks a night for that? To land your helicopter, said Chris.

They set off. *Easy Rider* on cheap scooters. They could get another bass tomorrow, Chris yelled into the wind. Or Mick could take over on guitar, because Tom had to go to the mainland, family business. For Mick, driving past the rubber forests in the dark was one of the island's special effects. The temperature suddenly dropped, the air was humid and musty, and you were surrounded by this strange rubber smell that made your pulse rise, as if you were in danger. Once you passed the plantations and were back in the warmth, you had this incredible high, like you'd sneaked past this giant, stinking monster without waking him up. He looked at Chris's back in front of him and had the rare feeling of conscious happiness. Man, am I happy, he thought.

At the resort, they were greeted by two young women with orchids in their hair. Behind them, the king of Thailand smiled down at them. They were driven around the resort in a golf caddy, by a man in the sandy-yellow uniform of a dictator. It looked like a fairy-tale village with chalets scattered across hills and tucked in between the remnants of the cut-back jungle. Welcome to Smurfville, Chris said. They drove to the main building where the internet was. And where they had Heineken, which cost as much as a night's accommodation on the other side of the island. Chris plunged into his emails like a man dying of thirst, while Mick logged on like it was a task he had to do rather than wanted to do. What would anyone have to tell him? The fact that no one missed him was only pleasant as long as he didn't question it. Advertising, newsletters, nothing, nothing, nothing. Nothing from Delia. He could write to her. But the idea of emailing her felt like a one-off opportunity, which amounted to the kind of pressure he couldn't face right now.

He looked over at Chris, who had found time during his week of raving for a trip to the hairdresser. His beard was gone, his now exposed, angular jawline and his equally angular haircut, longer on top, shaved undercut, made him look less feral, it looked good on him, although it wasn't entirely clear what he was trying to achieve with this dynamic look right here and now. Chris's thighs bobbed up and down, and he ran his fingers through his hair, and fidgeted in his chair, clearing his throat at such regular intervals that it sounded like a tick. Since he'd got back, his nonchalance had given way to a certain tension that was unmissable, and Mick would later wonder how he had failed to notice before.

Load up already, you piece of shite, Chris said through his teeth and clicked the mouse like a maniac, and even then Mick thought nothing of it. He logged out – five bucks for the information that nobody gave a fuck about him – sat back, and took a swig of his beer. Outside, a gangly youth swept the terrace with a witch's broom. An old White couple walked past him arm in arm. The woman supported the man, who took tiny steps, and then they both laughed. Would anyone ever look after him like that, Mick wondered, turned in his chair and looked straight into Chris's furious glare.

Then Chris put down his Heineken, stood up, and punched Mick square in the eye.

A young employee who was walking through the room with a teak tray laden with bright white towels stopped in shock, and the boy on the terrace turned around. Mick must have made a noise. Chris raised his hands and smiled at the young lad with the towels. Chris could beam like the sun.

Only fun, Chris said in English, his smile even bigger. A joke between me and my friend, you know?

The young employee nodded, not entirely convinced. How is my friend? he asked.

Good question. Behind Mick's squinting eyes was a firework display of little white stars, and the disquieting thought of men in pretend uniforms being summoned, who in turn would summon men in real uniforms. Public disturbance in paradise. Mick felt a surge of nausea, and the urge to laugh hysterically. He suppressed both, and jerked upright in the chair.

I'm okay. I'm fine. Just fun. Ha ha.

Hesitantly, the young lad found his smile again, that smile that made the whole world love his country, even though no one knew what it really meant, and went outside to join his colleague.

Read this, my friend. Chris pulled Mick's chair over to face the hotel computer with his emails open, picked up his beer, and walked out, his posture strangely stiff.

Mick couldn't take his hand away from his left eye, while with his right he scrolled down through an email thread with the subject line *Hi hi!* which he hoped, indeed fully assumed, had nothing to do with him. To the side, a tray of rolled-up towels was held out to him, just within his limited field of vision. He looked up at the lad's smooth baby face, a masterpiece of neutrality. He took a towel, unsure what he was supposed to use it for.

Thank you.

Mick pressed the damp, fragrant cloth to his eye, then started to read. He hadn't noticed the plinky plonky music when they walked into the hotel. But now it pressed itself into his mind, a kind of sonic torture, as if his nerves were the strings being plucked in that infuriating way that was presumably supposed to sound meditative. His instinct was to stop reading mid-sentence, go outside, and tell Chris to forget it. Put the whole thing behind them. Stephanie was probably drunk when she sent it, upset, and lonely. She'd probably just lost it by one-thirty in the morning. She was in a bad way, and if Mick understood correctly, it sounded like Chris had called her that evening and had a go at her, and Stephanie had responded like a desperate toddler and lashed out screaming. Mick wondered: if someone sent him a tirade like this, would he show it to someone else? Um, no.

Then he read on, where Stephanie called the father of her child a waster and an incompetent no-hoper in bed, a scathing assessment that she expanded on for an entire paragraph, before she got to her second point, which she introduced – in English for no apparent reason – in all caps: SIZE CARES!!!!

Mick, who was momentarily lost at this point, scrolled on, one-eyed and on edge at the irritating wellness soundtrack, and read an onslaught of insults directed at Chris's penis. More specifically, it was a detailed list of the most spiteful petty criticisms. Ah, you mean *size matters*, you wally, Mick thought. He wondered why Chris had taken this seriously for even a second, and then he found out a few lines down, when Stephanie revealed who had made Chris's abysmal performance and penis qualities so obvious to her: Mick.

Never in his life had he wanted praise as little as this. His ears were burning. Shame was so unpleasant because it was so hard to repress, because unlike guilt, you couldn't look at it from a different angle and put it into perspective. Shame simply overcame you, and when it finally subsided, it was still tucked away forever along with memories that probably even advanced dementia wouldn't erase.

He took the damp towel off his emerging shiner. Now what? He closed Chris's emails and staggered outside.

The hotel was duty bound to offer more than a run-of-the-mill beach, which it achieved with canopy-covered lounge beds and tiki torches, despite it being both off-season and monsoon season. Ignoring the loungers, Chris was sitting on the sand. The sound of the surf soothed Mick's ears, and perhaps Chris had also calmed down by now, sitting there throwing sand like a child. He also reminded Mick of a child in that red hoodie: the scariest kid in movie history, that creepy kid in the little red coat chasing Donald Sutherland around Venice. And Mick, always ready to be distracted, now gave himself over to the idea that this hooded figure might turn around any minute and instead of a nice Chris face, it would have the face of a murderous horror-movie monster. He walked up to the creature and stopped behind it.

Chris. You're not taking this seriously, are you? Please don't.

Chris – it was Chris – looked up at him like he was some irritating guy selling jewellery, then turned back toward the dark waves.

Listen, mate, I didn't tell you about Stephanie because I didn't take it seriously. Cos it wasn't serious . . . it was nothing.

Mm-hm.

And what she wrote there, of course, that's a load of bullshit.

Mick, stay out of this. The last thing I need right now is a what-Stephanie-means analysis.

Okay.

I can't believe the idiots I surround myself with. That maniac woman and now you.

Let's just forget it, okay?

Stop saying okay, there's nothing okay here.

Okay.

I'll punch you if you don't shut up.

You already did. Mick laughed. Unintentionally.

Mick, do me a favour and just fuck off.

Chris . . .

No, stop it, and next time don't think about *if* you're going to fuck, cos obviously that would never happen, but maybe give some thought to *who* you're going to fuck.

Listen, you guys haven't been together for years . . .

No, you listen. There are enough women in the world to just stay away from the few who are family or close friends.

Mick dropped to the sand, capitulating.

Don't act like it's just me, like *she* had no willpower.

Shit, that was a mistake, Mick thought, as Chris suddenly jumped up, holding his forearms over his head in an expression of misery.

Yeah, right, said Chris, his voice scathing. No one can resist you. It must be unbearable being permanently lusted after!

Mick stared at the beach in the flickering torchlight. He couldn't think of anything else to say.

You know, I never thought I'd say this, but not even the most cynical woman could think up someone as cock-fucking-fixated as you.

Okay, okay. I wasn't thinking. I thought you didn't care about Stephanie. At least as a woman, I mean . . .

Never mind. That's enough. I'm not going to stand here and fight about Stephanie. I'm going to look after Fee and that's it. And you two can do whatever the fuck you want.

There isn't an 'us two'.

I don't care.

Chris shook the sand out of his clothes, stood at the water's edge, and looked out to sea. It was strange how obviously pissed off someone could look when you could only see them from behind.

This dick contest – forced on him by someone else, that he hadn't gone looking for – this was a fleeting rift, right? Not the end? Mick combed his fingers through the damp sand and thought about what he wanted to say to Chris. He could only think of things that would make it worse. He kept his mouth shut.

Let's get out of here, Chris said, and Mick rose to put his arm around his shoulder, but Chris bent down for his flip-flops and strode off.

The similarity of the situations was astonishing. The only difference was the setting and the accuser. Mick wasn't going to take this excoriating scrutiny again, never mind if it was Delia or Chris flaunting their moral authority. And while we're on the subject of guilt, wasn't it Chris who was to blame for his hearing problems? No, that was an accident. Couldn't the Stephanie slip-up also be classified in the category of accidents?

Chris didn't want to classify or discuss anything anymore. He arranged his days to be emphatically alone. He wasn't unkind to Mick, he just treated him like any other tourist. The band rehearsed without him. Chris didn't need to kick him out, he just didn't get a second bass. It was hard to believe that their time together in Thailand had come to an end, not to mention their friendship. Mick imagined them getting stoned and finding something to laugh about, one of those extended laughing fits, and all the stress would be gone. But Chris didn't say a word to him except: nice weather today. Yeah, thanks, super informative.

Sober and alone. Mick's life on the island had become the exact antithesis of the past few years. It was as if he received a huge delivery of time every morning. Here's your time, please use it wisely. If previously he sat around with Chris and the band, now he sat by himself on the beach or lay in the hammock in front of his cabin, flicking through Mr Sunny's holiday library, a large basket of books in all the European languages. *War and Peace*, *The Red and the Black*, *Ulysses*, and *The Man Without Qualities* had been lugged around the world before being abandoned here. He leafed through the classics a bit, then picked up *The Beach*. With sobriety came taciturnity.

Some days he just nodded to a few people. Occasionally he exchanged a few words with the woman in the next bungalow, that was about it. After all, Agata – a tall, athletic Pole from the Giant Mountains; you could always hear her coming with her jangling carabiners – went climbing with Chris every morning, which made her a no-go zone for Mick. The seriousness with which they pursued their climbing reinforced Mick's sense of uselessness. Apathy. Idleness. Agony. These aimless days began to feel oppressive. This time off, this break, begged the question of what he was actually taking a break from. Hanging around had always been one of his top skills, but he seemed to have forgotten how to do it properly.

Mr Sunny always had something in his hand that emphasised his manliness, like an outboard motor, or a harpoon, or a machete, apparently he was once the Thai champion in Thai boxing. He ate chicken soup with rice for breakfast every morning, read the previous day's *Bangkok Post*, and then went about his day, greeting Mick as he passed his hammock.

It was Mr Sunny who indirectly brought about the coming together of Mick's past and future.

Could he help him, Mick asked him, facing yet another day of sunny emptiness. No problem, said Mr Sunny, and left it to Mick to interpret if that meant, No problem, I don't need any help, No problem, because I generally don't have any problems, or No problem, sure, you can help. His pick-up was loaded with long wooden slats, and just getting in and driving away gave Mick the pleasant feeling of having something to do. The construction site was behind a palm grove on a plateau with a picture postcard view of the sea. Two other men were already there, operating a circular saw.

Sawing, hammering, sanding. At thirty-four degrees, with the radio blaring out. In between: laughter, drinking water, being friendly in a nonverbal way. When two women drove up on scooters in the midday sun and brought food, he felt as good as those days in the reggae band. The construction that emerged looked like a covered stage. Shala, Mr Sunny called it, holding a pencil-drawn plan. An open-air temple, perhaps, Mick thought. He enjoyed the work even more once the men saw that he wasn't just a bored tourist, but that he actually knew how to work with wood. I'm a carpenter whether I finished my apprenticeship or not, he thought. In the evening he headed back to his bungalow, and although he didn't sleep through the night, he slept better than he had in months.

The world didn't revolve around him. It was more a sense of relief than a realisation; a sense that set in once he'd been working for a few days and that only vanished again when Chris reappeared outside his bungalow with his backpack. Chris had brought him here and now he was leaving him behind. Perhaps he would have gone on without me anyway, Mick thought, as they shared a tentative hug, because Chris was going with Agata to another island to find more limestone to climb.

See you in Berlin, he said in farewell, and when Chris didn't answer, he thought, maybe, maybe not.

Sunrise, Mr Sunny had said when they finished, pointing to the horizon. Mick thought he would give the pavilion some kind of inauguration, because somehow it belonged to him too. Even though he had nothing to do again, his days felt better than the days before the job when he'd had nothing to do. He went to the beach and after dinner he didn't go back to his bungalow, but walked up the hill to the temple, as he thought of it, and lay down. He lay back amid a symphony of jungle noises and the sound of the sea and slept peacefully until sunrise. The next evening he went up there again, and then again. Every day he expected to be sent away by someone who wanted to use the space, but no one came. On the island, time seemed to gather up and stretch out differently to time at home, so that later he no longer knew whether he spent a few days like that or two weeks.

When he woke up one morning and found a man sitting next to him, Mick was amazed at how little it surprised him.

Hi, I'm Jay, the man said, as if they had arranged to meet. A White man, but darker than Mick, who looked old and young at the same time, with intriguing wrinkles and a dancer's build. Without using his hands, he stood up from his cross-legged position and walked across the space, his feet brushing the wooden planks. He tilted his head back, then nodded. He was dressed like Mick, bare torso with baggy Thai fishing pants. It's turned out nice, he said at one point, and Mick nodded. Then he crouched down next to him again and for a while they just sat there and said nothing.

Jay didn't say: Let's greet the sun with Surya Namaskar, he said: All that's missing are some mosquito nets.

It wasn't a magical moment of epiphany; it was friendliness between peaceful strangers.

It wasn't a footstep onto a new path; it was just trying out something new, because Mick had nothing, genuinely nothing else planned.

Even the sunrise wasn't as impressive as it had been the last few days, it was a bit hazy.

But when Mick later decided that this morning was the starting point of his new life, he chose the more meaningful interpretation. Why not. After all, everything really was going to be different from now on. The next wave was there and he did what he had always done: he let himself be carried along. It was May 2000, and he was thirty years old.

INTERMEZZO

Idris

So, thought Idris, as he boarded the train to Paris in Stuttgart, that was Germany. He couldn't take his mind off the previous night. He felt old, so in that respect it made sense that a young man wanted to help him with his suitcase. Very attentive, he thought, but looks can deceive you: I'm fifty-five and in good shape. He declined the offer. Oumar waited on the platform, arm in arm with his wife, the key to his Mercedes in his hand.

Once upon a time you would have lowered the window, stuck your head out, and talked and held hands until the train pulled away. These days you grinned and made hand gestures. Call me. Yes, I'll call you. Idris sat down by the window and laughed, looking out. About time to go now, he thought. That's enough waving.

When the train finally started to pull away, Oumar ran a stretch of the platform at a surprising speed. Christine stayed where she was, her hands in her coat pockets, and winked at Idris as if she were the only person in the world who could see through him. *I don't need to justify myself to you, Christine.*

Love to Amadou, Oumar called out, his hands by his mouth, then he let himself fall back. They had known each other since school, he, Oumar, and Amadou: so long they felt like family. When Oumar and Christine were out of sight, he leaned back into his seat with relief. He had underestimated how tiring memories are. Too much of the past makes you old, Idris concluded, and closed his eyes.

It had been ages since his last trip back to Germany, and three days was too short for three cities. Oumar had a conference in Berlin, so he met him there. Wonderful that the Germans had taken the Wall down, Idris thought. How long ago was it now? About ten years? Wasn't that what they had always wanted, most people anyway? That was how it had seemed back then, at least. Just to cross over and bring their girlfriends clothes and LPs.

He hardly recognised the East. With the passage of time, as well as the political changes. He hadn't been back since the eighties, now it was 2000. They looked around Berlin, visited an old acquaintance, and stayed in Schöneberg, the district in the West that had been their favourite stomping ground back then. The next day they travelled on to Leipzig, ate lunch in the city centre, and again compared how it was now with how it was back then. Idris wondered if he would still know his way around in the city.

For my Leipzig I have only praise; it's a little Paris that educates its people. That line from Goethe's *Faust*, which the people of Leipzig had mounted as an illuminated sign on a building near their huge station to remind themselves how much their poet king had admired their city. The building was still there and so was the quotation. Idris had always been fond of the city, even if he hadn't anticipated spending much time there. He had his eye on France, the real Paris, and he dreamed of America. But who was interested in the dreams of an African schoolboy? A university place in the GDR, at no cost to his parents, plus a scholarship thrown in: the stuff of dreams. Back then, he didn't have any particular preconception of Germany. And then it turned out there were two Germanies and they had ended up in the poorer one. All the same, thought Idris, we were the lucky ones, the chosen ones.

Do you remember when we arrived here? Oumar asked him, as they stood in front of their old student halls. It had been rebuilt as a retirement home. Yes, he remembered. It was the first time he had been on a plane. He wasn't the son of a minister or a diplomat like some of the others. His father had two grocery stores, and he was lucky to have been the only son whom his father went out of his way to send to the Lycée Français and then abroad to study. When he thought of that flight, he pictured little boys giggling with excitement.

They landed in Berlin-Schönefeld and were loaded onto buses and taken on to Leipzig. They came from different countries, different ethnicities at any rate. Not that anyone in Europe cared precisely where they were from. That had never mattered and never would. Many of them had state scholarships, others had applied privately for a university place, but for the Germans, they were simply a bunch of Black kids. For the authorities, they were African students from the young nation states. Newly independent nations that had thrown off the colonies. Military dictatorships, maybe, but the main thing was they were no longer under British, Portuguese, Belgian, or French control, and therefore had the potential to be won over to the socialist side. In Leipzig, they were taken straight to the university, Karl Marx University, KMU for short. It had only had that name since the fifties, but it had existed as a university since 1409. Idris remembered the date because he had been so impressed. They were shown around the faculty, shown their future lecture halls, the cafeteria, the sports facilities. They shook the hands of lots of important old men and were flooded by so many impressions at once that in retrospect it was a wonder that none of them fainted. Besides this, of course, their future professors, tutors, and supervisors were invariably German. That is, White. They all knew a few White people back home, but here everyone looked like that. He remembered pale faces in the cool neon light. They wouldn't have been able to tell us apart either at first, Idris thought; we were mostly male and about the same age, skinny Black lads around twenty.

On their shoulders, they were told, rested not only the hopes of the GDR, a nation that in its infinite generosity and solidarity had offered them their university places, on their shoulders also rested the hopes of their home countries, exploited by colonialism, imperialism, etc, etc. But all that was set to change. In part, thanks to them. Because they would go back home, straight after graduating. Oh, is that right? They would have nodded. None of them had been aware when they arrived that they were invited as future creators of a new, post-colonial Africa. They were struck by the idealism of these GDR officials, even if the delivery was somewhat lacking in charisma. Everyone was constantly reading from a script. These people knew nothing about Africa, but their euphoria about the future had something infectious about it, Idris found, at least to start with.

Not only did their hosts have no idea about Africa, neither did they know what their African guests thought about it all. For all that they were invested with the hope of future Pan-African socialism, these students' focus was less long term, less complicated. Their thinking was straightforward: the important thing was Europe. It wasn't for fun that their parents had sent them to the best schools. This was compounded by another misunderstanding: while the officials most likely expected a degree of humility from them, these delegates from impoverished countries, many of them in fact saw themselves as the *crème de la crème*, given their background and education. And yet, the idea didn't occur to them that as well-educated men they bore some responsibility for progress in their countries. Though when you thought about it, it did make sense.

His mobile rang. He quickly pulled it out of the inside pocket of his jacket and turned the sound off. He still found it unbearable when people burdened others with their self-importance. It was the clinic, though he had impressed upon his staff that they should call him only in an emergency. He would call them back when he got there. He was looking forward to Paris and to seeing Amadou.

When, after graduation, they were all flung in different directions like a nuclear reaction, he was one of the few who went back, thereby fulfilling the official plan, if not his personal one. He was always reminded of that when he saw his old friends. Amadou, a slacker back then, had found himself a licence to print money with his orthopaedic clinic in Paris. Backs, knees, and the house speciality: hip replacements. A thriving granny repair shop in the French capital: you could hardly do better than that. Oumar was a consultant at a large hospital in Stuttgart. How ironic that he, the only one who had really complained of being homesick and who had nearly thrown in the towel, had ended up staying here, had become German, with a passport, a suburban house, a German wife, and two children. Very well, thank you, was Oumar's reply to the question of how they were doing. Christine's teaching job was going well; she'd been promoted to civil servant status. Well, good for them, thought Idris. He heard the muffled murmur of German being spoken in the train compartment and grinned to himself. The only thing about Oumar that wasn't German was his looks. And he, Idris, who had never been homesick, who had always imagined himself staying in Europe, had gone back to Africa. Isn't life absurd?

He put his phone away, sat back, and watched Germany pass by. Tidy, peaceful, green. It was a long time since he had been on a train and he had forgotten how relaxing it could be. When did he ever have time to think about the past?

He came here in 1967. He moved from Leipzig to West Berlin in late 1970. To start with, his grades ranged from satisfactory to good; later, when he came to realise that it was all or nothing, he got top marks. After general medicine came the dentistry state examination, then his specialism and doctorate. He had dreamed of cardiology but ended up in oral and maxillofacial surgery. With no regrets. There was no question that going back home had worked out for the best. He wasn't the eternal outsider. He hadn't had to pour precious energy into wearisome justifications: look, I'm a civilised being with a PhD, an acceptable sort of Black man. It wasn't to be underestimated, the toll it takes to expend that amount of energy your whole life long, thought Idris, especially when in the end you remained an outsider, a well-liked one, when things were going well, even a welcome one, but ultimately an outsider, all the same. Besides, with his clinic, he wasn't just one of many, like he would be here, but the best in Dakar. Everyone came to Dr Cissé. The rich and the diplomats anyway. He could justifiably call himself an artist, not that he needed to, his patients took care of his excellent reputation. His poorer clients didn't get Hollywood pearly whites, but he offered basic treatment through his smaller practice for very little, or even no fee at all. No, Idris had nothing to regret. He was doing well and he contributed to the common good. Differently perhaps from how his socialist hosts had envisaged it back then, not that they were around now to judge. All the same, he had gone back home to where good doctors were needed.

His nostalgia for Europe subsided a little. All was well. Or was it? He opened his newspaper only to fold it up again immediately. Too tired to read. He had had to submit to Oumar's schedule, which dragged him first to Berlin, then Leipzig, then finally Stuttgart. Next time I'll plan my own itinerary, and I'll stay longer, he thought. Maybe take the train right across Germany. It's so easy here, after all.

Sleet lashed against the window. He thought back to his first German winter. Once, the heating broke down, the only luxury even he really couldn't do without. He loved the winter clothes he bought back then. He never went anywhere without his knitted sweater and woolly hat. He'd learned to appreciate the benefit of long johns. One evening, he was studying for his exams, when he looked up from his book and saw a miracle. Something white was tumbling down from the sky. Frozen rain, lightness, silence. He woke Amadou, his roommate, who was unimpressed. He merely glanced outside for a moment, then turned back to the wall with a yawn. His father was a trade attaché and he had been to Europe plenty of times before. Idris ran out into the corridor, into the other rooms and called Alphonse, Mohamed, Seydou, Ousmane, Jean, and all the others, and they joined him, giggling in disbelief, as if seeing a magical spirit. They had long abandoned the university's culturally meaningful leisure activity schedule that they were supposed to follow. They did what they wanted. They went to dance halls and pubs, played football, socialised with Germans, and hosted parties in their miniscule bedrooms, relaxed and free of ideology. That evening, they ran down the corridors like children, laughing their heads off. One little, two little, three little Black boys … and their first snow.

Everything was new when they arrived. The way people looked and spoke, the food, the trams. Their bedding awaited them, piled up on the bunk beds: pillows, woollen blankets, and button-up duvet covers. One of their group climbed into the cover like a sleeping bag and buttoned himself into it, with only his head sticking out: Oumar, if Idris remembered correctly. But when Idris reminded him of it, laughing, Oumar's reaction was surly.

I'm not some idiot who doesn't know what a duvet cover is for.

Idris shrugged. Maybe it was another Oumar, after all.

We had no idea about anything, he'd said to Oumar, his tone neutral. It was the truth, after all.

The Germans had no idea either, Oumar had said. No one had a clue. We were students in a pre-globalised world. It was still the Eastern bloc; no one could travel anywhere. They made grand speeches about their socialist brothers and then asked us if we had cannibals back home.

Idris didn't remember it like that. In all honesty, he hadn't found people all that clueless. He had made some fantastic German friends and acquaintances. Artists, classmates, colleagues, even some of the old people were actually pretty cool.

Considering that they were Germans, they had, after all, come a long way if they were treating us Africans as if they had always believed in human equality, he said to Oumar, who had lost his youthful lightness, and not just physically.

I, for one, had my best times in the GDR. I'd almost say I liked it there better than in West Berlin. It was somehow warmer. It was human.

Compared to West Berlin, it was definitely more racist, said Oumar.

Maybe racism is human nature, Idris said. Oumar stopped and looked at him as if he had to remind himself who he was looking at. Idris, the provocateur. Idris grinned. Oumar did not. As young men, they had often shouted at each other, always confident that they would make up again later. If they ever came to blows, which was quite possible when you had known each other since you were ten, then they had successfully forgotten about it. Oumar patted him on the shoulder and shook his head. They carried on walking. Later, on the way out of the city, Idris remembered something he hadn't thought about in ages.

It was one of his first house calls, in the suburbs, one of the greener districts that looked like the countryside. Some of the people there still kept livestock, which he liked because it reminded him of back home. People are the same everywhere, he thought, they take great care of their animals and eventually they eat them. The first time he visited this patient, he went with an elderly German doctor. An old lady had had an accident and had extensive scalding. She must have been in terrible pain. It was obvious that he was the first Black person she had ever seen. She lay in her large double bed with her eyes wide open. He worked away, cleaning her wounds, changing the bandages, and so on. The German doctor talked to the old woman, who didn't stop staring at Idris the entire time, like he was the eighth wonder of the world. The following week he had to go and see her again. This time he was alone, but she wasn't. She had invited all her friends around to be there for his visit. Idris was the star attraction for a gathering of grannies. These old biddies were born in the nineteenth century; they hadn't even seen the countries theirs bordered with. For them he was a man from a foreign world, nothing more. They made him have coffee and cake with them, asked if they could touch his hair, asked what it was like in Africa, the lions, the heat, the hunger, the whole shebang. It was all perfectly friendly, almost bashful, and somehow endearing. The grannies whispered as he changed the bandage for their friend, his patient, smiling to himself.

You don't want to know what they will have said after you'd gone, Oumar said.

No, I don't, and what difference does it make to me?

Idris saw Oumar every year or two when Oumar was back in Dakar to see his mother and siblings. But he hadn't seen Christine since the late eighties, half an eternity. Their children both came over for dinner. Grown-up people whom he would not have recognised in the street. Valérie was already thirty-two, Cédric a little younger. He was a slimmer version of Oumar. An upbeat young man, athletic, warm, down-to-earth. When Idris remembered that he was his godson, he briefly worried that he might have been expecting a gift. What could I have given him? He's grown up, he's doing fine, he works at Porsche, he thought. Christine had snapped up Oumar, who was thin as a rake back then, and had never let him go. People always said it was the other way around: the Black guys coming over here snapping up the German girls. Ha, thought Idris, the German girls knew what they wanted better than we did, that much was clear. Apart from graduating and having a good time, he hadn't really wanted anything back then. He ticked both of those off his list, anyway.

Christine had very vivid memories of him; that's what she said right after they hugged. Idris always was a smooth operator, she said, with a laugh. A bit macho, too, of course. And rather disorganised, always keeping everyone else waiting outside the cinema. He borrowed things and never gave them back. It went on like that all evening, and he laughed along. He could take a joke, after all.

At dinner, she asked if there was anyone he was still in regular contact with. Who would I stay in regular contact with? he thought. I'm a busy man. It's over twenty years since I've been back to Europe, I have a practice and a clinic, goodness knows how many patients. What do you think I do all day, Christine? Write postcards to old acquaintances?

I'd rather come and visit my old friends, he said instead, raising his glass. Compliments to the chef, he said, as beautiful and charming as ever!

Later they sat by the fire with a glass of wine, looking at old photos, having a laugh at their seventies chic. Oumar finally let out his signature whinnying laugh, and Christine's laughter boomed like a goddess of thunder. A lovely couple. It really was a very nice evening.

It was also Christine who knew what had become of the young faces in the pictures. Most sounded successful, and even if he had lost track of who was who, he was glad to hear their stories. He wasn't someone who yearned for the past, but when he saw them like this – Oumar, who used to be so shy but dressed like a parrot in yellow bell-bottoms and psychedelic shirts, Amadou in his brown corduroy suit that made him practically monochrome, and Idris with his moustache, sideburns and size 28 jeans – at that moment, he missed those kids in the photos. Their innocence, the feeling of having their whole lives still ahead of them.

Christine, you must make me a print of this one. I have to show my daughters that I was cool once.

With pleasure, my dear. If you need a photo to prove it . . .

She gave him some photos to take with him. A whole bundle of them. Christine had had artistic ambitions back then. She'd set up a darkroom in her parents' basement, he remembered. Here on the train, Idris stood up and reached for his briefcase, and taking out the photos, he placed them on the fold-out table in front of him. A child came wandering down the aisle, snotty nose and a cookie in his hand. He stopped beside Idris. Nothing to see here, kid, Idris thought. Idris closed his eyes and nodded off into a short, exhausted sleep full of faces, voices, questions. When he woke up again shortly after Strasbourg, his nostalgia had turned to irritation.

His head fuzzy, he rummaged through his pockets for some aspirin and washed them down with half a bottle of water.

The sleeping pills of the previous night hadn't worn off yet. He took another swig of water and stared out the window without really taking the scenery in. It was a while before he realised the cause of his irritation. Not so much Christine, who seemed to see herself as his conscience. He was much more annoyed with himself.

Christine didn't have to do anything, she just had to be the way she was, and inevitably he found himself thinking about Moni. Monika. It was this resemblance between the two women that had probably made him remember them as friends.

Moni had found it too oppressive in the GDR. Understandable. Don't overestimate the West, he might have told her, but that would have been presumptuous. Everyone had the right to imagine they would find happiness elsewhere. As an African, he could tell her a thing or two about that.

Instead, all he had done was to encourage her to finish her degree, no matter what. What had she studied? Philosophy? Or was it called Marxist-Leninist Studies, or something like that? They dealt with the other philosophers only to refute them; Marx and Lenin were the be-all and end-all. Monika didn't have to work for her place at university; as a child of the proletariat, it fell into her lap, or so she claimed. She busied herself with Kant, Hegel, Schopenhauer, Nietzsche, Kierkegaard, drank red wine, and held her cigarettes with such flair that it made you desperate to take up smoking. It's all such a load of crap, she said. Philosophers who aren't allowed to think what they want? Are they actually out of their minds? And what am I supposed to do with it later? Teach? Agitate?

Finish it and get your degree, he said. The fact that you don't know what you'll do with it afterwards proves that it's a luxury. What I'm doing is basically a training course for a profession. But philosophy is a course for broadening horizons. Anywhere else in the world, it's a luxury only people who don't have to work can afford.

I can't drop out anyway, at least not as long as my dad's alive, Moni said. It would kill him.

He remembered her words well, because in many ways she seemed like she didn't give a damn about the world, but then again there was this loyalty. And he had always assumed that people in Europe – whether in the East or in the West – faced less pressure from their elders. It turned out that wasn't true. Moni's father was a Communist who toed the line and whose worldview was corroborated by the existence of the GDR, and even more so by his only daughter's choice of university degree. Idris liked what she told him about her dad, because it had the air of heroic legend, though at the same time it scared him. Germans with a conviction were terrifying, no matter what their conviction was.

They had never talked about a future together. Moni didn't want to marry him. No, Moni didn't want to marry anyone, at least not back then. That was part of her identity as a modern woman. The last few times he visited, he was already living in West Berlin but he didn't stay overnight. She was living in an old *Hinterhof* apartment, tucked away in the second courtyard of a block. In the summer, when her parents left Berlin for the country, she moved into their apartment in Treptow. From the S-Bahn, you could see the high-rises of Gropiusstadt, as if the Wall wasn't even there. She had named him Michael, he himself had called him Michel. A round, content baby who lay in his little crib, looking at his tiny hands and barely making a sound, while Monika hammered out her philosophy essays on her typewriter.

Michael. Michel. The last time he saw him, he could walk but wasn't talking yet. He had seen this child laugh but never cry. Was that true? For years, Monika sent him photos. Idris wondered for the first time in ages if he still had them. He didn't pursue the question of what had become of the boy.

He and Moni had passed each other greetings through mutual acquaintances. They stayed on good terms. Wasn't that how it had always been? He stopped writing to her from West Berlin. She was having difficulties. With the university? With the Stasi? He certainly didn't want to cause any trouble for her. Apart from that, she always gave the impression that she was doing just fine without him. A woman like Moni wouldn't have stayed single for long. It would have been challenging to present any of his successors as the child's biological father, unless he also happened to be Black. Idris wondered why he had never thought about it. She would have known what was right for her and the boy, he thought. At some point he heard through their acquaintances that she did marry in the end and had gone to the West. Monika got what she wanted. She always did.

Before the evening took a less pleasant turn, they had sat by the fire for a long time, he and Oumar and Christine. He then went upstairs, went straight off to sleep, and dreamed of a big old apartment. He was walking down a long, dark hallway, following voices, and Moni was sitting in the living room, the baby in her arms. Idris couldn't see his face; he just heard him laughing. He laughed like an adult. Why does he have fair hair, Moni? He's not yours, don't worry, she said.

He woke up, and realised he was in Oumar's guest room. He went downstairs to get a glass of water. Christine was still awake. She was kneeling on the floor in her white bathrobe, going through the large box of photos, arranging them in piles on the carpet. The television was on. A Persian cat he had never seen before was asleep on the settee.

Idris. Come and sit with me. Do you want some tea? Nice pyjamas.

Thank you.

He sat down by the fire again. Christine held a photo under his nose and smiled at him. A family photo. Oumar is carrying Valérie on his shoulders, Christine standing next to him with her hair in a long plait and Cédric on her front in a sling.

That was new at the time. It's the oldest way to carry a child, but it hadn't really caught on here yet. Do you remember?

To be honest, it never made much difference to me, he thought. Pram or sling – it's up to the mother, isn't it?

Cédric was an unusually beautiful child, he said.

I got nasty comments in the street because of my mixed-race baby.

Who wouldn't love that child, said Idris, who had never liked the German term *Mischling*. It sounded contemptuous. And it sounded like *Frischling*, a little wild boar.

Anyway, we weren't always popular, quite the opposite, as you know. These people killed their neighbours, and they were White. Do you think all of that would disappear all of a sudden just because they pretended that all the bad guys were over there in the West?

Christine had definitely wanted children with Oumar, and now, thirty years later, she was hinting to Idris – shifting into a more political tone – that their relationship was met with disapproval from certain ageing Nazis. Why was she telling him this? He took a sip of his tea. He'd go back to sleep after this.

You've always been good at blocking things out, Idris, he heard her say. It had been like this the whole evening. Idris: out of sight, out of mind. Idris, who made the world bend to fit his needs. Idris this, Idris that. Now he just sat there, drinking tea and gazing at the fire.

Where is that picture now, Christine asked herself, playing solitaire with the photos.

Listen, Christine, he said after a while, I have of course stayed in touch with a few people. It's just that I had to leave. That wasn't much fun. You know how complicated it all was.

Christine looked at him over her reading glasses and nodded.

Monika, for example, you must mean her. She left for the West in the eighties and got married, happily, as far as I know, he said.

Which Monika? Christine asked, taking off her glasses.

Which Monika? Were there so many Monikas? Well, yes, a lot of women were called Monika back then. But Christine genuinely didn't know who they were talking about, he could see it in her face. The fire had given her face the colour of raspberry yoghurt. A beautiful, light pink woman. He must have looked at her like an imbecile.

I don't know what made you think of this woman. Or let's put it another way: you must have your reasons to be happy for her.

She looked him up and down with her teacher's smile.

Not Monika, of course. Gabriela. His memory had tricked him. It had heaped Monika and Christine together: two tall, fair-haired, resolute women. But Monika was from Berlin and Christine from Leipzig. The tall Christine had been friends with little Gabriela. Gabriela, who didn't like being called Gabi. She liked it when he pronounced her name the French way: Gabrielle. Or Gabriellchen – little Gabrielle – that suited her. She had been studying draughtsmanship. And maybe I can study architecture later on, she had said. She didn't get a place to study architecture the first time round, but she didn't rail against it like Monika did with philosophy. She loved life. That sounded like a platitude, but it was true. She drove around in her father's Lada, jammed in cheerfully behind the wheel, with the driver's seat as far forward as it would go. If anyone needed the luxury of a car, she was there. She also had her own moped and would give him a lift on the back. He could picture her cute profile, framed by a helmet. Her dark fringe peeked out under the visor. That fringe that she was always blowing out of her eyes. Hold on tight, Idris.

He couldn't stop staring into the fire. Christine was still kneeling on the carpet, looking at him.

I meant Gabriela, he said after what felt like an eternity. How is she?

You're asking me? We left in 1976. You're surely not telling me you haven't heard from her since then?

Idris couldn't remember the last time he had heard from Gabriela, but he did remember that Christine's voice had always been too loud.

After that, we wrote to each other two or three more times, said Christine. Then that was it. I often think of her. I never heard from her again. The last time I went to Leipzig, there was a sushi restaurant where her father's shop used to be.

Leipzig. Sushi restaurant. Idris could only understand a few isolated words, as if he had forgotten his German. They looked at each other.

It was all so long ago, he said.

That's right, Idris, the boy must be about thirty by now. A long time ago – you can't explain everything away with that! Other people have managed to stay in touch.

I don't have to justify myself to you, Christine, he said, sounding colder than he intended.

No, you don't. It's not me you need to justify yourself to.

And suddenly Idris had the sense of a dream within a dream. He had met Moni, got up, walked down the stairs in this large, unfamiliar house, thinking he was awake. But he wasn't awake, he was still dreaming. In this dream within a dream Christine walked over and placed a photo in his lap and said, here, this is the one I was looking for. You can have it if you want.

He took the photo and stood up, like you do in a dream.

I thought of it when we were talking about beautiful babies, said Christine.

He headed towards the stairs.

I didn't mean that cynically, Idris. I really would like you to have it, Christine said, to his back.

He had no answer to that. He needed to be alone.

He didn't need to defend himself against Christine. She and Oumar had done things one way. He and Gabriela had done things differently.

I have to leave, Gabriellchen, he had told her, shortly before he left for good.

I can't, she said. My sister Brigitte ran away. In the boot of a car. Our Gitti. Never saw her again.

She shook her head, laughing about the car boot trick, and at the same time still mourning the loss of her sister.

Perhaps, he thought later, he was so fond of the people in the East because they were more like him in being resigned to their fate than the people in the West?

Gitti had been looking for freedom, and had found it, which meant that Gabriela had to stay. In the country and with her parents. Perhaps – and actually, the more he thought about it, the more sure he was – her sister's escape was also the reason why she hadn't been allowed to go to university. She had told him about the pregnancy, but he couldn't remember if she was distraught or overjoyed, and neither could he remember his own reaction. He wouldn't have been dancing for joy, that much was certain. This wasn't the first time he'd been told precisely the same news: that, unplanned, he was going to be father.

He never imagined that seeing Oumar's wife would rob him of his sleep. First he tried calling Odette to reassure himself that his life in Dakar carried on as usual. But she didn't answer. Then he sat on the edge of the bed and let the confusion, the women, the places, the years, loop around in his head until he silenced them with two sleeping pills.

Idris stretched his legs out with a sigh. Ought he to have explained himself to Christine? He knew he didn't need to, but even if he had wanted to, he wouldn't have been able to last night. The truth was, there had been good reason for him and Gabriela to have lost touch. Many good reasons. And now that he could think about it uninterrupted, they all came back to him.

He didn't know why he had been summoned by the police. It was hard to tell what would count as a crime in their eyes. German students seemed to get into trouble for the smallest things. West German television, the wrong posters in their rooms, the wrong clothes, wrong friends. Foreigners were mostly left alone. He had a French passport, as he was born in 1945 in what was then a French colony. Do what you like, he thought, feeling pleasantly unaffected by the German East-West squabble.

He had made friends with a couple from Leipzig, both artists. Gisela and Klaus. They were ten or fifteen years older than him. She was a sculptor, he a painter. To start with, he took letters from them to West Berlin, and later Klaus's paintings, which he delivered to a gallery owner there. Or was it a collector? He couldn't remember the details, but this well-dressed gentleman also gave him the money for the paintings. On one of these trips, with several thousand marks on him – West German marks – he was stopped at the Friedrichstrasse crossing, and his response was to do what he did best, even when he was shaking with fear. He talked those poor border guards' ears off. He churned out all the international friendship stuff that they were always going on about, and he told them how grateful he was for his first-class education in their fabulous country. Is that right? And why are you travelling to West Berlin so often, then? Love, consumerism, nightlife . . . all legal, yet not exactly what they wanted to hear. His feverish thinking must have finally brought him to the best place to go for any kind of fever. The Tropical Institute at FU Berlin, the Free University. An institution that genuinely did only exist in the western part. Where he, as a future physician in tropical climes, would have to complete the appropriate training. That much was true. Just not at that precise moment in time. They nodded and scribbled their notes. He couldn't tell if they would call the institute and enquire about him, or if that would mean showing weakness in front of the people in the West. He felt relieved even before there was any reason for relief. There he was, sitting in this little hovel that smelled of stale coffee, bodies, and cigarettes, his pockets full of West German money, which he was now claiming to have withdrawn from the bank. Funding from his state, his student grant in hard currency. For him and a few colleagues, hence the relatively large sum. Maybe they wanted to avoid any trouble on the diplomatic side, but he must have got away with it somehow, because if he had needed to tell Klaus about it, and explain how several thousand DM had gone missing, then that would be a conversation he would remember, wouldn't it? Or at least Klaus's face? It was actually quite a good story. I should definitely tell the girls when I get the chance, Idris thought.

And the bust-up, which he had forgotten about until Oumar mentioned it. It wasn't about girls or White guys versus Black guys, they were just drunk. Idris, a drunken young man, had broken the nose of another drunken young man. It felt like it, anyway, and that was how it looked. They were standing under the yellow light of a streetlamp in Leipzig and didn't know what to do or where to go. There were Christmas trees lying on the pavement next to them, so it must have been January. He was alone and had just vividly demonstrated that he was not to be messed with. The guy with the broken nose had his friend with him who was so blotto that he had to lean on his injured buddy while he hurled abuse at Idris. Look at that, you bastard, he kept yelling, pointing at the other guy, who was writhing in pain. Idris stood there frozen to the spot, listening to this guy's threats. He would come and find him, they'd get him back, he would beat the living daylights out of him as payback for this – he pointed to his friend's nose. Of course, they called them *niggers* and all that. If he hadn't been Black, they would have found some other reason to pick a fight with him. They would have been after his money, or they might have taken objection to how he had acted in the pub, a touch too confident, buying a few rounds. They had their eye on his leather coat. We're confiscating your Gestapo coat, one of them kept squawking like a crazed rooster. The *what* coat? Idris had always been a passable runner, but he didn't run. Something paralysed him. Was it fear? Probably pride. When they caught up with him at some point and he felt a hand on his shoulder, he just turned and punched. Right hook, direct hit, crack. You idiot, he told himself in the weeks that followed. Because apart from how much his cock dominated his life at that time, his hands were by far the most important part of his body. He wanted to be a cardiac surgeon; that was his goal above anything else. Idris didn't see himself as a husband, much less as a father; he even only vaguely pictured himself as a wealthy man, a natural consequence of his illustrious career as a surgeon. He imagined himself at the operating table, and he was obsessed with looking after his hands. And in the heat of the moment he had almost wrecked one of his anatomical masterpieces.

There they were under the streetlamp, Idris trembling and mute, the other two swearing and whimpering, until a window opened above them and a hoarse male voice screeched at them, quiet down there, you ruffians, or I'll call the police. Ah shut it, Grandpa, shouted his new enemy. At the word police, he finally understood what he had to do. He ran through the night in the wrong direction until he found a cab with a grouchy driver who eyed him suspiciously until he persuaded him with ten West German marks to drive him to the dorm, where he lay in bed for two days with ice packs on his irreplaceable hand. Whether the guy reported him or not, he didn't know, but every day he feared running into him again. The ease with which he had moved around the city for years until that point was gone.

Had he glorified his time in the GDR? He still maintained that it had been good, he'd liked it there, but it was also a long time since he had remembered just how urgently he had needed to leave.

It was a paradox, but the girls had also been a reason for him to get away. Or rather, their fathers. Moni with her Communist dad, firstly. How was Idris to know if her dad was some big shot, if he had the power to finish him off? And then there was Gabriela's dad, who seemed to be some kind of private entrepreneur and knew everyone in Leipzig. Old boy network, old school. She spoke of him only in the very fondest terms. Papa always says, Papa bought this for me. She was as good as a boy at making and repairing things. Of course, her dad had taught her that, too. This man wouldn't let his daughter be taken away from him, not after his other daughter was gone. Especially not by a Black man.

Gabriela still lived with her parents. They had a telephone, but he hardly ever called her because they always knew when they would see each other again. When he had decided he needed to leave, he tried to call her, and her legendary dad answered the phone. He answered with a lively *Loth speaking!*, heard Idris's accent, asked him his name twice, and then paused, silent.

Hello, he said, are you still there? Is Gabriela there? May I speak to her, please?

I hereby forbid you any further contact with my daughter Gabriela, he finally said. He didn't say it in a nasty way. It was very formal, which made the command even more unmistakable. Now Idris was silent.

Do you understand me?

He no longer remembered if he said yes. He hung up. What should I have done? Idris asked himself. He'd had no other way of contacting her. Did she try to reach him? He assumed she did, but shortly after that phone call he was no longer around. He was gone.

The summons, the incident at the border, one smashed-up German nose, and two women. One with a baby, one claiming she was pregnant. What if he'd been kicked out of the university and sent back, possibly at his father's expense? That would have been catastrophic. He would have been stuck at home, condemned to becoming a farmer. So he packed his bags and headed to France, where this nice young man from the former colony was asked if he had completed his military service. That was something he hadn't considered: as a French citizen he had not only rights, but also duties. So, back to West Berlin, where foreigners who had studied in the East could enrol and continue their studies relatively easily. When he heard that Gabriela had decided to keep the baby, he was already studying at FU Berlin and working well-paid night shifts at the hospital.

He sent her packages, again and again, until he left Germany. He tucked money in among the gifts. He wanted to help her, even though she had always given the impression that she had everything she needed. She had an aunt in the US and relatives in West Germany. His packages were sent back. Whether her father returned them, or whether she was sending them back herself, he would never know.

I'd just really like to travel, she used to say. See the world, see where you're from, Idris. Or at least know that I *could*.

Gabriela was never angry, she was amazed. Amazed that the world seemed so different from herself. That – and he didn't know if he was aware of this at the time – had frightened him. He could handle Monika's anger better. With Gabriela, he couldn't even say that he had run away from a responsibility for which he was too young and beneath which he felt crushed, because for that she would have had to hand him that responsibility. But she didn't ask anything of him, except that they got on, at least he didn't remember anything else. The way Gabriela approached life – and he should have told the self-righteous Christine this – she had a state of mind that you self-proclaimed hippies would probably want to put into pills and hand out at parties. She hadn't thought it up to declare a new era or to annoy her parents, that was just how she was.

He blew his nose. He was worked up and alone. He hadn't felt like this in a long time. He put the photo down in front of him on the folding table. It was really beautiful. In his imagination, German women had always looked like Christine or Monika. But Gabriela had dark hair. He had never touched such smooth hair. With her straight fringe, small nose and high cheekbones, she looked almost Asian, but her eyes were light, sometimes blue, sometimes almost green, fascinating, also something he had never seen before. Now the Wall was gone, she was free. She could travel. Perhaps she had even become an architect, after all. He hoped she had.

In the photo, she has the baby in her arms. Black straight hair like hers, pale skin like hers. He smiles up at her, she down at him. His little fist grips her necklace. She always wore a small gold cross.

Idris Ernst Gabriel, born on 8 November 1970, Idris read on the back of the photo. She had named the boy after him, after her father, and after herself. It was that little line of her neat handwriting in pencil that kept him awake all night. Now, without Christine's questioning presence, he was no longer shaken by the memory of her. He sat back and enjoyed it. That was my Gabriellchen, he thought, that was how I knew her. Everything she did, she did with care and love. The train was speeding toward Paris, and he thought of how they both were back then, so long ago. Young people with no idea what the future held, who were happy to have met. He was glad he was sitting alone on this train. He was glad that he was about to embrace his oldest friend, Amadou. Briefly, he felt like he did back then, when every trip was still an adventure. He looked at the photo once more before slipping it back into the envelope and was suddenly sure that the boy would have turned out like her. Not an Idris, not an Ernst, but a Gabriel. An angel, like his mother.

PART II

THE STRANGER

He was alone in the world, but not without roots. A considerable part of his energy went into maintaining the conviction that his life was perfect.

Gabriel

And suddenly I was White. Me. It wasn't the only distortion of facts that day, but it was the most preposterous. Not that the tabloids explicitly described me as White. They didn't need to. I became White when they refrained from writing that I wasn't.

They knew my name. In any other context, that was fine with me. I had done everything I could for twenty years to reach this point. Architects are rarely household names or celebrities you'd recognise by sight, but to give the average tabloid reader a hint at how to picture me, all they needed to do was show a few photos of our most significant building projects and refer to me as the renowned architect, and they had summed me up as one of those men who imagined that the world belonged to them and that they could get away with anything. I had never thought that. Our company had built so much, including bungalows for slum dwellers. But of course a skyscraper, ergo a phallus, worked better in this context.

It was made to look as if my entire life had been moving towards this incident, a causal chain so inevitable that even the dimmest reader would think: typical. Had I been unlucky? Was I in the wrong place at the wrong time? Didn't that amount to the same thing essentially? In the same way that you could say that my stars were misaligned or my energy field was weakened. After the incident I span in circles grappling for a cause and effect, a formula to explain what I should have done differently. Thoughts arose that sounded like something my wife would say. Had I failed to heed my inner voice? Was it trying to warn me? Was I pushing my luck by trying to add something else on top of everything? No, I wasn't. I don't believe in fate, so how could I tempt it? Or humbly win it over to my side? I believe in my work and the well-deserved impact of what I do. I had no doubts whatsoever about being appointed at the university. The timing was perfect. For me both as a man and as an architect. I had something to say. I had experience and ideas. As a student, I would have gone to my seminars. If I were head of faculty, I would have given me the post. My wife suggested I write a book instead, reasoning that a book demanded my professional competencies but less in the way of social skills. Should I have listened to her? I'm always interested in her opinion, even if I don't necessarily share it. I love Fleur, but I'm not Fleur. I'm Gabriel.

My student's reaction went far beyond what I might have imagined or feared. Presumably she was desperate for attention, looking for a platform of some kind. Which she found by presenting herself in the media as a victim. She didn't seem to care that she was also dragging herself through the mire. Fame or not, would someone really want that? She may have thought that people would eventually forget where they knew her from; the main thing was that people had heard of her. I don't know. What's clear is that she saw this as her big chance. But she might herself have been surprised at the way the incident was shoehorned into every possible kind of debate. On the other hand, perhaps she was also depending on the multifaceted nature of her victimhood. Gender, education system, class, skin colour: every topic had its moment in the spotlight. The tabloids ascribed to me more power, more money and more influence than I could ever dream of achieving. Some comments read as if I were Dominique Strauss-Kahn. Who still remembers him? He was soon eclipsed by Hollywood and Harvey Weinstein. All the same, my reputation was irreversibly tarnished.

There was nothing sexual about my outburst, though I could hardly prove that. I refrained from mentioning that for a moment I thought the girl was a transvestite; I'd only have turned another group against me if I'd said that. I didn't stand a chance. Anything I said would have made things worse. It would have meant throwing the proverbial shit into the fan: a repulsive metaphor that had never been so apt. I became public enemy number one for the press and every conceivable anti-discrimination group.

The university put on an official stance of contrition, which didn't surprise me in the slightest. The more media-savvy their statements became, the less they had a personal impact, which isn't to say that they didn't cause me considerable harm in other ways. We place the utmost importance on respectful interaction between students and faculty, yeah, yeah. I was a visiting lecturer, not on the staff, and I couldn't count on the support of my colleagues. After all, they hardly knew me. But I certainly didn't expect the opposite: colleagues who apparently felt the need to jump on the bandwagon. I had no interest in university affairs beyond my lectures, which is why I explicitly unsubscribed from all the email lists that were cluttering up my inbox. For my own projects, I had set up project-specific email addresses and telephone numbers, otherwise I could be reached on the main landline. I generally avoid social networks. I didn't see why I should join in with the whole campus nonsense, which I disliked enough when I was a student myself. The fact that I limited myself solely to my seminars confirmed the general suspicion that I was some kind of weirdo sociopath. The one social occasion I let myself be talked into joining, an evening in a bar, promptly became my undoing, because I made the mistake of talking to a female colleague about our students. I said that at times I felt more like I was teaching in a school than a university, thinking of the disturbing lack of interest shown by some of the students. The impression they made on me was that they hadn't chosen the subject they were studying, that they were lumped with slogging away at a subject for which they had no talent whatsoever, but which regrettably appeared on their timetable. I didn't mean just any students, but a group of young women in particular, which happened to include my so-called victim. I honestly wondered what had led them to study architecture. I had a few unfounded theories, none of which I was entirely convinced by. Maybe it was to meet men, maybe it was because it was their parents' aspiration for them, maybe they had embarked on their degree course with a misconception of what it entailed. It wasn't uncommon and neither was it too late to change. These girls seemed not only on the wrong course, but also out of their depth. I found it deeply irritating the way they acted like they were doing time, but it wasn't my role to suggest they switch courses. And if I was completely honest, and I was completely honest – by this point, I had moved on from beer to whiskey and another female colleague had joined us – I was irritated by everything about how these girls presented themselves. Starting with their appearance, which would be more at home on a TV talent show or in a nail salon, or goodness knows where. Now if it were combined with stellar performance in their studies, dressing like that would have been a statement. But as it was, I felt like a social worker in a suburb without aspirations. My colleagues agreed with me. Then I made the mistake of imitating one of the girls, or, to be more precise, her vacant facial expression, which was so extraordinarily idiotic that you almost wondered if this was her trademark selfie face that she also wore into my seminar. This facial expression was so recognisable that my colleagues immediately knew who I meant without any names being mentioned. I knew my pastiche wasn't very nice, and I'm quite sure I've no talent as a comedian, so I was surprised to see these women bent over with laughter and asking me to do the pout over and over, until it became awkward and I changed the subject. The atmosphere stayed like that the rest of the evening, with that sort of giddy jolliness that I normally go out of my way to avoid. In retrospect, I suppose it was lucky that Fleur picked me up; she had been at a restaurant nearby with friends. A cab ride with my over-excited, tipsy female colleagues would certainly have offered more scope for public accusations, regardless of what had happened. Too keen or too aloof, take your pick. No, thanks. And as it turned out, those two hours at the bar had been ample opportunity to judge my character. I don't know which of the two women sold this evening to the press as further evidence against me, but I was quoted later as saying: zero education, zero interest, zero talent.

Soon after that, some excerpts surfaced from an interview I had given to the BBC over ten years ago, where it sounded like I was denying poor people not the right to live in dignity but the capacity to do so. Just like that, they managed to portray me as the enemy of precisely the people I had spent years working and advocating for. All they had to do was choose the right places to wrench what I had said from its context. My office responded by publishing the interview in full. Context is everything. But context also requires effort, and who would make an effort if you didn't have to? That was how I was presented and that wasn't going to change. Along with all the other revelations about me, the public now had an eminently cohesive overall picture of an asshole.

There was nothing I could do about the fact that I was a man, that I was her lecturer, that I was financially better off than she was. But they were happy to overlook the fact that I wasn't White myself. I had attacked a Black twenty-year-old who was circumstantially dependent on me. Which also wasn't entirely accurate, because my course was optional (taking us back to the question of what she was doing there in the first place). The fact was she was twenty and Black, and she dragged her father into the public eye, a minicab driver who was captioned with touching descriptions like Mr So-and-So worked double shifts for twenty years to give his children a good education. *I always wanted to go to university, but it wasn't possible. My daughters are doing it for me*, and so on. Accompanied with childhood photos of my student and her two sisters, primary school girls in little dresses and pigtails. Slim chance that a photo like that would fail to tug at readers' heart strings. The mother wasn't mentioned, maybe for tactical reasons, or maybe she really wasn't around. For me, they used a passport photo that could have passed for a mug shot: middle-aged man staring into the camera with as blank an expression as possible, as required for a biometric passport. Round head, very short hair, receding hairline, blank expression, a broad neck emerging from a white collar and tie. An overexposed, nondescript male. No room for sympathy. The girl's father, this amiable older man with salt-and-pepper sideburns, who probably wasn't much older than me, was posited as the dear, virtuous father and shining light of the immigrant community, confronted with the perfect nemesis: the evil German. And the beauty of it is that it's okay to say that. Germans aren't a protected minority. There are heaps of them, they demonstrably have skeletons in the closet, yet they're doing just fine.

The British comic profile of a typical German is rather basic and not particularly up to date, which doesn't stop anyone from using it. The alleged battle over the sun loungers at the pool, football, and always Hitler. It all comes out spontaneously, always brushed off straight away as a harmless joke. If you don't laugh, then you've got no sense of humour and you're probably from Germany. At first I was amused. I hadn't come across the ludicrous thing with the towels and the sun loungers before, because I hadn't been on any package holidays to Torremolinos, but I could picture German tourists doing that. Football is football. And my comeback to the constant references to history's worst German was: *Don't mention the war*. Where was that from – Monty Python? Fawlty Towers? Anyway, they found it hilarious. In fact they found me hilarious because I could quote a line from some ancient TV series.

But as a rule I wasn't the German they imagined. Just as after the Wall came down, I wasn't the East German people imagined. People looked at me and didn't expect a German accent, and consequently they didn't hear one. I found that fascinating. Although I definitely have a German accent. Why wouldn't I?

But now, not only was I definitely a German again – after all, who could be more suitable as the culprit in a juicy story like this than a German? – I was also a racist. If someone had predicted any of this, I would have laughed at them.

I got back from Greece very early that morning. We had been sailing in the Aegean. One of our clients had spent so much time with us that he called us his friends and invited us to go sailing with him. He was, if anything, more Mark's friend, but I liked him enough to spend my free time with him. When I was studying architecture, I had only ever imagined buildings, never people. But at some point my life was suddenly full of people. City planners, mayors, sponsors, entrepreneurs, company directors, and wealthy people of all kinds. There was an ever-growing chasm between my closest circle of friends and family and my broadest circle of acquaintances. I intentionally had such a small inner circle that it was basically only Fleur, Mark, my brother-in-law, and, at most, a handful of other friends, while I could easily have celebrated a milestone birthday with a guest list that the paparazzi would go crazy for. That's not bragging: it's a side effect of success that, as we all know, vanishes as soon as the novelty of that success wears off. Some clients disappeared again as soon as their house was built, while others seemed to have the sense that we had accompanied them through the most important step in their lives. Todd was in this latter category. He was an artist we had worked with on an installation for the Venice Biennale and who subsequently commissioned us to build him a house with a convertible roof. Our question to him was not why he wanted a house with a roof that could be opened completely, our question was why he wanted one in London. Our proposal, that we bring this project to life somewhere drier and warmer, and build him a house in London with a conventional roof, sparked in Todd an admiration for our foresight that eventually evolved into friendship.

Mark thought he was funny. I was confused. Surely he had to think about materials and weather conditions in his line of work. Or did his assistants do all that for him?

He only thinks about stuff related to his art, said Mark. It's odd, yes, but also effective, don't you think?

Todd had been talking about this trip for three years, but it wasn't until this summer that we found a date we could all do. It was the first time in years that I didn't have any plans with my family. The chronicles of Albert's puberty had reached new heights, and Fleur was pissed off with me.

Todd had talked about the yacht cruise as a men's getaway, but then he brought Linda along, his wife at the time. It was an outrage, which Mark brushed off as eccentricity. Eventually we accepted it, as if it was as arranged. Also on board was Elmo, Mark's eighteen-year-old stepson, whom I've known since he was eight. By now he was as tall as Mark and as handsome as his mother. He was clearly making an effort to communicate like an adult, but he still seemed perplexed about what he was doing on this boat with us all. He was bored in our company, even though Mark had made sure there were copious amounts of pot and booze on board, plus seemingly never-ending contemporary playlists. Elmo was suffering from an internet cold turkey of the first degree, which I recognised from when Albert had withdrawal symptoms, but beyond that you hardly noticed he was there. Todd was making an effort with Linda, the mother of his children, but she was more interested in talking to me and Mark. We were clearly part of her strategy to make it obvious that she was ignoring Todd, which was rather annoying. Not to mention unnerving talking to a woman I hardly knew and who had nothing on except a pair of bikini bottoms. My problem with naked people is their insistence on being treated as if they weren't naked. There's a considerable difference, for me at least, if I have a pair of jeans or a T-shirt in my field of vision while I'm in conversation, or if I'm faced with the penis of a complete stranger or the breasts of a passing acquaintance. Whether they're pleasing or not is hardly the point. Pleasure, displeasure, arousal, horror – each option ruled out the possibility of a relaxed conversation. Especially a parenting conversation, because Linda talked incessantly about her sons. I stayed out of her way as best I could on a yacht. Which is to say, with difficulty. After a few days, we had all got used to each other, and at last there was the peace and quiet that I had come for. I read a bit of *The Iliad*, gazing out at the sea, which had looked the same in Homer's day, a soothing thought that helped me unwind. Todd, Mark, and Linda shifted into the sleep cycle of late-night revellers, while Erik, the skipper, Elmo, and I made up the quiet day shift. The skipper was a Danish man who was almost absurdly good-looking and whose attention had probably also been the focus of Linda's minimalist choice of attire.

After resigning myself to a holiday that looked to be much less relaxed than I had hoped, I did actually start to unwind. And when Linda finally left early, it didn't make any difference to me. For the first time in a long time, I found myself in a state I remembered feeling as a child after eight weeks of no school, when I was desperate for something to do again. Although we had only been away for two weeks, I couldn't wait to get back to my daily routine.

I was in such a hurry that I cancelled the last day in Athens. Albert baulked at anything to do with history or culture, but I thought perhaps Elmo might be more open to learning about the ancients. On the other hand, his cultural education wasn't my responsibility. I booked myself onto the first flight back to London. Acropolis, adieu.

My flight came in at about 6 am. On the way into London, I had this triumphant feeling that the city belonged to me. It was slowly getting light, and here I was hurtling into the stirring hustle and bustle that might well have stressed me out after our peaceful odyssey, but in fact it made me feel alert and euphoric. My family was still asleep, and I didn't want to wake them, but neither did I want to creep around the house like a burglar. I wheeled my bike out of the garage. Hampstead Heath or Richmond Park? I decided to take the long route to Richmond Park. The idea lifted my spirits even more. I was back home, I'd soon be riding my favourite route, and, if I was lucky, I might see some fallow deer in the morning sun. And I would have time to prepare myself mentally for breakfast with my wife and son. As much as I was glad to be back, I was happy to put off seeing them. Every time we spoke on the phone, we hadn't said much more than: we'll talk about it when I get back. No point talking about it on the phone.

What good would it do anyway? Albert was pubescent in a way that was completely out of our control, and in any case Fleur and I couldn't agree on how to deal with him. I toyed with the idea of riding straight from Richmond Park to the office. Then I thought about talking to Fleur alone, and briefly imagined sleeping with her. I went back into the house, but it wasn't the best time. Fleur, who can also sleep through anything – you could be sanding the floor and she wouldn't wake up – had put on her sleeping mask, which she always wore together with earplugs. This meant that I wasn't to speak to her or touch her. A softly breathing Keep Off sign in a pair of tired-looking men's pyjamas. Which surprised me because she knew roughly what time I was due back. I left a cup of tea on her bedside table. She didn't stir. As I got changed, it occurred to me that the holiday had been worth it. I was feeling good and pain-free. I stood in front of the mirror, feeling pleased at how healthy I felt. I was bleary eyed and yet felt so light that I said to my reflection, we can do this. By which I meant everything: the conversation we needed to have, Albert's future, Fleur's mood swings, my need to catch up on family time.

I went outside. It was chilly. Leaning over the handlebars, I saw the shit. I looked up and saw the dog a little further ahead, sniffing the fence. A beautiful, large, black, short-haired beast that had abused my bicycle like it was a tree. My tyre was in the middle of its sizeable, ochre-coloured heap. I would have said something even if it had only been my fence. Or the pavement. The woman was still within earshot. She stopped when I called her. When she saw why I was calling her, she whistled to the dog and kept walking.

I wasn't angry with the dog. That enthusiastic joy in obedience that only dogs have, and how his ears flapped as he leapt toward her – it was briefly moving, in spite of my anger. She pulled him by the collar, bent over him, and tried to put him on the leash. The dog kept moving. The woman cursed and put her beer can down on the pavement to have both hands free. Her long hair, glossy black with pink tips, was falling in her face, and she carried on swearing. I didn't care about the beer. I didn't care how she was dressed. I cared about her behaviour as a dog owner, not about her as a person. I didn't expect to know her, and neither did I recognise her. I politely asked her several times to please pick up what her dog had left on my property. Then I shouted that she should take her shit with her. I followed her and kept on shouting. Without turning to face me, she shouted back that I should shut up and fuck off, and she held up her hand, her middle finger raised. She picked up her pace, which the dog misunderstood, and was now racing along and tugging so hard on the leash that she could barely keep up with him in her high heels. Annoyed, she pulled him towards her to let him off the leash again, and I kept on trying to get her attention, while she ignored me as if she were a normal passer-by being harassed by a lunatic. And suddenly I had had enough. I was sick of this tone, sick of this insolence, sick of all of it. I went back and grabbed a handful of the shit.

What's most shocking to me is the way I didn't pause to think but just stuck both hands in to grab this still warm, soft, stinking heap of shit. Especially since the actual trigger of my rage, apart from this girl's outrageous behaviour, was, after all, my disgust. There's a lot of things I find disgusting, intensely so. When Albert was a baby, I was relieved to discover that I could handle drool and vomit quite well. Changing nappies took some effort; I could barely overcome my repulsion, and I was grateful that Fleur didn't often ask me to do it. My pet hair allergy saved me from any discussions about getting a dog. Why would you want to stick your forearm down another creature's throat, I always wondered when I saw my wife wrestling with dogs. She let them eat out of her hand and lick her face as if she couldn't care less where the dog's snout had been. I could hardly look.

And then I went and picked up this shit as if it was something neutral, like a building material, and ran after the woman with it. Like an armed policeman I shouted that she should stop, I was warning her, but she just laughed again, not turning around. She had bare legs and was wearing one of those pretentious parkas with a real fur hood. This oversized balcony of fur was the first thing I could grab. Until that point I didn't even know what I intended to do with the shit. I probably just wanted to hold it under her nose. As proof of her misdemeanour. Idiotic, but not implausible. It wasn't until I had grabbed her that I knew what would happen next. Shouting at her, I spread the dog shit on the fur of her parka and then on her head. Me, who hates it when people touch my hair. The head is sacred; no one should be allowed to touch your head without permission. That should be true in every culture, I thought – in a normal state. And then I broke this taboo in such a savage way that even today I still can't make sense of it. Later, I realised that I had behaved like a monkey in the zoo. As a child, I used to go to Leipzig Zoo almost every week, and we'd always go straight to the gorillas. They used to throw their own shit at each other, but unlike me that morning, they used it as a plaything and not as a weapon, and I always wondered if it was their natural behaviour, a typical gorilla pastime, or if it was an expression of their desperation and boredom as lifelong captives. I looked at them, fascinated and repulsed at the same time. And because these creatures are so human, I was also ashamed on their behalf and hoped, rather irrationally, that the female gorillas stayed out of it.

The woman began to shriek like a lunatic and flailed around. She tossed her beer can to the side and tried to shake me off. She waved her arms and kicked back at me, but it was too late. By now my desire to punish her had turned into something playful, which was no better for her, because my initial idea of shoving the mound into her hood had turned into an ambition to defeat her, to smear her as much as possible. We used to call it 'soaping up' when we ambushed the girls with snow after school. I never found this game particularly exciting, but it was the done thing whenever it snowed. And now, forty years later, here I was making another girl scream.

Imagine, she told the press later, you're just out taking your dog for a walk, listening to music, when suddenly someone throws himself at you from behind and smears you with shit! She didn't have earphones in. Neither was she singing along to rap lyrics, as she later claimed as justification for her vulgar language. It hadn't occurred to her, or me, that there was hardly a corner of London left where you wouldn't be caught on CCTV. It was beyond doubt that she had attacked me verbally.

But that was no longer significant in the overall assessment of the case. Whether she was drunk or under the influence of drugs was also irrelevant, because the attacker here was me.

I didn't realise this until her shrieking became a whimper. When the fit of anger ebbed away, I came back around and saw I had gone too far, that I had been in the right a few seconds before but now I wasn't.

Unable to move, I stood there beside her. She was wearing a wig, that I had almost pulled off. A silver lining for her, because at least I hadn't smeared her scalp. She straightened her sunglasses and gingerly felt her artificial hair, as if it was burning. Stunned, she stared first at her fingers, then at me. In disgust, I backed away, although I stank just as much myself. *You*, she gasped again and again, as if she couldn't think of the next word to say. You pig? Yes, me. I had done this to her and I had to get away. She'll survive, I thought, it's repugnant, but no one is hurt. I'll keep going around the block and head home through the back garden. I backed away, leaving the girl standing on the pavement in the lovely morning light, shivering, smeared with shit, and as shocked as I was. She span around. The dog was nowhere to be seen. When I turned away to run, I heard her screech *rapist*. Or was it *racist*? Rapist or racist – both alarming accusations. I sped up, making a run for it like a little boy who in all seriousness thought running away would protect him from the consequences. Idiot.

I had left my several-thousand-pound racing bike outside. Stupidly, it was out of the range of the CCTV, and logically, later it was gone.

I went in the house through the back door, took off my shoes, and ran upstairs to where my wife had locked herself in our bathroom. I stormed into my son's ensuite. With his toothbrush in his mouth, he had his face pressed up again the mirror, inspecting his skin. An intimate moment. His instinctive response was to throw me out. Not a trace of joy that I was back from my holiday, just a startled: jeez! Before he could start whinging, I interrupted him with a staccato that he understood immediately: out, this is an emergency, we'll talk later. Albert, the king of the contemptuous glare, looked at my shit-smeared hands. If he had laughed, I'd have slapped him. Good thing he shuffled off without comment. Better for all of us.

While I was scrubbing my hands, it occurred to me what I had just seen walking through Albert's room. I stepped out of the bathroom. Albert had probably gone to our ensuite to finish brushing his teeth with his mother. There was a boy I didn't recognise lying in his bed and eyeing me sleepily. I didn't know if this had been discussed with my wife. Had my son already told her that he was into men? Or was this lad just a fellow gamer or stoner who hadn't made it home? At least he can't get him pregnant, I thought. But I'd had enough of this house-share free-for-all that my wife and son had set up in my house. I'd had enough of strangers in my private space, and I'd had enough of young people staring at me in horror. Please leave my house immediately, I said to the lad, the covers pulled up to his chin. He didn't move. Oh never mind, I thought, and went back into the ensuite, where I decided to take a shower.

I had a long, hot shower. When I came out of the bathroom, the boy was gone and I lay down on Albert's bed. Except for all the crumbs, I was amazed to find it was more comfortable than ours, and I dozed off into the best sleep I'd had in ages. I woke up when the front doorbell rang, and staggered into my dressing room, pulled on a pair of jeans and a sweatshirt, and went downstairs. Fleur was leaning against the kitchen counter, her arms crossed. Albert seemed entranced by the Nutella jar on the table. His guest was sitting next to him, biting his thumbnail and eyeing the two police officers who were standing in the middle of the kitchen: a very young White man and a small, Black woman, slightly older than her colleague and probably his superior. Good morning, sir, she said, as if we had an appointment. I took in the scene and presumed it was Albert who the police were here to see. Or both boys. Even my next thought only indirectly had anything to do with me: the boy sitting next to Albert must be his friend from France. Why had no one told me he was coming?

What can I do for you? I asked the police officers. In emphatically formal language, the woman now presented me with an outrageous claim. I had been accused of a sexual, racially motivated assault on one of my female students. I wouldn't have laughed in consternation had I comprehended the situation. I laughed like it was a mistake that would quickly be cleared up. There were surely no grounds for an accusation of this kind against me; I was never, at any time, alone with any of my students.

Stoically, the policewoman repeated the accusations, this time going into detail, taking care to use the word *faeces* instead of *shit*. And she named the place and time. The girl had recognised me. I hadn't recognised her. The truth flooded through me and made my knees go soft. You didn't need to be on university premises to attack a student; you could also meet her by chance one morning in front of your own house.

The police officers both had straight faces. Not the slightest gesture that might hint at what they thought of it all personally, whether they saw my student as victim and me as psychopath, or me as a victim of libel and her as hysterical.

This is a misunderstanding, I said to their blank faces. That's as may be, in which case all the more important to set things straight at the station, said the policewoman. My wife and son communicated with one another in silence, as they so often do. What the hell? asked Albert's eyes. Shhh, please, urged Fleur's. Albert's friend shook some cornflakes into a bowl and carefully poured milk over them.

I'm not going anywhere, I said, unable to stop my incredulous laughter. I stood there, barefoot, my arms crossed. No one said anything. What now, I wondered. Do I leave my family standing here in the kitchen with two police officers, and wait upstairs until they call for armed back-up to come and drag me out of the house?

The story of the man with the chair leg suddenly popped into my head. I'd read about it in one of the free papers you get on the Tube, the ones that seem to report exclusively on murder and manslaughter cases. I used to be amazed at London's crime rate, which wasn't something I had a sense of from my surroundings at all, until I realised that some of the incidents they reported on had happened over a decade ago. It didn't need to be news to feature in those papers, it just had to keep readers engaged for the Tube ride. People don't need the truth, they need sensation, so the same murder ballad was churned out again and again, as long as it was gory enough to keep readers' interest. One of these stories was about a man who had resisted arrest in a pub. I couldn't remember why. He hid behind the bar while the cops repeatedly warned him to surrender. But he didn't surrender, instead he opened fire, or pretended to, at which point one officer lost his nerve and shot him dead. It turned out that the man didn't have a gun, just a chair leg. Maybe he was drunk. Maybe he had reached the point where he couldn't give up, even if he had wanted to. I remembered that feeling as a child. It felt like my defiance was completely uncoupled from my free will. That morning, I needed to not reach that point.

The policewoman explained to me once again that I needed to come to the station now. She addressed me as sir three times in one sentence. I assumed that this was a technique from their training on how to de-escalate a situation. I had become grounds for de-escalation. Her colleague tried to move as slowly as possible, his jacket rustling as he went to pull something out of his pocket, presumably his walkie-talkie. Of course, we'll come, said Fleur all of a sudden. My wife was laying down the law now. Now it was Albert and I who were glancing at each other. She went to fetch our coats and placed a clean pair of shoes at my feet. As she moved about, she carried on chatting away to the police officers, asking them to meet us around the back. No matter the outcome of all this, if they came out the front the neighbours would see it as a double arrest, and that would live on forever in the collective memory of the street. Did that make sense? The policemen looked at each other and nodded. The younger officer went outside to bring the car around the back. The two boys sat in silence at the kitchen table, vigilantly following our every move like meerkats. My husband isn't racist, Fleur said as we headed out. It's burnout. He's sick.

Fleur

I would never have imagined him freaking out in such spectacular fashion. And yet, looking back, it was inevitable that something would happen at some point. I have a thing for predictions, especially in hindsight, which is even more absurd, so I usually keep them to myself.

The night before Gabriel got back, I was out in the car with Albert and his French friend Julien. The boys were sitting in the back, and Albert was just telling Julien what he didn't like about my driving when I hit a black cat.

I will never forget the scream of the old woman whose cat it was. Her pain was so intense that I thought she was about to collapse on the pavement and die. At the same time I couldn't stop thinking, thank God it wasn't a child, thank God it wasn't a child. Maybe I even said it out loud. The boys sprang into action. Julien looked after the cat; Albert googled the nearest vet. I dragged myself out of the car and almost fell to my knees in front of the old woman, I was so sorry for everything. My Buster, my Buster, my Buster, she whimpered, while I said sorry over and over. Two cracked discs, it was horrible. The cat was alive but we had no time to lose, and her owner was frail and in her dressing gown, so we promised to bring the cat back as soon as possible, and we drove off with it. If it hadn't been illegal, I would have let my fifteen-year-old son drive, because by now I really was driving like a maniac. As always when I get worked up, I no longer knew left from right. I clung to the steering wheel, trembling, while Albert navigated, muttering reassuringly to the cat in between instructions. Go left, not right! Okay, then take the next left up ahead. Buster, we're almost there, hang in there, mate.

His T-shirt and hands were covered in Buster's blood, and I was so impressed with him. He usually runs away screaming when it comes to other people's bodily fluids. We waited in the corridor while the cat was being treated.

I always wanted a black cat, but my dad wouldn't let me, Albert told Julien.

First I'd heard of this – Albert's wish or Gabriel's refusal. There's a childhood photo of Gabriel with a large black cat with white paws. He's so tiny that, in contrast, the cat beside him looks like a tiger.

He had a black cat himself, I said. It was called Mohrle. Funny, huh?

Albert just looked at me and asked, in his economical way: Really?

What does that mean? asked Julien, who didn't know Gabriel, who didn't know the whole subject of Gabriel and his background, because although Albert described himself as Black, he didn't look it.

Mohr is German for moor, an old word for a Black man, I explained to Julien in French. Same root as the name Maurice. Not a word people use nowadays, I added.

Why, of all people, did *he* name his cat that? Albert asked.

I imagine it was his grandparents who named it that. It was just a popular name for black cats, like Blacky.

Okay, cool, I'll call myself Mohr from now on, Albert said. Because I'm not allowed to use the n-word anymore, not even for myself, he explained to Julien, who looked at him thoughtfully. It was the kind of moment when I should have said something of pedagogical value, but thankfully the vet's assistant finally came out.

The cat survived. I didn't interpret it as a bad omen or anything. I don't see any signs at all in cats. I was mainly worried that from now on I would be even more reluctant to drive than I already was. We drove back from the vet's clinic to Buster's owner, gave her the all-clear, and then the boys got to gorge themselves on burgers while I sat there thinking that maybe it wasn't all so bad. Gabriel was having his time off; Albert had stopped treating me like his nemesis. Perhaps it was the presence of the refreshingly mild-mannered Julien that meant I felt less anxious than usual. I even left my phone in my handbag, uncharged, so I didn't get the message that Gabriel had decided to take an earlier flight and was looking forward to having breakfast with us. Later, I wondered if everything might have been different if I hadn't been fast asleep like Mummy Bear when he got in but, instead, had welcomed him home like a wife who was happy to see him again.

Gabriel

When I moved to London, I felt I could only stay here if I could prove myself worthy. I didn't have that feeling at all in Berlin. Why would I, with the pace of life and the prices? My last months there had felt like I was sitting in a stuffy waiting room. I had finished my bachelor's degree at TU Berlin and was living in a badly converted attic in Tiergarten, where it was unbearably hot in summer. That was when I discovered the stock market. Every day I lay around in my underpants in front of the muted TV, watching the fate of my shares and listening to Bach, who suited my mood well. A perfectionist who must have struggled with his God who kept taking his children away from him. My problems were minor in comparison: heartbreak. At twenty-five, I was rather late to seeing what the big deal was. But now I knew, when the woman I loved broke my heart. Although in truth, I didn't really know what I saw in her. Not that that made it any less painful when she coldly booted me out of her life. I was grateful to her in retrospect, though, because that was the point when I realised again that I wanted to leave Germany. I decided to do my Master of Architecture in London. The best decision of my life.

New in London, I felt like I was applying for a job. I wanted to do everything right. I became obsessed with fitting in. Like anyone adopting a new identity, I closely observed Londoners and their customs. Rushing and waiting followed very different patterns of behaviour to German cities. I launched myself in the swarm of people and learned to swim along with the flow. At first, I stared at other people. As discreetly as possible, but I stared all the same. I wasn't as sophisticated and worldly wise as I liked to think I was. I had grown up in a country with a predominantly homogeneous population. In other words, everyone was from the same tribe. With relatively few exceptions, like me, for example. By the nineties it was starting to be different in Berlin, but still no comparison with London, where for the first time I understood the people who used to drive me crazy with their gawking when I was a child. It isn't very cosmopolitan to stare at other people like they're aliens, but on the other hand, what's more fascinating than other people? Whenever I was on the Tube, I wondered if there was any type of person you wouldn't see there. No, if some group seemed to be missing, sooner or later they'd get on. A trip around the world on the Central Line. It wasn't long until I appreciated that part of the social survival strategy was giving each other a wide berth and, as far as possible, avoiding catching anyone's eye. Our brains can only cope with a limited number of faces. What I had initially misinterpreted as insensitivity was an intuitive self-defence against going mad.

In the years after we qualified, and before we set up our first office, we worked almost around the clock for Higgs & Partners. Sir Alan Higgs had everything I dreamed of: the right commissions worldwide, a Pritzker Prize, a Stirling Prize, and an OBE – the title of the Most Excellent Order of the British Empire. He had earned all that from his sometimes innovative, sometimes revolutionary, and sometimes just impressive projects, developed in his offices in London, Boston, and Hong Kong, which were crammed full of the staff who implemented his ideas: us. Hard-working termites in black polo-necks, ninety per cent male, who poured one hundred per cent of their manpower into the superorganism. If we had been a state, we would have created the model of communism. Or an autocracy of aesthetics. The wonderful thing about the marvellous world of Sir Alan was that I was genuinely glad for him, even though I coveted his success for myself. He came from a poor background in the north of England, a setting where, in the early 1940s no one had the leisure to care about beauty or light, and now here he was enthroned on the top floor of his own skyscraper in the City, eye to eye with the sun. An ascent so metaphorical and real at the same time that decades later its spirit still wafted through his office spaces as though through a lofty cathedral. I enjoyed working for Sir Alan and his visions. In a smaller office I would have been more visible as an individual, but his name was important for my CV, as much as he as a person was good for my own faith in my future.

When I think back to that time, I see myself sitting in that office, working on my renderings, the London sky full of cranes looming beyond the tinted windows, and Mark Barnett always somewhere nearby. Higgs was the second company where I had worked with Mark, after we met during our master's. We were faced with the question of whether our aim was to become partners – higher-ranking termites – or whether we should jump ship and start again under our own names. We were out drinking every night between nine in the evening and two in the morning. After that we'd sleep, and then the same cycle the next day. We survived that heady era with exclusively good results. There is no other way to put it. First, we went from being classmates to friends. Then, our hangovers left us in a state of frustration with the delusions of grandeur, from which the only escape was to finally start our own company. We were in our late twenties and had the sense that time was racing by. In fact, we were the ones who were racing.

The question of where I'm from seemed irrelevant like never before in my life, until the day they handed me that form. For a few days, I hadn't quite registered that my throat was more sore than normal, that I had tonsillitis. I vaguely remembered a suggestion of them being removed when I was a child and my grandfather refusing. The boy would stay whole, he insisted. But I was in so much pain now that I was having to spit surreptitiously into the bin at work, because every time I gulped it felt like swallowing razors. Until Higgs personally sent me to the doctor. The company driver took me to an NHS walk-in centre in Soho. Free health insurance for all: how socialist, I thought. Hopefully I would soon have private insurance and could go to a doctor in Harley Street.

So, I walked into this health centre that looked exactly as I imagined – state-owned, austere, and oversubscribed – and went up to the reception desk, where an older Black lady with elaborate cornrows handed me a form to fill in. It was the most astonishing official document I had ever seen. Not because they were enquiring about previous illnesses, allergies, or addictions. No, the astonishing thing was the question about the ethnicity to which you belonged.

Category A was White. White people had to tick whether they were British, Irish, Irish Travellers, that is without fixed abode, White EU citizens, or *other White*. There was an extra box for EU White people from Ireland. It was absurd; I assumed the lady had accidentally given me a form intended for internal use.

Category B covered *mixed/multiple ethnic groups*, that is, me. Here they distinguished between White and Black from the Caribbean, White and Black from Africa, White and Asian, and other mixes, which presumably would include the combination of Black and Asian, though it wasn't cited.

Asians, ethnic group C, were subdivided into people from India, Pakistan, Bangladesh, China, and other Asians.

Category D divided Black into Caribbean, African, and British Black. Plus: *any other Black*.

E was the group for others, split into Arabs and any other.

I sat in this neon-lit room that so perfectly encapsulated London: every one of the groups listed on the form was represented here in this waiting room. Every one of these groups was featured among my new work colleagues; I saw them walking down Oxford Street; they were gourmets of fine dining and fast food junkies. Some were homeless, some were billionaires, and some were totally ordinary people stuck in traffic. That was why I was here in London. With everyone else. I had never seen so many different kinds of people genuinely interacting with each other; neither had I ever seen so many mixed couples. So unlike the supposed melting pot of New York, where it was more a matter of diverse coexistence than a genuine mix. I always found the almost religious veneration of New York a bit suspect. My German friends assumed I would feel especially comfortable in the States, as though I had finally found a place where I belonged. So colourful over there! Finally I would no longer be the only one. True, I now belonged to a group. My belonging was cast in cement. But over there in the States, before I was an architect, before I was European, before I was allowed to be something, I was Black. Hundred per cent. I belonged to that group of people for whom taxi drivers never stopped, who really fucked up real estate prices if they bought a property in the area, who – when things really went wrong – made the police trigger happy. Was that what I wanted? I had grown up among White people, and it was obvious that I wasn't White. But in the USA it no longer mattered that my mum was White. Look at Barack

Obama: his White mum almost never got a mention. Fifty per cent White by ethnicity, hundred per cent by education, but it was almost as if she didn't exist; for Black people and White alike, this man was Black. What annoyed me wasn't being seen as Black; it was the obsession with colour in the States and the one-drop rule. I've always wondered why White people assume that their highly prized genetic material should completely disappear after one generation. Obama's success presumably lay in the fact that he was from abroad, that his father wasn't a US Black American. So he wasn't part of the curse that plagued that history. When, around the millennium, I was asked to go to Boston with Higgs & Partners, I declined. I had no desire to be a 'one of my best friends is Black' token Black man. I would rather stay in London, where I get asked at the doctor's surgery which Black and White combination I consist of.

I hadn't expected a questionnaire like this at the time. London was no paradise, but it felt so post-racist that it was tempting to assume it was really just about money. It's for the census, said the receptionist when I asked her what it was all about and what she thought of it. She looked at me as if we were in a restaurant and I was asking why she was handing me a menu.

So the NHS employee, herself a category D, found me more dubious than this form, even though large employers were constantly bombarding their employees with seminars, workshops, and communications on every variety of political correctness. Strange.

My statistics brain launched into action. I must have spent at least two hours in that waiting room. I stared at the form and at the other people waiting, thinking it over and over. The whole concept of ethnicity didn't work when you looked closely at these awkward categories: if you took continent of origin as a basis then Arabs were Asians, just like Indians, Pakistanis, or Chinese. Ethnically, on the other hand, that is in terms of skin colour, they were White, like Iranians, Central Asians, Turks. In France, Arabs would be people from the Maghreb, that is, in terms of the continent, Africans, but not Black Africans, emphatically so, like with Hispanics, who didn't feature here in England, because this wasn't the US where non-English-speaking Americans were shoehorned into the category of Hispanics, and therefore seen as non-White regardless of their skin colour, which must really wind up the Whites among them, while perhaps the Black and indigenous people couldn't care less.

The concept of ethnicity still didn't work even if you divided the White people into EU White and other White backgrounds, or if you put the EU Whites from Ireland into a subcategory, and added the subgroup of Travellers, i.e. a distinction based on way of life. The White category was most clearly based on a racial distinction; on the other hand, it was Category A, presumably because it constituted the largest percentage.

That in turn would have meant that the second largest population group in Britain would have fallen under category B: mixed, like me. Was it by colour after all, or by proportion of Whiteness? This questionnaire was so flawed that I forgot about the pain I was in, but it put me in an almost manic mood. I felt like I was at a maths Olympiad but knowing that the problem we'd been set couldn't be solved. There were no clear delineations.

As I thought about how I would improve this survey, because that should always be the focus when you complain about something, I noticed how much I was sweating. My boss had given me a painkiller and had slipped it to me in such a covert, conspiratorial way, as if it were an illicit party drug, and maybe it was, because he said *bon voyage*. Here I was sitting in this hideous light surrounded by sick people from all over the world, who wanted to see a doctor here in Soho, but would probably end up seeing a nurse, trying to reform the way the British categorised ethnic groups.

There was so much coughing around me and mucus being secreted, that I wouldn't have been able to stick it out without having the questionnaire to focus on. One of the problems was that all the categories were intermingled. But a population could be multi-ethnic and include different state affiliations. So therefore the creators of this form couldn't simply ask: Are you a British citizen (A) or foreign (B), and if (B), please state your nationality. Instead it opened up endless ways to offend people, given the way categories are ordered, named, not named, the use of the word 'other'. There was no logical, rigorous way to do this.

This ethnicity form was a revelation, because I had never thought in so much detail before about how people might define themselves. Country, continent, language, common struggle, religion. With some it seems straightforward, with others not at all. Would an Uzbek feel Asian, White, Muslim, or, as resident of a former republic of the Soviet Union, would they feel European? What would an Israeli put down here? What did Irish and Irish Travellers think about their special boxes? Maybe they joked about it, perhaps they were unfazed by the question, perhaps they insisted on this distinction and had even lobbied for it. I had no idea. Though it seemed to me you were at an advantage if you didn't care about these questions.

I did care about them. But it hadn't occurred to me that I would be asked them again. At least not here. I was sitting in a room where a good third of the people present had my skin colour. Brown. As a child, people often told me I had a beautiful skin colour, by which they meant that at least I wasn't completely Black. Sometimes they even said that. They said it with the full confidence that they were paying me a compliment. And would have been shocked if I had questioned it or even called it out as racist. Which, of course, I didn't do. I was little and I thought the world I lived in was normal. And I was alone. If I had had Black relatives, I would have read more into what people said. Sometimes when I saw Black people in town, mostly men, and they gave me a conspiratorial wink or said hello, I wondered if they were thinking the same: at least you're not all White. One of us left you here, kiddo. I was like Gulliver, either too *this* or too *that*. That all sounds more dramatic than it is. It's not like I was incessantly agonising over the question of identity. Nor did I particularly care what other people said. They were coming from an evaluation system that they weren't even aware of. An evaluation system that ultimately is based on not trusting the clan from the neighbouring village. All that notwithstanding, even if I couldn't articulate this at that time, when anyone praised my skin colour it always felt unpleasant, because I understood the subliminal message: *it could be even worse*. I wished that none of this was an issue at all. That wasn't me being idealistic. It was me thinking: can't you just leave me in peace?

Officials in Germany never asked questions about ethnicity, presumably for historical reasons. Not in the East or the West, not even today. All the same, when I received my first ID card at the age of fourteen, I had expected to see a reference to my otherness. But in the line next to *Special Characteristics* it said: none. I asked the woman at the office what sort of thing would be mentioned there. She said, a scar or a glass eye, for example.

After an eternity of thinking about it, I finally ticked the boxes making up my combination. EU White and African Black. Later, I wondered which boxes my son might tick: a Brit who was three-quarters White with a Black grandfather he didn't know. So I was a B, though I had always considered myself an A-type. No more questions. It was a racial questionnaire and made no effort to disguise the fact, for example, with follow-up questions about health, education, income, or place of residence. I would have liked to fill in my postcode: W1. After all, at the time almost my entire income went on having that postcode. I had achieved all this without my parents and they were the ones being asked about here. I was almost thirty years old, and it seemed as though the question of where I was from would never go away.

Fleur

With most people, you have to get to know them before you realise that they're utter bastards. With Gabriel it's the other way around. You have to get to know him before you find out that he's not.

After the attack on the girl, making him look like a bastard was no challenge at all. That's the fate of overachievers: people don't trust them. People wonder where their weakness lies, the abyss that tempts them. Their elaborate way of mastering life is a constant humiliation for others. People think swots are capable of anything. They imagine the worst inner demons, maybe even wish them on them. Not necessarily out of schadenfreude, but for the sake of balance. Too much of a good thing is like too much yin. Or yang?

Gabriel had already lost his balance long ago – something he did not like to hear. Just as little as he wanted to hear the words *overworked*, *overloaded*, *overwhelmed*, words that added up to the term *burnout*, which he also couldn't stand. If it had been diabetes, he'd have taken it seriously, but burnout was nothing more than a lifestyle word for him. Take some time off, I often said to him. I meant it seriously, but it was completely useless advice. You might just as well tell an addict to change his addictive behaviour. When I thought about how Gabriel had got to this point, it struck me that he'd had no choice. He wouldn't have had the success he'd had if he wasn't the way he was.

That's why time off made no difference. I remember the exhausting weeks we spent in remote places. Gabriel, running up and down, impatiently waiting for his long-planned high-speed relaxation to come into effect. Gabriel, no longer talking, but barking into his phone, because the more tired he was, the more the control freak came out. When he finally lay on a sun lounger, it didn't look like he was reading so much as thinking: I'm reading a book, I'm reading a book, I'm having time off, so I'm reading. A book.

When I met Gabriel, he seemed heaven-sent. He acted like he hadn't even existed before he became an architect. As though he had invented himself and set himself to work. He had composed himself of qualities he admired and that were useful to him, which made him less of an organic whole than someone with a privileged background, but that was what I liked about him. He was alone in the world, but not without roots. On the contrary. He slotted into the world. He was content. With where he lived, with his job, and with us, with me and Albert. Because he wanted it that way. A considerable part of his energy went into maintaining the conviction that his life was perfect.

I was born in London, but he was the one who felt at home here. My parents were ophthalmologists, and I spent my childhood in East Africa. I always thought I would go back there. Not necessarily Kenya, where we lived most of the time, but definitely somewhere where you have to sit out the midday heat inside in the cool. That was my only concept of the future. A hazy image of me lying on a white bed under a whirring fan. I never quite worked out what I would be lying there recovering from.

Right after I graduated, I started translating, just because that's how things turned out. Thanks to my last name, I started straight out with books that got some attention. The fact that I had grown up multilingual and had studied literature should have freed me from feeling like an impostor. But what are facts in the face of feelings? So I busied myself with literary stars and heavyweights who reinforced my sense that I myself was worthless. At the same time, I loved what I was doing. I was doing something I knew how to do. I translated my mother's French into my father's English, taking care not to lose anything along the way. None of the poetry, the wit, the slang, the spirit, the sound. For an insignificantly brief period I also wrote for a newspaper, first in the editorial office, then from home, then finally not at all. Every day, I'd get up when I wanted, put on what I wanted, and sit down to work where I wanted, and with every day the possibility of ever working in an office or on a team again started to evaporate, until eventually it vanished altogether. When I met Gabriel, the possibility of living anywhere other than London also vanished.

I'm from Germany, said the man who fell from the heavens. In Germany, the question of where he was from had been much more painful and tedious to answer. Yes, you speak German and you seem to have been born here, but where are you *really* from? He detested that, just as much as he hated questions about his father, which was quite understandable since he had no answers.

I'm from Kenya, I'd say, when I came back to England at fourteen for my final years of school. I didn't say it to give myself airs – it was quite obvious that I was from somewhere else. Especially at an age when everyone defined themselves by their favourite bands or by TV shows I'd never heard of. I adapted to their language and the way they dressed pretty quickly, but I never quite shook off the feeling of having just arrived. Perhaps because I liked it that way. Gabriel lived here because that was his plan, and yet we both remained immigrants. He with his accent, and me who never stopped getting lost, the eternal newcomer.

Seen in terms of skin colour, our primary school photos are almost a mirror image. At the time, my parents were working on their life's mission, building a medical centre in a Kenyan provincial town, which didn't have an international school, so I was enrolled at the local school. We children look as if we had had it drilled into us not to waste the photographer's time. We're standing there all prim and proper, staring into the camera. On the far right is the only White face, in front of our teacher's black nun's habit. I peer out from under my fringe like a shy ghost. There's less of a contrast between Gabriel's skin colour and his classmates', but he still stands out. In his class photo, it looks as if someone had shouted to the children: smile! While Gabriel is the only one who was told: stand still! He's standing straight as a post, looking directly into the camera. He still does the same. His look seems to say: you lot are you and I am me.

He's cute, my friend Bella said after I'd introduced her to him. He always wore black back then, preferably Yamamoto, and a pair of Le Corbusier glasses, which robbed his face of any approachability. Once we were really going out I wouldn't let him wear them. He also worked a fourteen-hour day, and although he was really trying to show an interest in my friend, he yawned a tad too often.

Maybe not cute exactly, I replied.

Yeah, but you've finally found someone to share your passion for Africa with, she said.

I was already really into him, but even this impression was deceptive.

Gabriel

When we launched our own business, I worked as much as Mark, and drank as much too, but I had more time. Because Mark was a ladies' man, while I had a problem with communication. All that call back, don't call back, second date, hold off for a while, breaking up diplomatically and gallantly, splitting up amicably – I saw it all the time with Mark, but I couldn't do it. He wanted sex; I wanted to get married. I was on a hopeless quest for the perfect match. Dream on, I said to myself, but I still wasn't ready to compromise. I seemed to completely lack that natural gift, without which the human race would have long since died out, that capacity to present myself to women as a man free of superstructure, and preferred topics, and a long, complicated list of things we had to have in common. Women who saw through all that and took the initiative were great in theory, but in reality their domineering approach was too far from my firmly defined ideals. Later on I realised what a fool I was not to make the most of that time. While I waited to find the perfect woman, why didn't I play the field a bit more? I was young, looked acceptable, something I sadly only appreciated in hindsight, was earning relatively well, and I used to go around London with Mark Barnett, which felt like walking through a wasps' nest carrying a cake. But instead of taking advantage of these favourable conditions, I always just presumed that any women buzzing around us had their sights set just on Mark. I had no awareness of myself as a person. At least not as a sexual being. I made up for this compulsive abstinence with work. I was waiting for Fleur, though I didn't know her yet.

I'm a romantic, I said.

You're a freak, said Mark.

Then I was introduced to Sybil, and it was immediately obvious why. One of my colleagues was getting married, and everyone at the entire wedding seemed to agree that the person I was sat next to at the dinner and I were a match made in heaven. Ah, I see, the table plan is arranged by skin colour, Sybil said, as she sat down next to me, and I couldn't help but like her. Sybil's mother was from Ghana, and it was from Sybil that I learned about the imaginative colour spectrum the cosmetics industry had dreamed up for our skin tone: Golden Almond, Honey, Chestnut. Butter Pecan. Caramel, Praline, Brulée, Toffee. Dark Ginger. Camel. Desert Beige. Beige Noisette or Beige Châtaigne. Rattan. Ambre Dorée. And Cardboard? That was my complexion back then, a time when I tended to neglect my health. I assumed that the lighter tones were Alabaster, Pearl or Panna Cotta, and the darker ones Espresso, Dark Chocolate, or Liquorice. These were the thoughts I had when I had to fight my way through the mountains of cosmetics in Sybil's pigsty of a bathroom, because her apartment was so small that I retreated there when I needed a short rest from her or had to make a phone call. I had met the messiest woman in the world. She was an amazing person and I enjoyed every hour with her, but only because I knew our time was limited. Sybil, the Thrill, as Mark called her, never missed an opportunity to remind me that she wasn't interested in a long-term relationship with a square like me. Great, I thought, that saved me from needing to think about whether or not she met my standards. I was spending my spare time with a beautiful, smart woman, and

I didn't have to tell myself inwardly that it wasn't forever, because she already made that quite explicit.

However, the only way in which our relationship differed from a steady relationship was that we claimed it wasn't. And then there were a few dos and don'ts, defined exclusively by Sybil. No parental contact, which was fine with me because it would have been one-sided, anyway, and it might have suggested something long term to her parents, Alice and Norman, who lived in Kent, which wasn't our intention. Another aspect of our non-relationship was never using 'we' when speaking about us as a couple. In other contexts, Sybil used 'we' all the time, using it to mean us as a tribe. A tribe that was allowed to expand, contract, and rename itself at will. We were the non-Whites, the half-castes, biracial, or mixed-race people, people of colour, brown people, yellow people, or simply just Black people, and, of course, brothers and sisters. We were the oppressed, the underrepresented, the discriminated against, the members of a minority, the disenfranchised. This obsessive 'we' was something totally new for me, an idea I found attractive at first. This is how it might have been if I had had siblings. This is how it might have been if I had grown up in another country. But my status as a lone wolf was undermined by being included in Sybil's group, and it wasn't long before it started to feel like collective punishment, because actually, I was used to being the only one, and I had no desire to form a Black empowerment partnership.

Sybil, you're not Black; your father is White.

But no one cares about that.

I do, and presumably your father does, too.

Oh, shut up, Oreo.

At first I thought she said Orpheo, and that she was confusing Orpheus and Othello, until I realised she was referring to me as a black cookie with a white filling. According to her, I was a wannabe White guy, battling on an almost daily basis with what she saw as the truth and what I saw as paranoia.

Sybil, the guy wasn't racist, he was just annoyed that your credit card didn't work.

Sybil, we couldn't get a table because the restaurant was full. And anyway, it wasn't a video call, was it?

He could tell from my voice. What do you think?

Voice, hair, skin, soul. The colour of our skin was imposed onto every topic and turned every topic into an argument.

Sorry, Sybil, I don't walk around all day thinking, I'm Black, I'm Black, oh God, I'm Black! I also don't think all day about the fact that I'm a man, that there are tiny organisms living on my eyelashes, that at some point I was squeezed through a birth canal. It's all fascinating, but I also have other things to think about besides those God-given facts. Don't you see?

I felt sorry for Sybil and the way she was constantly downgrading her own existence. She sounded like someone planning a slave revolt, but she was a middle-class British woman who worked in a large modelling agency and only ever wore designer clothes. She hated me for reminding her of this. But I actually admired the way she juggled her two worlds. She approached the fashion world and the fight against discrimination with the same passion.

I had come to London to become one of many. Now I was one of many, although the precise group to which I belonged was defined by my girlfriend who didn't want to be my girlfriend. I had intended to deal exclusively with objects and people I cared about and to feel at home in a city that would let me be myself. Now it felt like I had to rewrite my perspective on my own life, to my own disadvantage. No, you're not a well-dressed guy who dines at fancy restaurants;

you're branded, and you're in hostile territory. Sybil made London out to be pre-1994 Johannesburg or some southern state backwater teeming with the Ku Klux Klan.

And then with Sybil I had the skin colour stress from the other direction, which was no less depressing. We were taking a minicab, and it was clear the driver and Sybil hated each other from the first second. No, this isn't some kind of brother-sister thing, I thought to myself. People either like each other or they don't, that's all there is to it. The driver was bad-tempered, his car was filthy, his driving style was abysmal, his route was a ruse. Everything about it was so obviously bad that I wondered if Sybil would let him get away with it because he was Black. But no. He made the cardinal mistake of playing music that was too idiotic for Sybil and too loud for me. His fusty Honda was like being trapped in a cage with a predator. Sybil scolded him with her husky voice that I usually found so sexy. The driver drowned her out with his falsetto shriek that was at odds with his bulky torso, calling her a yellow bitch-cunt-slut, every insult he could think of. The key aspect seemed to be the fact that she was lighter skinned than him. He carried on shouting, saying she was from the Caribbean, which wasn't true, that she was descended from slaves unlike him, and that she was the last one with the right to give him orders. Speechless, I handed him his money, pressed it into his flailing hands and dragged Sybil out of the car. As he drove off, he shook his head indignantly, rolled his eyes and pointed at Sybil, as if to say, no offence, man, but get a grip on your girl! Sybil had her phone pressed to her ear, cursing all the while, as she tried to get through to the switchboard to complain. I stood there beside her, shaken, on a drafty street corner in a run-down neighbourhood, wondering if we were nothing but a few billion vicious creatures whose sole purpose was to make each other's lives a living hell. No, I decided, as we got into the next cab, driven by a normal human being, there's surely the same proportion of complete dickheads in any population. That was what I was constantly trying to tell Sybil. Our daily arguments were keeping us up at night and were wearing me out. And at some point, I became firmly convinced of an opinion that I had adopted at first purely for the sake of winding her up.

You want to make it all about colour? Leave me out of it. And I'll tell you why. Because skin colour as a criterion for discrimination is the basis for every kind of racism. The only people who are led by it are avowed racists. But if this distinction is complete nonsense, as it has indeed been proven to be, why should I be led by it? Why should I allow myself to be assigned to a group that doesn't even exist?

Because it might not exist scientifically, but socially it does. Just accept it. You can't just walk away from identity issues when you're part of a marginalised group, shouted Sybil, who depending on the context could sound like a library or a prison canteen. Did I love her? Most of the time, yes.

I'll say it again: I don't want to be pigeonholed. White people pick and choose what matters to them and what doesn't. I'm also claiming that privilege.

Okay. Your father wasn't there, you don't know your people, so you don't feel emotionally obligated. Or maybe you're angry at your father and that's why you reject your Black side.

My missing father was her knock-out argument. When she saw my full name on my driver's licence, she started calling me Idris, although I asked her not to. I am not Idris; I am Gabriel. I was asking myself more and more often why I put myself through this. Why, after a long day at work, did I need her insisting I was a trauma patient with an identity problem, resistance personified, or an Uncle Tom? It seemed to me that every conversation ended up in the same place. Again and again I told her, every which way, that the best way for people to define themselves and unite around a cause was by any characteristic other than skin colour. The last time we lay side by side, naked, I said: another person is not my brother because of something physical we have in common, in this case our skin pigmentation. On the other hand, all people are my brothers.

A brotherhood of men! Sybil laughed.

Exactly. Just imagine.

The truth was that Sybil had actually become more like a sister. I enjoyed her physical closeness, but I didn't want to sleep with her anymore, and neither did I want to think about why that was. I could hate her and love her again almost straight away, a seamless transition I had never experienced with anyone else. When I came to London, I briefly imagined that families like hers were what my childhood could have looked like: a mixed couple who stayed together and raised their children together. A normal family. Perhaps it was a psychological disaster that Sybil and I were in constant comparison in this way, but that's how it was.

Her parents had bought her a flat in a council estate in Lambeth, which bothered me more than the question of why a certain service provider didn't look at us nicely enough. I'd always been in favour of a free market but was strangely irritated by the idea of turning public housing into private property in this expensive city. The question of empathy for people who essentially had nothing to do with you: that was always the ultimate bone of contention. If I can say one thing about Sybil, it was that she constantly pressed me on topics to which I would otherwise have given very little thought. I still have the books she gave me: Frantz Fanon, Frederick Douglass,

James Baldwin, Dany Laferrière, Toni Morrison. Of them all, I only really read Laferrière: *How to Make Love to a Negro Without Getting Tired*. But did I care about Black Hollywood stars and celebrity models? No. I wasn't interested in their White counterparts either. But the thought of selling off apartments that were supposed to be reserved for the destitute, that was what really got me worked up. That was what I always tried to make her understand: everyone has their issues they care about, and mine was urban coexistence. This wasn't about skin colour; it was about money. When she showed me her new apartment, we met an old man in the lift in his Sunday best, a suit he had clearly treasured for many years. He had a silk handkerchief in his breast pocket and a bag of rubbish in his hand. When he reached the ground floor, he nodded to us and walked out. Sybil needed to go straight back upstairs because she had left her sunglasses in the empty apartment. I followed the old man outside and wondered if I should offer to take his rubbish out for him. No, I decided, he didn't need my sympathy. I went to the car, he to the rubbish bins. We drove past him on his way to the station, Sybil full of plans for her new place, and me worrying about gentrification, for the first time not as a purely theoretical topic. I watched the old man as we drove past and had the feeling that he nodded to me again.

He should be glad it's not gangsters moving in but workaholics like me, Sybil said. Anyway, aren't you guys building some massive place with a helipad on the roof? Who knows how many old cronies were evicted to make space for that? Since when did you become so sentimental?

I couldn't say. I saw at least twenty homeless people every day, but this old man clinging on to his Sunday best as much as to the era when he had bought it, before he was forgotten and overrun, suddenly seemed like this symbolic figure. Symbolic of what exactly, I didn't know. Perhaps this was the moment when I realised that I myself would eventually be old, too.

What's the matter, Oreo, are you thinking about your grandfather? asked Sybil.

Maybe, I said.

I invoked my status as her non-boyfriend and reminded her of her status as an independent woman. I didn't help her with moving into the flat, or with doing it up, which turned out to be a bigger job than she had expected. Sybil – who saw herself as either Ashanti warrior or damsel in distress depending on her mood – was furious. The warrior threatened me, while Little Miss Helpless acted like she couldn't even decide where to put her dining table without me. After I said in no uncertain terms that I was an architect and not an interior decorator, there was a silence between us that I found to be a pleasant respite. I was flying to China for the first time. She was off to Ghana. Fine, I thought, we'll head off around the world and meet again in London. Almost ten years after the fall of the Berlin Wall, I was grateful for my continuing capacity for gratitude. I was thankful for my freedom of movement, thankful for my job, thankful for the people whom I could only meet here in this life, including Sybil.

She broke off all contact. She wrote me a terse email that closed with a warning not to call her ever again. I saw her again once, at a launch event for a flagship store. She was standing among a few people of a similar height as her, models from her agency, I assumed. They towered over the black-clad crowd like poplars. When our eyes met, she shook her head slowly and turned back to face the person she was talking to. No one spoke to Sybil unless she wanted to be addressed. Especially not in public. Why did she reject me so radically? To this day, I still don't know.

Fleur

Call Mark's friend, I had written in my Filofax. I knew Mark Barnett in passing, I didn't know his friend at all, but he'd been so kind as to take me home when I was wasted so – as Mark shouted in my ear at a party – I owed him a drink, at least, didn't I? Oh yeah, I said, sure, absolutely.

Gabriel (Mark B's friend) – 3 pm, it said in my Filofax the day we finally met up. He didn't compliment me, he sized me up. As though he needed a moment to decide if he liked me or not. If I had expected something from this date, I might have been put off by his strange behaviour, but as it was I found it amusing. He was the one who wanted to meet me so badly, and he was a distraction from Sean, who I still thought of as the man of my life at that point. If I heard from Sean, it was a good day, a bad one if I didn't. Gabriel had caught me on a bad day. I hoped it would at least turn out a neutral day, that I'd get drunk enough to forget about Sean.

I summoned him to a pub near me and made it screamingly obvious in my choice of clothes that I was not out to seduce him. A code that usually even the dimmest men can read, though clearly not Gabriel. You'd think I was wearing a ball gown from the way he acted. His English gentleman look was flawless, he'd clearly worked hard at it. And yet he was a total mismatch. His German uptightness didn't match his appearance; his chivalrous manners didn't match his brutal frankness. When he was rude it wasn't a flirting tactic – this man who would later become my husband did not flirt. When he was rude it was just his way of expressing what he thought.

And if what he thought seemed unutterable even by him, he'd package it as an example from a French film or Greek mythology. My attempts to add a touch of laidback irony to our conversation just bounced off unnoticed. All the same, I liked him more from one beer to the next. The more he seemed to disapprove of my clothes, and my drinking, and my smoking, the more comfortable I felt.

He paid me a compliment at Nagoya, probably not even realising it. It was late afternoon, and the restaurant was empty. Except for us and Mick Jagger, who was sitting there with a couple of other people, who were practically invisible because this was Mick Jagger. I interrupted Gabriel, shhh, look around. Gabriel looked around, but straight away turned back to me and repeated his question. It wasn't that he was pretending an A-list celebrity didn't impress him, he was genuinely waiting for my answer. My intention had been to have a nice time with no strings attached, which he had interpreted as an obligation for us to genuinely get to know each other. He created a sort of hermetic space around us to achieve this, which only the waiters could briefly enter. And it worked. It was the longest continuous period of time in months that I didn't think about Sean. When he talked about architecture, he had that sparkle you get only with people who are doing something they really love. I didn't have that something in my life, so I was fascinated seeing his eyes twinkle. It was only later when he spoke about his father, prompted by my question, that he drew back and sounded like he was giving a brief overview of a subject that had nothing to do with him. People like his father, who had the fortune – or perhaps misfortune – of studying in East Germany were supposed to leave the country again after the standard duration of a degree course, and they usually did. An almost forgotten aspect of Eastern Bloc history: the strategy of luring the new independent states over to their side now that they were no longer colonies. Why not try a little socialism? A political gambit without victims, for once: just a few thousand graduates who left the GDR to go who knows where. And a few thousand women left behind with children, as always happens when men appear and then disappear again.

He looked at me like he wasn't one of those kids. My father studied medicine, he added, and gave us both a refill.

Mine, too. Have you ever been to Africa? I saw that he knew the question well and hated it.

I have no special interest in Africa. I have an evenly distributed interest in the whole world, he said. A perfect encapsulation of his hubris.

I do, I said, I grew up there.

He nodded. Our food came. We carried on talking. He was a good listener, so good that I was almost embarrassed to look at him and his captivated expression. Then I stepped on the next landmine. I started talking about music and asked him what he liked. He carefully bathed a piece of tuna in the soy sauce. As if he needed time to ponder this blah blah question.

I only listen to classical music, he said.

Ah, I said.

I'm not at all surprised that you're astonished.

If I looked at him in astonishment, it wasn't because he listened to classical music, but because of his strange, reverent way of eating sashimi. I wondered whether he followed the dietary rule of chewing every mouthful thirty-two times. Stuck-up poser, I thought, and poured myself a refill of saké.

Why should I be surprised that you only listen to classical music?

Because stereotypes are there to be fulfilled. I know the music question, it's feel-good racism. It's where White people tell Black people what they want to hear for once: music-wise, you really nailed it. Nice one, guys. It makes White people feel better about themselves and it makes Black people happy, even if they have nothing to do with music.

Like you, I said, laughing, a bit baffled. Was he always like this?

Exactly, he said, entirely without irony.

And now? I asked myself. Do I act offended? Argue? Or insist on having a nice time with a man I don't know? He gently placed a piece of fish on my plate and nodded at me.

Okay, next topic, he said.

Okay. Let me think . . . did you see that new movie with Denzel Washington? Or what was that other guy's name – Morgan Freeman?

He stared at me for a moment, then laughed. Involuntarily, almost bashfully, as if he was being tickled. I don't know what would have become of the evening if he hadn't laughed.

We carried on talking about this and that, and at some point I asked him if he ever missed Germany.

To start with, now and then, but then less and less. At the moment, not at all. I'm right here where I belong.

He gazed at me for so long that I had to clear my throat. It wasn't clear whether by *right here* he meant in London, or here with me in this restaurant, or both, and I didn't ask. I was fine with grandiose sentiments, but I was uncomfortable being the one they were addressed to. And I wouldn't put it past Gabriel to speak to me like the hero of an epic poem. Something was opening up between us that started to feel like the barely perceptible version of flirting, and meanwhile, beyond Gabriel's serious expression, Mick Jagger was getting up and saying goodbye to the owner of the restaurant.

He's been wearing the same size jeans for over forty years, I said. Only now did Gabriel seem to notice Mick Jagger's mickjaggerness, watching with interest as he left the restaurant and got into his limousine.

Remarkable man! You White folks should be real proud of him.

Yo, you bet we are, I said.

With the lapse in seriousness, there was a mischievous glint in his eyes which was gone as quickly as it had appeared. He seemed unaware of the weather phenomena that had fleeted over his face, I liked that. We grinned at one another.

That was great, he said, referring to the food. Exactly what I needed. Thanks for suggesting it, Fleur.

Putting aside the fact that he suspected racism in harmless questions, there was a contentedness about him that seemed kind of sexy. He didn't even seem to wonder whether or not I liked him. Outside, it had started raining.

Gabriel wanted to top up our saké, but the earthenware bottle was almost empty. I got the last drop. When he asked for the bill and looked at his watch, I realised that the tables had turned over the course of three and a half hours. He had been the one who'd wanted to meet me, now I was the one who didn't want to let him go.

What shall we do now? I asked Gabriel, who was reading the bill, and didn't notice that I sounded like I was calling the emergency services.

What would you like to do? A shame it's raining, otherwise we could go for a walk in the park.

It's challenging when shy people meet polite people. Tedious, even. I told myself I had nothing to lose.

Let's go back to mine, I said, less casually than I'd planned.

Gabriel looked at me and let slip a little *ahem?* just as the waitress approached our table again. Another extremely polite person. She handed Gabriel the little credit card folder with both hands and a little bow, Gabriel thanked her politely and signed. She thanked him even more politely. He thanked her again. She said goodbye to him. He said goodbye to her. She said goodbye to me, I said goodbye to her. She said goodbye to Gabriel again. Endless sayonara. Out of sheer politeness, we watched her in silence until she disappeared into the kitchen. Then he looked at me again.

I'd love to, he said. That was all.

He stayed exactly one day. In those twenty-four hours he didn't exactly make himself at home at mine, but he made a space for himself. He hung up his suit and shirt carefully, while my clothes were sprawled all over the bedroom, he polished two wine glasses for us, and when I came back from the bathroom, he was lying on the side of my bed that he presumed was the right one. It was the side I usually slept on. When he answered the phone to Mark Barnett the next morning, there was nothing he could have said that wouldn't have annoyed me. It occurred to me the moment he said he had to answer it. I absolutely did not want him to tell Mark who he was lying next to. At the same time, I also absolutely did not want him to deny being with me. So he spoke to Mark, who back then had a reputation for being irresistible, while I switched my breathing to inaudible and thought about going to the bathroom. Gabriel took my hand and laid it on his chest, stroked it and kissed the back of my hand while he listened to Mark. He gave me my hand back and suggested a couple of slots for an appointment. Then he looked me straight in the eye, thought for a moment, and told Mark: no, not before 3 pm tomorrow afternoon. Then he kissed me.

Gabriel

To me, Fleur looked like she had never touched a beer in her life, let alone had sex. The truth was that she was drifting around the party completely off her head. She was drunk and under the influence of several pills, including the morning-after. It was a house party at some friends of Mark's and it was well stocked with intoxicants, overflowing even. She glided through the crowd as if no physical obstacle stood in her way. She seemed to me like some being from another dimension. I hoped she would pause next to someone I knew, then I lost sight of her and didn't see her again until I was outside in the garden saying goodbye to some people who were leaving. She was crouching by a small pond and seemed to be gazing at her own reflection. I went over to her and asked if everything was okay, but I didn't hear her answer because she looked at me like no one had ever looked at me before. A magical moment of realisation. If one-sided. Because all Fleur realised in that moment was that I was more sober than she was. So I became the saviour of this enigmatic nymph, who later told me that she hadn't been staring pensively into the water, but had had to squat next to the pond as a precaution, because she couldn't face pushing her way through the party trying to find a vacant toilet every time she felt like she needed to throw up. There was also a simple explanation for her otherworldly choice of attire. My future wife, who was usually well dressed but not in this dreamy, feminine way, had come from another party with a midsummer theme, the birthday party of a Swedish friend, hence the look. A long, gauzy dress, combined with flowers in her hair and her detached gaze, which I misinterpreted. I didn't need to take ecstasy. The high I got from Fleur's breath and her touch was everything that people had raved about. Except that at that moment, I couldn't draw any conclusions about drugs, only about myself. When I bent down to talk to her, she had her nausea under control for a moment and was genuinely glad to see me. At least that's what she told me later. Just before I showed up she had spent an indeterminate amount of time wondering what would happen if she got up and danced. It would be good, she had decided in her little time capsule, because dancing or at least standing would get her circulation going again. Pull me up, she said, and I offered her my hands. Her friends had gone, and so had he, whoever he was, presumably the subject of all the drama and, I assume, the reason for the morning-after pill. He didn't show up again. Not at this party and not later, as far as I knew. I never found out who he was. Her sweaty hand in mine, I let myself be dragged through the house looking for her handbag. I also seemed to have moved beyond any kind of solid state. I flowed along behind her, staring at her bare back and her – back then still long – dark hair. On the way out we ran into Mark, who whispered to Fleur suggestively that she had managed to pick up the best guy in town. I suddenly came around. The outside world was back, loud, and drunk. But Fleur just glanced at me for a second and said, deadly serious: I know.

She lost her balance trying to get into the cab and fell out again backwards, hitting the back of her head on a metal railing. She didn't seem to register any pain. The cab driver decided she was too drunk for his cab and refused to take us. I got angry, while Fleur leaned on me and laughed. I was in love. I looked down at her dishevelled wreath of flowers and kissed her on her centre parting. Let's get out of here, she slurred. I alternated between dragging and carrying her, first through a dark stretch of park, then through streets I didn't know. She was much heavier than she looked. With all the chivalry I could muster, I carried her in front of me, my arms bent, her arms round my neck, which didn't make it easier, but I could hardly throw her over my shoulder. We're nearly there, she said, about two miles, and whenever I had to put her down for a moment, we both laughed. Who knows why we had to go through the park. Why didn't we just call another cab? Meanwhile Fleur had no memory of how she got home. Leave the light off, she said, and I hoped that she might want to sleep with me in the dark, but she was already asleep by the time I found her bed and laid her down. I didn't dare undress her, so I just took off her shoes, pulled the cover up over her, and left a note with my number next to her phone, which she never called. It was Mark who bumped into her a few weeks later and asked if she wasn't going to thank me, which she then did. It was also Mark who told me the significance of her surname, although it turned out later that it wasn't her father who was the famous eccentric with the publishing company, but a distant relative. It was 2000, and although Google existed, it wasn't much use for personal searches, but I wasn't surprised to learn that this being from another realm also came from another realm financially. When she finally called me, over two months later, I was surprised by the timing, but not by the fact that she was calling. Fleur, I said, finally!

I hardly recognised her. She had a new haircut, very short. Okay. She is one of those women who can get away with a man's haircut. To go with it, she was wearing some kind of bus driver trousers, brogues, and a Nordic sweater covered in elks and snowflakes. I'm not usually attracted to women dressed like Norwegian trolls, but I had had almost a quarter of a year to fall in love with Fleur in her absence, and I had made the most of it. I adapted to her new look within minutes. Even the distracting thought, who does she remind me of? was only briefly annoying. We were sitting in a bar in Primrose Hill and she was telling me something about her childhood in Africa, which I couldn't concentrate on, because I was flicking through images in my mind trying to find her lookalike. For me, this wasn't a date, but a life-changing moment. Fleur's presence ought to have made me nervous. I was nervous, but not like a man with the urge to conquer a woman, rather a detective who is missing a crucial piece of the puzzle. When it occurred to me, I interrupted her African monologue. I didn't know Africa. If she was looking for common ground, it was a good sign, but the wrong approach.

Ah, I know, I said, clicking my fingers.

What? asked Fleur.

I ordered another round of beers. I don't particularly like beer, but I loved this woman, and I could hardly tell her that she reminded me of a man. A very beautiful man, the young Alain Delon, but still, I assumed she wouldn't want to hear that. Instead I asked her if she had heard of wabi-sabi. I was more interested in Japan than in Africa. I explained to her the concept of imperfect beauty. When she asked what I was trying to say, I started waffling on, telling her that what makes her perfect is the chipped nail polish on her index finger, and what makes her face perfect is the way her lower incisor is slightly crooked. Thank you, she said, those are really nice compliments, you should make a haiku out of them. She seemed unsure whether or not to laugh, and when she did, she tried to hide her teeth. That I had met a woman I thought was flawless didn't mean the feeling was mutual. There was still the very tangible possibility that she didn't even like me. Another chip in her perfection was the way she glugged down her beer. If we don't leave now, you'll have to carry me again, she said, with a quiet burp. Any time, I said, fully serious. She nodded, eyeing me with a touch of disdain. I held her gaze. I wasn't going anywhere. Wabi-sabi had put her in the mood for dinner, something Japanese. We drove to Marylebone to a Japanese restaurant where we saw Mick Jagger and carried on talking about ourselves. We had almost nothing in common, but Fleur, who had met me that afternoon thinking she would quickly shake me off, gave me an extension of another seventeen years.

Fleur

Gabriel called regularly and had this natural authority that I found hard to resist. But I couldn't stay away from Sean because I was in love with him.

It wasn't until my late twenties, when many of my friends were already discussing work and mortgages over wine, that I realised I still had more living to do. For a few years, I had a thing for mass events and enjoyed dancing alone in the crowds. One year, at Notting Hill Carnival, I bumped into an acquaintance who was out with Sean. Fleur-Sean, Sean-Fleur, a little wave. It was too loud to shout against the booming bass, and we didn't know at that point that we wouldn't have much to say to each other anyway. Cornrows weren't the best choice for his hair, I thought, they made his head look too small compared to his upper body, which was certainly impressive but that wasn't what interested me. Every other man was going around topless. We spent hours together dancing skin to skin, until it was too dark for his ugly sunglasses. Exhausted, we stood in the queue for a drink, and already I would have preferred it if he never talked, coughed, chewed, or laughed ever again.

Whenever I saw Sean's face at rest, I believed for a moment in God, the almighty artist. He was working on his career as the next Tricky. Or Goldie? I've since completely erased his music from my memory, though I was an adoring groupie back then. His greatest success was a remix: a remix of a remix. Whenever he was staring at his computer, headphones on and a spliff in the corner of his mouth, I'd lie around reading. I'm the perfect woman for him, I told myself, who else would give him this freedom? I'm here, and I ask nothing of him. It never even occurred to me that a few demands here and there might have done him good, he might even have liked it. All the same, I tried everything, and got nowhere. Because Sean, the Jamaican with the denim-blue eyes, was a fortress that was sufficient unto itself, conquerable only briefly and through direct contact of the mucous membranes. So I slept with him as often as I could. I tried not to give in too often to the thought that he didn't care about me, but I took it as a good sign that he didn't care about my family either. Great guy, not for sale. My being White didn't seem to bother him in the slightest. He would have had every right to be appalled at any suggestion he was in any way scoring points with my skin colour. The unpleasantness of such a thought was of course put into perspective if you took into account how much I was in love with him. All the same, the idea that he might be happier about my being head over heels in love with him than a White man would be, or that my infatuation with him was somehow worth more to him than if I had been a Black woman, was so despicable that I was ashamed it had even existed somewhere deep within me. Like most of my friends, I thought of myself as colour blind, we didn't really care about skin colour. This not-really-caring was something we were so comfortable with that for a few short years we thought the whole world was on the verge of thinking like we did. We had no idea until much later just how tiny that world was.

At first glance, no one would have objected to the idea of Fleur and Sean as a couple. Nor Fleur and Gabriel. But Fleur with both of them? Never mind what was behind it all, whether I was fucked up, a nymphomaniac or downright cool: my predatory preferences could hardly be more obvious, could they? But the two of them had nothing in common. Their origins, language, character, philosophy, voice, physique, smell, taste … everything about them could not have been more different. The texture of their skin was so different, as I sometimes couldn't help noticing, fascinated, at every touch.

Regardless of all the contrasts, from the outside it would be seen as being all about colour again. Even friends who were supposedly over it long ago, they would have remarked on it: ah, Fleur's seeing two men, both Black. In fact, ironically, there wasn't even a match in skin tone. Gabriel, who hid himself away in his office almost around the clock, was an ashy yellow; Sean had a gleaming bronze hue. The only thing these men had in common was me. And I kept quiet.

I saw Sean again a few years ago. I was on the Tube with Albert, wondering how I used to be able to bear it, when a boy, about eight years old, sat down opposite us and looked me straight in the eye. Like Albert at that age, I thought, and before my memory could dredge up who the boy actually reminded me of, I saw his father nudging his way through the crowd to sit beside him. Sean. A flabbier version of Sean, with that drained look people get when they have to take public transport every day during rush hour and have resigned themselves to the fact that life isn't going to get any better. Maybe if I'd stayed sitting there I might have seen something of that spark that had sent me into that lovestruck delirium. Maybe the old Sean was still shining somewhere behind that dull façade, the way he was when I knew him, maybe shortly before his breakthrough to stardom, who knows. I didn't look at him long enough to find out; I wrenched my son up from his seat and manoeuvred us off the train at the last moment. I stood on the platform trembling, Albert asking me if I'd gone mad, feeling Sean's gaze on my back as the train pulled away.

I was just some woman that he used to know. He would have said something friendly like, Hi Claire, um sorry, Fleur, right, Fleur, how are you? I glanced around stealthily and saw him jammed in among other people hurtling into the tunnel, a tired, slightly flabby, haphazardly dressed man, someone I had once idolised like no one else before or since. My son tugged my sleeve. Who was that?

No one, I said.

Gabriel

Fleur didn't lie to me. She didn't lead me on or make any particular effort to make me like her. It all came from me. I projected my ideas and desires onto this woman, and it worked. She actually had a lot of what I craved. Her mother is Belgian, her father British. I wanted that naturalness with which she moved in the world. Brussels and London aren't so far apart that you have to spin the globe, but I sensed in Fleur's life a vastness that I myself had always missed. A stable family home, growing up on another continent, financial security. The fact that she carried herself as if she wasn't of this world somehow also fitted perfectly as far as I was concerned.

My parents aren't my parents, she told me at some point relatively early on. She wasn't the daughter of the famous publisher, nor, strictly speaking, was she the daughter of his cousin. The publisher's cousin and his wife had adopted her as a baby and named her Fleur after her new mother's godmother. Auntie Fleur had been a painter who never married and who died in a mental asylum; a story Fleur was fond of, as though it gave her food for thought. Art and the funny farm: Fleur had an affinity for such things. As someone with an engineering mind, I just had to accept that, and indeed I did. I loved that about her, as I did everything about her.

Her childhood was so harmonious that it was only out of a sense of ethical obligation that Richard and Danielle, my future parents-in-law, decided to inform Fleur, shortly before her eighteenth birthday, that they were not her biological parents. Unlike other adoptees, Fleur had lived her childhood without the slightest inkling or suspicion. Their announcement that they had something to tell her was so out of the blue that she prepared herself for all sorts of revelations. They can't seriously think I need a conversation about sex, she thought. She reckoned on the news that the family was broke and pictured herself going to a local university instead of Cambridge, a fate to which she had resigned herself within seconds. It was even plausible that her parents were separating. They hadn't given that impression, but you never know. Whatever it is, we'll manage, Fleur told herself.

Everything is fine the way it is, and that's the way it will stay, her parents said. And yet, everything changed in an instant. It was a Big Bang that blew everything apart. She had to rewind her life story and make sense of it all from the beginning. She recalled her grandmother telling her to play with her little brother. That's what she was there for, after all, she had said. Because of course: if you're adopted by a couple who subsequently have a biological baby, Fleur concluded, then you should consider yourself lucky to be allowed to stay. She had never loved her English grandmother as much as her Belgian one, but it was only now that she realised how that snooty woman had been looking down at her, like a foreign brat. Fleur now remembered herself as always disobedient, clumsy, ungrateful. She recalled her adoptive father's mother saying she must get this or that trait from her mother, and now she understood retrospectively that these weren't digs at her daughter-in-law, but assumptions about an unknown woman. To Danielle and Richard's relief, Fleur didn't want to make contact with her birth mother. She listened to what her parents could tell her about this woman, which, besides the fact that she had been very young, amounted to almost nothing. And then no one mentioned her again for another twenty years. Of course that didn't stop Fleur from thinking about her. What kind of women gave their babies away, she asked herself. Drug addicts, prisoners, minors, women who were mentally ill or homeless. No one else would. Not here. You would decide in advance against having the child.

Fleur's enigmatic, bright eyes and almost black hair, her angular face, her delicate limbs, her eloquence, the individual elements that made up Fleur: overnight it seemed they had nothing to do with the two families from which she had assumed she was descended. Her brother, the biological child of her parents, resembled neither his father nor his mother. For Henry, there was no reason to worry about the lack of family resemblance. Worrying in general wasn't really part of Henry's psychological make-up. Fleur, on the other hand, shaped by her parents' commitment to Africa, had developed an indestructible combination of gratitude and guilt about her privileged origins, only to learn that she had been born underprivileged, and that she was possibly the main charitable project of this philanthropic family.

I knew all her questions. They haunted her like ghosts and then disappeared again. At those moments, Fleur knew full well where she was from. She was the very modest, understated daughter of a well-to-do family. That was part of her, too. I always wished that this state would last. But she couldn't choose when that feeling came around again that she was an outsider.

It was complicated. Fleur wondered where she came from, who she was. She struggled with the idea that she was carrying around some early childhood trauma that would never be resolved. She had every feeling her parents had wanted to spare her. Because at the same time, everything was simple: she had parents, and they loved her.

I kept telling her that. And I wished my in-laws had kept their mouths shut back then.

Fleur

Whenever I arrived, he was already there. I was always late. I'd come rushing in and he'd look up from his newspaper, smile and tell me what he'd just read. Or he would stand on the platform and meet me as if he had been waiting for years. For me, who didn't even call him back if it didn't fit with my plans. He regularly put up with me standing him up. He'd go and do something else instead. While I waited for Sean to call me back, I guess Gabriel was waiting for me. Or maybe he was smart enough not to wait for anything. Maybe he was doing exactly what any agony aunt would advise in this situation: he got on and lived his life.

This went on for almost a year. I could sometimes look back and remember our early days fondly, or as enjoyable as Gabriel found them, but for that I had to synchronise my memories of them with his. Memories that only started with me getting off the train at Vauxhall. Because most of the time I came straight from Sean. While I put on my clothes from the night before, he'd stay there in bed, chatting on the phone to whoever must have been Britain's funniest person – why else would he be crying with laughter after having exchanged barely three sentences with me in the past forty-eight hours? Sean laughed, gesturing with his free hand that I should close his battered apartment door firmly behind me, and winked at me. The Walk of Shame as my friends and I called it: setting out the next morning after staying over, in your sweaty and smoky clothes from the night before. The shame wasn't being in your thirties and still not being in a committed relationship.

No, the shame was the fact that I kept coming back, again and again, to the same flat that I didn't have a key to, and where I left not even the slightest trace, not even in the form of a clean pair of knickers. Later, I heard that the woman Sean met after me had moved in with him after just a few weeks, with everything she possessed including her three-year-old son. I hadn't been able to leave even a toothbrush at this man's place. That said nothing about him, a lot about me. Sean didn't see things in terms of patterns, or a structure, he just saw me when he was in the mood. He would regularly hack up my heart and make a steak tartare of it. Whenever I asked him to. It gave me plenty to muse on, but it didn't occur to me to change anything. Instead, I rummaged around inside myself and came to the depressing conclusion that as a child given up for adoption, I was doomed to chase after people who didn't want me.

Interesting that you see it that way, my therapist said. That was her standard response to all my theories because she didn't have any herself. Her appearance matched my emotional state better than my own: a dishevelled emu, head up high, peering around in surprise, apparently wondering how it had ended up in this beautiful practice. She was the only person I told what was going on in my life. A woman who got nervous patches on her neck when I mentioned sex, and who generally seemed to have the life experience of a five-year-old. All the same, I liked her. It made no difference to me that I didn't come away with any useful advice, I wouldn't have followed it anyway.

I came out of Sean's apartment, walked along the outside corridor to the occasionally functioning, grotty lift. The residents' attempts to improve the entrance area made it look even more depressing, and I thought, this is where I belong. Not just because I was in love, but also because I was firmly convinced that I came from this kind of housing estate. This is where my life began, where I was conceived. No doubt by teenagers, in shabby, cramped conditions, surrounded by junk. It didn't matter where it was, poverty is the same everywhere. I walked past worn-out shoes, strollers, and third-hand tricycles while Sean lay in his flat, laughing, barely noticing me leave. Even if my abrupt departures were prompting him to ask me more often when we would see each other again. He could sense Gabriel, while Gabriel never seemed to wonder why I looked the way I did, namely like I'd been up half the night, and why I smelled the way I did, namely of Sean, masked only by Sean's shower gel, usually Axe.

After a few times, I started taking my cello with me, because I'd told Gabriel I was giving lessons to socially disadvantaged children. He thought that was wonderful, and of course he insisted on carrying the cello. Once he almost got into a fight because some guy who was drunk in the pub accidentally knocked it over. I can't do this anymore, I thought, even though he was the one who got smacked in the face. *La Fleur du mal.* I felt bad, of course. And carried on doing it. The cello was one of my adolescent ideas. A geeky alternative to shoplifting or mindless tattoos. It turned out I was too old and lazy. I never practised. With any other instrument I could have formed an amateur band, but as it was, it stood there at my parents' house reminding everyone that I had been a complicated teen whose musical talent was overestimated. When I went to theirs to pick it up, I was thirty years old, and seeing two men. I needed the cello to help me across the border from Sean land into Gabriel land. From the Banana Republic to Switzerland. And there he stood, overworked and so happy to see me that I felt ashamed, and gave me everything that I was longing for from someone else. I had never seen anyone show their love in such a fearless way, and not for a second look like an idiot. Sadly that wasn't a compliment I could say to his face. When other women looked at him or if they gave us both a knowing look, I knew I was turning down a prized gift. Well, I wasn't rejecting it outright. I just couldn't accept it in all its dimensions.

Gabriel

He won't be frail, I thought as I flew over to see him after his heart attack. He would either recover or he would die. There was nothing in between for Ernst, my grandpa. I assumed he thought the same, at least he acted like he did. The doctors wanted to keep him in the hospital, but he insisted on being discharged. They advised him to go into supported care. He refused. He wouldn't even entertain the idea of living somewhere else than in his house. I expected nothing else.

When I arrived at his house, he was lounging in front of the TV in his pine-green bathrobe. He had a meal delivered once a day that he poked at contemptuously, and he could get himself to the bathroom. I don't know if I could have washed him. I probably could have, but I was relieved that it didn't come to that.

When I shaved him, it was the first time in a very long time that I had been so close to him physically. I suggested it the second morning when I saw his wet shaving kit in the bathroom. I wet his face with a hot flannel, lathered him up, stood behind him with the blade like a barber, and took my time.

My hair needs a trim too, he said, at the back. I looked down at his head. He had had the same haircut for as long as I could remember. Shaved at the back, longer on top, combed back. White and straight. For the first time, it struck me that despite the difference in our hair texture, I had the same receding hairline.

He used to take me to his barber. Herr Stahl, an agelessly elderly man in a blue-grey smock, was commanded to 'trim the fuzz'. And Mr Stahl, who presumably had no ambition of becoming an international hairdresser, became an expert in short haircuts for African hair. At first he stroked my head sceptically as if considering a rare deformity, but with time he cut my hair as well as my hairdresser in London for under 10 GDR marks. His successors kept his name and his old neon sign, and expanded it. The salon became Stahl & Klinge with its young new owners, who installed a music system fit for a night club.

Do you still go there? I asked my grandfather.

In the beginning, yes, but I didn't like it there at all anymore, he said, and when I laughed, he laughed too: a short, dismissive hmm.

I went out and bought him a grab handle and a slip mat for the bathtub, both of which he also acknowledged with a disapproving hmm. Then I cut his hair, which I managed with more finesse than either of us expected.

Thank you, my boy. I'm presentable again now.

I had brought him the contents of an entire deli counter from London. But my grandfather, once a devourer of charcuterie, had changed his dietary preferences. He now ate only porridge oats with milk and sugar and sliced bread with plum jam. We sat in front of the television, he with his sugary snacks, me with my huge and entirely superfluous selection of the best cheeses, pâtés, and cold meats.

When he got worked up about something on TV, I took it as a sign that all was well health-wise. Change the channel then, I said.

It's the same crap on all of them, he said.

When he asked me to bring his accounts over to him on the sofa, I noticed that he was charging ludicrously low rents. It looked like I wasn't the only one who wished my grandfather could live forever. I went through his bank statements and his rent book, which he kept by hand, and it all tallied down to the last penny. He was like clockwork. A slide rule. A spirit level. And as long as he stayed that way, nothing changed. All the same, I suggested I could let the tenants know I'm coming for an inspection, see what state the flats are in, and think about recalculating the rents. He was against it.

No. We're not racketeers.

But we're not the Salvation Army either. And even if you're not going to make a profit, the house at least has to pay for itself.

He didn't need me to tell him that. He obstinately justified his philanthropy by saying that he didn't want to put people through yet another change. By this he meant his last remaining old tenants, people who had rented from him for over half a century. He had always been their landlord, not their acquaintance, but by now the length of time had created a bond that was also benefitting the younger high-income earners because he couldn't charge them double for the same apartment, could he? Yes, he could, I thought. These people knew exactly how lucky they were to live in a Jugendstil house in Leipzig's Waldstrassen Quarter at that price. They would happily pay twice as much. But I didn't say anything. He grumbled, but he let me at least go and have a look round.

They'll need to get used to you anyway, he said.

I didn't mean anything by it, but that's how he took it. I no longer fended off his not-long-to-go-now hints. He was eighty-five. It wasn't his job to make me feel that death existed only as a distant possibility.

As long as I had known him, he was always busy. Even when he watched television, he was always repairing things, or doing paperwork, or a crossword puzzle. His hand trembled so much now that he couldn't write in the boxes. A mood arose between us that didn't suit either of us. It was as if the room was full of questions. Big ones and mundane ones. His tidy wardrobe, for example, and his ironed shirts and polished shoes. And how clean the floors were. It surely couldn't be that a man in his mid-eighties was doing all this on his own, could it? He was popular among the widows, whom he mentioned on the phone only as Mrs So-and-So, never mentioning them by first name. The discretion he maintained seemed like a kind of intimacy, so I didn't want to probe. I missed my last chance to ask him who had been there for him, and I regretted it later. If I had known who it was, I would have given her something, at least a memento of him.

His family doctor and old friend Gerhard kept going as long as he could, until he made a few disastrous mistakes and had to hand over his practice to a younger female doctor. It was like with his hairdresser and also with Grandpa's own shop, which he had already rented out when he was in his late seventies, at an appropriate rate, to a Vietnamese family who were opening a Japanese restaurant. His world hadn't disappeared. It had just been recorded over like a video tape. The doctor, whom he called 'the new doctor', although she had been treating him for almost ten years, came twice during my visit and was satisfied with his condition.

She likes you, he said once she was gone. She's capable and attractive, what more could you want?

He had never winked at me before. This doctor, an athletic blonde woman of about forty, had been friendly in a professional capacity, nothing more, and she had been wearing a large, gold wedding ring.

I told you, I've got a girlfriend. And we're going to get married.

Fleur was the opposite of what he would call capable, but he would like her.

Why do you want to rush like we did back then? You've got time, enjoy life.

Because that's what I want. I want to enjoy my life, with her.

You've always been so resolute. You get that from me.

He looked at me thoughtfully. His now very thick glasses gave his gaze an innocence that didn't suit his character.

I'll bring her next time, I said.

Did you know that your grandmother fell in love with another man while I was away? he asked. It was so out of the blue that I thought I had misheard.

I didn't know. My grandparents were always a fixed entity for me, not a couple confronted with the question of falling in love. Besides, he was a storyteller whose stories were rarely about himself. If he talked about his time as a prisoner of war, he tended to sound like a historian, not a survivor. Or, like now, he had simply been 'away'. I didn't say anything. Breathing heavily, he folded up his newspaper and tucked it into the magazine rack next to the sofa.

You couldn't blame her for that, could you? She didn't know if I was even still alive. The last she had heard from me was in 1944. What was she supposed to do, wait until hell froze over?

He looked at me as if he expected an answer from me. A politician was answering the presenter on TV.

You numbskull, my grandfather tutted, and turned off the sound. Then there was a pause when we were probably both thinking about my grandmother, who smiled down at us from a beautiful, Ingrid Bergman-esque black-and-white photo. No revelations now, please, I thought. Please don't tell me now that I'm the grandson of the unknown soldier. I interrupted the silence.

When did you get back from Russia?

1948. Late summer.

I nodded. My mother was born in 1950, which didn't necessarily mean anything. Again, he stopped to think for so long that I thought he had fallen asleep, then he sat up and started speaking more loudly than before.

Oh, I see. No, no. Lene and I, we could trust each other. My children were both mine.

When I had to go to the airport the next morning, he was so fit that he woke me up with a hard-boiled egg. A month later, he came down with pneumonia. One of his tenants told me he had spent two days out in the rain scrubbing off graffiti and trimming the hedges.

Fleur

I only realised how much I had got used to our regular contact when Gabriel suddenly disappeared. It wasn't deliberate; he rushed to Germany because his grandfather was in hospital, and he forgot to take his charger.

Of course he asked me if I wanted to go with him, and I didn't even hesitate before saying no. He wanted me to meet his grandfather, his only close relative, who had taken the place of his parents. I could lie, disappear, sleep with Sean, but I could not, under any circumstances, go and be introduced to an old man I didn't know as Gabriel's future bride. It was the first time I had ever seemed to really hurt him. So I thought up a trip to Haworth to the Brontë Parsonage. This story was harder than my imaginary cello pupils from challenging homes. Partly because Gabriel was so pleased that I was finally getting back to my PhD research. He still asked me if I could join him afterwards, though. No, I couldn't. Because I was flying to Ibiza with Sean and a few other people the day he was going to Leipzig. The extreme contrast between going on a bender in the Balearics with meeting an old man in East Germany was just too much. I dreamt up a stomach bug a few days before he set off, so I wouldn't have to lie to his face. The day he was flying I picked him up unannounced at five in the morning to drive him to the airport. It was the first time I had done anything for him. You're an angel, Fleur, he said as he got into my car, so tired and so happy at the surprise, that it was all I could do to stop myself shattering the illusion. Not because I didn't like him anymore, but because I could no longer keep persuading myself that what I was doing was okay. I went back to my place, packed my things, and headed out to the airport again, this time by train, and flew to Ibiza. Completely exhausted and angry at Gabriel, although it was hardly his fault that I was running out of steam for my two-timing. How did bigamists do it?

After two days, I turned my phone back on, and as he hadn't called or texted, I assumed he was exercising his right to be offended. We did the full Ibiza: nightclubs, pool, beach, dinner, more clubs. I seemed to be enough for Sean those few brief days in the sun. When Gabriel still hadn't been in touch after four days, I sent him an SMS, and a day and a half later I found myself staring at my phone like I normally did waiting for word from Sean. How could it be that I was going through the same phone torture but with Gabriel now? Everything I knew as a constant was falling away.

After almost six days, the longest interval since we'd been going out, I had a call from an unknown number. I didn't get out of the pool in time. The next time, I was sitting next to Sean in the car. The caller had left me a message that I couldn't listen to because in those days you had to enter some kind of code to get voicemail messages when you were abroad. I felt like I'd been cursed. By now he must have heard from the dial tone that I wasn't in England, but that was secondary now. When the unknown number called me again, I answered straight away, even though Sean was lying next to me. I knew it was him before he said anything. Wait, just a second, I whispered, as I rummaged through a pile of clothes for something to put on. When Sean grunted in his sleep like a predatory growl, I grabbed a towel and rushed out of the room naked. I don't know if Gabriel noticed how wired I was; it was ten in the morning and I hadn't slept yet. I don't know if he noticed that all I cared about was myself and my redemption: oh I'm so glad you called, I couldn't get through to you, I've been thinking I should have come with you after all, me, me, me… Now, when he asks me where I am, I'll tell him, I thought. Gabriel didn't say anything. He coughed into the receiver. How are you doing? I asked him at last.

Not so good, he said.

When will we see each other again? I asked him.

I don't know when I'll be back, he said, and I felt dizzy.

If I fly back now, I'll regret it. I might not see my grandfather again. Do you understand?

Platitudes rushed through my head. I'm so sorry, I wish you strength, he's a good age, it's so nice that you can say goodbye to him. I was on the verge of asking him if I should come after all, even though I still didn't want to, but from the little he said it didn't sound like I mattered anymore, he was in another place right now. He was with the man who had raised him. The woman he couldn't rely on, as he must surely have realised by now, must have seemed very distant.

Have you got anyone with you? I asked him.

At that moment Catherine, my only friend from Sean's gang, came out of her room. Covered in sweat, in her dress from the night before, a yoghurt drink in one hand, a cigarette in the other. I held my finger over the mic and ran out onto the patio. When I could listen again but couldn't hear anything down the line, I could tell that he hadn't said anything, and was instead quietly crying.

Again I wondered if I should fly out to join him. Looking for a quiet spot in the grounds of the villa where I wouldn't run into any party corpses, I eventually turned out of the driveway. I came to a lemon grove, where I sat down on the ground under a tree and looked down the hill. There were a few minutes of silence, but I knew he was still there. It's strange how difficult it is for some people to cry and how easy it is for others, like me. Gabriel didn't seem to have expected it, and it sounded like he was holding the phone at a distance.

Gabriel? I asked, and all I heard was him slowly breathing out. If he hangs up now, I thought, because he's embarrassed or because he's realised that he's just as alone with me as he is without me, then that's it, he's gone.

Later, I often wondered what gave me the final push to tell him. Did I suddenly feel responsible for him? Was I relieved, desperate, determined? I can't remember. All I knew was that I suddenly wanted him to stay.

Gabriel, please don't hang up, I have to tell you something, I said.

Hmm, he said. He kept trying to sound like he wasn't crying. I would have liked to tell him to just cry. Instead I said, tell your grandfather that he's going to be a great-grandfather, okay?

When he didn't respond, I thought for a moment that my decision would be taken away from me again. Maybe Gabriel hadn't heard me or had misunderstood. Maybe it was a sign, a silent command to retreat. As you were. I didn't want to say it again. He sniffed. And then I did say it again, in other words.

I'm pregnant, I said. He might be happy to know.

I'd known for three days. There had been growing evidence even before I flew to Ibiza, but I'd avoided reaching the right conclusion. I'd been sleeping and eating erratically, fibbing my way through life, teetering from one hangover to the next, so it was no surprise that I needed to throw up now and then. Then here I was with my so-called friends and Sean, my so-called boyfriend, at this lavish finca in Ibiza, waiting for my period and for a sign of life from Gabriel. And as it became a certainty, I could already see myself coming out of an abortion clinic and getting into Catherine's Mini. A scenario I didn't need to imagine, because it had already happened the year before.

There's nothing I can do here anyway, I thought. I can't decide now. And then Gabriel's grief took my decision away.

Later, when we were at loggerheads, when I was looking for a wrecking ball to tear down his stable, concrete world, I was often on the verge of telling him my version of our early days. Listen, Gabriel, you might not believe it, but your harmonious Gabriel life, your happy family existence, in fact rested on the whims of a woman who wasn't even really your girlfriend at the time. An unhinged woman who peed on a test strip before kneeling on the bathroom floor tiles and praying for the second line in the control panel to please, please not appear. And who, when the second strip did indeed appear, washed down all the party drugs she could get her hands on with Red Bull and danced to Carl Cox, in the hope that in view of the quite clearly not ideal conditions, the fertilised egg would change its mind and leave this inhospitable body.

That woman no longer exists. Her story had to be rewritten. Not for the sake of preserving Gabriel's contentment but because it was the beginning of my son's life. He has a right to have been wanted, we all do. And with a few months delay he finally was.

Gabriel

It was hard for me to pack away his personal things, but I didn't know what else to do with them. I had already packed a few boxes of books and valuables, which I had sent to London, only to put them straight into storage. The only things I would wear as a memento of him were his signet ring and his cufflinks. He had taken care of his belongings, kept them in good nick, as he put it, and now they were turning from possessions into junk. That hurt. Ernst wouldn't have minded if I'd just called a house clearance company so I could get on with my life. Pull yourself together, my boy, and get rid of the lot of it, he would have said. At least, that's what I told myself he would have said. I kept thinking that phrase over and over, in his voice, as I clambered around in the attic, sorting things out. I had to see the stuff before I let strangers at it. I was from a discreet family. Tucked inside a photo album I found a family tree drawn by my grandfather in the early 1940s. I recognised his handwriting. I knew it well. In fact, I could mimic it perfectly. I had written my own sick notes for long enough. The family tree was part of a so-called Aryan certificate, the *Ariernachweis*. I read the names of the dead, who were also my ancestors, the dates of their baptism, marriage, and death, and wondered what it was supposed to certify. I knew only the penultimate and final generation. My grandparents and their first child, Brigitte, who didn't have any children. She was the end of this so-called Aryan family. My mother was born five years after the war, and the family tree would have continued with me, the intruder, the first dark spot in this pristine White genealogy. Now, I was the last one who would continue it. It had never occurred to me to ask my grandparents what they thought of their daughter having a baby. Unplanned, out of wedlock, and by a Black man. What they thought of me before they knew me. It was such an obvious question to ask, and yet at the same time it wasn't at all, because everything was self-evidently right the way it was.

We were so stupid back then, you lot can't even imagine it today, Grandma would sometimes say, but you had to fill in the details yourself: when *then* was and who *you lot* were, but then she was already onto the next topic: apples. The White Transparents are a joy this year! Ernst was more opinionated, but he wasn't any more personal. He talked about *them* and meant, depending on the chronological context, the Browns or the Reds, both as much idiots as the other. He never belonged to either. At some point during one of my aunt's rare visits – by which point I was already almost an adult – she told me how hard it had been back then, a tragedy even. They had kicked my mother out, and it was only later, after I was born, that they let her move back. I became their sunshine. Then my mother, who still looked like a high school student although she already had a seven-year-old son, had her accident. She was riding her moped to work, as she did every morning, and later everyone said she died instantly. After the accident, I became their everything. No one gave any more thought to what they had said or done before, which was characteristic of that generation. How else could they have lived with themselves, Gitti said, with contempt. I had no reason to think about what they had thought and said before I was born. I had no reason to doubt that they loved me.

They didn't lie. They preferred to say nothing. They had nothing to say about my father, because they knew little more than I did. My mother was the only one who could have told me anything about him, and who perhaps had pictures of him. I only found photos of her in the attic. Young and beautiful: she didn't exist in any other form. With her sister, with friends, with me. Not a single Black person to be seen. Your dad couldn't stay with us, he had to go away, far away, to Africa, she had told me. It was the child-friendly, short version of the story, I suppose. She would have told me more at some point. She didn't seem to be angry with him, at least not when I was born, otherwise she wouldn't have given me his name, along with her father's and her own: Idris Ernst Gabriel. He cut and ran, said Ernst, which was fine with us, in hindsight, because we wanted to keep you, without having to argue with a stranger.

I stood there like a stranger at his funeral. Grandpa Ernst had died where he had always lived, and the church was full of people who wanted to pay their last respects. It was funny how satisfying that felt, almost gratifying, as if this gathering of people was a confirmation of his existence. However, the man whose life the pastor recounted in between the psalms was not someone I recognised. The man I knew had stayed in the church because he was a traditionalist and because it was important to him to distance himself from those he despised as a godless rabble. He was never pious; if he was spiritual, then only in his own way, not avowedly so. Now he was being portrayed like someone from the Old Testament, who had endured his losses without complaint, because the Lord gave and the Lord hath taken away. On the tombstone were the names of his wife and his daughter, my mother. I stared at the years – *1919–1985, 1950–1977* – and played around with the digits, adding them together, subtracting, finding common factors, barely able to look away as the mourners passed me by. I had needed to cry after my phone call with Fleur, but he was still alive then.

I took the family tree, all the photos and his letters to my grandma from the war, and then called a house clearance team. Grandpa Ernst had known a few and he appreciated them, even if he called them vultures because they lived off the estates of the deceased and not from carefully selected purchases, like him, a respectable antiques dealer and collector. I stood in the middle of the large attic, where one last old tenant still hung her laundry. I was going to have it converted to a yuppie loft studio. I had had the building permit for years. That's great, my boy, we'll do that, we'll keep up with the times, I heard him say.

Fleur

Gabriel told me not to come until after the funeral, that I should take it easy and no need to burden myself with a grief that wasn't mine. We then drove around Germany for a few weeks. My memory of that trip is like a travel documentary, in muted colours. He dragged me around the country like a Japanese tour group, talking incessantly about history and architecture. He himself also acted like a well-read tourist, not like someone who had grown up there. The only things he reacted to on a personal level were the architectural abominations. Poorly renovated, stupidly planned, unimaginatively built – it sounded as if a once beautiful country had been wrecked in his absence. Otherwise, his connection to this country seemed to have died with his grandfather.

We saw a new city every day: this crash course and this pace were his way of grieving. After I stressed that I was only twelve weeks pregnant, and he didn't have to treat me like I was just about to give birth, he lined us up a genuinely full itinerary, and dared be intimate again. We felt our way towards each other those days we were on the road. Sometimes we talked like old friends, then we'd be so awkward again that it scared me. What were we doing here? I noticed that his jawline had become more angular. He told me he was on the nicotine gum. It wasn't that long ago that he'd started smoking, and he'd quickly got up to a pack a day; smoking and working went so well together, after all. Then after that call when I was in Haworth (Ibiza), he stopped again straight away. Can you think of a better reason to quit smoking? he asked, and for the first time I saw that he was happy. I knew he hated anyone touching his hair, but I reached over and ruffled the back of his head, and he let me. As always, he was entirely, fully present. He was processing death and getting ready to welcome new life. While I sat at his side, imagining head-on collisions with lorries on the wrong side of the road. I didn't choose this. Like the several thousand thoughts of sex that supposedly flood men's brains every day, with me – this fledgling carrier of new life – it was uncontrollable, fleeting thoughts of death. At a service station in front of a dark coniferous forest, I secretly smoked a cigarette. Gabriel had gone off to make a few phone calls. He'd warned me it could take a while. I had already checked my voicemail that morning in the bathroom. Once Sean had realised that I was probably gone, he had become a persistent caller. I almost had to laugh at the pathetic predictability of this development. All I'd needed to do over the past few years was not call him back. Now all of a sudden he was desperate to know how I was doing. He hoped everything was good. From message number four, he missed me. There were so many things he would like to do with me. Uh-huh, wouldn't you just. Message number five consisted of a sad sigh, and messages six to ten were please at least just tell him what was going on. Great fucking timing to suddenly be interested in me. What if he showed up on my doorstep in London? Or sent Catherine over? Though fortunately this time I'd spared her from staring at my pregnancy test with me. No one knew where I was, why, or with whom. I was standing in a semi-circular car park between two trucks, where I lit an Ultralight and called Sean back.

Where are you, in Belgium? he asked.

Germany.

Oh. Okay. I see, he said. I was worried, you know?

No need. I'm fine, but we won't see each other again.

Do you want to come over and talk about it? I'll cook us something – what do you say?

Nobody likes having things taken away from them. Everyone likes a range of choices, open doors, access. The fear in his voice had nothing to do with me. My narcissistic wishful thinking (he loves me but has trouble showing it) was suddenly gone.

Sean, it was all bullshit from the beginning. It was a mistake.

I heard him inhale sharply through his nose. Take that, I thought. This woman who was ecstatic at every second she spent with you, like a parish priest getting an audience with the Pope, was now declaring it as null and void.

What makes you say that? he asked. When you get back, we'll talk about everything, okay?

We've had enough opportunities to talk, Sean. I don't want to talk anymore.

What do you want?

I want to be with someone who loves me.

A curious cliché, a spontaneous truth. I coughed.

Who says I don't love you?

He tried a laugh. A weak comeback. A summation of the shit that thankfully was now over.

I wish you all the best, I said, flicking my cigarette into a puddle that could have been petrol, but wasn't.

Now I'm at his mercy, I thought as I walked back to Gabriel's rental car. Or: now I'm stuck with him. Irrevocably. If you consider the unpleasant but universally valid schema whereby desire is fuelled by hopeless prospects, it seemed inevitable that he would now lose interest in me. The service station, a popular place to abandon pets and children, didn't help. The car wasn't there. I knew it wasn't possible, and yet I was almost hyperventilating. Here I was in this godforsaken place, feeling the full force of the truth that I had so deftly masked with the distraction of German high culture since I'd arrived in the country: I don't even know this guy. I'm having a baby with a stranger, and there's no going back. The alternative would have been to have a baby with a man I'd invested so much thought and emotion in that for a while I'd been under the illusion that I knew him, and that wasn't any better. Other alternatives would have been to have the baby on my own, or not at all.

Feeling detached from my legs, I walked on autopilot towards the petrol station, and then saw the car parked further back than I expected. The adrenaline that rushed through my terrified body was probably more harmful than the cigarette. For the first time I felt an inseparable connection to the child. I took a deep breath and stroked my belly, which still felt the same as always.

Gabriel was leaning against the boot of the car, looking at his shoes and talking on the phone. When I came to stand next to him, he took my hand, registered that it was ice cold, and slipped it under his jumper. He looked at me for a few seconds, then when he started to speak he was looking through me again. It sounded as though his German persona was less friendly than his English one, but I might have been imagining it. Exactly, he said a few times. *Genau*. Germans were always saying that. I leaned against him, enjoying the warmth of his body and the adrenaline subsiding after that scare. He was still there. I had to get used to him being there with me.

He would keep the tenement blocks in Leipzig and buy out his aunt and great-aunt, he told me when we were driving again. I had seen them, an imposing Art Nouveau house and a smaller one where his grandfather ran his antique shop: two townhouses that anywhere else would have made him a millionaire, but not in Leipzig, not yet anyway, though it was only a matter of time. I didn't know that it had been possible for individuals to own apartment buildings in East Germany, but then I'd never thought about it. They had retaken ownership of one of the houses after the Wall came down, the other had been in their possession the whole time. It had been a win-win situation for the state, Gabriel explained. Maintenance was as expensive as anywhere else, and rents were more or less a token gesture. The owners were faced with the choice of either making losses or throwing in the towel; there was no profit in it. Nothing but stone-cold expropriation, he said. But now it was different. Thanks to his grandfather's tenacity. Then came the numbers part of his lecture. Increase in value, rental income, mortgages, interest, renovation costs, plus this, minus that. He'd told me before that he did maths to relax. He liked solving equations most of all. They were his antidote to the absence of logic in life. He did sums when he couldn't fall asleep, when he was lying in the bath, maths puzzles were his way of daydreaming. Now he was sharing his daydreams with me. It was unbelievably dull, yet also endearing because he seemed so content as he told me. I wondered if he felt he had to present himself to me as a capable breadwinner. I had never been in this earnest realm with any man. My family was less wealthy than our name suggested, the big money hung on a different branch of the family tree, though our side wasn't exactly poor. So I might more likely have faced the problem of meeting a man who looked to me as the provider. Gabriel didn't seem interested in anyone else's money, but he was fascinated with his own. He had begun to speak of us as 'we', which sometimes warmed me inside, then felt almost suffocating again. My moods, which tossed me back and forth even in my normal state, had expanded their scale in both directions. We'd move in together for the time being, at his place. Good that we both had a good credit rating. Good that we both had such good degrees. Good thing we were both the kind of people who knew what they wanted. For a moment, even I knew what I wanted.

Can we please stop listening to Wagner?

He looked at me, annoyed. All that pathos isn't good for me or the baby, I said, sounding way too touchy and whiny. He took it with composure, switched to the radio, and neither of us said any more on the topic. I kept forgetting that he was grieving. There was a handwritten note inside the Wagner CD box. It wasn't hard to read, I could translate it. *Dear Grandpa, I know you prefer your records, but you can listen to this one in the car. See you soon, Gabriel.*

It was October, and the sky hung over us like a herd of elephants. I only noticed the differences between the East and the West when Gabriel explicitly pointed them out to me. I assumed it was because the Wall had been gone for over ten years and only Germans could see the differences now. Some places looked more spruced up, others more dilapidated. Some people went out of their way to be friendly to us, some were unutterably surly. Not unlike Belgium, I thought. Belgium can also pelt you with culture one minute, and then the next minute it's so grim that you have to break the speed limit through the villages to avoid feeling suicidal. Besides, Belgium is also a divided country in its own way, like so many countries. Apparently, it is in the nature of man to find his immediate neighbours particularly odious.

When he led me to the enclosed inner courtyard of an old house in Berlin and we stared up into the dark blue square of evening sky, I briefly felt like I was in the right place at the right time. Our fingers intertwined, he lifted our hands and kissed the back of mine. If there was a moment in those days when I felt at home, it was then. There were only two stars visible. The left one is a satellite, Gabriel said. Then he spun us around in circles, looking at the four tall, dark walls surrounding the courtyard and said, we could buy something here. I didn't think *we* should buy an apartment in a grotty old house in East Berlin, but I liked him more and more. He was truly at home with himself, my neurotic friends would have said, and now he was at home with me, too. The arched entrance to the courtyard was like a portal to another time. Behind us smelled of cabbages and old potatoes, ahead smelled of Vietnamese food and mojitos. I enjoyed peering in bars, where I had no business to be anymore, and watching the people giddily drinking themselves into the night. I ignored the shops for young parents with money and taste, which Gabriel didn't even notice because he was surveying the facades and whinging as if he had himself commissioned the houses. We sat down at a Japanese restaurant, because at that point I didn't know that pregnant women weren't supposed to eat raw fish. Every Berliner I talked to advised me to come back in May or June next time. The city would be so absurdly more beautiful that every year even the locals can hardly believe it. I briefly thought of a parting gift for Sean: he'd be happy here, I thought. I should let him know how easy and cheap it would be for him to rent a whole studio here, and how relaxed the people seemed. They didn't even expect you to speak German. To avoid any possibility of this happening, I deleted his number shortly before Hamburg.

As strange as Gabriel often seemed to me, we did share something, some common ground. Whether he liked to see it that way or not, we both had phantom parents we carried around with us. We both went through life with the stigma of having been unwelcome. No, that wasn't him. No, he didn't see it that way. I think he would have been more comfortable with me stabbing my nail file into his thigh than using the word 'stigma'. He tucked his chin in like a soldier standing to attention and drove a few miles in that pose. He was sick of other people prescribing how he was supposed to feel. Everyone seemed to think they knew exactly how he felt, how he ought to feel. So presumptuous of them. Yes, he had spent his childhood answering other people's tedious questions. His father was to blame, or rather his physical appearance, and his absence. Which didn't necessarily mean that Gabriel missed him as a person. He had missed his mother, of course he had. But his father, someone he didn't know? He would rather have had siblings. Would have, could have, would have been – whatever. He had got through it, and in the best way possible, because he'd had people around him who cared about him and supported him. Yet still, people constantly asked him how he had coped in the East, with all the racists, and they always seemed to assume that his father was such an important part of his heritage, this great man, surely, whom he absolutely ought to get to know.

Why? When he was so kind as to never make contact with his son? Because it was through meeting him that Gabriel would finally find his roots? In that case, Gabriel argued, someone's going to need to explain how these so-called 'roots' are to be defined in the first place. He turned to me and smiled to make it clear that his hostile tone wasn't directed at me. He took a piece of gum and handed me one.

Parenting is about being there, he said, loudly and conclusively like a family court judge. If that's how he sees it, so be it, I thought, and just nodded. He had no idea of the barrier he had just built between us.

During that interminable drive through Germany, I found out what he was like in the morning. He'd open his eyes and he was immediately awake; he even looked the same as always. I learned how insufferable he could be when he was hungry, how annoyed he got by people who, in his opinion, were grossly unsuited to the jobs they were in. Not that he was ever patronising to anyone, he just genuinely wondered how people could be so badly miscast. I calculated how long I had known him. Nine months, a pregnancy long, if you will. I could have already known all his quirks and his specialist disciplines if they had interested me beforehand.

What's up? he'd ask if he caught me staring at him in wonder. He hated being stared at. You could call it a childhood trauma; best not to in his presence. They look at you because you're very special, his grandparents had told him. What beautiful reasoning, I thought, so loving and wise. And as you could see from Gabriel, it worked, too. All the same, he had developed an aversion to the provinces, even though he realised at some point that people gawped at everyone like they were an intruder and not just him. Nothing, I'd say, everything's fine. He'd yawn, fill up the petrol tank, read the menu, back out of a parking space, and I'd watch him with wonder like he had magical powers. I might almost have said, I just pictured myself as a little girl and you as my dad. He would have laughed and asked, and? How do I do? But instead I asked him, wasn't he also a bit scared of what was coming? He just shook his head as if I'd asked him if he found *Jaws* scary. He had no doubts, while I still found it impossible to grasp the fact that soon there would be someone for whom we would both be the most important people in the world, the ones who knew everything because they had always been there and had always been together.

I was thirty-one and felt like a runaway hiding a teenage pregnancy. He was thirty and thought the timing was good, though not perfect because after all it had been rather sudden. He had anticipated that I'd been using family planning. He didn't say contraception, he didn't say 'being careful', he said family planning. I wasn't in the slightest surprised that he thought that was my job. No, I was once again surprised by his choice of words, which were at times so stuffy and bourgeois that at first I thought it was his way of being ironic.

Thanks to his merciless love of the truth, I also learned that he had envisaged that the best age to become a father would be around forty. I was eating an ice cream during this lecture. Always when I think of that Germany trip, I see Gabriel staring at the road ahead talking and me eating. Forty was the ideal age, partly because he expected to have reached the point financially that he had in mind. I, on the other hand, had no conception of myself as a forty-year-old, neither would I have expected to spend the next ten years with Gabriel. As I've said, I had no plan at all, except for the vague idea of a dissertation on the Brontë siblings, which was actually also just an expression of my general lack of any plan. I assumed that in Gabriel's meticulously calculated future, the mother of his future children would ideally have been younger than I was. I threw the question out there in the overheated rental car. He looked at me, then back at the road, and said, Fleur, you're perfect.

Gabriel

The Wall came down shortly after I finished high school. I went to a grammar school with a Classics specialism. It was home to the Thomanerchor, Leipzig's St Thomas Choir. I might have been in that famous choir, if I'd had any talent for singing. I got a place at the school on academic grounds, although good grades didn't necessarily mean anything when it came to the final exams. My grandfather was a self-employed troublemaker, my aunt had made a run for it over the border, my mother was dead, and my father was from a non-socialist foreign country, which might not have been mentioned anywhere officially, but unofficially it was most certainly noted, everywhere from school documents to Stasi files.

In spite of all that, I got the university place I wanted, at the College of Architecture and Civil Engineering in Weimar, which was renamed the Bauhaus University again shortly after. Before that I was faced with three years in the army, as was the custom, but which in the final years of school seemed to me like I was about to be sent off into space after my exams. I only fully realised what it would have meant when the Wall came down, and military service was reduced to one and a half years instead of three. That was when I realised that I didn't want to serve at all, not in the National People's Army or the German Armed Forces, and neither did I plan on doing civilian service. I didn't want to waste any more time. How dare you decide how I spend my life, I thought, and I enrolled at the Technical University in West Berlin in 1990.

Grandpa would have preferred Weimar. The distance was almost the same, but he would have liked it if I'd studied at the Bauhaus University, and he didn't like Berlin. He raised it once when I visited him, but not in the way I expected. He wasn't tall, but he held himself like someone with authority. He stood before me and told me, wagging his finger at me, that I should never even for a second mould my future plans around him, that I should never put something off or avoid something for his sake. Do you understand, he asked in conclusion, as if he had given me a telling off. Yes, I said, and we changed the subject. He was in his mid-seventies, but he never repeated himself. He had thought carefully about this message. And I, who in the early nineties already had the feeling that I could go anywhere right then, only grasped much later how much easier he had made it for me with those words.

He had tried to shape his life around the GDR and had succeeded against the odds. He managed the tenement that his father had built in 1900, which he had been allowed to keep, as well as his two businesses. He sold his antiques and remained in the middle-class independent party, the LDPD, which at times claimed to be the only party that opposed the Socialist Unity Party, the SED. Whenever membership of a party was advantageous, Ernst would show up with his LDPD membership card insisting on his rights. It was more difficult to throw him out than someone with no party affiliation, but they pushed him around all the same. He also insisted on the privacy of his correspondence and refused to tolerate anyone opening his letters or parcels from the West, as I know from a Stasi file. Most of the time he acted as though he was living in a state governed by the rule of law. That didn't always work, but it worked more often than an outsider might assume. His sister had married a US officer after the war, his daughter Brigitte had gone first to the West and then on to Spain, and my grandmother's siblings also lived in West Germany. If we all bugger off, that'll be it for our houses, he would say. They're not getting their hands on them, oh no, Comrades, not while I'm still around. He lived in the firm belief that the GDR was an interim solution that had to be sat out. He wasn't wrong there, except that it was an interim solution that dragged on for forty years. None of that meant that he was fundamentally dissatisfied. He simply withdrew from the current era into his antiques. People from the West, who paid twenty-five deutschmarks a day to visit, commissioned him to buy collectibles for which they would have to pay much more back home. Sometimes he would have celebrities come and see him, mostly pop singers from the West, who would be paid for a concert in East German marks and didn't know what to do with the cash that would be worthless over the border. There's nothing to buy here, is there? as people were always saying in the East. But at Mr Loth's, there was always something worth spending your money on, because Mr Loth had an eye for things that would gain in value. When they walked through his door, his customers soon forgot they were in the land of scarcity. How about an Art Deco necklace? Some Meissen porcelain? A big game hunter's trophy? Hot stuff, this, keep this one just between you and me. Or a sideboard from Deutsche Werkstätten Hellerau? They knew what they were doing back then, even before the Bauhaus, he'd say, you'll like this.

He was seventy-four when the Wall fell. He had been allowed to travel since he was sixty-five. If you don't count from the founding of the GDR in 1949, but from when the Wall went up in 1961, he had only been stuck there for a total of seventeen years. In that sense, his tactic of sitting it out had worked out.

Well, it worked out however you looked at it, because he was always of the opinion that he had done everything right. He left me his properties and his values. In his own special way, he was even funny. Of course I missed him.

Ernst's sister Margarete – Aunt Gretel, as we called her – was living in a retirement community in Florida by this point. On the phone, I had the feeling that she was already in a place where neither pain nor time existed. My dear Ernst, she whispered thoughtfully, when's he coming back, then? You give him my love and my best wishes, won't you?

Brigitte, my mother's sister and my closest remaining relative, was now living in Andalusia, making ceramic tableware and saying she was done with Germany. Her decision to not even get on a plane for her father's funeral emphasised even more starkly what I already knew: I was now alone.

Fleur

Two years before my own wedding, I was bridesmaid for Bella, my father's goddaughter. I went all out at the hen party, acting like I'd never partied like that before. At the wedding I wore a lime green satin dress like the other three bridesmaids, and by the time Bella tossed the bouquet, I was even drunker than at the hen party. I stared hypnotically at my Nokia, waiting for a text from Sean, which, as expected, never came. My oldest friend's hyper-organised, detail-obsessed wedding felt to me like having the TV on in the background. Bella's father, Nicholas, a school friend of my dad's, had been a hippie, or so he claimed, before becoming a foreign correspondent. His memorable wedding speech came back to me when the time came to introduce Gabriel to my parents. An asinine effort full of copy and pasted jokes. Basically your standard wedding speech. One of the drole anecdotes from Bella's life went like this: Nicholas, father of the bride, man of the world, and top journalist, had naturally raised his daughters Isabella and Fiona to see all people as equal. Poor or rich? Illiterate or professor? Black or White? Such questions would never be asked in a house like his! Of course not! But then, during their time in Washington, DC, it turned out that his girls, who otherwise so rarely listened to their old dad, had taken one of his principles to heart in particular. Meaningful pause. A sheepish titter across the room. I had hoped Sean would reply and drive over from London to Winchester for the evening part of the wedding. It would have been our first official appearance together. I would introduce him as my boyfriend. Then came the sublime punchline from Uncle Nick, and I was relieved that he had passed up the chance, perhaps even slept through it: Bella and Fiona took their dad at his word, and within a year that big house in Washington wasn't just full of Black kids, ha ha ha, no, they also both had Black boyfriends. Imagine: Black sons-in-law-to-be! I looked around. The guests filled his pause with obedient laughter. Even the guests from the Middle East, Asia, and South America. They weren't Black people from Washington, DC, but they might well have shared in the general confusion about what the joke was precisely. The bride's dark and murky past? But, ha ha ha, all's well that ends well, and no one could fail to grasp that bit, because here was Bella sitting next to a deeply tanned White man, hurrah! Would Black guests have applauded a cheap gag about Asians? I assumed, yes, sadly. It seemed like everyone was happy as long as he himself wasn't being targeted.

Bella took a sip of champagne and raised her eyebrows; Russell, her groom, tried out an amused expression. Fiona, at that point, hadn't told her parents that instead of a Black son-in-law she would soon be presenting them with a future daughter-in-law.

Nick would sell his own granny for a joke, my dad said the next morning, you know that.

My mum just shook her head – about what, as usual, she didn't elaborate.

There we were, a year and a half later, faced with the son-in-law question, or rather, I was faced with this question because Gabriel dismissed out of hand the idea that his existence might raise any doubts. I wondered how much of an Uncle Nick my parents had inside them. They had spent almost their entire working lives in Africa and felt more at home there than in Europe. Their friends were scattered all over the world, they were non-racists on principle, and they genuinely loved humanity, possibly the main thing they had in common. But that didn't necessarily mean they would be delighted at the prospect of a Black son-in-law. After all, they had adopted me, a White baby, because they wanted a child who looked like them. I was ready for anything. Racism happens to the best of people, I thought.

My parents loved Gabriel. I had underestimated them. It hadn't occurred to me that it was less about him or themselves, than about me. Gabriel's resolute and unwavering way of loving me convinced them from day one. It helped that he was so polite and successful. They would have vehemently denied it, but it also helped that he refused to be pigeonholed into the English class system. No slang, a German accent. He wasn't poor, but the presents he gave weren't gimmicky, they were carefully curated acts of kindness: first editions, records, concert tickets, wine. It helped that he had a profession that people could relate to. It helped that he was Gabriel and not Sean.

Regardless of the questionable circumstances – after my Ibiza trip I had flown straight to Germany, from where I eventually returned pregnant and practically married – my friends thought it all sounded terribly romantic. Enviable and almost cinematically spontaneous. They congratulated us on our determination. Why wait, it wouldn't make anything better. How long have you known each other, anyway? Just over a year. Oh, for so long? How come we're only hearing about your dishy fiancé now?

We managed to get married two months before Albert's arrival. Big belly, small wedding. Gabriel booked a table at a Michelin-starred restaurant for us, our witnesses, and my parents. He dressed impeccably and hired a well-known cellist for the ceremony. She started playing as my father walked me down the aisle, and Gabriel turned to me, nodded almost imperceptibly in her direction, and winked at me. The cello was a message just for me. Remember? Yes, I remember. I'd get off the train, sullied, my cello with me as an alibi, which you, Gabriel, would take from me and lug around the city because you thought it was important to me and was part of me. Flooded with hormones and utterly delirious, overtired and, to my mind, uglier than ever – because the pregnancy was making my hair fall out and had pushed my hairline back five centimetres – I was bawling by the time Dad handed me over to Gabriel.

For years I tried to destroy our wedding picture, without success. Gabriel must have hidden the negative away in a safe deposit box, because it keeps resurfacing. It reminded me of Jan van Eyck's *The Arnolfini Wedding*. A picture that fascinated me as a child because the bride was pregnant, and I knew that in the past, you weren't allowed to have children until after the wedding. Later I read that her pregnancy wasn't a realistic depiction, but a representation of fertility. Anyway, in our wedding photo my belly is as obvious as Arnolfini's bride's, and my ghastly bald forehead and puffy face complete the Renaissance look. Gabriel doesn't look like Arnolfini, who was straight out of a horror movie, but just like the couple in the painting, we look neither at the viewer or at each other. Two people, overrun by circumstances, who don't know what they're getting themselves into. After I removed it from our living room for the first time, I took him to the National Gallery to show him the painting. He was even more thrilled with the photo after that, convinced it was a recreation of the van Eyck, an inspired composition by the photographer, whom he had obviously underestimated. We are looking to our future, said Gabriel, who still has this monstrous photograph on his desk today. In a way, yes, I thought, seeing my gaunt face, because that was the day I became Mrs Loth: Lot's wife, the woman who must not under any circumstances turn and look back at Sodom and Gomorrah.

Gabriel

After Albert was born, I realised how little I knew about myself as a young boy. You were a relatively easy baby, that was how my grandfather summed up that period of my life. We were missing the chroniclers, my mother and grandmother, who would have been able to expand on whether I was cute, or what I had done that was funny. Of course I had some baby and toddler pictures of myself, but I didn't know whether I had started walking and talking early or late, what I liked, what I was scared of, and I knew almost no childhood anecdotes about myself. I didn't miss them, but when everyone piled in around Albert, it occurred to me that it was probably the only time in your life when you prompt such unrestrained enthusiasm in others. A time that you will only know from other people's stories.

Albert would definitely have a bit of both of us in him, said Danielle, Fleur's mother, who had documented Fleur's childhood with great care. If you really looked, you could indeed see hints of us both, although I found that from the beginning he had his own distinct features that, fascinatingly, changed from week to week. His pale eyes, which everyone said were still finding their colour, became darker, but not brown, more a slate blue. He peered around at the world with those eyes, as if he already knew it all. Then, when Fleur's mother said he also had a certain resemblance to Henry, Fleur's brother, we glanced at each other. Fleur aghast, me amused. We never asked Danielle if she had actually forgotten for a moment that Fleur and Henry weren't biological siblings. He looks like you, people always told me when we were out on our walks. Whenever I could, I would skip my lunch break and instead go home and take Albert out for a bit. Not as often as I would have liked, I later thought, but still. The only time I tried to sing him a lullaby, he had his first laughing fit. He cooed and kicked until he was red in the face, that's how funny he found it. I called Fleur to come and see, and the three of us laughed together. My singing sounds like dodecaphony, so it was a compliment that he didn't cry. This wasn't going to be my way of soothing him. But he calmed down when I spoke. So I'd talk on the phone or sometimes talk through my projects to him when he was at my side or when I was out pushing him. No one walked around talking out loud back then, so maybe I looked like a homeless nut job pushing his stuff around in a pram. I didn't care. I hadn't realised how often people would come and talk to you when you're out and about with a baby. People would make room for me, they'd let me go first in the queue, they smiled at me, they liked me, because of him. Maybe strangers used to like me that much at that age, I thought. Before he could say his name, Albert and I had walked the length and breadth of London. And I had a much better idea of where I wanted to live in the future and where I definitely didn't.

One drizzly afternoon Fleur called me and asked me to pick up a few things. I left Albert in front of Waitrose with his rain cover over the pram, went inside, and when I came back out with the shopping, his pram was surrounded by an outraged mob. At first I thought they were just admiring him, until I realised they thought he'd been abandoned. They'd pulled their phones out and one woman was leaning into the pram, about to spread her germs onto my clean son. I pushed her aside. He wasn't Moses floating down the Nile in a basket; he was a baby sleeping in his high-end pram outside a supermarket, where one of his parents had popped in for a few essentials. The pram laden with brand new baby stuff, today's newspaper, the supermarket, the neighbourhood, the baby sleeping peacefully – it was all so obvious that I couldn't believe that a mob of fretting busybodies had amassed in such a short time. Thank you, I said, it's all fine, I'm here now, this is my son. What were you thinking, I heard. We were so worried. When I heard someone mutter about how irresponsible I was and that I could at least thank them, that was too much. A few metres away there were two beggars in their regular spot. Right under a cash machine, making anyone getting money out practically have to stand on their beds. I pointed to them.

Why don't you go and ask them if they're all right? Or aren't they sweet and cuddly enough for you? Then I walked away, the collective resentment of the superfluous saviours tutting away behind me. Okay, I thought, as Albert slept on, this was a busy High Street in London and I was acting like a clueless mother in the small-town Leipzig of the seventies. Didn't everyone leave their prams outside the shops back then? Along with dogs and older children who were also left to wait outside? Didn't the shops even have signs in the window with crossed out dogs and prams? I wasn't sure, and anyway, it didn't matter. Different time, different place. A child could be kidnapped anywhere, I thought. I got it. All the same, it was a lot of fuss about nothing, right? When I told Fleur about it, she told me about a case from the nineties. Two children kidnapped a toddler from a shopping centre and killed him. Even the abridged version was one of the most gruesome stories I had ever heard, but Fleur didn't spare me the details, like the fact that they didn't kill the kid right away. It was a mixture of morbid fascination and parenting advice.

The next day, when a young staff member said he felt more vulnerable than ever before, I immediately agreed with him, even though I loathed small talk in the men's bathroom. It was the autumn of 2001, and it was only later that I realised he had been talking about 9/11. Anyway, when I walked around with Albert, he never cried, and it helped me clear my head. I found I had the best ideas. Fleur gave him thousands of nicknames; I called him partner. A shame he can't remember that.

Fleur

If you want to make God laugh, tell Him your plans. This saying didn't seem to apply to Gabriel – his plans were working out fine. It was a good thing I didn't have any, at least not at that point. That's not sarcasm, it's what explains the harmony that existed between us for years. Albert's birth re-emphasised our domains, which were already clearly delineated. I had a job that could be done from home. Gabriel, spurred on by his sense of himself as provider, worked eighty-hour weeks. If there were setbacks or problems, he would fire up an emergency generator that kept him going in top gear for days on end with hardly a wink of sleep. He worked on planes, he worked with jet lag, he worked at night and started again as soon as he got up, even while he was busy making the perfect omelette. I'd watch him, baby on my hip, unable to multitask even being a mother and having a haircut at the same time. If we ever asked ourselves (we never did in any serious way), who was responsible for going out into the world and whose remit was nursing a feverish child at night, those roles were already set in stone by this stage.

Gabriel, an avowed opponent of socialist ideas who liked to play the neoliberal at dinner parties, had discovered his socially conscious streak as an architect. He had developed a super-functional prefabricated house that could be built in slums, a bungalow made of modules that could be combined and slotted together like an IKEA kitchen, a comparison he didn't appreciate. Aesthetics and materials were adapted to the environment and climate, and the houses exuded precisely the lightness that everyday life in a slum did not. The first prototypes in a favela, surrounded by tropical plants, looked like a holiday resort for surfers. While I was playing with wooden blocks, Gabriel, who had been obsessed with model-making since he was a child, tinkered with the miniature version of his designer shanty house. If I wasn't beaming with happiness at that time, it was because I had resigned myself to the fact that radiant happiness simply wasn't in my nature, and because I understood that there was something worth striving for more than happiness: warm, stable contentment.

So Gabriel threw himself into the idea of cost-effective, dignified living. He abhorred small talk and conversations that were, as he put it, unproductive. Once, I called the host of a seated dinner beforehand and asked her to please seat him next to someone who might interest him thematically. I didn't like doing it, but on the other hand, I knew I was doing us all a favour. Otherwise he would have inflicted his waves of unfiltered, bored contempt on the entire table of ten. It was different when it came to his projects. He could have left the communication to his staff, but the manufacturers and suppliers of mosquito screens, solar panels and non-splintering Plexiglas became his favourite people to talk to. He was proud of the projects they completed and the accolades he received for his ideas, but it wasn't a priority for him to be there on site. He flew to Brazil twice; he loved that country – in his own way. It was the home of Oscar Niemeyer, after all. He skipped the two projects in Africa, even though I had suggested I could accompany him. He didn't have time, he said, and it was true: he genuinely never had enough time.

When he was asked in a BBC interview why we didn't see more of these housing solutions for the poor, he said that, on the contrary, there were many intelligent designs for dignified housing for the very poor. One major obstacle, he said, often lay with the residents themselves, who, against the background of their precarious living conditions, often couldn't make the most of what was on offer and soon misused them. He said he assumed that the context of their challenging living conditions meant it wouldn't be long before the residents of his homes dismantled them to sell individual parts or burn them as fuel, or that the bathrooms would be converted into chicken coops, and the houses would end up overcrowded. The presenter seemed to wonder whether this was some unusual kind of humour and asked him what made him think that. It sounded, well, creative, but was that really what he had in mind for his houses?

No, Gabriel said, but I'm not a dreamer, I'm a realist.

He then listed a few examples from the twentieth century that showed the extent to which the social ideas of architects and the reality of poor people's lives had drifted apart, which is why most of these projects were doomed to failure. The moderator coughed in consternation and moved on to the next question, which concerned Gabriel's latest project, a museum to house the art collection of a Central Asian billionaire. I could hear Gabriel's friendly tone, the smile in his voice as he spoke, which lingered throughout the interview because he loved to talk about his work. It made no difference whether it was about a megalomaniac temple to art in the steppes, or about his passion project, which he had with such professional prudence just kicked into the bin. I knew Gabriel, but hearing him speak from the car radio alienated me even more than the moderator, who brought this madness to a smooth conclusion: yes, what contrasting worlds you move between as an architect. Mr Loth, thank you very much for this conversation.

That must have been in 2003 or 2004. Fortunately, before the time of the guaranteed shitstorm, before the era when everyone was constantly quoting and commenting on everything anyone said, which didn't mean it was all forgotten. Gabriel had made one of his merciless judgments, targeting the poor, who, you might understand him as insinuating, were partly to blame for their own plight and were not in a position to be helped. The worst thing about it wasn't even his destructive impulse for frankness, no, the worst thing was that he had been invited onto the show as a visionary, a bearer of hope.

Albert and I waited for him outside the BBC building. When he got into the car and asked me how he was, I suggested he leave the press work to Mark. He immediately agreed with me. That was Gabriel, too: he had asked me for my opinion, not praise, and my opinion, I was always amazed to discover, was actually important to him.

Do you think people are bothered by my accent? he asked me. He was self-critical, indeed as hard on himself as he was on others, but when it came to assessing where his faults lay from other people's perspective, he was so limited that it almost bordered on a disability.

No one minds your accent, Gabriel. Besides, if there's one profession where a German accent fits, it's architect.

So what was the problem? he asked me, turning around to grin at Albert, who was sitting in the back in his car seat, staring spellbound at the passing cars.

The problem was *what* you said. You've just won two awards for improving living conditions in slums. And then you say in an interview that these people aren't in a position to live better?

Did you listen to the whole interview? Did you hear my examples? That's not my opinion, darling, that's the truth.

I would have liked to put my hands on my face and groan into them, but I was driving.

And on the BBC, the world's most revered network, there should be room for the truth, I think, and also the maturity to hear it and take it on board, don't you think?

I think Mark should be the one to deal with the press.

Okay, said Gabriel, thinking about it seriously for a moment, before saying again, okay.

Gabriel

Taking in the full vista of the site, I felt like a commander in some epic movie. It was my first construction site in the open countryside. The railway station we were building was the vanguard, the city would follow. In Europe, something like this would take decades, but this was China. This was the implementation of an idea I had developed, I thought to myself, proud, happy, almost megalomaniac. Then I tried to forget everything I knew and look at the scene anew. What was this here, really? Green hills on the horizon, before them the outskirts of a town; beneath my feet, three hundred and sixty degrees of mud and swarming activity. Many, many people hard at work. Not legionaries but construction workers, not weapons but construction equipment, not horses but Chinese copycats of European and Japanese cars, not a field camp but a workers' slum hanging off the construction site like an appendix.

When we won the tender, we might have understood what the deal was even without the translators: you, dear friends from the land of the setting sun, have a blank canvas. Go wild. You can build a monument of concrete and glass in a city that not so long ago was just farms and fields. In the past, cattle once grazed here. We are bulldozing away the present day with its exceptionally drab functional architecture. We are giving you a blank canvas for the future, with the new high-speed train that will race into your station, and your responsibility is to make it a reality without delay. Needless to say, it's none of your business how we treat our workers or what we pay them. No politics, as you put it so nicely in your country. We are the money and the power, you are the architects, the executors of our will. This was a Faustian pact, and we could hardly have expected anything else. The written part of our contract consisted of a schedule, which in Europe would be what you might allow for a largeish bus shelter, and the finance plan, which at first glance looked realistic. For us, it was all about the station and the prestige, less about the money. A project like this, implemented in a country with a low wage and low price structure, had a much lower total volume than it would in the UK and was therefore far less lucrative than you might expect from the scale. The low wages meant that people earned too little to live anywhere other than on the construction site. It also meant that they couldn't travel home to their villages whenever there was a pause in construction because the ground was frozen. It meant that they worked in conditions that we had to overlook, although of course we couldn't help but see. This wasn't Denmark, we knew that beforehand, nor was it exclusively about altruism. But I liked to think that along with all the technical problems we had to solve constantly, it should also be possible to build ethically. And that should be true regardless of whether you were in an EU country, a sultanate, or a turbo-capitalist Communist Party dictatorship. Our non-intervention pact commanded me not to ask anyone personally how they were doing. But after a few visits to the construction site, where I had seen their huts in the distance, I had a batch of my pop-up tents delivered.

After my prefab house, which had to be transported on a pickup truck, I had designed a thermal pop-up tent. If all the homeless people in a major city put one up at night, they would turn the city into a gigantic igloo colony. But when I designed the tent, I wasn't thinking of homeless people but of construction workers. People like these who I saw working in a three-shift system. Their only protection consisted of helmets. The different colours showed which team they were on. Otherwise, they wore all kinds of clothes, including old suits and sandals.

The tent initiative was logistically extravagant, and well-intentioned, but ultimately futile. Not one single tent was opened as far as I could see. It seemed crass to demand gratitude, so I said nothing. On my next visit, they had disappeared, and I hoped that people had taken them back to their villages or at least got some decent money selling them on. The subject never came up again. And I never found out if my actions resulted in that loss of face that was so dreaded in Asia, and whether the way they smiled at me at the next meeting was a look of pity, disdain, or just a simple smile.

I could stop asking myself questions like this once we were joined by Yu Yan. Everything changed with her on the team. Yu Yan, whom we called June, was our interpreter. She was of a similar age to Mark and me, and she had grown up in England where she started studying architecture, before stopping when she had her two children. After her divorce, she applied to us for a role, but we didn't have any part-time positions, so we turned her down. To start with, in China we worked with the local interpreters our clients hired, and although Mark didn't have a problem with them, I did. I feared too much was lost in translation. I felt like a simpleton who was only passed on whatever information it suited them to pass on. Mark remembered June, I assume because he had saved her under the category 'hot', and it was a huge improvement all round. Shop talk went like clockwork because not only did she speak both languages, but she also understood the context. Besides, June's presence meant that certain other questions simply vanished into thin air. The social codes and hierarchies remained inscrutable, but I no longer lost time and sleep worrying about it. I also stopped talking to people who understood English, insisting that she translate everything for me, even the most trivial customer service requests at the hotel reception. In the evening at the bar, I had her go over that day's meetings with me again, explaining who had said what and how. When did yes mean no, what made them laugh like that, who was in the government, who was a new capitalist, who were the really important figures, and who were just bums on seats? I completely abandoned any effort to communicate directly, whether it was a business matter or something that only concerned me. You could say that I was being a moron.

It didn't seem to make any difference to our Chinese partners. Mark made jokes; June did her job. I asked my questions directly to her perfectly symmetrical face, from which the answers also came. We rose from our meal, and her shiny black ponytail guided me to the exit. We're going to another bar? Fine. We're heading back to our rooms? Great. We're taking a private jet to another major city that we've never heard of? Okay.

It was six months before I diagnosed myself with a particularly feverish case of infatuation. An island fever that set in the moment I arrived in China and instantly subsided when I arrived back in London, when I would say goodbye to the lotus blossom and go home to my English rose. This flower comparison alone was evidence that I had lost the plot. This went on for a few days at a time every couple of months for a period of over two years. It was sometimes stimulating, often unbearable, but most of the time I tried to accept it as an inevitable side effect of the project. Whenever I saw June in the London office, I still saw that her face had the golden ratio, but it didn't distract me, and I didn't feel the same urge to follow her everywhere like I did in China. Even more stressful than this desire was my anxiety about how much of it she noticed. After all, June translated not only our words, but she also picked up the slightest vibration in the room, which was invaluable for us on a business level, but for me personally, it could have meant that she knew how I felt long before I was even aware of it. She could read everything and yet herself remained unreadable.

You find your interpreter attractive, which she is, you don't flirt with her, you're happy when she orders a cup of tea for you in a motherly way – it's fine, don't be so hard on yourself; everyone's entitled to a bit of distraction. Think of it as a luxury and stop creating a problem where there isn't one. I kept telling myself this, but it didn't help. My casual approach to the matter was getting on my nerves more than the matter itself. June had taken over my mind. I couldn't sleep, and when I did my disrupted dreams looked like Wong Kar-wai movies. This can't go on, I thought, when I was jolted awake by my own snoring on the flight home after one visit. I'm going to have to fire her. But by the time we said goodbye at Heathrow with a friendly hug between colleagues, I was already cooling off again.

Have you had chicken pox? Fleur asked when I got home.

This abrupt change of mood did me good, even though I had no idea what she was talking about. I had a vague memory of being sick as a child, with small spots, but it could have been measles, rubella, chicken pox, who knows. Although on the plane I would change seats as soon as anyone near me so much as coughed, I generally presumed I had good immunity to any kind of virus that my son might bring home from nursery. Albert, this youthful extension of my own organism, was covered in spots, which Fleur had smeared with a white lotion. Otherwise, he seemed well enough. After two days I looked the same, except that I couldn't get out of bed for three weeks, which I would have liked to call precious family time if I hadn't been so ill. Childhood diseases are so much more dangerous in adults, didn't you know that? That's why parents hold chicken pox or rubella parties, so they can be sure their kids get it when they're young. No, I didn't know that. Lying there, feverish, I had regular updates from Mark and June on the latest. As always after our trips, June turned from an obsession back into an employee who called me to summarise the conference calls with China. Chicken pox, ha ha, she said, those weeks stuck at home! Mine both had it, one straight after the other. What joy. You mustn't scratch or it'll scar, and that would be a shame for your lovely complexion.

While I lay in bed, I listened to Fleur and Albert's daily comings and goings. I learned what a long, tedious process getting dressed was. He was like a wolf cub forced into human clothing. I heard how much he loved being tickled by Bojana, our cleaning lady, how animated he was when he chatted away to himself, how loudly he stomped around the house. He made an impressive noise for his size. I heard Indian and African pop music blaring out from the stereo, alternating with Motown, all Fleur's picks, and Shaggy and Shakira on repeat, at insufferable frequency, which Albert demanded. If it went quiet, without first hearing the front door or the car, it meant Fleur was working and Albert would be sitting on the floor painting with headphones on. This ritual was new to me, too.

Their well-tuned routine made me grumpy and happy at the same time. Grumpy because they didn't seem to miss me, happy because I felt so at home listening to them. After all, this was also my life that they were living.

Fleur

Emmanuèle, my main author from France, had always been prolific, but now she was churning manuscripts out like a machine. I was translating a book a year by her by this point, and because of her colossal sales figures, I was also being asked to translate her backlist. It made me about as successful as a translator could be. From time to time, I was mentioned in the reviews for my 'congenial translation', and I was once awarded a prize for my work. Emma touched readers by showing them the wretchedness of their existence with such virtuosity that they didn't know whether to laugh or cry. She struck a masterful balance. Although her characters all seemed very similar in terms of their frame of mind. Emma saw little reason to think of anything beyond these invariably depressive protagonists; her readers were hooked on them. I sometimes wondered whether she never changed anything because she didn't want to or because she couldn't. So I spent my mornings and sometimes also nights inside the heads of sexually frustrated middle-aged academics who viewed the world through an excruciatingly cynical lens while smoking and drinking themselves to death, and was surrounded the rest of the time by two people who were perfectly content with their lives. One was on his way to becoming a celebrity architect, the other was getting more cute and cuddly by the day. I hopped back and forth between these mindsets and appreciated them both. I didn't talk about it, but I saw myself as the ideal translator for Emma's texts. That could be me, I thought, immersing myself into her dark lakes of hopelessness. At other moments, I thought, it's your own fault, you degenerate first-world psychos. Enough for today, I have to look after my boy now.

Gabriel had become the father he had probably always imagined himself as. When he was there. He had explained the world to Albert before he could even tie his shoelaces, and for a few days at a time he would be the loving but strict stickler for principles before he disappeared again. I felt that life would get serious soon enough, so I read and sang with Albert, but I kept the early learning to the bare minimum. Also because I hated driving and I found going out in public with a child who was prone to unexpected outbursts of rage all a bit much. Albert's angelic looks conquered our hearts. When he started screaming though, no one looked at his distorted features but glared at me, sometimes with pity, usually expecting me to do something to shut him up. Well, if there was a magic word that could turn the raging Rumpelstiltskin back into my sweet little boy, I never found it. Afraid of confrontation, I sat out this phase at home. Gabriel didn't mind that he was more often the one Albert was cross with. At home as with work, for him it was all about getting the best possible result. That's why he wanted an au pair, and I didn't. Why would a man who is never at home want an au pair? For him it was simply good form, something to round off the image he worked at day and night. I, on the other hand, saw no benefit to having a stranger living in my house. A young woman whose main priority was presumably to find a cheap way to stay in London, and to that end had to pretend that she could think of no better way to spend her days than with someone else's toddler. Even if we found someone who was genuinely interested in Albert, I had no idea which part of my duties I would be expected to entrust to her. I would have had to sacrifice my freedom to a schedule, only to be faced with the question of what I was supposed to do with my Albert-free time. Why expend so much interpersonal effort for someone whose function was effectively a dogwalker? Except for our cleaner, Bojana, and my mother, we didn't have any regular babysitters. I didn't see the point of going out only to spend the entire evening talking about the babysitter: we have to go now, yes, we need to relieve the babysitter, thank you, that's kind, but no more for me please, yes, it's a shame, but it's almost eleven, yes exactly: the babysitter. I hated those evenings and would rather stay at home.

My mum encouraged me to enjoy every second. He'll never be so cute again, she reminded me. I knew I was getting weirder by the day, but I couldn't help it. My charming little man and I spent our days playing and dancing. Because dancing was the only thing I missed from the previous phase of my life, and he loved it. I'd crank up the stereo and put him on my hip at first, later I put him on the floor and bounced around with him until we both squealed with delight. He hated his recorder, he loved painting, he was like me with crafts – messy – but he was an adorable dancer. I took a back seat when it came to nurturing talents, but my son's sense of rhythm was obvious. It's in his blood, said Bojana, who idolised him, and I was glad that Gabriel wasn't there. Dancing all day, having *it* in his blood, all that was missing were the drums. And then the drums came. Albert wasn't interested in any instruments besides the drums. He was the Little Drummer Boy, whether it suited his Afrophobic father or not. He would have preferred to see him with a violin, that much was obvious. But as far as I was concerned, anyone who, like Gabriel, claimed to be non-musical and was even proud of the fact, forfeited his right to have a say when it came to choosing an instrument for his son. Besides, he was hardly ever at home. Together with my brother, I bought Albert an impressive collection of percussion instruments from around the world, in his size. The tribal beast of rhythm moved in with us and stayed.

I knew Gabriel would bring it up at some point, the only question was when. When it happened, I knew before he did, and I was annoyed before it even kicked off.

We were upstairs in his room, Albert and I, when Gabriel came home. I was fascinated by his concentration when he drummed – my son who was usually so easily bored. Where are my darlings, my husband called and came in. I usually did bedtime, and I spent most of the days with him, and I don't think I realised how rarely Gabriel was in Albert's room. It struck me when he stood there on the toy-strewn carpet in his cliché architect outfit like a black monolith. He gave us both a kiss, straightened up again, and surveyed the nursery as if it were one of his construction sites. One that had been tampered with. We'd decorated and reorganised since he was last in here. I knew it was too colourful for him and above all too untidy. I left the two of them alone and went downstairs. Gabriel came down again soon after, while Albert went back to his tablas.

Can't he learn a more beautiful instrument?

I not only expected the question, I even knew how it would be worded.

Every instrument is beautiful if you can play it. And for his age, he's really good.

I sawed away at a ham, avoiding the cumbersome slicer he'd bought, a typical Gabriel acquisition, as if we were an Italian deli. He poured us wine. We sidled furtively around each other.

He's having fun and he's talented, I said.

Grumpily, he chewed on a piece of ham and washed it down with red wine. He can drink with such contempt. I drank with an emphatic contentedness.

Why don't you teach him the cello, he asked me.

Because he doesn't want to. (And because I don't actually play the cello, darling.)

He's five. He doesn't want to brush his teeth either.

Then give me one reason why he should learn an instrument he doesn't like, when he can learn one that he loves.

He said nothing. Aggressively we nibbled and sipped away, nudging past each other. Can I please, thank you, drawer, fridge, tap, on, off. Sigh. I poured us more wine and drank in big gulps. I tried to wash down my hostile thoughts, but instead flushed them up to the surface.

Gabriel's entire approach to life was based around not fulfilling stereotypes. To that end, he had assembled an impressive collection of counter-clichés: from his alleged love of classical music and the full array of conservative status symbols to his emphatically rigid body language. Everything he represented, bought, and claimed to like was a statement. If they existed at all, the prejudices he was so anxious to debunk were one-dimensional and found only in the minds of people he didn't even need to care about. I had watched this tense struggle for years, finding it sometimes amusing, sometimes painful, but I had never told him how obvious it was that that is what he was doing. Now I summarised it in one bilious sentence.

Not liking drumming doesn't make you White, Gabriel.

I beg your pardon? We had often been strangers, but never enemies.

What I'm trying to say is that the Black man you refuse to be is a crude caricature. Do you really think people see you that way? It's an insult to the people around you who don't think that way at all. If you constantly anticipate these clichéd thoughts, you keep them alive all the more!

He was silent.

Do you understand what I mean?

I wasn't sure I had expressed myself at all clearly, I was agitated, and at the same time I felt horribly sorry for everything at that very moment, but his neurosis also affected our lives, Albert's and mine. Gabriel made me wait for a response. With all the coldness he could summon up, he said: no.

I remembered a rule – I didn't know where I had read it – which had unfortunately slipped my mind for a moment: only argue about the thing you're actually arguing about. And that was Albert.

I may have found a teacher for him. We should be grateful if he – Mr Singh – will take on such a young pupil.

Gabriel had sat down and was staring into his lap. It was briefly quiet. Then we heard Albert.

By the way, what he's playing are tablas. They're from India, not Africa, if that's your problem.

I don't have a problem with Africa, I have a problem with the noise, he said. He spoke to me as if he needed to calm me down.

We could hear ourselves chewing and swallowing. I suffer from almost neurotic noise sensitivity, just not with my son.

Our neighbour Anke had recently complained about the noise.

We were still living in our beautiful Victorian semi then, sharing a thin party wall with Geoffrey and Anke, a German who Gabriel couldn't stand. Germans, I had learned, didn't fall into a comradely embrace when they met other Germans outside Germany. That is, Anke had actually been looking forward to meeting a fellow countryman and had no reason to suspect the extent to which Gabriel saw her as a disruption to his London identity. After the first and only meal we had at theirs, I had to listen to Gabriel rant for an hour about everything she had said or done wrong. A German East-West rift had opened up in the middle of Notting Hill. When Anke learned that he had grown up in the GDR, she asked him a few questions, and even I was struck by her blithe naiveté. I learned more about the German-German problem that evening than I had in six years with a German man. Because I knew that tone of voice. You heard it when you met Europeans in Africa. Not people with experience, but newbies. Recent arrivals, still wide-eyed and amazed by everything. Anke clearly had a similarly enthusiastic, patronising impression of a country that was now hers, too.

How can she not know Weimar? Gabriel snorted, and his disdain for our neighbour billowed out of every pore. Goethe? Schiller? Bauhaus? Or how about the Weimar Republic? Never heard of it, Anke? The woman earns seven figures, and she's not even ashamed of her ineffable stupidity.

I think six, I corrected him. But a six-figure annual salary has nothing to do with education – and everything to do with the sector you're in.

Thank you, honey, why do I keep forgetting that? He gave me a quick hug, then continued his rant. On this subject, he seemed to have lost his usual talent for not letting people get to him. Thoroughly irked, he stomped around our deluxe German kitchen and worked through the problem of his country of birth.

I was so happy not to have to hear this bullshit the last few years, he blustered. The West Germans are acting like occupiers. And in the East they feel like they're not being taken seriously, sometimes rightly so, but on the other hand, they also can't stop whining about their already internalised second-class status, taking every opportunity to fulfil the cliché they're so upset about. It's an unbearable spiral of snobbery and snivelling sentimentalism, and this in a country that is doing so well. I'm glad I'm out of there, very glad!

The next day there was a cheesecake on our doorstep, but Anke had made it with quark rather than cream cheese, which made it a German cheesecake. She had also written a nice card, which I read to Gabriel, who avoided her cheesecake like the plague, and who never said anything to Anke again beyond a mandatory hello. I was all the more annoyed that her sensitivities, of all things, were more important to him than Albert's talent.

She would also complain if he practised the violin or the piano. She would always complain, not because it's loud, but because she's Anke, I said.

He looked through me, absently. I looked at his beautiful, manicured fingers drumming away on the dining room table. He didn't even realise he did this all the time, that was how distant he often was, even from himself. I said nothing.

We should move, he muttered.

But not because of her. Since when do you even care what she says?

It's fine, he said, do what you want. You already have...

He capitulated. Still bristling slightly, he let me sit on his lap. We made up again. He never said anything again about my insinuation that he wished he was White, which really wasn't true. A few weeks later, he came home with a DVD and showed me what Albert's phase reminded him of. We watched *The Tin Drum*, a movie every cinephile knows and certainly every German. The story of a boy with wide-set eyes, who doesn't grow, doesn't speak, doesn't play with other children, who just drums and shrieks until glass shatters. The fact that he associated Albert with this fictitious misfit upset me even more than his drum phobia. My goodness, I thought, I'm not about to start a discussion about the metaphorical statements of Günter Grass, especially since I hadn't actually read him. I took it upon myself to rectify that.

Gabriel

My endlessly deliberated and discarded options concerning June became superfluous in the spring of 2007. I didn't have to sack her, ignore her, or get her into bed with her after all, because it turned out June was marrying Mark. I had missed the fourteen-month build-up to this finale, because I was so preoccupied with myself. And because June had compelled Mark to absolute discretion. She had also made it quite clear that there would be no messing around with her. Okay, Mark told himself, then actually no. And then just okay, yes, and he broke up with his long-time girlfriend Karen. This was the first time our taste in women had overlapped, which no one but me knew about, because we weren't Jules and Jim, and normally I found even the phrase 'taste in women' distasteful. I was happy for Mark and June, and for me and Fleur, who had nothing at all to do with it. In fact I was almost ecstatically happy, which was unusual for me but it truly came from the heart.

Their ceremony was to be small like ours was; June had already had her pompous white wedding. I was Mark's best man, and standing next to the two of them, I didn't feel even a whisper of melancholy. June was like a sister-in-law to me now, and Mark looked happy. Fleur, who was like a rare species of orchid and only bloomed in very select conditions, stood behind us in a tightly pleated, concrete-grey silk dress, holding Albert by the hand and dabbing at her lower eyelids. All was well.

That was the summer when I found our house. It needed to be somewhere I could relax, including aesthetically. I wanted to build the future and live in a house from the late nineteenth century; I always had, and I knew that sooner or later I would find it. In my stocks and shares phase, I had discovered something about myself: I wasn't prone to hysteria. I could bide my time. Here I was in my – for an architect – unspectacular house, resisting the temptation to get swept away by the frenzy on the property market. The time would come.

The price was a steal for the size and location. We wouldn't have been able to afford it if it hadn't gone to auction. The previous owner, a young guy, had bought it from an elderly gentleman with no heirs and had only lived in it for two years before he was forced to sell up. Fleur thought this felt like bad karma and was wary about buying a house at auction. It didn't worry me. It wasn't repossessed, after all. We didn't know exactly what had gone wrong. All we knew was that the owner had set himself up with a sort of Neverland ranch at the peak of a rapid rise to success, which was then followed by a crash. Some kind of psychiatric diagnosis, not for us to speculate. Fortunately, he hadn't had time to completely wreck the house. We stood inside, Fleur horrified, me thrilled. I could picture how it would look after I had stripped it back. All Fleur could see was the clutter. The previous owner had surrounded himself as quickly as possible with all the paraphernalia he must have presumed was appropriate to his new income bracket. He was clearly inspired mainly by Hollywood movies and had installed an oversized marble staircase that made a complete mess of the floor plan. He had a confessional booth installed as a lift, a pool, and a dance floor in the basement. Name a bachelor cliché, he had it. There was hardly a surface that couldn't be raised or lowered electronically, an extravagance fit for a Bond villain, for which he had lost the remote controls.

Naturally, he had also collected art, or had art foisted on him. Looking through, all you could say the works had in common was that they were clearly bought by someone who was easily influenced and prone to pronounced mood swings. The few lucky hits he had scored, while randomly shooting in the dark, now belonged to us as we had bought the house 'sold as seen'. When his brother showed up at our house to ask gingerly if we'd consider returning a few items, he had the enormous good fortune of encountering not me, but Fleur. She decided to give it all back to him, and even helped him sell some items on. I tried not to listen when she named the sums involved. Her charity diminished our bargain somewhat, but I told myself, okay, never mind. She called it karma; I saw it as kindness. We had bought the real estate, the house; he could have some of its contents back for all I cared. He wouldn't thank us for it, but Fleur needed to feel she had done the right thing, and I loved Fleur.

David, the brother, had nowhere to put the stuff, so he had potential buyers come to the house, thus extending Fleur's involvement by months. She must have seemed like a fairy godmother. In the midst of legal claims and demands he couldn't meet, here out of the blue was a woman who was eager to help, even to her own cost. She was so generous that you had to wonder if she was even of sound mind. He told her about his brother, who had been a bit ahead of his time with his mobile phone apps start-up. To begin with, an impressive number of investors believed in his enthusiastic vision of the future but then dropped him just before he could prove the concept. His story was even more tragic when you considered that what he was suggesting was as obvious as electric windows once the first iPhone came out. When they finally found him, he had been hiding away for months in the smallest room of the house living off canned goods and pizza deliveries. A task force of police, a psychiatrist, and two social workers had to break into the house and found him lying naked on a filthy mattress, surrounded by utter squalor, reading comics.

When I got home, David would jump up as if I had caught him red-handed. He would disappear shortly after, only to be back the next day sitting in the kitchen with Fleur. If even I could see he was in love with her, surely Fleur had realised too, but she just acted as though she had a new job and a new co-worker. I didn't say anything. I saw this sexy Good Samaritan through the eyes of a twenty-five-year-old and felt lucky that she was my wife.

At some point the house was empty, and he was gone and forgotten. As was the brother, and his fall from grace, which I had no cause to reflect on until years later.

Fleur

When, at some point, Albert started answering me only in English, tossing aside our *maman-bébé* French like a picture book he had grown out of, I simply let it happen.

His neglectful hippie mother had let it lapse. I hadn't stuck firmly to the rule of only speaking French with him, because I hadn't been aware how much the rule mattered. I asked my mum – who also spoke only English with Albert – how they had managed it with us. We always spoke whichever language worked best at the moment, and you children took it all on in your playful way, she said, glorifying that time, and us, as well. She smiled at me pensively. Her hair was long as always, and now it was white as snow which oddly enough didn't make her look older. Danielle, *ma belle*, my dad had called her for over forty years. I would never be able to get out of the habit of comparing my looks with hers, of thinking I would look like her one day. If you believed what she said, children absorbed the languages around them by osmosis. But sadly it wasn't quite that simple. Every child is different, Dad shouted from the background, a platitude that also happened to be true. My brother speaks less French than I do and hardly any Flemish, in fact he only really speaks English, while I can also speak Swahili, although not as well as I used to. Our languages weren't a gift, they were a suggestion that I had accepted and my brother hadn't. As my parents always said, Albert might not be his biological nephew, but isn't he like Henry? In terms of languages, he certainly seemed to resemble him.

The Petite École Française, probably Albert's last chance to learn French as a matter of course, was by then out of the picture, because in choosing a preschool I'd latched onto an acquaintance with a child of the same age and prioritised logistics. Gabriel was persuaded by my choice, perhaps even more so by the fees.

Albert had been at school a while before Gabriel noticed that he wasn't bilingual. And it was only then that I became aware again of the lapse. We were in France, and it was as if Gabriel had unmasked a spy. He asked Albert: What does this mean? How do you say that again? When we passed a road sign, he would ask him about the numbers. Albert didn't answer. Not answering was as much a part of Albert as his curls, it didn't mean he didn't know. He ordered his ice cream in English and didn't respond to anyone who addressed him in French, not the nice adults, and certainly not the other children. For several days, Gabriel looked on and seemed to be wondering what was down to Albert's character and what was down to some other problem. On our last night in Biarritz, we had a babysitter and went out on our own to find a restaurant. On the way, I told him.

He's kind of dropped his French. I would have liked it to be different, but he can't speak it anymore.

Gabriel was horrified. The day before, Albert had hit another kid on the beach with his spade. Out of nowhere, said the other child's mother, and I believed her. My sweet-looking son has a propensity to be a thug. Gabriel told him off, a little half-heartedly, but that incident had upset him less than realising Albert was monolingual.

Kind of dropped it? How can he drop his first language if you speak it with him? What went wrong? What did you do? I don't understand.

Jeez. What did I do? He was talking about years of our life together as if I had burned the lasagne.

First of all, French is my first language, not his. Secondly, not everyone has a talent for languages, Gabriel.

Why would he need a talent? He just needed you to talk to him.

I did. I've been speaking French to him for years, all that time we barely got to see you.

Be fair, please.

Angrily, he scratched the back of his head. The silver in his hair had doubled, glistening in the evening sun. It had seemed for some time that he was becoming more attractive by the day. An impression which unfortunately I didn't have of myself.

You could have taught him German if his multilingualism is so important to you.

He ignored that and stopped to read the menu outside one of the waterfront restaurants. He had to be careful not to get a gin & tonic face. From the side you could see his upper eyelids and his cheeks were puffier. Other than that, he was in full bloom. Did other women see that too? We carried on walking. He put his arm around me. He could be physically affectionate and verbally indignant at the same time.

No one cares about German, he said, coming back to the topic. On the other hand, right, why not. In that sense, he could have learned Flemish. He had the ideal conditions. Shit.

Speaking isn't really his thing in general. I'm sorry. But that's the way it is.

Gabriel stopped, inspected the next restaurant, and nodded contentedly. This would be it. He took me by the elbow and steered me inside.

It doesn't work that way, Fleur. We can't let his wilfulness and your indulgence ruin his future prospects. If everyone thought like that, no one would eat with a knife and fork. What's the point?

His future prospects aren't in tatters because he's not multilingual at seven. That's typical overachiever nonsense, I said, even though I knew what he meant.

Une table pour deux, s'il vous plaît, he said in his textbook French.

The waiter made a joke that only I understood and took us to our table. We read the menu in silence. Then Gabriel closed his with a snap and said, you've just slept through the opportunity, Fleur. Admit it and let's figure out how to get out of this mess.

He had relied on the fact that in his absence everything was going according to plan. A solution had to be found. His route out of this so-called mess was a Swiss boarding school. Something else from the list of things he assumed he would have liked for his own life. Bullshit, I thought.

I was to blame, at least it felt that way, but I had my reasons to disagree, too. My own boarding school past, for example: a relatively short phase that I'd suppressed. As an adult, it's good form to claim that you were the child who was teased by everyone at school. Because, by implication, it also means that you stood out from the crowd. No one wants to look back and see themselves as one of the common mob. I didn't either, but it was what it was. My parents stayed in Kenya but sent my brother and me back to England to boarding schools for the last few years of school. I was fourteen, had the charisma of a broomstick and didn't have the faintest idea what my classmates were talking about. At times, I didn't even understand the words they used. The chances were high that

I might be branded the uncoolest girl in the school, except they had already agreed on another victim before I showed up. I didn't help her; I prioritised saving my own skinny ass by becoming part of the nasty mob. Kids are monsters. Nothing will have changed about this ghastly group dynamic. There's no motivation at all for the strongest and the most popular to forgo this ready-made entertainment. My throat tightened at the idea that my son could be on the other side, that he could be the one sitting alone at his table, having to pretend not to notice that they were throwing food at him. And Albert, being the way he was, wouldn't even tell us, I thought, almost crying, while Gabriel went to go and see the fish on display.

He's too young, I said, when he sat down again.

I don't think so at all, but let's sleep on it.

A few days later he flew to Central Asia, where his worries about Albert were drowned out for a few weeks by a major construction site. By the time he was back, the new school year had already begun.

Gabriel

China always felt like a long-distance race that we were damn well going to win. The post-Soviet space, on the other hand, was more like a low-level but constantly rumbling earthquake. I always had the feeling I had overlooked or forgotten something. And yet everything was going well. After we had managed a small but impressive museum and a large hotel without any scheduling or financing difficulties, we were blessed with a warm rain shower of Central Asian contracts. A shopping mall, the redevelopment of a stadium, a covered bazaar, a research centre. No airport yet. I dreamed of an airport and an opera house. My mind flitted between the financial, aesthetic, formal, legal, and ethical aspects of these projects, and even though we had a large team, I felt like a naked Atlas groaning under the weight of the entire globe. Being a control freak (according to Fleur) and a hopeless delegator (according to Mark), I started sleeping badly during this time.

During the day I would walk around with the distorted sense that I ought to know how things worked here. In my distant and outdated GDR schooling, they made us learn everything about the Soviet Union. Geography, culture, epic history: the Soviet Union had bypassed the capitalist stage of social development and had leapt straight from feudalistic tsarist empire to victorious socialism. Thirty years later, it was highly feudal and hyper-capitalist. Nothing in the world was as it was back then, so why should here be any different? I wondered why this realisation made me so melancholy. I had only known these countries from books, and they mattered no more and no less to me than they did to Mark, who had taken on most of our projects in the former Soviet republics. He smelled of old money, English money. The new money he attracted was forward-looking and, strictly speaking, not even new. It was fossil money, bubbling up from gas and oil wells. What had changed since my schooldays was that it no longer flowed into central coffers, but into private hands. Hands that we had the chance to shake. Dainty hands, ordinary hands, massive paws: always men's hands. We might not be changing the world but we would change the way it looked. What we needed was land and money. When both were on offer, our architects' hearts sang. With a polite yet mischievous smile, all Mark had to do was clear his throat and say, great, and the meeting room would be filled with a general feeling of good will that was of such value to our company. Mark's father was a banker, one of the good ones he was keen to stress, and whatever he meant by that, he had offered us the best credit terms to help us get the company off the ground. Mark's mother ran a school for deaf children. They were comfortably off, upper middle class but with none of the House of Lords and fox-hunting culture that people abroad tended to associate with Mark, and which he only noted with a grin. Along with nonchalance in the face of any kind of cliché, he was distinguished by his impartiality. It made no difference to him who owned what, had owned what before, and had done what in the past. The ideal characteristics for negotiating a good deal, which I didn't have, as much as I would have liked to.

I clung to Mark's geniality and yet had the sense that I had bitten off more than I could chew, and I risked being caught at any moment. Me, who had always had endless faith in myself. Me, who gave a wide berth to anything paranormal and yet now had this constant uneasy gut feeling for which there was no justification whatsoever. Once one of our clients told us a story about Ivan the Terrible. When St. Basil's Cathedral was completed in Moscow, it was considered the most beautiful building anyone had ever seen. Ivan asked the architect if he would be able to build an even more beautiful one. The architect replied yes, an unfortunate reply as Ivan lived up to his moniker and had the man's eyes gouged out to eliminate that risk. Our client told us this brief, belligerent anecdote, not in the evening over a whiskey but one morning out on site. We were almost blown off the scaffolding by the wind, and a childish refrain popped into my head: I want to go home. Interesting, said Mark, the most English of all English responses. We weren't in the Middle Ages, we weren't even in Russia, but I took the story to heart as if it had been a crudely coded personal threat. The client was no ruffian, though, but an affable bear of a man who just enjoyed showing off his general knowledge. Do we want all this? I asked Mark on the way to the airport. It felt as though we were constantly on the way to and from the airport. Yes, said Mark, with the emphasis on *all*. Our job is to build. Whether it's a kindergarten, prison, or triumphal arch – we do it and it turns out well. If anything goes wrong here, I said, we'll be crushed. But I needn't have worried. It was never about us. We were contractors, mercenaries, vassals, nothing more. The problematic issues that troubled me existed whether we were here or not. One of our clients was implicated in a corruption scandal, which didn't necessarily mean that he was corrupt. The science centre was to be built on an area where there were territorial tensions between local ethnic groups. My favourite project, the stadium, was being contested by locals, for whom I felt more sympathy than the people who had commissioned us. They wanted what critics of waste and squander always want: better schools and hospitals. The construction site was sabotaged, and after that it was guarded by a heavily armed security service. I could still read Cyrillic, which was of no use to me because although I could pronounce the graffiti that was sprayed on the walls, I couldn't understand any of it. I could imagine, though, what was scrawled on the concrete, something to the effect of: fuck off. Accompanied by some artistically successful depictions of Kalashnikovs.

There is no construction project without unforeseen incidents, no matter where you are in the world. I knew I ought to be grateful for the positives: the direct line to the money, the lack of bureaucracy, the unconditional, almost manic desire to build. Our bazaar was celebrated as a shining example of the successful combination of tradition and modernity. Mark and I looked like Bert and Ernie in the press photo that all the media used at the time, and which has since then lingered on the internet, never to be erased. Mark, tall and slim, was Bert; unfortunately I lacked Ernie's cheerful demeanour. I looked like some chubby coach potato. I didn't ask who it was that had the temerity to send that photo – out of a series of over twenty pictures they could have chosen from – but the fact that I had neglected to pay attention to which photos of me were being used was clear evidence that I wasn't on good form.

You're acting like an ageing model, Mark said. He was right, an unflattering picture was a trifle compared to everything that was going well, but I couldn't help being annoyed. And I was still so tired. In the mornings, at the hotel, I envied the retired middle-class Europeans who were waiting for their Studiosus tour buses. I want to visit the nomads, too, I thought. Fleur, who had once loved to travel, was now saying more and more often that she had had her fill of long-distance travel, that she'd done enough for several lifetimes. She took Albert to Provence, and I joined them there.

At that time, in 2009, I was still a long way from asking myself what I could do about my exhaustion. I was convinced that a short holiday would leave me feeling like a new person. That effect never materialised, which didn't stop me from counting on it twice a year. Fleur had rented a gîte this time: a cavernous box of a house with poky, shabby little bedrooms. Fleur's friends Bella and Russell came too, which was fine, no problem, nice people, with a daughter, Chloe, the same age as Albert, although he flatly refused to play her. Also, the rancid feel of the house bothered me less than the words used by the others to talk it up. What, if you please, is 'authentic' about a decades-old, dark-yellow rim in the bathtub? To rule out any laissez-faire behaviour, the landlord had smothered every surface with Post-it notes. Don't swat mosquitoes against the walls. Don't take the white towels to the beach. Don't put glasses down without a coaster. For goodness' sake, I thought, but also: okay, whatever. I lay back in a hammock and waited for the relaxation to set in, in whatever form it might take. Sleepiness, a desire to read, an appetite for food, for sex. But I couldn't sleep with my wife if I had to listen to Bella and her daughter on the same floor. I couldn't sleep with my wife because of irritating noises from the bed. I lifted the sheet and found a thick layer of plastic.

Fleur, how is it we've paid more for this dump than we did at the Eden Roc and we're sleeping on an incontinence mattress?!

Don't exaggerate.

Fleur shook her head with disdain. She ran an epilator over her lower legs and plucked out a few individual hairs with tweezers. Why couldn't she allow me the illusion that she had permanently smooth legs and have it done in a salon? I knew that cut toenails, cotton buds, used tissues, callus removers, and tongue scrapers existed, but I didn't want to see them. I couldn't sleep with my wife because she was always doing something that made me not want to. So I slept as much as I could and Fleur told me that while I did, I talked, kicked, and ground my teeth.

Besides, France reminded us again of our failure as parents. Me much more than Fleur. Albert didn't care in the slightest that Chloe, a year younger than him, could speak a passable child's French with which she could melt the toughest waiter's heart. He watched her do it as if she were fetching a stick – well done, but what did that have to do with him? When he was smaller and it turned out he had perfect pitch, while he didn't seem to care about anything except his own narrowly defined range of interests, Fleur sometimes worried he was a savant. A suspicion that was never confirmed, but which Fleur also never completely let go of. No doctor ever uttered the word autism, a diagnosis I hadn't come across before but could have accepted, not that I would have had a choice in the matter. Albert's fine, I kept saying, with genuine conviction, he's just not overly interested in other people. Then we fell silent, and I know what Fleur was thinking: like you!

Now, at eight, he was also far from being a particularly sociable child, but he seemed more purposeful and focused rather than reclusive. At least, he certainly displayed determination when it came to steadfastly rejecting what he saw as entirely unnecessary school subjects, a topic that Fleur and Bella mulled over again and again throughout the week. Also typical for Albert was that we kept having to go out and look for him.

The morning after I arrived, he came with me in the car to the bakery in the village, heard an intriguing instrument being played somewhere nearby, and after lunch he walked back there by himself. We found him near a campsite, where he was being taught to play the didgeridoo by a couple of young guys. He wasn't in the slightest bit interested in Chloe and thoroughly ignored her, which added to Fleur's stress. Neither of us was particularly relaxed during this holiday, although everything was actually fine. I was bothered by the presence of the other family, while Fleur told me off for not hiding how dull I found their conversation. As soon as someone started speaking, it was obvious from my furrowed brow that I would rather be talking to a Russian structural engineer. I appreciated Fleur's examples. It's true, I would have preferred a conversation with a structural engineer, even a warlord if necessary. The main thing is having someone to talk to who knows what he's talking about. And I couldn't stand all that navel-gazing of talking about oneself.

Fleur was the first person I had ever wanted to explain myself to. The first and only. Her friends, on the other hand, always had this endless need to share and communicate what was going on with them psychologically. All that I feel so…, perhaps because I still feel this hurt…, because I need this or that from my partner…, because I have this or that deficit. As an only child, with divorced parents, as the oldest, as the middle child, as the daughter of a mother who did something, or failed to do something else. None of this sounded particularly painful, and in any case, it sounded like they'd already found the release they craved. And rarely were they presenting their insights for the first time. That week in the house in Provence, it was Bella who steered every dinnertime conversation towards psychotherapy.

I personally had nothing to contribute. So, once everyone had declared their allergies, intolerances and food-related traumas, I volunteered to be the chef for our evening meals. It gave me a way to stay busy during the day, going out exploring the local shops, farms, and markets. I took Albert with me on some of the trips, who fortunately was an omnivore. I kept my mouth shut for the most part at dinner and carried on trying to relax. With Fleur's lovely feet on my lap, signalling a request to stay and sit with them after dinner and not go and make phone calls, I drank wine and Armagnac and let everyone's voices wash over me like a tapestry of sound. It was mostly just the female voices, as Russell would be busy until the children's bedtime with his daughter, and Albert if he allowed it. In previous years, we had gone on holidays with my in-laws, who have the rare gift of being interested in other people while also leaving them in peace. I had never had a problem with Bella and Russell when I saw them very occasionally in London. To be precise, Russell's presence didn't bother me in Provence, either. It was Bella whose high-pitched voice and nutritional anxiety were a massive obstacle to my relaxation. And it was also Bella whom I was officially not allowed to dislike because Fleur was so attached to her. But why would you go to France and not eat anything? Why would you drag your child into this terror? When I saw the prison food she put out for Chloe and Albert for lunch, I asked Fleur, why should healthy children eat like a neurotic woman in her mid-forties? But Fleur just gave me her shut-it glare and called for the children.

I talked more that evening than on previous days. I suppose it had to come out at some point. The conversation wasn't about the influence of Fleur and Bella's childhoods this time; it was about the current children. A reasonable topic when you were on holiday with them and they were in bed. I listened for a while. I waited for the tone to lighten up. I waited for some humour. After pastis and wine, I was back on the Armagnac.

Then I asked Bella if she wasn't perhaps encouraging her child to do too much, and pushing her too hard, and Bella, usually so eager to discuss things, acted as though she couldn't even imagine what I meant.

Okay, Bella, I said, let's not talk about Chloe in particular. Let's just ask ourselves in general terms if it isn't us that's the problem.

Fleur took her legs off my thighs and stretched them out under the table with a creak. Russell refilled Bella and Fleur's glasses and went back into the kitchen with the remains of my cassoulet, which Bella had praised, but not touched.

With everything that we do and offer them, everything that we are or think we are, is there even the possibility of mediocrity? I asked.

Bella looked at me as if she found it difficult to believe that someone saying such things could even be sitting at a table with her. Then she regained her composure, took a large gulp of red wine, and turned directly to Fleur as if I wasn't there. Back to Chloe: talented, but she wasn't living up to her potential, not enough focus, could be a sign of not being challenged, gifted or highly gifted, hard to say, learning Mandarin, best time to learn. And yet, the child was unbearable for days on end, perhaps meditation would help? It was self-adulation thinly disguised as a catalogue of woes. It was the deliberate negation of my question: shouldn't we simply let children be children? An effective strategy I use in negotiations is repetition. To please Mark, I call it Doing a Cato, after Cato the Elder who rounded off each of his speeches with the same phrase. *Furthermore, I am of the opinion that Carthage must be destroyed.* It worked. So I said it again.

Wouldn't it perhaps be an exercise in love and humility to admit that one has brought an average child into the world?

I wasn't playing devil's advocate. If anything I saw myself as an advocate for my son. I would have loved to storm into

Albert's room, take him in my arms, and tell him that he would never again have to do anything that he didn't want to do. I felt the wine and the Armagnac, and softened my tone. I meant us by what I said next, but I couched it in general terms.

I think most parents tell themselves their child can achieve anything if the desire is there. It's easier to accept laziness and defiance than to admit that their child simply isn't bright enough.

I was met with an uncomfortable silence. Of course, I was aware that wasn't what they wanted to hear. Because we were on holiday, because the mistral was blowing through our hair, because we were sitting together for a meal they praised for its delicious simplicity, even though every day I had spent several hundred euros on food and wine and had cooked for hours so we could feel like God in France. God, who in France pretends to be a peasant. I yawned.

Then you send your child to a mediocre school and let him live a mediocre life, because I certainly won't! countered Bella, holding her hand over her glass when I tried to top it up. Fleur put her hand on mine, which meant leave it. It was my exhaustion that always got me so wound up. I got up and made a toast to our children. Loudly, I declared that it wasn't up to us what would become of them, anyway, and that we should all brace ourselves for a surprise. So far, so incontestable. Without much enthusiasm, the others raised their glasses. Then I added, there had to be saleswomen, too, after all.

At that point we cleared the table.

Well, that was entirely unnecessary, Fleur said when we were up in our room. And the crap about saleswomen was truly the cherry on the cake. My problem was I had a problem with harmony, she said. I laughed. The saleswoman popped into my head because that afternoon I'd bought a chateaubriand from a female butcher who was the most cheerful person I'd met since I had arrived in Provence. Still fully dressed, I threw myself on the bed, glad to be alone with Fleur.

In East Germany, saleswomen were more powerful than many academics. They sat at the interface of distribution and could be as bad-tempered and rude as they felt like, I called cheerily to Fleur in the ensuite. For once, I was tipsy, on the merry side.

Standing in the doorway, Fleur just shook her head and poked her toothbrush around in her mouth so hard that it was painful to watch. No? No what? No, that's not a job befitting of Bella's daughter?

I still maintain that Chloe is a bog-standard normal kid who is being hyped up as a genius. She's clearly not going to be a saleswoman, so why all this fuss over something that's not even up for debate? She won't even need to work, we all know that.

It wasn't about Chloe, Fleur shouted, her muffled voice coming through the wall of the ensuite. I got up and stood in the doorway.

Oh, really? Then I misunderstood. Who was it about then?

Fleur rinsed her mouth and held her palm out to me as if she were banishing a curse from within me. Be gone, foul demon!

It was about Albert. Bella was making it sound like she had as much trouble with Chloe as we do with him.

Why would she do that?

Out of politeness. Empathy. Connection. Call it what you want.

I fell back onto the bed.

I'd call it next level phoniness, I said. She pities your son so much that she has to pretend she can't handle her daughter? Then assumes she's doing you a favour? That's one stage too complicated for me. I'm sorry. Do you see what I mean?

Yes, Gabriel, I do. But you know, not everyone has such an intimate relationship with the truth as you do.

I don't have a fundamental problem with lying. But I can't help wondering, who is this farce supposed to comfort: them or you? And also, what exactly is empathetic about it?

Let's put it this way: it's just not your way of communicating. You enjoy your holiday and let everyone else enjoy theirs, okay?

I went to the window, opened it, and looked out at the rustling darkness. Then I took a cigarette from Fleur's pack and went out on the balcony to smoke.

Let's not fight, okay, I said, turning to face her.

Fleur spritzed herself with mosquito spray and nodded. A chemical blast to wipe out the goodness of decades of meticulously controlled diet. She pulled her sleep mask over her eyes and muttered, you're just completely overworked. Good night.

Overwork and exhaustion were the male equivalent of the female monthly cycle, as I had learned. It explained misbehaviour and was hard to disprove. Especially if you did actually work long hours. I didn't say anything. Because that bothered me less than the underlying theme of this holiday they were discussing in such a convoluted way: that Albert had been declared a disaster and Fleur was accepting it. I flicked the cigarette butt out into the Festival of the Cicadas.

Russell and Bella welcomed us the next morning with an opulent breakfast intended to let the previous evening be thoroughly forgotten. They had even rustled up a rusty champagne bucket from the kitchen of this overpriced Villa Villekulla. Nice touch. Fleur was worried they had overheard our argument, while for me the evening was reduced to a mere few unpleasant highlights: Bella's piqued look, Russell's weary one, Fleur's reproachful one. I was drunk. What of it? When I had staggered through the house at night in search of water, I had had an idea that I still liked now I was sober. I would spend the second week of my holiday with Albert, just the two of us. It would improve the mood in the house, because even if they really tried, Fleur's difficult husband and solitary son were never going to be the perfect holiday companions, were they?

And this has nothing to do with last night? Fleur asked. She was sitting on the edge of our anti-erection bed, her chin on her knees, removing the nail polish from her toenails.

No. And even if it was, it wouldn't matter. But really it would be good to spend some time alone with Albert again.

Okay, Fleur said, pushing her hair off her face. We looked at each other, and at the same time both realised how bad everything was. I had been away so much and then came here, only to disappear again a few days later with our son. And she just said, okay. Next door Russell murmured something and Bella giggled.

Okay, Fleur said again, then I'll have a bit of time for myself. I might go and see Emma in the Dordogne on the way home.

Okay, I said, too. Her poorly concealed relief that we were leaving didn't feel great, but it had been my suggestion, I suppose. The idea that she might have had something else in mind didn't occur to me. How could it? I sat down next to her on the edge of the bed and inhaled the acetone smell of her nail polish remover. We said nothing until Albert came in.

I presented him with a *fait accompli*. A method that was out of fashion at that time, but which for thousands of years had enormously simplified dealing with children. He wanted one last morning with his didgeridoo friends, but he liked the idea of us going off on our own. He listened to me, nodded, and let Fleur pack his suitcase. Fleur was against Disney, the man as much as the corporation, so this was a trip we would have had to do without her anyway.

Why did you tell Chloe we were going to Granny and Grandpa's? I asked Albert, when the two of us were on our way to Paris.

Had Fleur perhaps suggested it? I didn't know.

He just shrugged and looked out the window.

She might have cried if I'd told her we were going to Disneyland, he said, after thinking about it for an entire song.

Good boy. He wasn't interested in Chloe, but he didn't want to upset her. I recognised that. I turned the music up and drove the way we liked it, faster than Fleur. After I had seen it on road signs what felt like a hundred times, I asked myself, but why Paris, anyway?

I thought about it for a while, and with each passing kilometre, my world began to open up again.

Disneyland Paris or Disneyland Florida? I asked, and glanced at his face, behind which the cogs were turning. He wasn't predictable, that's what I liked about him. And now we'd see if he opted for the quicker option or the bigger one. I looked at the road ahead and for the first time since I had landed in France, I felt happy. Happy to be on the road with him, happy to be a father who could make dreams come true.

Florida, he said after a relatively long moment to think, and we grinned at each other. He hadn't expected it, and I think he was still waiting for a but or a condition of some kind. I put my phone on speakerphone, called my office, and asked them to book the tickets for me. Yippee, Albert said quietly to himself, pressing his nose against the window. I wanted to tell Fleur about our change of plans, but it was engaged, and later her phone was switched off.

Fleur

I'm going to see my mum, I said when they called me from Orlando. Albert sounded a bit hyper, getting to stay up and stuff himself with junk food, and Gabriel was happy to see Albert so happy. Say hi from me, Gabriel said, automatically, thinking of Danielle, my mother that he knew.

I hadn't lied. I was driving to meet my mother. The other one. She lived near Brighton. Divorced. One son, Matt, my half-brother, about whom she had said very little and who knew nothing of my existence. She had suggested a café on the pier, where she was waiting for me outside. When I walked up to her and realised it must be her, she was standing there, her hands in her coat pockets and the wind behind her almost blowing her towards me, that was how light she seemed.

She was one up on me. From the outset, she had no illusions that there would be any connection between us. Formally, she held her hand out for me to shake and eyed me reticently. You're doing well, she said, good to see. She didn't know what I wanted from her, she'd said on the phone. I just wanted to see her, if only so that I could draw a line under the question of who my parents were. Again and again, I'd encouraged Gabriel to do the same, but I had actually meant myself. With unusual persistence for me, I insisted on meeting her, and she, perhaps because she was as fragile and weak-willed as I was, finally agreed. Our positions had been defined in advance: I wanted something from her, not she from me. Well then, she said, as we sat down. She had reserved a table, the café was full of tourists, and I saw that she didn't really know the place, and neither was she someone who often reserved a table in a café. I told her a bit about my childhood and growing up, she nodded now and then and said, things have turned out well. I couldn't place her tone of voice, but neither could I discern any joy or relief in it. She was simply acknowledging. I ordered a white wine to help with my nerves, a Sauvignon Blanc. She listened as I went over the wine list with the waitress, and then said, your family are French, right? My mother is Belgian, I said. I had to clear my throat after saying *my mother*, but she just nodded and seemed pleased with herself and her memory. I would never meet my birth father because, unlike her, he didn't even exist in the adoption records. She had never named him, and she wasn't going to now. A school friend, a married man, possibly a relative. I would never know. It was all a long time ago, she said, and if it had been easy, it wouldn't have turned out the way it did, would it?

She worked part-time in a bookshop. Oh, I said, how nice, I translate books. She forced a smile at my desperate attempt to find common ground. I would have liked to make better use of my brief time with her. To have let myself look at her more closely, to search for myself in her more openly, perhaps more shamelessly, but I didn't dare. I was so intimidated by her reticence that I rabbited on and on, making shrill proclamations about things that neither of us cared about. All the same, I knew I would never forget her. How could I? A pale, delicate woman, only sixteen years older than me, hardened by life, who had perhaps always been like that, what did I know, and who wasn't going to tell me why she had decided against keeping me back then. Maybe she'd had someone she could confide in, someone who could help her find solace; the more I thought about it, the more I hoped she had. I was the last person she was going to open up to. When she moved her hands from her lap and placed them on the table, I saw the first, and only, real proof that she was my birth mother. Our hands were just a few inches apart, with only the plastic napkin stand between them, and I didn't even dare touch the woman who had given birth to me, perhaps even breastfed me. Her wariness didn't even fade when she ordered herself a wine, too. I can't pronounce it as beautifully as you, she said, and we shared a fleeting smile. An amicable smile like travellers who know they won't see each other again. On the way there, I had imagined we might go for a walk along the seafront, perhaps arm in arm, and we'd talk. But I understood that this meeting at the café would not be followed by anything, and I asked for the bill. She looked out the window while I paid. Can't you at least pretend for a moment that I interest you, I thought. As we left the café, I lapsed into the mumsy chattiness of the playground conversations at Albert's school. Look at us, I said, both in beige trench coats. She raised her eyebrows and nodded. Like a shy child, she let me hug her in the carpark. I'm glad to see you're doing well, Fleur, she said again by way of a farewell. As I drove away, she stood there waving so dutifully that it was me who looked away first and stared at the road. My thoughts were drowned out by the last thing she'd said. *Fleur*. I had always wanted to know what my name would have been. I took the next exit and texted her.

What name did you give me?

She replied straight away: they said it would be better not to give you a name.

Shortly after, she wrote: Fleur is a pretty name.

I sat there at a petrol station somewhere between Brighton and London and cried. Until someone came up and knocked on my window.

She'll never forgive you for the fact that she gave you away, Gabriel said. He was back from Florida, pleased with how the father and son trip had gone and shocked that I had gone alone. He didn't ask, why didn't you tell me? He said, I should have been there.

The only person I had spoken to about it was Dad. He understood that this was something I needed to do, before I turned forty and while he and Mum were still around. He also knew that he would be the one I would turn to. Since the age of eighteen I had dragged a phantom mother around with me, but he had remained my only father. A couple wouldn't give a child up for adoption, it's always a single woman who gives her baby away or has her baby taken away from her. I didn't know the statistics, but I thought about it that way so often that I was convinced of it. After Brighton, I called Dad and told him that there was no need to worry Mum; my biological mother wouldn't feature again in my life, everything would remain as before. Even if she had been different, nothing would have changed between us, but I didn't need to tell him that.

Are you okay? he asked. I nodded into the phone like a two-year-old.

It's good that you met her, darling, he said, then he left it there, and switched to talking about Kenya, where my parents were visiting their old friends and colleagues, and about Mum's health.

If I'd been with Dad, I would have curled up against his bony chest until the bad melted into the good like a dollop of crème fraîche in a bowl of soup. He had been my shoulder to cry on for as long as I could remember. A major task with a child who cried as much as I did. Danielle had had an undramatic and efficient way of comforting me, of quickly getting a smile back on my face. Hers was an impatient, upbeat character. Now I wondered if a sombre woman could have been so unconditionally supportive as an adoptive mother. Someone like me.

You know, Gabriel said, kissing me on the crown of my head, we mustn't let Hollywood tell us how to feel, that inevitably leads to disappointment.

He was shaping meatballs the size of table tennis balls. Albert had asked for Königsberger Klopse, one of the rare times we had a German guest appearance in the kitchen. I leaned against him and drank wine, glad that he was back. He looked at me and rubbed his forehead with his wrist. His fingers were sticky with minced veal.

It must have hurt that this woman didn't rush to embrace you. But have you ever thought what it would have meant if she had?

What he said didn't comfort me, but what would have done?

At least she was honest. After all it sounds like she's not stupid. She doesn't seem to think that every hopeless situation somehow gives way to a TV-style happy ending, he said, shaking his head. Not disparagingly, just yet again in disbelief at the spectacular lack of common sense in this world.

There was nothing she could do, Fleur, he carried on. She had to talk herself out of being your mother, and then you come along and want to change that? You're her skeleton in the closet.

No, you really couldn't accuse Gabriel of letting Hollywood dictate anything. I felt like I was dangling upside down on a rope and slamming into a cliff over and over again. This woman. Hopeless situation. Skeleton in the closet. Thud. Thud. Thud.

I freed myself with a little cough. I knew him, after all. His analysis was an expression of concern, he was on my side. It was sometimes hard to believe, but always true.

Thank you for your thoughts about *this woman*. Makes me feel much better.

He took his head out of the cupboard and pressed me against him. Much too tight. Gabriel.

I'm so sorry she hurt you, he said into my hair. I wish I could have spared you that.

That's why I didn't tell you, I thought.

You might not like to hear this either, but we live in a class-based society, and you were born into a different class than the one you grew up in. She will always hold that against you, too. None of it has anything to do with you.

Who else does it have to do with, I wondered, crying into the shoulder of his bright pink shirt. He stroked my back. Then he raised his arm and said, just a minute. Go upstairs, will you?

He was shooing away Albert, who must have appeared behind me like a hungry puppy. I couldn't turn around to face my son.

You know, she will always tell herself that your parents had it so easy, that they were lucky enough to have a baby when they wanted one, while she was doomed to have one that she hadn't chosen. Any deviation from that idea, any regret, would break her.

I had heard enough. I nodded. It wasn't a debate. We were interpreting my background, each of us in our own way. What else could we do?

Do you look like her?

He knew how much this question had nagged at me.

You can tell that she's my mother. I have her hands. She's small like me. I probably won't get fat, just even thinner. But my eyes aren't from her.

I had been sure that the ambiguous colour of my eyes was from her.

All is well, Gabriel said. You are loved. She doesn't matter.

I nodded. That would be nice. It would be nice if you could inhale other people's truths and make them your own.

When Gabriel and Mark first launched their company, for a while they called themselves Concrete Rock. It was meant to come across as young and interdisciplinary, with a name you could print on T-shirts and beanies. That's what Mark Barnett thought. Too playful, insisted Gabriel, who argued for the more classic Loth & Barnett. But Gabriel was the one who was concrete rock personified. His inner workings might not be concrete, but his outer shell certainly was.

You know Fleur, it took me years – years! – to figure out who Gabriel reminds me of, Mark told me one evening when we were both downing back-to-back gin & tonics. My mother made me think of it. He reminds me of my father.

We were at a raucous party rounding off a riotously successful year for Loth & Barnett. Mark leaned down to me, his lips right up to my ear, and listed the similarities between Gabriel and his father.

Lost both parents before the age of ten. Survival strategies acquired as a child, unintentionally but very successfully. Assertive. No room for weakness. Definitely no room for any nonsense, or doubts, or melancholy. Bathed in dragon's blood.

Gabriel would have hated that if he'd heard it, that much was certain. Dragon's blood, is that right? I said, and he laughed at me. Blind drunk, red-faced, and yet seductive, like a raspberry sorbet. I was always very fond of Mark. Who wasn't? He raised his glass.

Here's to our Siegfried! The Song of the Nibelungs – isn't that his favourite?

I nodded and clinked my glass against his. For a few moments we stood thigh to thigh on a factory floor in Bermondsey, before we were jolted back to reality, because at that moment, high on the party atmosphere, Mark and I were united by the fatal desire to kiss. It was long overdue, but it was impossible. The stakes were too high. We would both be ostracised for life. Meanwhile, Gabriel stood behind us, oblivious, talking to his young fans about Zaha Hadid. Here's to you, Baroness, slurred Mark and pressed his moist temple against mine. I didn't like it when he called me that. No, I said, finally putting the appropriate distance between our bodies again, not to me, or to you, Mark. And once again we raised our glasses to the man we both loved.

Gabriel

I never understood why Albert hated going to school. But I did understand that he wasn't going to tell us. We wished he would. He could tell us anything. He knew that, but he didn't make use of it. It hurt me and Fleur even more so. But I understood it because I also tackled my childhood problems by myself. I had only just started school when my mother had her accident. My class teacher talked to my grandma about it, not my grandpa. She came to our house and suggested that I repeat a year because of it. I could stay home for the rest of the school year and recover, she said, maybe I could go to a children's sanitorium. I didn't know what a children's sanitorium was, so I thought she meant a children's home, like an orphanage. The ultimate horror for any child. I must have reacted strongly, because both women said, no, no, not a children's home, more like a hotel. Like going on holiday, you know?

I didn't want a holiday. I had understood the main part of the message correctly: they thought I should repeat a year at school. Never mind why, they wanted to dump me with the little kids. They were going to kick me out of my class and I'd have to start all over again, like a game of Ludo. It was so unfair. Grandma had never been very interested in having her own opinion. She had her husband for that. After my mother's accident, she turned into a nodding ghost. All she said was, fine, if you say so. I sat there while they talked about me right in front of me. When I started to cry, Grandma pulled me onto her lap, while my class teacher looked on sympathetically, probably thinking to herself, exactly, the poor little thing; that's what I mean.

Grandpa probably didn't care much for my teacher's opinion. I had that vague impression although I couldn't have articulated it at the time. A woman under thirty who walked around in tight, flared jeans (it was 1977) was, for him, not someone to be taken even remotely seriously.

Grandma, on the other hand, recognised her authority. The young woman had studied; she was a teacher, and she knew what she was talking about. The older woman in mourning, in a black pleated skirt and black blouse with a white collar, said goodbye to the young woman with the waist-length hair, and I, the dwarf in the dungarees, knew I was done for. I was small, it was true. And I had cried. A big mistake. That was worse than getting told off. Worse than a five, the lowest grade.

But then it wasn't me who went to the sanitorium in the end, but Grandma. We visited her on the Baltic coast. What's the point of going to the seaside in such cold weather? I asked myself. You can't even go in the water. I was afraid that she would remind Grandpa to take me out of school, so I left the two of them alone as little as possible. As a parting gift, I drew Grandma a picture that she was kind enough to hang up in her room. It was a picture of her: a black triangle with a head and limbs, against a background of grey waves and seagulls like sideways threes.

The teacher's suggestion was never mentioned in front of me again. My mother had taught me to read and count before I started school. I hope you won't be bored when you start, she said. I shook my head and demanded more letters and numbers. She was right, I was bored. I sat next to Pablo Alarcón from Chile. Who knows if it was intentional to put us exotic kids next to each other. We didn't look alike, but we both had dark hair and dark eyes, and sitting in the back row we formed a unit as far as the teachers were concerned.

Those little Black boys – they're worse than a sack of fleas! The little fidgets, always getting into mischief. Unlike mine, Pablo's outsider story was an adventure that everyone could understand: the bad guys had taken over in Chile, after all. Pablo's parents were on the good side, so they had had to leave their country in the middle of the night. They jumped onto a plane in the nick of time, without even knowing where it was going, as Pablo told us whenever we asked him, his story embellished with sumptuous new details each time. He had lots of things I would have liked: straight hair, a dog, two big brothers he either bragged about or invoked as a threat when needed. Even the fact that his mother hardly spoke German seemed beneficial. If the teacher needed to talk to her, she would come into school with Pablo's eldest brother Ramón, who was already sixteen, and he would interpret. Ramón could tell the teachers and his mother whatever he wanted, I thought, envying the Alarcóns their infinite possibilities.

If I stayed under Pablo's influence, I knew I would end up repeating a year. Snitching was for cowards, my mother had taught me, something I stood by firmly. So I told the teacher I couldn't see sitting at the back and was moved to the front row next to a girl who seemed incredibly dim. If you can't read the board, we'll have to check if you need glasses, said the teacher, presenting me with my next problem. If I had to wear glasses, or even worse, glasses with tape over one lens, I would look like a complete idiot. The notebook for communication between teachers and parents was called the *Muttiheft*, the mum book. The friendly reminder to see an optician had to go, so I buried my *Muttiheft* in the garden.

By now, I pursued my own agenda and at the top it said: no more crying. Even if there was often good cause to: disgusting food, bad grades, scratchy sweaters, being chased by bigger kids, forgetting my PE kit, getting told off, being laughed at. But all that was better than being a useless baby who couldn't even make it through first grade. It helped that the word *tapfer* – brave – was so important in my grandpa's value system. And perhaps the stress – a word that wasn't often used in connection with children at the time – made me forget I had any reason to cry. I couldn't tell if they were still reviewing my case and decided that it would be foolish to remind the adults. At the end of the school year, our teacher announced she was having a baby, and introduced us to her successor. The new teacher seemed ancient to us and had a noticeable overbite. As far as we were concerned, she wasn't a patch on our magical teacher with the long hair and flares. But for me, the petrified boy in the front row by the window, the main thing was that she knew nothing about me. I showed Grandpa my report card and asked him if I would still have to repeat a year. Not with my 1A report card, he said, and gave me twenty marks.

Albert's situation was nothing like mine. But all the same, he might have preferred to work out his problems by himself, like me. Just because he doesn't tell you everything, it doesn't necessarily mean he's unhappy, I told Fleur. The fact that we had very different relationships with him also seemed entirely normal to me. If he had grown up in the proverbial village that it takes to raise a child, he might have sought out even more roles. Possibly even someone he would open up to, although perhaps he didn't need anyone like that. That was what he seemed to have from me, a trait I hadn't imagined might be hereditary.

Albert should have what he wants, I thought. When appropriate, of course. Until he learned on his own that you don't need everything you want. Fleur had precisely the opposite opinion. For a while, she led a dogmatic crusade of anti-consumerism. She even developed an obsession with renunciation, which she also imposed on Albert. There could hardly have been a more diametrically opposed approach to raising a child, which Albert understood, turning to me instead of his mother with material requests. Fleur remained unusually austere. She put herself on a pedestal and preached her nonsense down to both of us. Nonsense that decreed, for example, that we should only give each other hand-made gifts for Christmas. Why, Fleur? Because shopping is so vulgar? Or because you're so good at crafts? Or because you seriously think I want to weave a straw star for our son instead of getting him the Lego Death Star he's asked for? I found this kind of affluent naiveté almost as annoying as the dinner table Communist claptrap about the ills of capitalism while quaffing expensive wine. But I was never annoyed with Fleur. Our debates felt like chess games that we took it in turns to win and that led on to sex. As long as that was all we were arguing about, everything was fine, I thought. I liked buying Albert toys, and even more than that I loved taking him to restaurants, watching with fascination to see how his tastes developed. Even as a child, he knew how to behave in a restaurant: never too demanding, or too meek. That might sound trivial, but it's true. This connection we had didn't change the fact that he always was and always would be a mummy's boy.

Fleur was the one he clung to like a little monkey, and she was the one who happily took on some of the traditional dad roles. She loved carrying him on her shoulders, playing football with him for hours on end, play-fighting with him with angelic patience, a role he only freed her from when he started playing rugby.

From the third year of school, I started driving him to school whenever I could. I would have done it from the beginning, had Fleur said something sooner. Dressing every morning to make a statement that's judged by people who I don't even care about – I can't stand it, she said, looking as miserable as if she had to fight a clan of hyenas every day. If she has to, she can function in the morning, but she only really participates in life from late morning. No problem, I thought, that was the point of being a couple after all. As far as the other parents were concerned, I was Albert's father, who showed up in the right car and in the right suit, in order to relieve Albert's mother, who either had me wrapped around her little finger or had a job to get to, or both. If there was some kind of insidious social Darwinism as Fleur perceived it, it didn't apply to me. Not my circus, not my monkeys, I thought.

My grandpa used to drive me to school every day in his dark green Lada. He enjoyed driving, and he knew I liked being in the car, too, and I suppose he decided that these daily rides should be what we now call our quality time. On the short trip, which was really just once round the block along a few one-way streets, and which would have been quicker on foot, he asked me what subjects I had that day, whether I had done my homework, and listened to what must have been my tedious childish chatter. Then he stopped and let me out into my day.

Albert found it an imposition if I attempted to talk to him about school. What are you doing in maths at the moment? I always found it so interesting! I saw his face in the rearview mirror. He hardly needed move a muscle in his face to express his contempt. Good technique, I thought, that will help in later life, when he has an adversary to vie with. It tickled me that he thought I was a freak for enjoying maths. During our morning commute, I started to see why Fleur allowed him everything, apart from TV and consumerism. I had assumed that she, with her hippie mentality and her eternally bad conscience, was simply too acquiescent. Not that I was wrong about that, but I had underestimated him. I hadn't realised how important his judgment was to me, his love, which I had assumed I was naturally entitled to. After a few weeks of him refusing to engage, I asked him if he would rather *not* talk to me. His merciless response was: yes. That was it. I was his rarely there father who believed that it wasn't the time itself that mattered, but how you used it. A liberating thought that, however, now came up against the concrete wall of his monosyllabic answers. My son took my truths and crushed them. A strong boy. I was proud of him.

At least I had the foresight not to ask if he wanted to put his headphones on. I regretted that I hadn't learned more about music theory. Music and maths went so well together, but Albert's approach to music was emotional, so I decided that we would listen to music together in the car. Alternating between his and mine. He wouldn't have chosen to listen to classical music, but he understood it immediately and pointed out things I had never heard before. When occasionally our tastes coincided, I was as thrilled as if I had won a tender. Then I would drop him off and let him out into his world, which he wouldn't let us have even a glimpse of.

I, too, had as a child assumed the right not to think about what adults wanted. My grandpa had watched me walk away just as I watched my son do. Did I turn around to wave? Did he expect me to? I don't know.

Fleur

At some point, my mother asked me if I didn't want to put in a little more effort. With what? I asked, whereupon she slowly nodded and gestured towards everything about me, from my hair down to the tips of my shoes.

You look like you're rebelling against Gabriel's dress sense, she said, gingerly, as if anticipating a defiant reaction from me. Gabriel dressed like a conservative cosmopolitan. If he were attacked by muggers, all they would have to do was undress him and they'd score a five-figure sum, not even counting his watch. I liked his vanity, but I didn't think I needed to dress like the head of a central bank.

You could ask him why he doesn't dress more like me.

Seriously? I like his style better. When you all got out of the car, I actually thought for a moment that Gabriel had two twelve-year-olds with him.

Apparently, I had visually assimilated to the person I spent most of my time with. I took note and changed the subject. I knew what Danielle meant, but in this case she was wrong about Gabriel, who usually got on everyone's nerves with his maddening aesthetic demands. I remained the exception, even after all this time with him. As long as I didn't accompany him to any dinners in my baggy trousers and hoodies, he didn't seem to have anything against how I looked. He had a terrific eye for what worked and would buy me clothes that always fitted perfectly and looked good on me. I usually wore them once, then sold them on to donate the money. He didn't know that his exquisite taste in fashion was helping other people's children get an education, and he never asked. If I overdid it with the homie look, he would let me know with a quick frown and by telling me how lucky he was that he got to see me naked. Which reminded me how lucky I was that I was with him.

I toyed more and more with the idea of moving to the country. Why would you want to? Gabriel asked. He was right to question it. I never did a stroke of work in our garden, barely ever went out into the countryside, but I longed for a quiet life in tracksuit bottoms and wellies away from watchful eyes. I was alone in that. Albert would have been against it, too, if I had asked him. He didn't need fields and forests to expand his radius, he had already started exploring the city on his own. Okay, I thought, I knew my way around Nairobi and Mombasa at his age, and not just the so-called safe neighbourhoods. Why should he see only Kensington and the back seats of other parents' SUVs? When he turned thirteen, he told me that he wanted to start having lessons again from his old tabla teacher, Mr Singh, who was in his mid-seventies by then and no longer liked driving around. So Albert had to visit him in Southall. I didn't call Mr Singh because he and Albert had had their own relationship from the beginning. A master-disciple relationship that the five-year-old Albert, who otherwise ignored hierarchies, had accepted from day one. And a kinship among musicians. When they used to practise together and I'd pop my head in for a moment, they sometimes glanced up at me and smiled, but they never let me interrupt their playing, the little one and the old one. Albert was very mature when it came to music and had a work ethic that reminded me of Gabriel's. That's a very good idea, send him my regards, I said and gave him the money. He did genuinely go to Mr Singh, but nowhere near as often as he claimed. Before he had an Oyster card, I could see from the tickets that he was travelling to other parts of London as well. I held back from calling Mr Singh, who was the only adult who had never complained about him. Besides, I didn't want to alienate Albert by giving free rein to the control freak in me. He had always been secretive, but he came home when he said he would and he was never completely out of reach, so I let him be. I heard him talking on the phone in his gangster slang and smiled to myself. Swallowed consonants, reduced grammar, and a *my nigger* here and there – it was possible he talked that way with the other spoiled, middle-class boys from his school because that was the mood they were in at the moment, but it was also possible that he had met some tougher guys. I remembered myself at that age and stuck to the idea that you were more likely to trust your parents if they weren't constantly pestering you. Once I went down to his basement, which by now looked like a professional recording studio, and there he stood, at not quite fourteen years of age, already taller than me, playing around on his 808 drum machine, a joint in the corner of his mouth. I stared at him until he asked: What? When he took what I thought was a joint out of his mouth, I saw that it was the cap of a pen – he was genuinely writing songs. I took the opportunity to tell him that if he was tempted to smoke weed, please wait until he was sixteen, or preferably even older. He looked at me like I wasn't all there. Does that seem reasonable? I asked. Sure, he said, but why are you talking about that now? And if you don't do it at all, you won't miss anything, believe me, I added, immediately hoping that this stuffy advice wouldn't backfire. He let me give him a hug, then he played me a tune. The friends he took down to his basement were always boys whose parents I knew at least by sight. I only heard about his new friends from time to time, but I didn't know where they lived, how old they were, or even where he knew them from. Some guys I know, he called them. Maybe he had met them online, maybe he met them on his travels around the city. I would have liked to know why he never brought them home. Was it because they belonged to a sphere that was none of our business, that he wanted to keep for himself? Or because he didn't want them to see that he wasn't really one of them? Who knows. Amidst all the worry, the reassuring thing was that my little loner had evolved into a social being. And by the looks of it, the circle he had grown up in was getting too small. When he wanted to go to a gig in Brixton, I suggested that I join him, and he immediately said yes. He seemed to have absolutely no problem with showing up at a club with his mum. The boys we met there didn't seem to think it was uncool that he had me with him, either. A weird generation, I thought, standing there with the kids and listening to the band, whose members were only a couple of years older than Albert and who sounded like Talking Heads. When I'm playing gigs, you should both come, he said on the way home.

It was these sparse comments that told me everything was all right, that he wasn't drifting away from us, just getting older. Gabriel barely noticed any of this development. He still saw him in the morning, but by the time he got home in the evening, Albert was usually back from his excursions. I never mentioned to either of them that I'd seen through the Mr Singh alibi. Maybe because it reminded me of myself back then with my cello.

Gabriel

There was never enough time for the life I had chosen. This crushing realisation came to me precisely when I did have time one day, when I was walking through the house in the morning sunlight. Fleur was out, I had a rare day off, and I was alone. A state I had not experienced for so long that it felt surreal. How long? When did it start? Irksome questions that had been coming thick and fast since I'd been seeing different doctors, each time hoping for a quick solution that never came. When did you start sleeping so badly? When did you first notice that juddering feeling inside? That constant feeling of terror, like you've just had the fright of your life – when did that start? I didn't know. The symptoms must have crept up on me gradually after feeling normal for years. Maybe I had been suppressing them, too, although I hate it when Fleur points out how good I am at suppressing things. But that morning, for once, I had nothing to complain about. I could catch up on some sleep, I told myself. Every night I woke up abruptly between three and four, as though punched in the face. I'd sit bolt upright in bed, pick up my phone, check the time, now wide awake. At first I told myself, my body must be set to a time zone where it's now seven or eight o'clock in the morning, and I would sit down at my desk in the study. I had the feeling that I was being granted extra time, time when I could take care of the things that were obviously depriving me of sleep. I didn't mind.

Fleur said at one point that I had changed. I used not to get annoyed by people; I would let things bounce off me – a gift she had envied in the past. And I wasn't punctual like I used to be, another quality she had admired in me. I had developed a tendency to grumble. I had always been indifferent about having to wait, as long as I could make phone calls or had something to read. Now it made me angry. I had become allergic to time wasting. But what wound me up most of all was anything associated with male entertainment: bars where people showed off their knowledge of whiskey and cigars, not to mention the depressing idea of enjoying the company of poorly paid anonymous women. It didn't matter in the slightest if it was with Central European planning officials or Central Asian gas oligarchs. The globally identical symbols of taste and success were more wearying in their lack of originality than endless meetings. So I stopped joining in.

This consolidated my reputation for being impatient and cranky. Of the two of us, Mark had always been the good cop, but as my fatigue worsened, that contrast intensified. This division of roles earned me the task of having to fire a number of employees. That was in 2012 and 2013. Two major projects had literally come to nothing, and another was plagued by a corruption scandal that got worse by the day; in the end we were relieved the contract was cancelled before the inquiry commission stepped in. That's construction for you, I told myself, but it was another cause for my insomnia. The layoffs were not totally unexpected. Those members of staff were young and talented and would move on, perhaps start their own business as Mark and I did back then, yet I felt like the messenger of an unjust god. I'm sorry, but I have something to tell you . . . I was genuinely sorry, and the nagging sense that they didn't believe me didn't help.

The slimmed-down staff meant less time, not more, especially since I was still working as a lecturer. But which tasks could I have delegated? I had read about an architect who had a two-hour sleep-wake rhythm like a baby. Two hours of work, two hours of sleep, and so on. After a hideous month, I knew this method would drive me to the brink of madness. So I learned how to get by on very little sleep at night and to treat myself to short naps in the day. It wasn't enough. I tried acupuncture. I went to a sleep laboratory where I was diagnosed with restless legs syndrome, which I already knew about from Fleur. My GP – Dr Drexel, whom Fleur called Dr Dre – prescribed me a drug with the active ingredient modafinil, which left me even more exhausted. He then prescribed Adderall, and for a while I went around like a Duracell bunny, until I realised how stupid it was to have avoided taking drugs as a young man only to get into amphetamines in middle age. I came off them after just a month. The doctor gave me vitamin B via an intramuscular injection – in the buttock – which he called grappa on the house. I didn't notice any difference. Dr Drexel's parting advice was: the best cure for fatigue is sleep.

I learned to snooze in taxis and on planes, which I couldn't do before. I learned to take a power nap on my in-laws' bathroom rug. I worked out that carbohydrates made me more tired than protein. For the first time, I could understand people who did coke, who started stuffing themselves with pills, trying to keep their pace up – whatever it takes. If any of these methods had worked for me, I would have used it, regardless of how legal or healthy or otherwise. I read about autogenic training and wondered where I was going to find the time to try it.

How do I get more time? I asked myself the same question that morning. I was on my own, lying on the sofa in the sitting room, the perfect position to catch the sun on my face. I ought to have felt happy, but instead I felt like I'd just been given some terrible news. I looked at my phone. Missed calls, text messages, questions waiting for me to answer later. When the doorbell rang I slid off the sofa and paused for a moment, kneeling on the carpet. I hadn't seen a cardiologist yet. When do people start doing that? I was breathing slowly – did it hurt, was it even beating? yes – when suddenly Albert appeared in my peripheral vision and was just as startled as I was.

What are you doing here? he asked.

Day off, I said. What are you doing here?

Day off, he said with a grin, and headed for the door. When did he get such broad shoulders, I wondered, though I should have been wondering why my heart was racing like this. I sat down on the edge of the sofa and looked down at my feet. I would have liked to go upstairs to bed, but I couldn't. A short time later, Albert came back with another boy, whom he nudged in front of him, whispering something to him. They went down to the party cellar, a relic from the previous owner that I had never got around to changing. Albert had made it his realm. I must have looked like a drunken wreck to this boy I didn't recognise. In a bathrobe at noon, breathing heavily on the sofa. Seeing me didn't seem to puzzle Albert in the slightest. After an indeterminate amount of time I heard him again, talking quietly as he led his friend back out. Unable to react, I stayed lying where I was. He's skipping school, I thought. How did I not know about this? I can't worry about that right now. I might be dying. At some point I sat up again. I stared at the wall, at the pictures hanging there, none of which I particularly liked. What did they call this state? Catatonic. It carried on until our cleaner, Bojana, came in.

What are you doing here? she also asked me.

Did you know that Albert was skipping school?

Bojana took off her coat, hung it carefully on a hanger, and opened all the windows.

Oh, yes, a difficult age. She let out a little laugh through her nose.

She stopped in front of me and blinked. But we were no better, were we?

I had never thought very hard about Bojana, certainly not Bojana as a schoolgirl. I suddenly had a realisation that every person who cleans other people's houses must have at some point had a different plan for their future. I watched her twirl her hair into a bun and pin it into place.

Day off? she said, her voice notably cheerful. It was clear that I was in her way, so I pulled myself together and went upstairs to the bathroom, where I stayed in the shower, unable to leave, all the while thinking: I can't do this. Or maybe I said it out loud: I can't do this. When I was drying myself and I asked myself *what* I couldn't do, I could think of only one answer: everything.

Then I left the house. I walked through Holland Park, then east, roughly in the direction of my doctor, not that I had an appointment, and kept on going. The last time I remembered walking through London like this was when Albert was still tiny. It was cloudy. I was soon tired from walking – I couldn't walk as long as I used to – but I would feel crushed in the Tube, suffocated in a taxi. So I kept going. In Soho, I strode purposefully into a bike shop as though it had been my plan for months. The sales team were euphoric to have such an eager customer. I felt better by the end, coming away with an orgy of accessories. Soon I would buy a road bike, an idea I had been toying with for years. I always found a solution for everything, didn't I? I was still puzzled about this crisis feeling, though, in the absence of any crisis to respond to.

I bought some red mullet and vegetables and found I was able to propel myself through a crowd of shoppers, so perhaps I could manage a cab home. At home, Fleur told me I looked well, like I'd had a really good rest. I left it at that and started filleting the fish. We forced Albert to come up out of his cellar and eat with us.

I spared him the question of why he had spent the morning at home, but I was interested in one thing that I had heard him whisper to his friend.

Tell me, did I hear you correctly earlier? I asked.

What, when?

Fleur looked back and forth between the two of us. I served some pieces of filleted fish onto her plate.

The gardener, I said.

Albert put his hand over his mouth so as not to squirt his juice all over the table, he thought it was so funny. Then he enlightened his mother.

I said to Ravi: You don't have to say hello to him, he's just the gardener. And Ravi was like: Really? What's he doing on your sofa? And I was like: My dad lets him chill here.

Fleur giggled, as if it was some hilarious joke. Albert couldn't hold in his laughter.

And the funniest thing was Ravi believed it!

Fleur

Our reasons for concern were as different as we are from one another. But this time Gabriel and I came to the same conclusion. Albert should go to boarding school.

He and some other boys had gone around Knightsbridge at night, pasting shop windows and billboards with gigantic dick pics. With what? Gabriel asked, and I unintentionally had a fit of laughter that turned into overwhelmed weeping. They had chosen one of London's swankiest areas to get some good video footage of their project – which Albert called guerrilla art critiquing consumerism – that they could share online. There were four of them, masked, and as quick and deft as professional bank robbers. Albert, who for reasons of coolness now only said *paper* when he meant money, had ordered the posters online and paid with plastic – Gabriel's credit card. The best possible resolution and paper quality because Albert, as we both knew, was far from a critic of consumerism. The print shop didn't seem to have had a problem with the subject matter; on the contrary, Gabriel was now a premium customer on account of the scale of the order. Albert was the only one in the gang whose involvement could be proven, but he definitely wasn't the mastermind. This prank wasn't his style: he made music, he didn't communicate through pictures, certainly not dick pics. I was the repressed one who had avoided going near his laptop, scared of checking his browsing history, while there he was leaving it all out in the open. It was absurd. His mum was terrified of a bit of porn, while he was out plastering it all over town. Not using pictures of himself, as Gabriel and I noted with relief. Gabriel didn't insist he named the others, since he had always told him no one likes a snitch. I wanted to know who was in on it – not because I was keen to see his friends punished but because I was now seriously wondering who he was hanging out with. Of course, he wouldn't tell me either, so there was no point asking. I almost longed for his childish selfishness again. Then, when I happened to see him naked and saw some large bruises that he reasoned away as *some guys and I had a bit of trouble with some other guys*, I got scared.

And so it was me this time who brought up the subject of boarding school. I didn't have to convince Gabriel, he would have been happy to send him right away to a Jesuit college in Paris, an elite school for future decision-makers, but Albert's achievements weren't quite elite enough for that. France, though. School names like Sacré-Cœur and Notre-Dame de So-and-So set off a symphony of right and proper in Gabriel's head, which I found ridiculous but definitely preferable to Albert's anonymous friends among the artists and heavies. We agreed on a bilingual boarding school near Rennes. That way, I persuaded myself, Albert would still be close. I wouldn't have to fly; I could go over and see him in Brittany at any time. The school had everything as far as Gabriel was concerned. Catholic background, although he was a non-practising Protestant and I was agnostic, horses, historic architecture, conservative school uniforms, and a monastery-style timetable with a one-hour-a-day limit on mobile phones and the internet. Gabriel was particularly enthusiastic about the promise that pupils were prepared for admission to Cambridge.

Albert was less shocked than I had expected. And we were less angry about his guerrilla operation than he had expected. Don't see it as punishment, Gabriel told him, see it as an option. Here in London you've been making trouble and getting bad grades, so now we're going to try something else. It's that simple. As for using his credit card, the most he could muster was a mumbled half a sentence like *next time let me know first, okay*?

After this conversation, he took him out to a restaurant with a nose-to-tail ethos, where they had dishes like sheep's head and lamb's Achilles tendon: things that sounded like a dare and therefore appealed to Albert's tastes. They came home late and in a good mood.

So, how was it? I asked. Any complaints?

Gabriel, who was once so tolerant, perhaps even uninterested in the faults of others, had become such a fastidious restaurant-goer, as if he were the man who doled out the Michelin stars.

No, it really was excellent, said Albert, in Gabriel's tone of voice and German accent. Everything was consistently to our absolute satisfaction. Gabriel just shook his head, and I laughed as I always did at my son's impressions. He could pick out every subtlety in an accent. His Ukrainian sounded different from his Russian, his Austrian different from his German. He was constantly regaling me with situations like an Italian tourist discovering the wine is corked, a Somali pharmacist refusing to part with some prescription medicine, or a cab driver from Martinique telling a joke and messing up the punchline – my personal favourite that I always asked him to do again. His masterpiece was, of course, a German demanding to speak to the manager. I was confident that he also regularly impersonated Gabriel on the phone. Depending on his mood that day, Gabriel would either laugh along or find it downright rude to make fun of people who, unlike Albert, spoke other languages.

Basically he speaks every language, I said at some point, only in English.

Oh, give it a rest, Gabriel snapped.

That evening, however, everything seemed fine. Albert had had a glass of wine, Gabriel had drunk the rest of the bottle, and my son continued to entertain me with his unique linguistic talent, his gift of the gab, until my husband couldn't help laughing along. Don't get melancholy now, I told myself.

Two weeks later we took him to France, and I was suddenly alone. I'd never had to justify what I'd done all day. Now I was asking myself. Gabriel was purporting to be happy about his lecturer position, and he kept talking about how much time we'd have for the two of us now, although really he didn't even have time for himself. While I had too much of it, which bothered me for the first time in my life.

Nobody cared two hoots about translators, usually not even the author. The publishers sent you a contract and you got on with it. And Emma was a money-making machine whose work someone had to prepare for the English-speaking market – and who had now specifically asked for another translator. I had been starting to wonder if something was amiss, as she hadn't replied after I wrote to her. And from time to time I wondered why the manuscript was so late this time, until I found out that a new translator had been working on it for months. After nine books, that hurt. Especially because I didn't understand what had happened. I wrote her a long email that I spent nights agonising over, revising it over and over. I wrote that it was fine for me to no longer be her translator and that the decision didn't need to change anything about the fact that we knew each other. I avoided the word friendship; nothing is more pathetic than a one-sided friendship. I asked her for an explanation, and all the while I could hear her reading my words to Azzedine, her husband. Scornful, pitying, irritated, maybe even astonished. What does this woman want from me? Every possibility I thought of was worse than the last. I sent nothing in the end. I waited for Emma's fiftieth, an opportunity to send her a birthday message. I got a reply in the form of a round robin email.

Spammers, friends, foes, and colleagues! You all know that I'm not a great fan of my birthday, but still you thought to badger me with your congratulations, and as polite as I am, I thank you! Here's to our good health, Emma.

That's it, just deal with it, I thought, and went to meet Morris, Emma's English publisher, for lunch.

We sat in a restaurant full of women. I assumed that the miniscule portions were a gender-specific adjustment for the guests, which at the same time had a positive impact on profits. Skinny clientele, happy management. The food was excellent.

Don't take it personally, Morris said, after a bit of beating about the bush. You know she changes publishers as often as her underwear, he added, skewering his last shiitake mushroom.

You know, Morris, I said with the horrible feeling I was going to sound like I was grovelling, I actually didn't want to talk about Emma, but to ask what the chances were of a freelance role with you.

Oh? Morris mimed drinking an espresso to the waiter and held up two fingers, flashing his long, white teeth.

We'll have to have a look. We certainly wouldn't want you to take a job below your station just because you're feeling cooped up in the short term. A job for the sake of a job, if you know what I mean.

I nodded.

Another not insignificant hurdle is your last name. As the daughter of a publisher, why would you take a second-rate role for a smaller house? How would that look? I mean from the outside, but also internally, that is, for all parties.

My father isn't a publisher, I said. That's a distant relative. Which Morris brushed off with a flick of his hand.

I'll be perfectly honest with you. I need young people with hunger and drive. Thirty-year-olds with ten years of experience under their belt, if you know what I mean.

I just nodded. What could I possibly say? I had for years lived a life where I had been sheltered from this kind of truth.

Two women had turned up to join their friends at the next table, prompting a noisy round of hellos and hugs. Morris turned to them and eyed them up and down, mentally ticking off the designer labels.

You know, Fleur, Morris turned back to me. You don't have to work, either. You should take comfort in that.

What do you mean, *either*?

The only people in this room who need to work are the waiters and me. If you want my advice, take a cue from this lot. Go full-time with the ladies who lunch. Have a rosé, gripe about your husband.

Maybe they're working.

Yeah. Maybe. And maybe I'm Miss Bahamas.

It's not just about money.

It's always and only about money. I'm sorry to have to bring you this news, which wouldn't be so new to you if you weren't so comfortably off. Be glad of your little German soldier. He'll keep on busting a gut for you, until he drops.

Hmm, like I needed to be reminded of that. Thank you, Morris.

My pleasure. But seriously, Fleur, said Morris, rummaging around in his thousands of jacket pockets, leave it to the younger generation. They need the work, you don't.

Let me get it, please, I said, waving to the waiter.

Thank you, and my warmest regards to the breadwinner. How is he doing, anyway?

He's working a lot, as usual.

Quite right, Morris said.

We stood outside under the awning and had a cigarette, huddled together like two students. Don't take it personally, Morris told me again, referring to both Emma, whom he was kind enough to dismiss as some kind of frog-guzzling witch, as well as to the fact that my market value had slumped to about zero.

That evening, I told Gabriel about the vacuum I found myself in. He tried to take it seriously and didn't quite succeed. The absurdly great gift I had had from him, ever since we had known each other, was that he never questioned me, but that also prevented him from recognising that I was less satisfied with my life than he was. Shopping, gardening, decorating – none of that was my thing, and he had never questioned that before, either. If I had to spend my time on these wifely pursuits, the least they could provide would be the deceit that my life had some meaning.

I have to do something, I said, or I'll disappear. And I thought, I'll punch him if he says, You're perfect, Fleur.

What about your PhD? he asked, tapping away on his phone.

And then what? I asked.

The next morning, he set off for the office without having to nag Albert for half an hour. Don't you miss him? I asked.

Of course, Gabriel said, but at some point he'll be gone for good.

Albert called me regularly to tell me that he wanted to come home, to get back to his normal life. Not just London, his stomping ground, but also his online profile that was like a job for him. When he had started at boarding school, he thought he'd be able to stay in touch with his followers and gaming friends. He was used to simply getting around bans, so it was a shock to discover that not only did they restrict students' use of the internet, they even took away their devices.

I can't respond to anyone anymore, he moaned. I don't have time to upload my stuff, the Wi-Fi here is so lame, it's like the Middle Ages. Everything I've built up has gone to shit. I'm literally dead!

Be like a celebrity, keep a low profile, and let them wait for you, I suggested.

A celebrity needs to be visible, said my millennial child. This isn't the eighties.

The eighties. Synonymous with all that was ancient. Everything that was so prehistoric that he could only perceive it through the prism of music. I knew I needed to take his problem seriously if I hoped to be taken seriously by him. That's not to say I could think of a solution; I could hardly offer to help out with his accounts until he had finished school.

My God, he'll survive, Gabriel said.

It might sound like nothing. But if I understand it correctly, he's built some kind of career online and it's important to him.

Career, Gabriel said. You're not seriously suggesting that he should sacrifice his education for this 'career'?

A gesture I had never seen him make before: quotation marks in the air. It didn't suit him. Then he looked back down at his laptop – just like Albert would if we let him.

No, but neither should we completely ignore what's important in his life. Imagine if you'd been banned from books or model aeroplanes. That must be what it must feel like for him.

I've been banned from all sorts of things. And I would have been laughed at if I'd talked about any of my childhood hobbies as a 'career'. Tell him to stop acting like he's been sent to a gulag. He can do the same things there that he did here. Drumming, for example. The only thing he's had to give up is the shady company he was keeping. And the fact that he is finding it so incredibly difficult only shows that we did the right thing. Think of him as temporarily not entirely compos mentis. If we give in now, he'll only blame us later.

And then Albert did suddenly give it a rest. For most of that school year, he even sounded almost happy. He'd made a friend, he told me. Julien this, Julien that. Interestingly, he couldn't think of anything he needed, whenever I asked him if he wanted us to send him anything. So I sent him money from time to time, amongst other things, so he didn't have an excuse not to call me.

There you go, said Gabriel, when I showed him an email from a content-sounding Albert, albeit one littered with spelling mistakes.

Three months later, he was at it again. We were summoned to France. Not everything is easier when there are two of you, but a conversation with a disgruntled headteacher is. I had always gone on my own to see his teachers and heads, and I had also handled the poster prank alone, at least the most difficult conversations about it. I had always been fine with Gabriel's absence, but now for the first time I thought it was his turn. Besides, he had taken some annual leave because he was going to Greece with Mark Barnett and some friends.

Is that okay with you? I asked, a purely rhetorical question.

He looked at me without saying anything, took off his glasses, and rubbed his eyes with his fists. Whenever he did that, I felt like I had a glimpse of what he must have looked like as a child. I don't know if I've ever told him how it makes me go soft inside when I see him do that. I don't think I have. I managed to stay firm by allowing myself two sleeping pills and going to bed at nine.

I slept as if I'd been knocked out by a sledgehammer. When I woke up, he was already gone. When he got back the next morning I was still asleep. He brought me tea in bed. His sailing friends were waiting for him in Athens, he had done his duty and was passing the baton back to me. After banging about in the dressing room for ten minutes, he stood by the bed, ready to go. Even on the plane it would be obvious that this was a man about to go sailing. Without my contacts in, I was looking at a blurry Ralph Lauren ad. He leaned down, kissed me, told me that our delinquent was sitting downstairs, and that he loved me. Then he called a cab.

When I came downstairs, Albert was lying on the sofa. At least, his body was there, his mind was elsewhere, touring the vastness of the internet. He had gone to a kitesurfing camp over the last school holiday and we didn't see him. So I had missed his latest growth spurt. A metamorphosis had taken place: my child was gone, and here instead, sprawled out on the sofa, was a broad-shouldered man who urgently needed to change his socks. I gave him a hug, which he submitted to for a moment, before fending me off.

And, I asked, any news?

The grapefruit juice tastes like incense, he said, nodding sparingly toward the coffee table where his glass stood.

He meant what he said, precisely. I had asked for his news, and this was his answer. It was usually a complaint with regard to his comfort. Anyone else might perhaps find other topics to discuss with their mother after being suspended from school. They might defend themselves, try to explain themselves, adopt a meeker tone, perhaps, but not Albert. He behaved consistently as if he had grown up with staff to attend to his needs. In a way, he did: me.

Anything else? I asked.

I hadn't seen his shrug for months, and I didn't like it one bit.

Albert, I asked you something. All this isn't great, and it would be nice if you would at least talk to me. We are, by the way, on your side.

He scratched himself and yawned.

What do you want to know? You already know everything.

Oh? Is that so?

I had always flattered myself on how well I understood him. It's not so hard, I thought. After all, I was his age once. Now, though, I had my doubts. Surely, I was never such a pain in the arse as this at fifteen? I was petulant, I was ungrateful, but I'm sure I never looked at my mother like an irritating fly. I snatched the iPad out of his hand and launched into a lecture that even I found annoying. I paced up and down beside the sofa, remonstrating with him about everything he had done wrong these last few years and, with mounting disappointment at myself as I did so. I enumerated for my own child the cost of his existence. I sounded like I had never wanted to sound: humourless and whiny. He interrupted me with his new, strange male voice.

Can you please stop with that shit. I know all this, why are you telling me?

He hauled himself out of the upholstery and stomped past me, his dirty dishes rattling on the table. I hate it when people crash about like Godzilla.

Hey! I'm not done yet.

I am! You're being annoying.

And you're not in the slightest bit annoying, of course.

I jumped up and followed him downstairs, still stunned at this undignified mother-teenager mini drama he was dragging us into.

Albert, I'm sorry, but I'm not going to leave you alone. We're going to talk now.

He yanked open the sliding door out to the pool and turned to look at me.

Can't you just shut up and smack me?

What?

Just slap me and be done with it.

You want me to hit you?

Yeah. Like Dad.

Like Dad?

Yes, Dad. I honestly preferred that to your nagging.

Your dad did what?

Albert shrugged and pushed the door shut behind him.

Gabriel

You hit my child? she shrieked when I called her back from Athens.

Fleur, calm down, please. I gave him a slap. Admittedly not the greatest parenting achievement of my life, but it's not child abuse.

She breathed dramatically down the line. I had been unsure about leaving her on her own, but this trip had been planned for a year, and I didn't see why we should put our entire lives on hold to bow to Albert and his antics.

And perhaps out of your infinite source of compassion, you could spare a drop for me, I carried on. Then you might see that I'm also at my wit's end with him. I really don't know what to say to him anymore. They don't want to teach him, never mind what we pay, and all he can think to do is to laugh in my face because now he finally has unlimited access to the internet again. What do you think I should have done?

I don't know either! She sounded like she was facing disaster.

Do you want me to come back? Or do you both want to come to Greece?

No, never mind. I want Albert to stay here for a while and settle down. Besides, my parents are coming tomorrow.

She wouldn't leave London because he didn't want to. Because the prince wanted to hang out in his magical cellar, feeding his followers with his nonsense.

You need to stop thinking that we have to buy his love. We don't. Children are scheming, but it's not like they only love their parents when everything goes their way. Be understanding about everything, for all I care, but don't let him blackmail you, okay?

You must never hit him again, promise me!

Again, a smack isn't hitting.

What is it then?

It's an outdated method of parenting, which nowadays is used only in extreme cases. And this was an extreme case.

We'll discuss this when you get back.

I called her a few more times, but she was always brusque with me. I didn't see why this was cause for disagreement. Albert's latest deed didn't leave room for a difference of opinion. He had gone too far, period.

In France, he had made friends with a day boy, someone who lived locally in one of the nearby towns or villages. So at least he isn't snobbish about who he's friends with, Fleur said. I didn't follow. How could he be a snob? That would require first of all that he took an interest in the fabric of society. Our son had his own class system. A dual one that consisted of the people who interested him, and the majority, whom he ignored. Actually, it was a radical perspective I could sympathise with. And his creativity. He was a nerd, and he was lucky to grow up in the era of the nerd. Although at times I would have preferred him to be an old-school nerd: a status that never caused me any harm. It didn't hold me back socially. I was in the chess club, made model aeroplanes, and wore corduroy trousers and sleeveless knits, while everyone else wore jeans. I let other kids copy my work. They either liked me or they didn't, but at least they left me alone. However,

Albert's expertise was limited to fields that were of little use to him at school. Sadly.

So he had this friend, Julien. Allegedly, they met up in the afternoons after school to play backgammon or hang out in the woods. What they actually did there was so bizarre that the prank with the so-called dick pics seemed almost funny in comparison. They had dug a huge pit in the forest. A grave. With two puny spades. They had spent days digging, making their hole bigger and deeper. A few times they even met at night and dug by torchlight. It was their game they kept coming back to, their project. Who knows what they chatted or laughed about as they dug, whether they were also smoking pot, or making up stories, or whether they were reenacting something they had seen. They wouldn't tell us anything. Of course, they also wouldn't say whether they had a plan from the start, or if they first dug the pit and then wondered what to do with it. Either way, they then stole a teacher's car, went joyriding for a while, before finally driving it into the forest and into their huge pit. The next few days – during which the students were all asked if they knew anything about what might have happened to the teacher's car – they carried on meeting up after school in the forest, where they finished filling in the hole again, and covering it over.

They were two quirky boys whose recreational activities, unfortunately, went far beyond the category of 'quirky'. If it had been an unpopular teacher, they would have been thrown out of the school as heroes. Madame Giordano was a Latin teacher, and Albert hadn't even had her for any lessons. When I apologised to her, she seemed to find the whole thing more puzzling than shocking. She said she knew Albert only by sight, a nice boy, she had assumed. What had come over him? I didn't know either. Madame Giordano was attractive. Closer to my age group than his, but that didn't rule anything out. It was possible that it was some elaborate way of hitting on her, albeit a method that backfired somewhat. I told her that I would make sure the claim was settled as soon as possible, and she smiled a thin forced smile that was probably meant to suggest that I had much bigger problems to face than a call to my insurance company. And she was absolutely right about that. Not only would they not pay out even a penny for my son's vandalism, but I also had no say whatsoever in the question of his remaining at the school, which had already been decided, as the principal explained, in a roundabout way and politely, but also unambiguously. As sorry as he was. Travelling there was like going to Canossa. I wondered why I even bothered. I could have apologised by phone and asked them to put my son on the next train, but instead here I was, sitting in the principal's office, looking into their pinched faces. The principal, whom I could see only in silhouette because the sun was shining directly on him from behind, used an ancient intercom system to request coffee for everyone, intended, presumably, to show how extremely cultivated they were at this establishment, even with the parents of the blackest sheep. Or would you prefer tea? No, thank you, I said. Next to me sat the mother of the other boy, Julien. I mistook her for another teacher at first, because she made no attempt to offer an apology, and in fact was glowing with as much reproach as the principal. I'm glad I didn't know at that point that her son was allowed to stay on at the school, as I might have said something I would have regretted later. The boy was on a scholarship, and his mother was alone with two sons. The school was most likely showing off its social conscience.

After a cup of what was by far the most unpleasant coffee of my life, we got into the caretaker's SUV and he drove us into the forest. The principal, Albert's class tutor, Julien's mother, and me. I looked out the window and avoided any contrived conversation. I wasn't going to see these people again, and now they were about to show me why. We walked through the damp woods to the place where the car had been hoisted out of the pit. A brand-new, sky-blue Fiat Cinquecento that perfectly suited the pretty Latin teacher. A car that stood for la Dolce Vita and which had now been exhumed like a buried corpse.

This so-called prank had come to light because Julien had accidentally let slip to his brother, prompting a few older boys to want to dig the car up and sell it. In the process, they were caught by some forestry staff who had been wondering, for weeks, who had cut down a few individual trees and left them lying there. The boys had cut them back to make room to drive the car right up to the hole. And Albert, the genius, had been stupid enough to leave his sweater in the car. The fact that his friend had blabbed had dire consequences for the two of them, but at least it showed that they were children and not fully mature psychopaths.

It was raining. With our hands in our coat pockets, we stood by this hole like actors in a thriller. I told myself to imagine I was at a construction site, not a grave. Workers were walking around in heavy boots, dragging the Fiat onto a tow truck, exuding a busyness that I liked better than the dramatic faces of the teachers present. Maybe the boys had seen one TV series too many. Perhaps the car had been the most innocuous of their ideas, and I should be glad it was only a car. My son had driven me up the wall on a regular basis, but I hadn't found him creepy until then.

Albert lay in his room reading. His bags were packed and stood at his side, waiting. The housemaster who had brought me up left us alone. Without greeting me, he asked about his mother. Without responding, I asked him about his hairstyle. He had dreadlocks, which didn't suit him at all. My coily hair and Fleur's silky, smooth hair had resulted in his big curls, which people called his angel curls when he was little and had more angelic features. His hair was too fine to be matted into real dreadlocks. A bit pathetic and with too much space between them, they dangled from his head, which looked small in comparison. I had hoped that this boarding school, chosen for its conservative regime, would have regulations to protect its students from their own disfigurement. Nope. Albert explained that he had even applied in writing for permission to have this hairstyle. With an ethnic or religious background as justification, you were allowed anything: kippah, headscarf, turban, dreadlocks. He had written to the school that he wanted this hairstyle to continue the tradition of his paternal grandfather, a Rastafarian, and was granted permission. Anything else would have been discrimination, which they couldn't get away with, Catholic or not, right? Actually, he could have gotten a special permit for marijuana as well, he said with a grin, that was part of the Rastafari religion and helped with communication with their god, Jah. I nodded with interest, as if we were having an adult conversation.

Mm-hm, Jah. I assume Jah stands for Jehovah?

He just looked at me, annoyed.

His African grandfather, my father, was granted cool status *in absentia.* Albert knew nothing about him. I had nothing I could have told him about this man, but apparently he provided a better surface for projecting onto than us adults who were present in his life. Maybe it was because of his passion for drums, or maybe it was simply that he found us nauseating, especially me.

It would have been nice if you had shown so much commitment and enthusiasm in other areas of your life, I said. Then I wouldn't be here now.

It would have been nice if you had asked me if I wanted to come here at all.

I had expected an answer along those lines. And of course he mirrored me by imitating my accent. Unfortunately, he was now missing Fleur, his appreciative audience. I had resolved to bring him home as peacefully as possible. We would discuss it later. When my anger had abated somewhat. For that I needed distance and I needed Fleur. There wasn't much that I didn't think I could do, but I found myself wondering more and more how people managed to raise their children alone. I thought of my grandpa, who I lived with, alone, at Albert's age. There was no one I would have liked to talk to more that day. Although I had always spared him situations like this. I wonder whether Albert would have been more considerate of us if one of us had been alone with him. Would he maybe have stopped to think before serving up this crap? Hard to say, but sadly I assumed probably not.

Are you ready? I said. Let's go.

He threw his book onto the bed and started taking his posters off the wall and rolling them up.

I sat down on his bed and picked up the book he had been reading. *Les Chants de Maldoror.* The first-person narrator, a devastated archangel of unspeakable beauty, is the ultimate incarnation of evil that descends to earth to the humanity he abhors and commits such heinous acts that make the real Satan look like a nice guy. I was under no illusions: my son read only when forced. And now this, what I assumed was some nineteenth-century syphilitic fantasy, which offered no doubt a mere nano portion of the evil he might otherwise garner on the internet. If that was even what he was into. It's all just a phase, I told myself. If he wanted to provoke me with his choice of reading, he would have to bring out bigger guns than that. I lay down on his bed and immediately sat up again. It was too tempting.

I'm glad you're interested in French literature, I said. He nodded. His way of nodding is from me, Fleur had once said. He just raises and lowers his head once, then keeps it down. I would have liked to hug him. No matter what he'd done, it was a desperate situation. He had manoeuvred himself into it, but these constant rejections had to hurt. He took his holdall and his wheeled suitcase. I carried an open cardboard box with his scant possessions like a security guard escorting a fired manager off the premises, and we left his room. It was indeed spartan, and it could be interpreted as punishment when compared to the paradise of possibilities at home. Well, that was how Fleur saw it. I thought it would do him good to concentrate on what was important. The school had been a golden opportunity that he had thrown out the window. We walked down the corridors, and he nodded to a few other students but didn't stop to talk to any of them. In his cardboard box there was a framed photo of his mother. Fleur, perhaps in her mid-twenties, lying on her front on the beach, propped up on her forearms like a sphinx, laughing at the camera. Yellow sand, golden Fleur, white bikini. My son had installed his mother in the room as a bikini-clad beauty. I wouldn't have been surprised if he had told the other boys she was his girlfriend. That made me wonder if anyone would still have a printed photo of their girlfriend nowadays. Then, among all the odds and ends, I saw a familiar model. It was a mock-up of one of our first bids in China. We had designed two skyscrapers that spiralled up into the sky like chains of DNA. So he had also brought something of me to keep in his room.

I had found us a Michelin-starred restaurant nearby at a country hotel. Not that I wanted to reward him for his behaviour. I wanted to reward myself. I needed a treat after all this opprobrium. Service station fare would have made me gag.

We're going to have a nice meal, okay? I said as we put his stuff in the boot. He raised his eyebrows with disdain. I resolved to keep talking to my son and not to this nasty piece of work.

Do you want to say goodbye to your friends?

He laughed as if I'd asked him if he still played with Lego.

Do you want to or not?

No, man, let's get out of here.

Would you please tell me what there is to laugh about?

I'm feeling good, man. What? Am I supposed to pretend I've enjoyed it here just because you paid for it? I'm glad to get out of here.

You could have had it another way.

Oh really? How? With a polite request to you, or what?

Okay, I actually wanted us to sleep on it and to discuss everything together with your mother. But maybe you'd feel better if I ask you the question now. What exactly were you thinking?

He shrugged. That shrug enraged Fleur but not me.

If that was supposed to be art again, then please explain it to me.

I was serious. If he was trying to tell us something with this morbid nonsense, I'd really like to understand. He laughed. An arrogant little laugh intended to make it clear that I understood nothing at all.

Good. You can figure out why you're so desperate to get kicked out of every school and what you're trying to tell us. Write it down if you have to.

An essay isn't really my style.

Then talk to me!

He crossed his arms and ran the tips of his shoes through the gravel. Then he looked me in the face again.

You can take the *nigger* out of the ghetto, but you can't take the ghetto out of the *nigger*, man.

And at that point my palm landed square on his impudent, mocking face.

We were facing each other in the car park. He had recently grown taller than me. Just a few centimetres, but I couldn't have kissed him on the forehead anymore without him leaning down toward me. I pushed aside the empty words of apology that raced through my head because they weren't mine. I only reproached myself for one thing: that it was that ridiculous quote that provoked me. I thought the slap itself was an appropriate response. Nothing is more repulsive than bullies who claim to hit out of love. I loved him, but at that moment I couldn't stand him. We were silent. He didn't give the impression that he felt he had been treated unfairly. He had wanted to sound out a boundary, and voilà, there it was.

Get in, I said. And he got in and fastened his seatbelt. I braced myself for a long journey in silence.

We would get through it.

Fleur

The two weeks of his sailing trip felt different from his usual trips. More definitive. Gabriel was always jetting off around the world and filling it with buildings, or so it seemed to me, and maybe to him too. He was happy and I was not unhappy – that was our happiness status. We were glad when we saw each other, and in between I was alone with Albert. The sailing trip was really nothing unusual, but while he was away, I thought about our years together in the way that you might think about a dead person, someone you've kept in loving memory.

And then I kept thinking back to that one evening. It was the last evening I'd spent with Emma, who came with her husband to visit us in London. Of course, later, after she had terminated my role without a word, I wondered if I had missed something that night. But now I was thinking about it because it was the last evening when Gabriel and I didn't act like a partnership of convenience faced with a list of jobs to do, things to sort out, buy, or get rid of. We were still just a couple. Allies who exchanged glances, who enjoyed the sight of each other, who looked forward to their guests leaving so they could have a laugh by themselves or make love immediately. If still able to. We weren't on that occasion. Too drunk. What mattered was that we both wanted to.

Emma had asked if we could stay in rather than going out for dinner. London is worse than Paris, she said, and I didn't need to ask what she meant. The people, the traffic, the weather, the restaurants, the smoking ban. I knew Emma – for her, it was all an imposition. For Gabriel, who hadn't read any of her books, and who wasn't familiar with either contemporary literature or the human abyss, Emma wasn't a celebrity, she was just someone I knew from France. He probably didn't even notice that she liked him right away. He behaved like he always did. Polite in his own way, but not overly charming. Also because he never asked questions unless he was interested in the answer. Other people's children, parents, holidays, and infirmities were a bottomless pit for which Gabriel had no spare capacity. Emma, on the other hand, didn't beat about the bush, she came straight out and asked him where he was from, who his parents were, what his childhood was like, whether he considered himself Black or White, how he felt about his roots – she asked him all the questions that used to make him clam up. When Emma asked him if he missed his father he said, only when people ask me about him, like now. Then I wish I had more answers.

Never mind, Emma said, the world is full of bastard children. I'm one, too, by the way. I met my biological father once and I could have done without it. An utter deadbeat. Can you believe, he only made contact after seeing me on a talk show? Blood is certainly not thicker than water. Speaking of which, is there any more wine?

Gabriel would never call himself a bastard. But he seemed impressed by Emma's tendency to use the harshest words. He even allowed her to constantly invade his physical space. For her, it was a show of warmth, but for him it would usually be sheer horror. He'd be preparing the fish and she'd be almost treading on his toes, he'd say something and she'd interrupt him and tap his chest with her index finger, he'd say something she liked, and she'd throw herself at him, kiss him on the ear, or slap his bottom while giving me a wink. Meanwhile, Azzedine, Emma's husband, responded to Albert's adolescent taciturnity by playing him his favourite drummers on YouTube.

By the end of the evening, we had become a conspiratorial bunch, reminding me of parties that unexpectedly got so out of hand that we started to feel like a group of hostages. Gabriel and I had never had guests in this big house that we missed already even before they'd left, when they were still putting on their coats. Usually one of us was relieved, at least, or had already gone to bed early. Azzedine arranged to meet Albert the next day at a record store somewhere in Camden. Emma said goodbye to Gabriel with a fumble that was so intense that I was glad I hadn't invited them to stay the night. There was a vibe that I had been feeling all evening, like a question hanging in the room. After waving their cab off, we embraced without a word and staggered like an eight-limbed monster into our bedroom, knocking over a standard lamp on the way, and ignoring it. Everything about that evening was out of the ordinary. I asked him about the vibe and expected a terse shake of the head. But he pointed his toothbrush at me and laughed.

You noticed that, too? Okay. That makes me feel better.

Noticed what? Emma's hands on your bum?

A hand on your bum is a hand on your bum. It raises fewer questions than what was left unsaid, don't you think?

I nodded. I wouldn't have been surprised if this hint of ambiguity had passed him by altogether. What did that mean? That I thought my husband was emotionally stunted? He rinsed out his toothbrush and then the sink with his usual thoroughness. Whenever he used something, he cleaned it afterwards as if he had to get rid of any trace of his DNA. I found this amusing or irritating, depending on my mood. That night, I loved it.

I have no interest whatsoever in appearing naked in one of her books.

But otherwise you would have gone for it?

Is that what you'd expect from me?

He closed the door to the bathroom behind him and stood there in the room, naked. I hadn't seen him like that in ages. After a few seconds he pulled his stomach in.

Would you have gone along with it if I'd gone along with it?

He looked to the side and thought. He was giving it serious thought. Me too. Nothing had changed about the fact that he wanted to fulfil my every wish, no matter how daft he thought it was. He was faithful. If you start from the assumption that men are not monogamous by nature, then he was faithful to me out of principle. For the first time it occurred to me that swingers bypass the question of fidelity by simply having their partner with them when they fuck someone else. The price would have been contact with another man. Gabriel wasn't homophobic, but like many men, he described himself, without being asked, as one hundred per cent heterosexual. As for the idea of having sex with Emma, I absolutely couldn't tell what he thought. No one could tell what he really wanted, possibly not even himself. My trick question lingered in the room. I had asked it out of genuine interest, but now I realised how dubious it was, like do you think she's pretty, would you sleep with any of my friends? He decided not to answer. Instead, he cracked his neck twice, took a run-up, and threw himself on me. I squealed. He nibbled my neck, kissed me, and then lay there, still, on top of me. Hey, I said, groaning under his weight, you owe me an answer. Depends on the people, he murmured into my neck. What people? I asked, laughing. You know, the people, he said, then he started snoring, and I realised that he had been talking in his sleep.

We may not have been an exceptionally happy couple, but we had the potential.

When Gabriel called me from Greece, we assured each other that we'd talk when he got back. I wondered: about what? About Albert's next school or about us? I hadn't told him that I'd said Julien – Albert's partner in crime – could come and spend the holiday with us, because I needed a break from the constant discussion about the right way to deal with him. That is, the strict way. Albert would get through all of this just fine because he had known what he wanted to be since he was five. We should stop using him as an excuse for the fact that we only ever spoke to each other like two social workers. Because, dear Gabriel, even if you don't like it, I thought, that is something we could do if we were divorced. Every day I'd play through our conversation over again while Albert showed his buddy around London. The more I thought about it, the more I had the feeling that something was about to change. Something I would need time for. Emma, if she had still been in my life, would have come straight out and asked: Don't you fuck anymore? Or has it been years since it was fun or made any sense? Then she would have given me advice that was equally forthright, which I might even have followed, in a milder form. I resolved to bring some of Emma's directness into our conversation when he got back. Most of all, I would have liked to ask him to extend his trip to Greece by a few weeks, to have longer to prepare myself.

On the morning of his return, when I heard him bringing me tea in bed, I just thought, not yet. Later. As patient as he was, he let me sleep, went out, and took everything he had been working towards for decades and threw it all away.

Gabriel

That morning in the summer of 2016 wiped out everything I had known until that point. It was like I had been sacked from every area of my life. Brexit provided the appropriate backdrop. Everything was about to change. My lecturing job was over. Mark and I decided I would step back from the business for a while. Of course, it remained our partnership, but we wanted to tread carefully, diplomatically. When his daughter was born, he had taken half a year off, and he felt, even though the reason for it was crappy, that now it should be my turn. Take a year, then it will definitely have blown over. A scandal never lasts more than a couple of weeks. You're not a royal, after all, he said. And no one can tell us how to run our company.

What do you mean by that? I asked him.

They might accuse us of having very few women working for us, he said. One, to be precise.

We're not responsible for gender statistics. We build houses.

Take some time off, Gabriel, Mark said.

After a few weeks of stunned silence, trying to get on with our life, Fleur came to the conclusion that the incident with the student was just one of many and that it was the symptom of an agitated depression, a so-called male depression. A theory I would have accepted if it helped me in court. Privately, I felt so misunderstood that I was at a loss for words. Yes, I had suffered from sleep deprivation, which surely in the last few years no one could miss. Exhaustion had worn down my old forbearance, something Fleur had always praised. I was finding it harder and harder to overlook things that had always irritated me really. In short, I was plain exhausted. Nevertheless I heard Fleur's diagnoses, which made me out to be someone who had lost any semblance of control over his life, and I fell into an if-you-say-so state that was so unlike me that the depression diagnosis became a self-fulfilling prophecy. When I once asked her, do you still love me? she answered, that's not what's important right now. It was the worst possible answer and it fitted perfectly into the overall picture.

Henry's presence took the pain out of our discussions. He didn't act like Fleur's brother, but like a mediator. It was bad enough that he felt he had to. Fleur suggested to me daily that I go to a burnout clinic. I refused. I wasn't sick. Then Henry suggested an anger management group. It's less time-consuming and it's anonymous, and it will do you good, especially since in your defence we'll be focusing on your, well, mental state, he said. I wasn't thrilled. Aside from the fact that I hated groups of any kind, anger management had never been an issue. Fleur then enumerated a list of situations that I had forgotten about but that she seemed to have recorded in meticulous detail. All of a sudden it was, remember the group in the restaurant that was too loud? Or the guy on the plane? Or that one, or that one, the one you complained to, rather more loudly and aggressively than necessary, remember? You have been a bit of a steaming kettle lately, haven't you? Excuse me? I've been a what? Fleur sounded like someone working out the grounds for divorce from her cantankerous grump of a husband.

Would you both mind leaving your emotions out of this debate, Henry said. It would make communication a darn sight easier. Also, it might possibly help if you both see that we all want the same thing.

Thanks for pointing that out, Henry, I said.

He nodded as he cleaned his glasses.

Okay, said Fleur, crossing her arms with a sigh. I was still stunned. Whenever I complained about something, it was always for our sake, often enough for Fleur's sake. I had asked people if things could be a little quieter because she was sensitive to noise and because she speaks so softly that it's practically impossible to have a conversation anywhere noisy. Yes, I forced a scruffy guy on the plane to put his damn shoes back on, which should have been the crew's job. Yes, I asked our neighbours, well after midnight, if they wouldn't mind moving their party indoors. It was always about things that everyone also found annoying but no one else was prepared to do anything about. Fleur would bristle with discomfort, I would call the waiter over. And again and again I defended our son, again and again it was me who had to explain why Albert was destroying things, ripping people's glasses off their faces, spitting, biting, throwing himself on the floor, and finally, when he was old enough to be out on his own, why he had become a notorious troublemaker. Albert wasn't interested in rules or consequences – which I saw as something sincere and authentic, which I tried to explain to others, mostly without success – only to be told now by Fleur that I hadn't been gentle or polite enough. Albert himself acted with unusual restraint ever since my problems began to dwarf his, although I would have been the perfect target for his wry sense of humour. I hadn't watched television for years, but now I did occasionally, and I liked it when he slouched on the sofa next to me, in silence. The three of us had agreed on a new boarding school, an hour and a half northwest of London, a boarding school with the internet and one of the few that was willing to accept him with his grades and his history. Fleur took him there, and when he said, don't let them wind you up, Dad, by way of a goodbye, I knew he was on my side.

Fleur

If someone had asked me if I recognised the people in the CCTV footage, I would have said no. I could see a tall, strongly built girl and a slightly shorter man. I wasn't a fan of his cycling gear and his beard, but they were at least familiar. It was his body language that was so unfamiliar. Aside from the fact that he looked White on the grainy black-and-white film – an effect enhanced by the fact that the girl was Black – he was also fatter than I knew him to be. His figure skater's bum looked flatter, but he now had a belly. The belly of an architect. I stared at him, baffled. I should have been wondering what had got into him, my husband who was usually so self-restrained. Instead, I was asking myself how my stylistically confident husband had come up with the idea of squeezing himself into such an undignified Lycra outfit. Nothing was right about this image. Nothing was right about that morning. I had the feeling that I ought to have been more shocked than I was. It was a strange feeling.

Then Henry asked to have the footage sent to him. There wasn't much there that might help Gabriel's case, but it was important that we could at least show that the girl had clearly shouted *fuck you* and so on. Gabriel never wanted to see it again, understandably. I watched it a few more times. I had to make sure it was really him. I watched this maniacal outburst over and over. I watched the man I had been married to for almost sixteen years evolve from self-control personified into a raging lunatic. I saw this short Lycra-clad sportsman hurl himself at the tall disco queen, only letting go of her when she fell to her knees, howling. I switched to slow motion and saw the horror on the young woman's face, and in my husband's face the firm conviction that he was in the right. Him. Attacking a stranger outside in broad daylight. With a handful of shit. I had to ask myself, had I missed something? Had his transformation taken place before my eyes? How had I not noticed it happening? Had he changed gradually while Albert was growing up and I had apparently dozed off for years? I recognised this hot-tempered, vituperative side to Gabriel of late – but verbally, not physically. I decided that what I was seeing here had to be a nervous breakdown. Another thing Gabriel didn't want to hear. Our argument over the proper term for attacking someone with a handful of dog shit was so ludicrous that all of us, Henry, Gabriel, and I, just said 'incident'. And finally, I asked myself, what could I have done differently? In general, not just that fateful morning.

Gabriel

I did what Henry suggested. I hadn't imagined myself ever involuntarily joining a group again. Two of the younger men were built like bouncers, one woman looked like a truck driver, and another kept suppressing a giggle. All the others seemed to be trying their best not to stand out. The more they tried to be inconspicuous, the more they humbly tried to sink into their chairs, the more obvious it was what they were thinking. At least that's how it seemed to me. Everyone was telling themselves they didn't need to be there. Because they didn't look like bar brawlers, because they were educated, because they were well-to-do, because they were actually civilised, pleasant-natured people who had ended up here by mistake. The higher the social status, the greater the distance between physical violence and one's self-image, and the more one's own aggression comes as a shock. I felt the same.

I was struck by how often people claimed to be peaceful. Always in the context of trouble or arguments. I'm a peaceful person, they always say, but I won't tolerate that; that's going too far. I had never thought about whether I'm a peaceful person or not. I place more value on the rules of coexistence. I believe in culture and in civilisation. Violence isn't a question of character, but the consequence of capitulation. If someone turns violent, they cast off their layers of education and civilisation and free their inner animal. But it's only in bed that we want our inner animal unleashed. And even there, ideally showered and somewhat tamed.

We didn't have to face an aggressor from the outside; we had to defeat our own inner aggressor. To recognise it in time and hold it in check. By breathing, taking pause, suppressing an impulse. By consciously recognising our triggers. Interrogating your inner self, as the course instructor put it: a wiry guy about my age, with a grey ponytail, who gave the impression that no one's story, no matter how brutal, could shock him. If you felt like expressing yourself, you were welcome to. In essence, this rueful umming and erring amounted to: the world had become too much for us. We were so overwhelmed that we chose the wrong form of communication. It wasn't until the third session that I understood that it wasn't just about physical attacks. Some of the people had been verbally abusive. One teacher had lost her job for continually shouting at her students. I thought about how often our teachers had yelled at us. None of them would have felt as ashamed as this haggard woman who cried a lot and described her behaviour as serious child abuse. If you had asked my teachers back then they would simply have said they needed to maintain quiet and discipline. They saw their yelling as an unpleasant necessity, for which they sometimes even blamed us children. Do I have to yell like that again today? I'm already hoarse. It's impossible with you lot! I can't imagine any of us complaining to our parents about it. It seemed to me that that wasn't so long ago. But in fact I went to school in another century. If a stranger had yelled at Albert, I would have sued him, like this pitiful woman. The instructor advised her, as he did all of us, to take up a martial art. Controlled, channelled aggression. One of the participants, a young guy in his twenties, said that there were no specific triggers. Everything made him aggressive. No therapeutic questioning could talk him around from this declaration.

I liked him. A kind of Themroc, who just couldn't stand anything anymore. Just like me.

Fleur

Gabriel hunkered down at home like a guest outstaying his welcome. Defiantly, I thought to myself, it's none of his business if I lie in the tub for an hour in the morning and then hang around for hours on the internet, not as a contributor like Albert, just a voyeur. What is it to him if I leave everything lying around until Bojana comes and tidies it away? Gabriel never said anything to that effect, and yet I felt watched. We could spend the entire day fucking, walk around naked, and order takeaways, I thought. We could pick cities neither of us had been to and fly there. We could look at each other with the same confused expressions as here. Maybe Gabriel could finally turn Albert's Michael Jackson cellar into a respectable basement. Albert would hate us for it, but I would explain the need, and he would understand: Gabriel is different from us, darling, he can't just sit around doing nothing.

I suggested it to him. Dutifully he went downstairs with me and looked around as if he were standing in someone else's house. Then he shook his head wearily. Albert likes it this way, and what would we do down here. Throw parties? Exercise? Accommodate asylum seekers? A room that's ripe for development, in his own house at that, and the only response he can think of is a lacklustre smile before he settles back in front of the TV with the newspaper, to work through every conceivable consequence of a possible Brexit – that really was a bad sign. He was like a balloon that had eventually burst with rage and drifted back down to the ground depleted of air. I wanted to call Mark and beg him to let Gabriel back into the office.

I claimed to have appointments. Bella became my Mr Singh. Unfortunately, I had to dress appropriately for this. I walked aimlessly around the city in my going-out-for-lunch outfits, like an employee who couldn't find her office again after her lunch break, waiting for an idea, any idea. When Morris graciously offered me a translation, I felt sick with relief. It was a pretentious novel that would have benefitted from being trimmed by a few hundred pages. I enjoyed working while at the same time developing an excessive and far too personal dislike of the young author. This will be my last translation, I told myself, feeling like I should thank this irritating writer for the kick up the backside. Gabriel was no longer cooking to relax, now he was cooking as if I were a top executive and he was my devoted layabout house husband. When he had set the table, he would knock almost timidly on the door of my study. Then we would sit across from each other, eat his elaborate dishes, and talk like the old couples we used to pity on our travels. Every few minutes, one of us would say something, and the other would agree amicably. The celery goes well with it. Mm-hm. It's getting colder. Yes. It will be even colder next week. I stopped constantly telling him I'd seen it coming. I'd annoyed him long enough by saying that.

And anyway, what's the use of wondering when something started going down the pan? It's nothing more than torture for brooders like me. You can spend years reinterpreting old decisions as fatal errors until you have your life marked out as a timeline that builds from misery to misery to the ultimate final catastrophe. If only I had insisted we leave London. If only I had encouraged Gabriel to write a book instead of working with students, knowing what his social skills were like. If I had paid more attention to my own interests, I could have written a book myself. If he hadn't been so overworked, he might have noticed how unhappy I was. If he had been home more often, he might have got on better with Albert. If I had expressed myself more clearly, he might have listened to me more. Mrs Would-Have and Mr Could-Have wouldn't need to ask themselves what they could have done differently. Mrs Would-Have and Mr Could-Have would still have been a happy couple.

Gabriel

Off we go, then, said Richard. All right, son, seat belt on? He said it, because the annoying warning signal wouldn't stop otherwise, and just as he called Fleur *my love*, he called me *son*, which I had always liked but at that moment his fatherly tone truly made me feel safe. My father-in-law was going to drive me to the airport and put me on a plane to São Paulo. He would wait until I had disappeared past security, then he would slowly stroll back to his car and have a nose around the departures hall like a tourist in a cathedral.

It was Mark who'd had the idea of my flying out to stay with Marcos for a bit. Marcos was one of our clients who had made his fortune in the early noughties selling nutritional supplements for the fit and beautiful. He had commissioned us to build him a holiday villa in the state of Santa Catarina. We were the same age and had got on well, and Marcos had stayed in touch with both of us, sending his annual alcoholic Christmas greetings. Mark had called me and suggested I head to Brazil for a proper summer break. Finally, some real R&R.

Why not, I thought, lacking any strong opinion in a way I never had before. What difference does it make if I hang around here doing nothing or there?

Henry was working on getting an out-of-court settlement, just transferring some money to the girl to save us all a tough time, but the girl was persevering. Nevertheless, I – a family man and partner in a company worth so and so – was allowed to leave the United Kingdom. Marcos, who spent most of his time in São Paulo, agreed immediately. Mark came over, brought me up to speed on work, mentioning only things that were going smoothly, and said goodbye to me as if I were emigrating. Fleur also liked the idea that I would be travelling alone. She seemed relieved. It was as if a crisis team had formed around me and had resolved to get me out of the country.

Go inside, my love, you'll catch a cold! Richard called to Fleur, who was standing in the driveway, freezing. She shook her head, jumped from one foot to the other and gestured to me: Bye-bye, kisses, phone. I wasn't a huge fan of the heart hand sign, but some confirmation of love would have been nice. As we drove off, she ran a little way after us, waving, skipping like a little girl. From cold or from happiness? I wondered, and finally fastened my seat belt.

I had forgotten how beautiful Brazil was. When we were working on Marcos's house, Mark had managed the build even though it had been my design. The last time I was here was to present one of my concepts for entry-level urban living: good quality favela houses. A visit full of handshakes and appointments that could have taken place in Angola or Azerbaijan. As a student in the mid-nineties, I had flown alone to Rio de Janeiro, from there to Belo Horizonte and then on to Brasilia. I went to see Niemeyer's ageing drawing-board city and wondered where else in the world a president would commission an architect to build a brand-new capital from scratch in the middle of nowhere. I didn't dare use the few scraps of Portuguese I had learned. But people were constantly talking to me, mistaking me for a Brazilian. I looked into their friendly and then baffled faces when I tried to explain that I was from Germany. German? You? Uh-huh. Really? I found a certain logic for those who spoke English: I'm a mixture of Europe and West Africa. Which was to say, yes, I could be one of you. At the same time, I felt more foreign than I had ever felt anywhere before. I was lonely, and I was homesick. But not necessarily for Germany in particular. In fact, that was when I decided I wasn't going to stay in Germany.

I had always thought I had an exceptional talent for being alone. Not so on my trip to Brazil. In a less beautiful country I might have resigned myself to my loneliness. But in Brazil, I missed having someone to share the country with me so much that it hurt.

Fleur was convinced that a break would be good for us. I tried to pretend I hadn't heard that. She was more discontented with me than I was with her, that was a fact. She might still love me, I told myself, but the thought was so self-pitying that I wouldn't let myself think it again. When finally, after three weeks of radio silence – the longest time since we had been together – she called me on the number that only she, Albert, and Mark knew, she sounded different from when we said goodbye. She reminded me of the woman who had only dated me for Mark's sake, who had taken months to decide if she even liked me, and whom I desperately hoped to marry. I didn't know what we were going to talk about, I was ready for anything, but if she had told me she was leaving me, it would have killed me. Instead, she told me she had found a new focus. The Fleur from before, that shimmering creature with the cello that I never heard her play, used to be the most enthusiastic museum-goer I knew. Then she had married a man and had a son who both blinkered out anything that didn't fall within their specific interests. It was only now that I realised how alone you could be with me and Albert. Without him, without me, and with no new book by Emma, she had gone to the National Portrait Gallery and discovered a painting that had intrigued her. A young man from a prominent family in what is now Senegal was travelling with his companion to buy or sell paper and slaves, and on the way home he was himself captured by members of another tribe, and was shorn, sold, and shipped to Maryland. His education helped and he was ransomed, and in London his portrait was painted by William Hoare in 1733. The painting has only been up since 2010, Fleur said pensively. I didn't know it, I haven't been there for so long. Anyway, I've started some research. I don't know yet what I want to do with it, but it's fascinating. I could hear from her voice that she was serious. And it sounded genuinely interesting. Fleur had been listening to my projects for years. And I had never had the feeling that she was missing something. Maybe she hadn't noticed it herself.

Why don't you send me what you've got so far, I suggested, and we can think about it together?

Okay, she said, maybe later. Stay offline for a while, okay?

She talked to me like a junkie in rehab. I was standing in the middle of Marcos's airy house, which I had designed without any interior walls. At that moment I would have liked a wall to kick. I said goodbye, less affectionately than I had intended, and hung up.

Marcos had commissioned us build to his house on a hill: an A-shaped villa, beautiful timber, lots of glass, surrounded by rainforest. A retreat for a luxury-loving hermit that was no longer as solitary as it was: there were now two neighbours in sight. People who shared his taste and who were also hardly ever there. Christoph was an Airbnb guest from Switzerland staying in one of the other houses. He and I stopped to talk a few times. My stay was suddenly less relaxing when he told me about the world's most venomous snake, which was said to live in the area. Small, brown, and as inconspicuous as a stick, with such a deadly venom that you would die within five minutes, which is why they called it the five-minute snake.

Like a good boy, I stuck to my internet ban and didn't google the snake. For safety's sake, I followed Christoph's advice of stomping firmly to scare it away before it could bite me in fright. Every day I stomped down the hill and back up again, no doubt looking ridiculous. At the bottom, a small asphalt road dwindled into a sandy path that led, without any warning, into one of the most stunning landscapes I had ever seen. A nameless marshland, as still as the moon and full of knee-deep water holes, each a self-contained biotope of tiny fish and plants. A few kilometres on, I came across fine sand and eventually reached a glorious, almost deserted beach. I showed it to Christoph and found it good to speak German again, good to have a longer conversation. At the same time, I had to skirt around one topic, his – as he put it – messy divorce, which he was having a rest from here in Brazil. Then really have a rest from thinking about it, I advised him, and we talked about other things: the state of the economy, politics, our work. After he had left, I realised I was finding it easier to be alone out here than when I first arrived. I jogged. I cooked. I spent days oiling the wooden floors and the veranda. I spent whole evenings drawing, dreaming up houses that no one had commissioned, wondering why I hadn't done this for years even though I loved it so much. In order not to hear the wildlife outside, I listened to my host's CD collection. Superstars and Brazilian musicians I had never heard of but who Fleur and Albert probably knew. I missed them both more when I listened to music than I did when it was quiet. I discovered an LP by Chico Buarque, *Construção*, which I listened to over and over, like Albert did when he liked something. I heard it so many times that eventually, with my rudimentary Portuguese, I worked out the lyrics to the title track. A man makes love like it's the last time, kisses his wife like it's the last time, climbs the scaffolding at a construction site, arranges the bricks into a magical pattern, drinks, dances, and stumbles into the sky, where he floats through the air until he lands on the pavement and then gets run over as he walks into the oncoming traffic. I had never seen myself before in a book, or a film, and certainly not in a song. But with this one, I thought, that's me.

I battled with giant cockroaches. I encountered the biggest spider I'd ever seen, so large I could hardly believe it was real. I felt paralysed at first, as if I were already immobilised by its neurotoxin, but I knew that only one of us could stay in the house. You don't kill animals, you take them outside. I thought about my mother more than I had in years. The spider was sitting on the white door to the pantry like a Halloween decoration. Praying it would stay there, I ran to the wardrobe in the hall, put on Marcos's raincoat and gardening gloves, and picked it up to carry it out. A hideous experience for both of us. The spider desperately fought to get out, sweat ran down my forehead into my eyes. I had no idea what its weapon was, stinging, biting, or spraying venom, so with outstretched arms I ran down the hill and then another half a kilometre or so, before I hurled it into a thicket, convinced that it would immediately find its way back to the house. I called Marcos, who claimed he had never seen any large spiders like that here before. We arranged to meet in São Paulo, but not until two weeks later, because he had his parents staying with him until then. I went on my own to Florianópolis for a look around and for the first time in weeks saw people dashing about. After dinner I drove quickly back to my retreat on the hill, fleeing my 1990s homesickness. I planned a trip to the Iguazú Falls, only to abandon the plan because it was a trip that seemed pointless without Albert. Albert didn't get in touch because he had school and could say hello to me via Fleur. Teenage heedlessness, teenage heartlessness. I called Fleur; she told me I sounded well. She spoke to me like a rehab patient. I could get on the next plane, be home tomorrow, and in the office the day after. What do you all want from me? I thought.

While she told me that Albert didn't really like it at his new school, it was a school after all, but that he seemed to be adapting quite well so far, and that she was trying to find a daily structure, which wasn't easy without the two of us, I worked on getting my resentment under control. I liked her the way she was before.

I had never told her that she had changed, although she had told me I had. And now I wondered who I was before. Confident in my success, I had always concentrated on the things I wanted and ignored everything else. I had come a long way with that approach. Why should it all be so wrong now? As we said goodbye, I asked her to send me what she had so far about the painting, and she promised she would.

I waited until the next day. There was Wi-Fi in the house; it had just been turned off, like my laptop. When I woke up, there was a butterfly on the windowpane. Inky black, with wings that would almost completely cover my face. It was more sinister in its beauty than the spider. It remained still as I moved closer. When it opened its wings and I saw that they shimmered not black but cobalt blue, I felt relieved, like some ominous danger had passed.

It was a morning that in London would have struck me as particularly sunny. Here it was simply a new day. I walked through the gleaming light, still thrilled, as I was every day, by this house I had designed for Marcos. I was in my early thirties back then and already knew what I was doing. The floor was scattered with my designs from the previous night. I drank coffee while listening to a Portuguese lesson. I repeated the sentences out loud in the silence of the house. Albert would have imitated me and split his sides laughing.

I've had enough of being on my own now, I thought as I logged on. I went straight to Fleur's email, looked at this cautiously smiling African from the eighteenth century, read what she had discovered so far, made some notes, and wrote a few questions for her. *He was one of the locals who were involved in the slave trade himself, right? Did he carry on with it after he returned? Who commissioned the portrait? Was it him?* Then I had a quick look through the rest of my unread inbox. The daily stream of emails had thinned out. They had stopped copying me in on every thread. The requests for keynotes or jury memberships suggested that no one outside England seemed to care about the so-called scandal, which was a relief. I read, replied, deleted. When I read *Greetings from Dakar*, my first thought was of spam, then Fleur's research. It took me a long time to realise who it was that was writing to me.

He would have liked to get in touch with me years ago, he wrote. I must surely be surprised to hear from him, he continued. I got up, went to Marcos's drinks cabinet and poured myself a whiskey. Then I read on.

He was delighted that I had become such a successful man. He had only recently become acquainted with the internet and had been amazed at how easy it was to find me. My mother would certainly be proud of me, after all, she had also wanted to be an architect. A wonderful woman. He hoped she was doing well.

I picked up my whiskey glass and went out to the pool. I was barefoot. I thought about the five-minute snake and imagined crossing paths with one now of all times. Then he would have both brought me into the world and finished me off too. With the least amount of presence possible. I sat back on a sun lounger and let myself be dazzled by the water. I had known at some point that my mother had wanted to be an architect, but I had forgotten. She would have been proud of me even if I'd done nothing at all, I thought. That was the only thing I could say for sure about her. She would have been sixty-seven that year. I didn't know how old he was, but I assumed he wasn't younger than her. I didn't owe him anything. I could just read the email and then move on with my life. I didn't even have to tell Fleur about it. I went back inside. The laptop had switched to the screensaver. I poured myself another whiskey. He didn't want to explain anything to me, at least not in this email. I was grateful to him for that. Apparently he didn't need an organ donation either. Or money. In the email signature were the addresses of a dental practice and a clinic in his name. He seemed to be doing well. I couldn't say why, but I was glad to see that he was doing well. He isn't looking for me because he wants something, I told myself. He's looking for me because he's old. It's as simple as that.

It would give him great pleasure to see me.

I had shut down for a whole month. My adrenaline and cortisol levels seemed to have settled down. Now I suddenly felt like I did before. I was cold, clammy. My body was buzzing again.

I told myself, I'm here, this is now. I'm not going back, certainly not to a time I can barely remember, to think about what might have been. If he had been there. If he had made contact sooner.

I lay on the floor and stared up at the ceiling fan. I didn't fit into his life. It was what it was. And he doesn't fit into mine now. It is what it is. Isn't it?

I felt the wood beneath the back of my head and thought about calling Fleur. Or Mark. Or maybe my father-in-law, a natural at being a father, a man who understood everything. No, I thought, this is something no one understands. I would be the one who would have to explain myself. I would have to explain why my response to this remarkable turn of events after all these years was to simply ignore it as if it were spam.

I don't have to do anything, I thought, and poured myself another finger of whiskey. Then I read again what Fleur had written about the life of the aristocratic African in the portrait by William Hoare. If she wants to go to Africa, no matter where and for how long, I'll go with her, I thought. Even if she wants us to split up, she'll still be my family.

Then I deleted his email.

The next morning I knew immediately that I had not been dreaming. My father is alive. That's good, but it's got nothing to do with me. I arranged my trip to São Paulo, from where I would fly back to London. End of the break, end of the story. For the last time I waded through the warm water holes to the beach and back. I was in Santa Catarina, a predominantly White region, but it seemed that day as if the majority of humanity was made up of old, Black men. I saw them at bus stops, in restaurants, at fruit stalls, in cars, alone, in families, in groups. An impression that persisted when I arrived in São Paulo.

Marcos did me a huge favour when he asked me what I thought of the old warehouse he had bought to become his new company headquarters. This question provided me with useful time in a huge city full of busy people who wanted nothing from me. We clambered around the old building. I stroked its brick walls and thought of my song on a loop: brick by brick, a magical design. *Construção*. I could manage without many things but never without architecture. When I sat down in Marcos's office to jot down some designs for the redevelopment, I immediately fell back into my old rhythm. His employees were nothing to do with me, but all the same, even here, I liked it best when everyone had gone home. I ordered sashimi and stayed. I tried calling Fleur on Skype and FaceTime. I finally wanted to see her again, but she didn't answer. Please let me book you a flight to São Paulo, I wrote to her. Then I took his email out of the trash. I didn't read it again. I wrote *My father, your grandfather* in the subject line and forwarded it to Albert.

EPILOGUE

2017

Mick

Do you remember me? How have you been? What did you study? Do you have a wife and children?

I'm on the phone to my father, Mick thought, in disbelief, I'm on the phone to my father. For the first time. He was two when Idris left. Disappeared, you could say. Now it seemed he had no time to lose. Call me, Mick had emailed him, after nine in the evening is ideal. Idris had called promptly, and was soon up to speed in terms of Mick's career and family.

He was listening to Idris, answering him without actually answering, pleased to realise that for all these years he hadn't just practised what he preached, but had actually internalised what he was telling people: the other person is you. Mick understood his father. He understood him so thoroughly that this inner realisation seemed more significant than the fact that this man had made contact after forty-five years. Mick had never been a moraliser, but since he had come to understand himself, he found he understood other people even better. That helped. People liked him. People had faith in him as a yoga teacher and as a life coach. He had a past life that he summarised in vague, self-deprecating terms, suggesting a confused, hectic, and haphazard odyssey, a life journey that made him an expert on every kind of personal crisis. The accumulated madness of his younger years, obviously never intended as an investment in the future, had in fact served a purpose.

There was an infinite amount to learn, and it earned you neither riches nor applause. That had become clear to him when he set out on his new path back then, after he was literally stranded in Thailand. Thanks to Jay, his first teacher. This was a path he had stayed on ever since, even if he didn't always manage generosity, struggled with humility, and had barely made a start on frugality. After a few years, influenced by his time in India, by various teachers, and by an absence of money, he came back to Berlin, to find his centre. Not the overworked inner centre that people were so obsessed with, but a midpoint between the earlier rascal and the later ascetic. He remembered the time before the miscreant, the child he had once been. A boy who, like all children, could busy himself for days on end with one thing, without any external stimulation, an ability he lost later on: the ability to be alone. Awakening his childhood abilities took Mick further than most of the workshops and retreats he attended. He had an exhausting relationship, then a long-distance relationship, which fizzled out by itself with the lack of commitment. After that he stayed single. He stopped asking himself constantly how he was doing.

I am, he thought now, and after those two words he placed a full stop.

When mindfulness and serenity became the ultimate non-material must-haves, Mick found his timing was spot on, for the first time in his life. Mindfulness was part of his new skillset, serenity one of his natural talents. He had never used that word, but he clearly had it in abundance – he'd been serene enough to do nothing at all for years, after all, he thought, laughing to himself. Looking back at how he had frittered away his youth, he viewed it with equal serenity – what else could he do? He developed a workshop, a seminar, a webinar, and when the time came, an app. Bodywork was more his thing, but he earned more from mindfulness, serenity, and sleep. He earned his living through sleep. It was a dream. It had been a long road to get to this point, but the guided meditation with binaural beats, his most successful product, had taken him less than a week to prepare, he recorded it in one afternoon. His warm baritone had become his greatest asset, maybe he should have realised that years ago, but he'd never thought of it that way. Once or twice he tried reanimating the old Mick by heading over to Berghain. He didn't bother with the intro, the never-ending Saturday night, and skipped straight to the Sunday morning. He was waved past the queue, his ego flattered by his veteran status, and he stood there stone-cold sober amidst the distinctly unsober crowd, waiting to see what happened. Not much. That feeling of stepping into a time machine didn't do much for him, it just felt dull. A shame, he thought, but on the other hand, what did I expect? Sometimes he felt like he had to pay for his nineties with a decade-long hangover. Thoughts of penitence that didn't really make any sense. No, this wasn't a punishment, he had just grown older and some things were over, some things carried on.

Delia was back in his life. You'll always have a place in my heart, she had said at some point, to which Mick replied, don't be so cheesy. That made her laugh. She was right. Almost three years of no contact, and then they met again at a massive fortieth in Sardinia. In 2004, he went to her wedding. From then on, he was there in her life again. In a different way. Better, as he found. He was there for her when she had two miscarriages in quick succession, he was there when she got divorced and came back to Berlin, and he went with her to Hanover several times when her father was terminally ill. When are you two clowns actually going to get married? asked Bernhard, who died in 2009. Shortly after that Mick became a dad. Out of nowhere. Pure Mick style.

The new Mick found it harder than usual to forgive the old Mick, the master of avoidance. A grandmaster: he had managed not to open or throw away an envelope for an entire decade. When his old friend Fabian had given him the envelope, he had just turned thirty. When it fell into his hands again, he was almost forty. He had just moved house. He had finally found a dilapidated, old coach house, completely run down and therefore still within his budget, in a great location, tucked away in the second courtyard of a block. His plan was to live upstairs, and downstairs he would set up his yoga and coaching space; he could also rent it out when money was tight, times he imagined weren't behind him. Cause for celebration, and cause for a clear-out. *Mick – Pending* was written on some of the shoeboxes, a collection that was still growing even after ten years of yoga practice and after training as a yoga instructor, as an industrial climber – which had helped enormously with his sense of balance – and as a life coach. Water under the bridge now, he thought as he opened up one of the boxes. And that was when he read that Lynn from London – sweet Lynn from the drum'n'bass cellar and the bed in Golders Green, where Mick hid away for a day and a half after the most idiotic event of his life – had never had any intention of suing him. For what again? His completely unfounded fears had revolved around her record reviews that he had translated and passed off as his own. No, Lynn had written to say that she had a daughter. From the one-night stand with a certain German, who had given her a false surname, but who she later recognised in an English music magazine as a Berlin club manager. Mick remembered the picture: three shiny moon faces against a vague, colourful background. Chris on the left, some upcoming celebrity DJ in the middle, and, on the far right, himself. The caption listed him as Mick E., his not particularly original *nom de guerre*. Lynn's letter read like one from an old acquaintance, free of despair, though that could be deceptive, and free of demands. She wrote that she had been looking for him but hadn't found him, that she was married now, it was 2000, and she thought she'd try again, who knows, maybe he might want to meet his daughter Tara. She had put a few photos in with the letter. The little girl was five at the time and was unmistakably his. His. He who shortly thereafter, in one of his few bouts of radicalism, had gone for the snip to make sure he couldn't bring a child into the world, or rather any more children, which had cost him his relationship with Delia. It was one of a series of Mick-ish actions and inactions, the consequences of which left him at times convinced that he was his own worst enemy. A stage he thought he was long past in 2010. He read Lynn's letter and noticed how all his repression and flight reflexes were reactivated simultaneously, accompanied by a fervent desire to get thoroughly wasted.

Our dramas and traumas are not necessarily our own fault, but we have to take responsibility for them, he told his students the next morning, the tough guys he was teaching yoga to in prison, one of his favourite projects. The next day, a bright Saturday, he borrowed a friend's sailing boat and spent an afternoon with Delia on the Wannsee, then invited her to dinner. He made short work of an aperitif and three-quarters of a bottle of white wine before he broke the news. The conception of the child clearly fell within their time as a couple, so there was no need for any particularly smart cogitation or calculations. A few years later, Delia's desire to have a baby, never fulfilled, had become louder and louder. Her friendship was one of the things the new, upbeat Mick valued most in his life, which didn't mean he couldn't still upset her. Pensively, Delia took this news on board with its remarkable time lag. She drank. Blinked into the sun. Breathed. Nodded.

It's our ego that so often gets in the way, he told his students. The ego question is as infinite as most egos are. Delia seemed to have hers under control.

I see, she said. And then: have you been in touch yet? How old is she now, fourteen, fifteen? Does she look like you? You're going over to see her, right?

Relieved, Mick sat through her volley of questions, which didn't feature the word *I* or *me* even once. He shook his head.

No. I wanted to talk to you first.

Ten years of not opening a letter, that's Mick in a nutshell, said Delia with a slight snort of a laugh.

He rubbed his head. Yes, you could see the whole thing as a joke. And him, too.

I told you then it would be crazy to have a baby with me, remember? Now you see what I meant.

She turned her chair to put her face in the sun.

It's a bit rich me giving anyone advice with all this, he said, thinking: shit.

Oh, I wouldn't say that. Plenty of men who have children and don't give a shit about them don't have any issue with their credibility or reputation. Not in any culture, not in any industry. Not in yours, either. Your CV starts with your first yoga class.

He was more concerned about his personal integrity than his public résumé, but he didn't say anything. He moved his chair next to hers, stretched out his legs, and leaned his head back.

So, Delia said after a while, now we both finally have what we never wanted. Nice work.

Since he had really got to know her, since they weren't a couple anymore, since they weren't forever locking horns, he'd found it easier to know what to do and not to do. In this case, for her this news required neither approval nor disapproval. Then she must be right. That was it, done, over. He turned back to the table and shared out the rest of the wine.

Cheers, he said, to us.

They sat in the September sun until it set. Four weeks later, he flew to London for the first time since 1994. Delia flew with him.

And now here was his own dad going one step further. Checking in after over forty years and then straight away asking him about his professional career – that was hard to top. That was also why, when he read Idris's email, Mick thought, that could be me.

That could be me, he also thought regularly when he practised yoga with his offenders. The group collectively added up to a few hundred years without parole: men whose lives had been a never-ending series of bad decisions, men who had wanted it easy and had made it a thousand times harder, men who had lost it, who had flipped out, until they were arrested and locked up. He didn't like all of them. The fact that he could have been one of them didn't mean that there weren't inveterate bastards among them.

But none of his jailbirds got on his nerves anything like as much as the people he was surrounded by when he found out that his father was alive and wanted to see him. His damaged ear had never quite got back to how it was before. Sometimes he heard too little, at other times too much. And he had become more sensitive in other ways, too. Days when so much came through that he almost wished he could have his old filter of apathy back. The noise level meant he really needed to stop meeting people at places with a power juicer, an espresso machine, and shouting, although he always forgot. But the most unbearable was the endless meeting and greeting all around him. The scrambled eggs were made from powdered eggs, the coffee was terrible, the waitress was as with it as the undead.

You shouldn't judge.

Being less judgmental or – if you were playing in the enlightened league – not judging at all made everything easier. It freed the mind, the gaze, the soul. Not judging could be seen as a direct ticket to nirvana, or if you wanted it a touch more humdrum, as a guide to a calmer approach to one's fellow human beings. If it were that easy, everyone would do it. It was more than an exercise, it was practically reprogramming.

He started by not judging Nina for being late. She had suggested the place, she had set the time, but okay. Mick planned to publish his years of expertise coaching groups of all kinds in a nonfiction book. The title was to be *Smells like Team Spirit*, and Nina would take on the job of ghostwriter, because Mick was more a talker than a writer. This is a business meeting, he told himself; you ought to be able to cope with getting out and meeting people once in a while. He took a deep breath. Nothing had changed his life as fundamentally as conscious breathing. That wasn't some twaddle, it was his lived experience. He looked around. Changed his perspective. Didn't see everyone else as puffed-up hipsters, he saw himself from the outside. With his beard, in a down jacket and trainers, he sat there with his bright green drink and looked at his iPhone. Nothing distinguished him from everyone else.

He tried to block out the noise, scrolled through his emails, bored, even reading the ones he usually deleted immediately. *Greetings from Dakar*. Ha, nice try.

That's exactly how we do it, great. I think that's our USP. I'll have the pulled chicken, but without quinoa, is that possible? That was what he heard.

Do you remember me, he read.

He read it over and over again. Still, nothing distinguished him from everyone else around him. Nothing except his heart rate and his history.

He actually did remember him. Whereas if Idris, his father, had made contact a few years earlier, he would have had to say no to this question. One side effect, or perhaps a central effect, of his regular meditation practice was that memories he thought were gone started to come to the surface. He couldn't consciously recall them, but he enjoyed the images as they swept through him. Like any miracle, it was difficult to put into words. In a way, it was a bit like being off your head, almost like before, only sober and no regrets. And then the memories were there. He sometimes saw himself from the outside, like in a dream. A few times he saw himself on a checked blanket. Small, very small. The Black man with the moustache at the desk had to be his father. Idris typed on a typewriter with two fingers, looked down at him, pulled a funny face, then went back to typing. End of memory.

Then he was looking down from above at black coily hair, holding on tight. To what? To ears. He must have been sitting on his shoulders.

My photos from that time, I must have left them back in the East, Monika said when he asked her. Bullshit, thought Mick, it was her best time, there's no era with so many photos of her. She just doesn't have any more photos of *him*. That's okay, Monika, totally understandable. He asked her a few questions and felt like an Alzheimer's patient. Was there a guy called Amadou? Were we on top of the television tower, were we at the zoo, me on my dad's shoulders? Was he wearing a leather coat and clogs?

A leather coat, yes, and maybe clogs, too, that's what people wore in those days, said Monika thoughtfully, what makes you think that now? You were too small to remember it.

That's what he'd thought, too. But not anymore. It was like he could remember his own prehistory, the time before language.

Just a question, ciao Mama, he said, and hung up, as always slightly sapped by the feeling of a love that was beyond doubt but complicated all the same.

On the day that Idris made an unexpected return to his life, Mick digested the news while enduring the racket and one more cup of coffee, then he called Nina to postpone their meeting. He made his way home on foot, flooded with unformulated, interwoven questions about his existence and its meaning. Depending on the phase of his life, his answers to these questions varied between coke-head philosophy, clinical diagnosis, and spiritualism. Sometimes a bit like a Yogi tea bag, said Delia. Now that he was almost running to get back to the peace and warmth of his coach house, all he could think was, I don't know what this is all about. Looking at it without any imposed superstructure, it came down to this: he, his daughter's absent father, was now about to meet his own absent father. At the age of forty-seven. Well fine, he thought, as he unlocked his front door. He got changed, made himself some tea, and sat down. Sitting down usually meant meditating or consciously sitting. Not this time. He just sat. He didn't feel any negative feelings. He had never been angry at his father, more at himself or what was referred to as 'the circumstances', but never at Idris. He wasn't now, either. Neither was he elated. He stayed sitting there. By the time darkness fell, he had grown accustomed to the fact that his father was back. He hadn't been waiting for him, but now, in the twilight, he felt as if he had always expected him.

He read the email again. Idris wrote to tell him that he had two sisters, one in Canada and one in France, and a brother who was an architect. And then he asked him if he would like to meet. He, Michael, could choose where.

I'm looking forward to meeting you, he wrote to his father. I would like to come to Dakar.

His old self and his new self agreed on one thing: the world was there waiting to be seen.

No one in the arrivals hall would have guessed that the two men embracing, at first tentatively and then with firmer conviction, had not seen each other for over forty years. No one would be surprised that they were father and son. The age gap made sense, and there was an unmistakable family resemblance. Not that anyone was there to speculate about the two men. This was Charles de Gaulle airport in Paris; people were busy enough with themselves.

My father cares about me, Mick thought, as Idris took his backpack from him and walked ahead, leading the way. Do I walk like him? Maybe not, not yet. Do I look like him? A bit. He seems fit, that's good.

Idris made a beeline for one of the airport bars, Mick followed, sat down with him and listened. Slightly dazed and at the same time hyper-focused, he looked at this face that he'd been able to remember in recent years in its younger version. It looked different from how he remembered it: rounder, clean-shaven, and with gold-rimmed glasses. No more black Afro, instead short grey hair and a high forehead. He's got the gift of the gab, like me, Mick thought, grinning as he looked around him. Busy people, all doing their thing, and here he was sitting with this older man who, in his rusty German, was summarising his last four and a half decades.

East, West, university, specialising, doctorate, Paris, then back home, worked like an animal, never looked back, Monika was convinced she could manage on her own, that's how she is, isn't it, his mother?

Mick nodded. They ordered tea and espresso. Idris kept talking. His clinic, which he was now gradually stepping back from, his wife, his daughters. Fatou and Bijou, Mick's half-sisters. Neither of them have turned out anything like how I had imagined, Idris said.

He laughed. It was meant to sound like a benign fatherly joke, but it didn't come across quite as lighthearted as intended. Mick looked at him and knew him. Sort of. He briefly wondered what they were doing in this airport bar. No one would come here if they weren't waiting for something.

Did his father just want to meet him for a cup of coffee, bring him up to date, and then leave again? It would be weird, but even that Mick would accept. He was content, complete, no one could touch him. A good state to be in. Idris looked at his watch. Good taste in watches. Expensive, not tacky. Mick, who had only a mala bracelet on his wrist, still had a connoisseur's eye for luxury. Idris kept talking. No, you couldn't stay in the GDR. Paris would have been nice. Speaking of which, we're going to meet Amadou. My oldest friend – he knew you as a baby – he was also friends with your mother. I've put you both up in a very wonderful hotel near Amadou. Very nice there.

So there would be more time after the airport bar, and Mick's meditation memories of a man named Amadou were confirmed. He would talk about that, maybe write something. Wait a minute: *you both*?

Your brother's not coming, Idris said, his spoon jingling loudly as he stirred his espresso.

Why not?

Well, Idris took a sip, he didn't want to see me. I find it a shame, but it is his right.

They looked at each other. Mick peered through the lenses of Idris's glasses into the eyes he had inherited. It was only now that he realised: his brother hadn't grown up with this man either. He hadn't grown up with their sisters. No. His brother was like him.

That's why I'm all the happier that you're here. It is a pleasure for me to hold my firstborn in my arms, if I may say so.

Idris awkwardly climbed down from his bar stool, hugged Mick, and asked the barista for the men's room.

Idris

He had to get used to their names. In his head, he called them Monika's son and Gabriela's son.

Michael was the one he knew. Gabriel he only knew from an old black-and-white photo. Gabriel was the one who hadn't answered his email. He hadn't rejected him; he simply hadn't said anything. For so long that Idris was on the verge of trying to call him when he was in his office, although he decided not to in the end. When his grandson Albert replied instead, he cried with happiness. Don't lay it on so thick, Idris, his wife Odette would say, nothing is worse than a pathetic old man, and she wasn't entirely wrong. But there he was, sitting in front of his computer, reading Albert's email written in beautifully clear, elegant French, and thinking, this is your life's happy ending, Idris.

He invited his son from Berlin and his grandson from London to Paris. Paris was in the middle, he knew his way around, and it was where his oldest daughter and his best friend lived. This weekend will be so exhausting, he told Amadou, I'll need a week of respite care afterwards!

Michael has a daughter, Tara, whom he met for the first time when she was fifteen. He doesn't see her often, they get on well, but as far as she's concerned her dad is her mum's husband. There's no doubt about that, and it's okay.

Maybe that was a dig at me, Idris thought, only to correct himself immediately. No, Monika's son wasn't the kind to take a dig at someone. He was every bit as gentle as he remembered him. He couldn't say that, so instead he babbled away about other things, but this boy really hadn't changed a bit. He sat next to him, upright and toned like an athlete, smiling at him now and then and looking as content as he did back then in Monika's *Hinterhof* apartment, that place that was always so draughty. He was a handsome man, his son. The women noticed him at once. He caught their glances like rays of sunshine but gave nothing back except the neutral smile he seemed to have for the whole world. This is where he probably doesn't take after me, Idris thought. It crossed his mind that his son might be gay.

So, do you love women? he asked him.

I love people. Not all of them, but I'm working on it.

He ran his hand over his short hair and smiled at him.

Okay, to answer your question. The most important woman in my life is not my wife, she's my best friend.

Uh-huh, Idris thought. Well, he has a daughter. I guess that means he knows how to sleep with women. And then he thought, be glad he is the way he is. And that he is letting you be who you are. There's not a hint of reproach emanating from this man. He could ask me where I've been all these years. He could demand money from me. He could criticise me for leaving his mother alone. But no. He asked if there were any hereditary diseases in the family.

No, Idris said, why? Do you want more children?

No, that's ruled out, he said, but isn't that what you'd like to know if you don't know one of your parents?

An interesting way of looking at it, Idris thought. The opposite of most people's rose-tinted approach to ancestry. And amazingly matter of fact, considering his clearly innate gift for seeing life as a wonderful journey full of friendly fellow travellers. Almost as if he were a scientist. He had already told him on the phone that he hadn't been to university. Such a smart boy, his mother a philosopher, his father a doctor, but he hadn't studied and he didn't seem to have a problem with it. The Germans, they were just content with things as they were. The main thing was to be healthy, right? Idris would have liked to order a pastis, but it was only noon, and he still had to chauffeur his new family into the city from Roissy in Amadou's all-singing, all-dancing SUV. He asked for a decaffeinated espresso, the most pointless drink in the world.

Every night for weeks, he had gone to his sons' websites, looked at their profile pictures, and wondered what he should write to them. After he had finally sent his emails, it was time for a conversation with his wife. For Odette, there was not the slightest reason to be upset about the sins of his youth. There had been two women long before her time – and? What was she supposed to say to that? In fact, she said nothing for a long time. Instead, she just pulled her snooty expression that she had regularly resorted to over their thirty-five years together to remind him that he had married up and she had married down. You've always been economical with the truth, Idris, she said. When he came home a few days later and heard her on the phone saying that her husband was flying to Paris without her to visit his children from his previous relationships, he took that as a sign that all was well on that front. Fatou, his oldest, had taken the whole week off when he told her he was coming to Paris, something he would never take for granted, and he was pleased. Then it turned out she had assumed he was terminally ill. What else was I to think, she said, the way you were being all hush-hush and saying in every call that we had to talk. No imminent demise of her father, then, but instead two German brothers. Idris was relieved when his daughter linked arms with him. Listen, Fatou, he started, because he had prepared himself for these conversations. He had an answer ready for every possible question. But Fatou interrupted him. And, does this settle the grandchild question? Is one a doctor or a CEO? The younger one is a well-known architect, Idris said. If she thought his fatherly pride was misplaced, she didn't show it. How does it feel to finally have sons? she asked, and she seemed genuinely happy for him, which meant that she was going to let it go for the time being, that she would save her questions for later. Fatou had earned her master's degree in sociology, focusing on the consequences of growing up without a father. The fate of single mothers in the banlieues seemed more important to her than starting a family of her own. He had had no idea what good those hours with Fatou would do him. As always, it bothered him that his Parisian daughter was so defiantly inelegant, and as always, she interrupted him and annoyed him with her cheeky sarcasm. But this time she was a bit less distant than usual when she hugged him goodbye, and she said that over the next few days she would be there whenever he wanted her. As she strolled off through the drizzle towards the Métro, back to her monk's cell of an apartment, Idris again remembered what he always wanted to say to her, every time he was alone with her: Fatou, I hope you know that I love you as much as I love your sister.

Was it even possible to love two people the same amount? It was definitely what was expected of parents. Another thing people said about love was that sorrow and suffering made it grow. Bijou wouldn't have survived half an hour if her mama hadn't been the daughter of a government minister and her dad hadn't put fillings in the teeth of everyone in Dakar who mattered. She was always his problem child in terms of health, but she was bright as a spark, his little bunny. Yes, he had been a different father to her than to Fatou. And yes, if he was asked the unfair question of who his favourite person was, it would be Bijou. Who even now spared him no suffering. She met her husband, Lamine, while she was studying in Canada. He was such a perfect fit, as if he had found him for her himself. Then, just one year after the wedding – a wedding that would have bankrupted another father, a year when Idris imagined himself as a grandfather, regularly flying over to Montréal – came the divorce. It was her fault. She acted like she had lost her mind. She dumped Lamine and moved in with some random guy she had met. Never mind if he was Black, White, yellow, single, or married, it didn't make the slightest difference, because after three months he was also passé. In the ensuing phone calls, she accused him, her disloyal father, of teaming up with her ex-husband against her. And worse. Idris didn't like to think about it. What good did it do? For the moment, anyway, Bijou preferred to speak only to her mother. He would leave it to Odette to tell her about her two half-White half-brothers.

What made you think of looking for me now? Monika's son asked him, reaching down to stroke a total stranger's dog. An exceptionally ugly French bulldog. Idris could hardly bear to look.

He had anticipated this question, too. The short time with his son-in-law had reminded him how much he would have liked to have had a son of his own, as much as he loved his daughters. When you're old, you can't have enough children, I suppose, Fatou had said. He wouldn't exactly put it that way, but the desire to get his life in order had seized him in his late fifties and had haunted him like a ghost ever since. What was he supposed to tell Michael?

Not a week has gone by that I haven't thought of you, he said.

Michael sat back down on his barstool and nodded thoughtfully.

Why don't we have a Pernod? To calm the nerves. To celebrate the day, the lifetime, even. What about you? Not for me, thanks, but go ahead. Michael gave him an affectionate pat on the shoulder. And they both laughed, in a private, tender way they never would with a woman. I'm late, but not too late, Idris thought.

When he told him that his brother wouldn't be coming, but that he was about to meet his nephew instead, he jolted Michael briefly out of his unflappable calm. His usually drifting gaze became focused, and Idris realised he hadn't mentioned this before. How was Michael to know he had a German brother?

Excuse me, I'll be right back. Idris placed his hands on Michael's firm upper arms, gave him a brief hug, and left him to sit a moment with this new family revelation. What else could he do? I think he is the strongest of my children, he thought as he walked through the bar. Oh Idris, don't talk nonsense, said a voice in his head. That's what Odette would say. Monika too, loud and clear. Gabriela wouldn't.

By the time he returned, Michael had digested the news. In profile, he looked like a dark, bearded version of his mother. How is Monika? he asked him.

The plane from London was an hour and a half late.

The time flew by. Michael talked about his work. A bit opaque, his professional life, but it seemed to make him happy. And at one point, his German son, who had travelled half the world but had never been to Africa, asked him which ethnic group they were from. Who his people were, as he put it. No one in Europe had ever asked him that. We are Fula, Idris said.

One not insignificant reason that he had been so pleased about the man his daughter Bjjou married was that Lamine was also a Fula. It had all seemed so ideal. Although Idris had imagined he had left that way of thinking behind. He had fathered two children with women in Germany; he wanted to live like a carefree White hippie, in the belief that his generation was going to change the world, that no one cared anymore where a person is from, and then, decades later, he was the one opening a bottle of champagne because the boy his daughter had brought home from North America was not only African, not only West African, but a Fula. What did that mean? That our horizons shrink as we grow older? That as we approach the end of our lives we want to get back home? He swirled his glass, letting the ice cubes clink, and looked at Michael's face. Maybe I want to die surrounded by my loved ones, he thought and raised the glass to him. To your future, my son.

By the time the plane from London finally landed, Idris felt like he was leaving the bar with his son, a son he had raised. That's how familiar he seemed, as he handed him his coat, took his backpack and said, well then, shall we go?

While they waited at arrivals, Michael asked if he could take his picture. Of course, Idris said, and posed. I am the only person I know my age who likes to have his picture taken, he thought with satisfaction. For Delia, my ex, Michael said. Why isn't she his wife? Idris wondered again but didn't say anything. He felt nervous at the sight of the arriving passengers streaming out. He knew he would recognise Monika's son. He would have spotted him in a crowd of thousands. He was the one he had held in his arms, the one he had had climbing on him, back when Idris was still breezily nonchalant about being a father. He would have recognised his second-born, too, the star architect who seemed not to want to allow his father to be proud of him. He would recognise him anywhere because he had exactly the same eyes as him, which Idris in turn had from his mother. A miracle and at the same time none at all. He also had Gabriela's high cheekbones, a serious man, arms folded in the photo, standing next to his business partner, a smiling Englishman, in front of a UFO-like museum in the former Soviet Union. But what would Gabriel's son look like? Any young lad coming through those doors could be Albert.

A group of nutcases ran their way, almost on a collision course with them. With extraordinary presence of mind, Michael glanced up from his phone, took Idris by the elbow and pulled him aside a fraction. Then he looked towards the arrivals. Over there, he said, is that him?

Idris didn't recognise Albert by his appearance. He recognised him by the woman who was with him. He stared into the stream of people, and there she was. She brushed her straight dark hair out of her eyes, saw him and waved to him just like back then in Leipzig. Yoo-hoo, Idris, over here. She could wave with her whole body. Gabriela always looked so happy to see him. So happy ...

Hey, his son Michael put his arm around his shoulder, are you okay?

Albert

This is exactly what Dad was keen to avoid, I thought, as my African grandfather waved around his ironed handkerchief, saying how much he had missed us. Missed us? Give me a break. Until a few weeks ago he didn't know about me or Mum. He didn't even know that Dad's mum had died. Dad would have turned and walked away. A melodrama? No siree. Not with my dad.

I was looking forward to meeting him, but I also knew that if he turned out to be a jerk, I'd just go and hang out in Paris. I was actually thinking I'd come on my own to meet him. I'm sixteen, almost. Dad, for once, agreed with me. He'd managed to find an office over there in São Paulo – that looked just like his London office – and he seemed to have got his act together again. At least he seemed pretty laid back when we skyped.

Let him go on his own, Fleur, he said, it's important at his age. If you're worried, you can call him twice a day. I can't see any problem with it. His entire desk was full of drinks cans and takeaway boxes. He sat back and tapped his Montblanc against his lips, like he always does when he's waiting or thinking.

Fleur? he said, leaning forward again.

No, Mum had insisted, somehow switching roles with him. You don't want to see your father, fine. But Albert's not going on his own.

We could meet in London, Berlin, or Paris, Idris had written to me, which would you prefer? I let Mum answer: Berlin? I knew people there, apparently so did he, and as it later turned out, I have an uncle there, too. So, the old man decided on

Paris. *Exactamente* like Dad, who refuses to accept that he's his son. First he asks you what you want, then he makes all the decisions on his own, and in the end he acts like everyone had agreed in a fair vote. What is that? Machiavelli? Or some dictator gene he inherited?

I liked him. Took a photo of him straight away. I like his style. Looks younger than Richard, my English grandpa. He's definitely younger. And very different to how I'd imagined him – but how was I to know what he'd be like? Within the first half hour he was crying, laughing, and giving off this ambience like we'd all known each other forever, as if this was a normal gathering of a normal family. Ah, he practically shouted, and tomorrow Fatou is coming for lunch, too! Cool. Who? Who knows if he's always like that or if it was because of us. Like Dad, he has no idea about music. But pretends he does. He struggled to find a radio station in the car, and he asked me if I knew Maître Gims, drumming on the steering wheel. Absolutely zero rhythm. At least he's not boring. I decided to make Dad a little film about his father. If he wants to, he can watch it, if not, he can delete it. If I were him, I'd watch it, but I'm not him. He would have his reasons. Dad doesn't do anything without a reason.

When we landed in Paris, Mum ran straight up to him, and right away the two of them started chatting away in French. As if they knew each other. He looked at her, hugged her, held her away from him, looked at her again, and shook his head, all choked up. Like *she* was his child. Weird. We stood by and grinned at each other, me and this tall man who was with him. Hi Albert, I'm Mick, your dad's brother, nice to meet you, he said and shook my hand. He didn't sound quite as *Kraftwerk* as Dad, but he clearly had a German accent. Wait a minute. Gabriel has a brother who's also from Germany? That was a whole other story besides the missing dad, right? Yeah, really nice to meet you, Mick. Then my grandfather came up to me and hugged me. *Mon cher Albert!* Over his shoulder I could see Mum saying hi to my uncle and checking him out. Yes, he looked like Gabriel, not a hundred per cent, but he was definitely his brother. We all had to go to a bar, my grandfather leading the way – he had left his car keys there. Inside, he stirred all the staff into action, tipped the man behind the bar, and then we were off. There were four of us, but there were more to meet another time. In Dakar, in Montréal, here in Paris, and I have a cousin in Shoreditch, as my uncle told me, leading me through the airport crowds like a tour guide, and pulling Fleur's mega suitcase. This is my dad's clan. He thought he had no family left except for one aunt, and now, with all these people showing up, he just wanted to stay in Brazil to build something again. What a headfuck. The whole thing's wild.

When would I come to Africa, my grandfather asked me. What about school? And what did I want to study? I would definitely come to Africa, I said. I'd already been once, but to the other side and with my other grandpa. The school question was annoying, but standard, and got the standard response. I answered him in his accent. He didn't seem to twig, or if he did, he didn't seem to mind. He nodded and drove out of the parking space – same technique as Danielle, my grandma. Must have had the same parking teacher. I saw Mum glaring at me in the rearview mirror, her *I'm warning you* look. Maybe I'll be a comedian, I said, still in my Senegalese cab driver accent.

Ah, said my grandfather, as a career?

My new uncle sat in the back next to me and laughed. He didn't make a sound but his whole body was shaking, he was laughing so hard. Great guy.

We have so much to talk about, my grandfather kept saying. For sure. Mum still had to tell him that Dad's mum had died, a long time ago. I assumed that was going to be a shock – he'd asked about my German grandmother in every email.

I get him, Mick said, with a sort of sad smile. But I can't just pretend he's only been away a short time. It doesn't work like that.

We spent the afternoon just the two of us, walking around, talking like we already knew each other. Not only did he understand my grandfather, he also understood that all I wanted to do was make music. He got it. Be happy that you know what you want, he said.

Do you want to say anything to my dad? I asked him on our way back to our hotel in the evening. He took my phone, walked beside me with his basketballer stride, and left a voicemail message that seemed to go on forever.

What was that about? I asked him when he was done.

You don't understand any German?

I made a zero with my thumb and forefinger. *Nada.*

Mick stopped and nodded a slow uh-huh but seemed to have no problem with my non-existent German. We were standing in a square in Paris. He put his hands in his pockets and looked up at the houses as if he was reading them, like my dad would. Then he looked at me again, also like Dad. The slightest smile, barely showing in his mouth.

I told him I was looking forward to meeting him.

That's it?

The rest was a thing between brothers.

I nodded. Sure.

ACKNOWLEDGEMENTS

Thanks to all the people who believed in me and my Brothers: Karsten Kredel (my German editor and publisher), Petra Eggers (my agent), my family and friends, all my readers who understood what I was saying/writing so well, and, of course Gersy Ifeanyi Ejimofo and Ruth Ahmedzai Kemp for the English edition.

Jackie Thomae – Author

I would like to thank Silke Lührmann, Katherine Van de Vate and Norm Kemp for helping with *Brothers*, and Alexandra Roesch for your support with the many projects you've helped me with over the years. I'm hugely grateful to Gersy Ifeanyi Ejimofo, Natasha Onwuemezi and Melanie Cotton, and especially to Jackie Thomae – thank you for trusting me with this very special book.

Ruth Ahmedzai Kemp - Translator